P9-DMW-872

"Gregory beautifully builds the suspense."
—*LIBRARY JOURNAL* (starred review)

"Will have readers spellbound."
—*NATIONAL EXAMINER*

"Gregory is . . . one of the very best writers of historical fiction. . . . The book reads like a thriller, and is impossible to put down, even if you know the outcome."
—**LIZ SMITH**

"Absorbing."
—*PUBLISHERS WEEKLY*

"Gregory puts readers at the scene with visceral details."
—*KIRKUS REVIEWS*

"Gregory does her usual excellent job of ratcheting up the intrigue and suspense."
—*BOOKLIST*

"This wives' tale takes on a new life under Gregory's whimsical pen."
—*NEW YORK POST*

"In historical-fiction-queen Gregory's latest, [Kateryn Parr] is unforgettable."
—*PEOPLE*

"Gregory is a historian with heart and wit who makes history accessible."
—*ROMANTIC TIMES*

"IMPOSSIBLE TO PUT DOWN." —LIZ SMITH

Praise for *The Taming of the Queen*
and #1 *New York Times* bestselling author Philippa Gregory

"Who's ever heard of Kateryn Parr? Henry VIII's sixth wife was smart, independent—and managed to outlive him. In historical-fiction-queen Gregory's latest, she's unforgettable."

—People

"Full of vivid details and fraught with the constant tension of a court run by a madman, this novel will appeal most to historical fiction readers and those who enjoyed *Wolf Hall*. . . . Gregory beautifully builds the suspense."

—Library Journal (starred review)

"Gregory manages to make history lively, fascinating, and real, even as she puts her own twist on what readers believe they know. The impeccable research shows in every page, while her wonderfully realistic dialogue and remarkable characters come to life. Gregory is a historian with heart and wit who makes history accessible."

—Romantic Times (Top Pick)

"This wives' tale takes on a new life under Gregory's whimsical pen."

—New York Post

"Gregory does her usual excellent job of ratcheting up the intrigue and suspense."

—Booklist

"This novel beautifully exemplifies [Kateryn Parr's] accomplishments while portraying an honest and emotional woman learning to survive in a dangerous royal court."

—Historical Novels Review

"Absorbing. . . . Gregory's portrait of the complex, aging king and his sensual, scholarly bride will satisfy Tudor enthusiasts."

—*Publishers Weekly*

"Gregory puts readers at the scene with visceral details."

—*Kirkus Reviews*

THE KING'S CURSE

"Infuses vitality into an oft-forgotten player in the aftermath of the War of the Roses—Margaret Poole, heiress to the defeated Plantagenet clan."

—*Closer* magazine

"[A] gripping and detailed chronicle, with plenty of court intrigue and politics to spice up the action. . . . Highly recommended."

—*Library Journal* (starred review)

"Nobody does dynastic history like Gregory."

—*Booklist*

"Gregory manages to keep us in suspense as to what will befall her characters. . . . Under [her] spell, we keep hoping history won't repeat itself."

—*Kirkus Reviews*

THE WHITE PRINCESS

"Loyalties are torn, paranoia festers, and you can almost hear the bray of royal trumpets as the period springs to life. It's a bloody irresistible read."

—*People*

"Bring on the blood, sex, and tears! . . . You name it, it's all here."

—*USA Today*

"*The White Princess* features one of the more intriguing theories about the possible fate of the princes."

—*The Washington Post*

"This is the most fascinating and complex of the series—not only in history but in the psychological makeup of the characters, the politics of the era, and the blending of actual and reimagined history. Gregory makes everything come to life. . . . This is why Gregory is a queen of the genre."

—*Romantic Times* (Top Pick)

"This rich tapestry brings to vivid life the court of Henry and Elizabeth. Meticulously drawn characters with a seamless blending of historical fact and fiction combine in a page-turning epic of a story. Tudor-fiction fans can never get enough, and they will snap this one up."

—*Library Journal* (starred review)

"As usual, Gregory delivers a spellbinding . . . exposé."

—*Kirkus Reviews*

"Elizabeth must navigate the treacherous waters of marriage, maternity, and mutiny in an age better at betrayal than childbirth. . . . At this novel's core lies a political marriage seen in all its complexity."

—*Publishers Weekly*

"Replete with intrigue and heartrending drama."

—*Booklist*

THE KINGMAKER'S DAUGHTER

"Gregory . . . always delivers the goods. Her latest novel wraps up her Cousins' War series of royal witches, philanderers, and king slayers with the story of King Richard III's wife, Anne Neville, who went from the marital bed of one royal prince to that of another king-to-be during this long family feud."

—*New York Post*

"Conspiracy and a fight to the death for love and power."

—*Los Angeles Times*

"Gregory is one of historical fiction's superstars, and *The Kingmaker's Daughter* shows why . . . providing intelligent escape, a trip through time to a dangerous past."

—*Historical Novels Review* (Editor's Choice)

"The bonds of sisterhood infuse Gregory's latest. . . . The stakes are high as Anne and Isabel Neville, daughters of the earl of Warwick ('the Kingmaker'), vie for their father's favor and a chance at the throne. . . . In addition to Gregory handling a complicated history, she convincingly details women's lives in the 1400s and the competitive love between sisters."

—Publishers Weekly

"Gregory delivers another vivid and satisfying novel of court intrigue, revenge, and superstition. Gregory's many fans as well as readers who enjoy lush, evocative writing, vividly drawn characters, and fascinating history told from a woman's point of view will love her latest work."

—Library Journal

"It's every man and woman for themselves in Gregory's latest, which offers reliable royal entertainment."

—Booklist

"Gregory creates suspense by raising intriguing questions about whether her characters will transcend their historical reputations."

—Kirkus Reviews

THE LADY OF THE RIVERS

"Showcasing the same intimate imaginative texture as her classic *The Other Boleyn Girl*, *The Lady of the Rivers* is Philippa Gregory back in rip-roaring form."

—USAToday.com

"Wielding magic again in her latest . . . Gregory demonstrates the passion and skill that has made her the queen of English historical fiction."

—Publishers Weekly (starred review)

"The best writers of historical fiction imbue the past with the rich tapestry of life and depth, and Gregory is surely counted among their number. . . . A worthy addition to this fascinating series, once again distinguished by excellent characterization, thorough research, and a deft touch with the written word."

—Library Journal

"The suspenseful pace never flags."

"The ethereal magic threaded throughout the story . . . contrasts nicely with the power politics."

—*Booklist*

"The best yet, a lively tale of witchcraft and romance set amid civil wars in England and France."

—Associated Press

"The beauty of Philippa Gregory's prose resides in her details. She paints scenes so vividly, so exquisitely."

—*Bergen Record*

THE RED QUEEN

"Sexy . . . Scandalous . . . Smart."

—*Redbook*

"[Gregory] again brings insight to English history, re-creating the power struggle between two of the nation's most notable women in a tale fresh for modern readers. There's no question that she is the best at what she does."

—Associated Press

"Nobody does the Tudors better than Gregory, so it should come as no surprise that her latest is confident, colorful, [and] convincing. . . . Like Margaret Beaufort, Gregory puts her many imitators to shame by dint of unequaled energy, focus, and unwavering execution."

—*Publishers Weekly*

"Like Gregory's other historicals, excellent characterization and a well-researched story will hold the interest of readers, especially for fans of the Tudor dynasty."

—*Library Journal*

"Gregory's vivid, confident storytelling makes this devout and ruthlessly determined woman a worthy heroine for her time."

—*Booklist*

"Gregory once again demonstrates her flair for dramatizing history."

—*Kirkus Reviews*

"Gregory is a consummate historical author. . . . A fascinating portrait."

—*Historical Novels Review*

THE WHITE QUEEN

"Philippa Gregory turns real-life historical royalty into royally entertaining novels."

—*Time*

"Engrossing . . . Gregory has a deft hand with historical imagination. . . . Bright, lyrical."

—*The Washington Post*

"Gregory's exhaustive research, lush detail, and deft storytelling are all in top form here. . . . Mesmerizing and historically rich."

—*People*

"A rattling good yarn, extremely well told . . . Gregory navigates herself faultlessly through the period with a fine sense of what was distinctive about it."

—*The Wall Street Journal*

"Fascinating."

—*USA Today*

"Gregory earned her international reputation evoking sex, violence, love, and betrayal among the Tudors; here she adds intimate relationships, political maneuvering, and battlefield conflicts as well as some well-drawn supernatural elements. . . . [Gregory] captures vividly the terrible inertia of war."

—*Publishers Weekly*

"Gregory shows a sure touch from beginning to end, weaving a compelling story with vivid characters."

—*Library Journal*

"It is a well-told story . . . richly detailed and fast-moving. Gregory's legion of fans will be delighted."

—*Booklist*

"As always Gregory fills out all the dark corners of history and creates a thrilling read, and again creates a portrait of female society that has more power (diamond-hard women who will see their sons and husbands rule at any cost) than is generally acknowledged."

—*Kirkus Reviews*

"[Gregory] delivers another riveting tale of a strong woman, making her life leap from the pages. History becomes an adventure, a mystery, a love story, and a powerful drama in her capable hands. This is what we read for."

—*Romantic Times*

"[Gregory] deftly develops Elizabeth into a sympathetic character from a history that is not always kind to her."

—*Historical Novels Review*

**These titles are also available
from Simon & Schuster Audio and as eBooks**

By the same author

History

The Women of
the Cousins' War:
The Duchess, the Queen,
and the King's Mother

The Cousins' War

The Lady of the Rivers
The White Queen
The Red Queen
The Kingmaker's Daughter
The White Princess
The King's Curse

The Tudor Court Novels

The Constant Princess
The Other Boleyn Girl
The Boleyn Inheritance
The Queen's Fool
The Virgin's Lover
The Other Queen

Order of Darkness Series

Changeling
Stormbringers
Fools' Gold

The Wideacre Trilogy

Wideacre
The Favored Child
Meridon

The Tradescant Series

Earthly Joys
Virgin Earth

Modern Novels

Alice Hartley's Happiness
Perfectly Correct
The Little House
Zelda's Cut

Short Stories

Bread and Chocolate

Other Historical Novels

The Wise Woman
Fallen Skies
A Respectable Trade

THE
TAMING
OF THE
QUEEN

PHILIPPA GREGORY

TOUCHSTONE

New York London Toronto Sydney New Delhi

Touchstone
An Imprint of Simon & Schuster, Inc.
1230 Avenue of the Americas
New York, NY 10020

This book is a work of fiction. Any references to historical events, real people, or real places are used fictitiously. Other names, characters, places, and events are products of the author's imagination, and any resemblance to actual events or places or persons, living or dead, is entirely coincidental.

Copyright © 2015 by Levon Publishing Ltd.

All rights reserved, including the right to reproduce this book or portions thereof in any form whatsoever. For information, address Touchstone Subsidiary Rights Department, 1230 Avenue of the Americas, New York, NY 10020.

First Touchstone trade paperback edition March 2016

TOUCHSTONE and colophon are registered trademarks of Simon & Schuster, Inc.

For information about special discounts for bulk purchases, please contact Simon & Schuster Special Sales at 1-866-506-1949 or business@simonandschuster.com.

The Simon & Schuster Speakers Bureau can bring authors to your live event. For more information or to book an event, contact the Simon & Schuster Speakers Bureau at 1-866-248-3049 or visit our website at www.simonspeakers.com.

Manufactured in the United States of America

1   3   5   7   9   10   8   6   4   2

The Library of Congress has cataloged the hardcover edition as follows:

Gregory, Philippa.
The taming of the queen / Philippa Gregory. — First Touchstone hardcover edition.
pages ; cm
1. Catharine Parr, Queen, consort of Henry VIII, King of England, 1512–1548—Fiction.   2. Henry VIII, King of England, 1491–1547—Fiction.   3. Queens—England—Fiction.   4. Great Britain—History—Henry VIII, 1509–1547—Fiction.   I. Title.
PR6057.R386T36   2015
823'.914—dc23   2015018375

ISBN 978-1-4767-5879-4
ISBN 978-1-4767-5881-7 (pbk)
ISBN 978-1-4767-5882-4 (ebook)

For

Maurice Hutt, 1928–2013
Geoffrey Carnall, 1927–2015

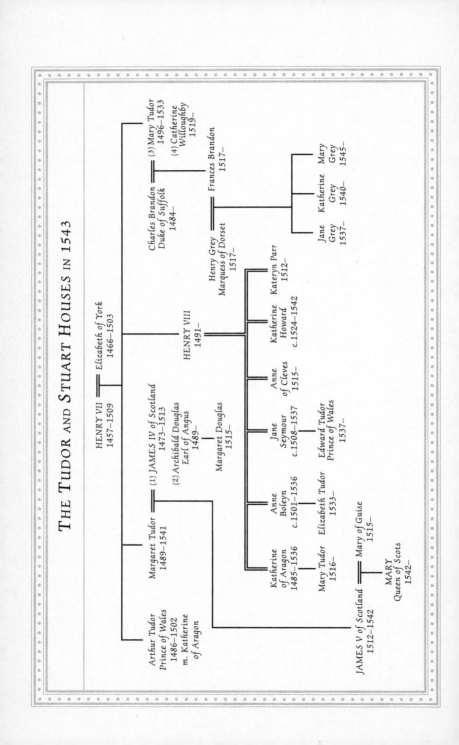

THE TUDOR AND STUART HOUSES IN 1543

HENRY VII == Elizabeth of York
1457–1509   1466–1503

Arthur Tudor
Prince of Wales
1486–1502
m. Katherine
of Aragon

Margaret Tudor == (1) JAMES IV of Scotland
1489–1541   1473–1513

(2) Archibald Douglas
Earl of Angus
1489–

Margaret Douglas
1515–

HENRY VIII
1491–

Mary Tudor (3) == Charles Brandon
1496–1533   Duke of Suffolk
                  1484–

(4) Catherine
Willoughby
1519–

Frances Brandon
1517–

Henry Grey ==
Marquess of Dorset
1517–

Katherine
of Aragon
1485–1536

Anne
Boleyn
c.1501–1536

Jane
Seymour
c.1508–1537

Anne
of Cleves
1515–

Katherine
Howard
c.1524–1542

Kateryn Parr
1512–

Mary Tudor
1516–

Elizabeth Tudor
1533–

Edward Tudor
Prince of Wales
1537–

Jane
Grey
1537–

Katherine
Grey
1540–

Mary
Grey
1545–

JAMES V of Scotland == Mary of Guise
1512–1542   1515–

MARY
Queen of Scots
1542–

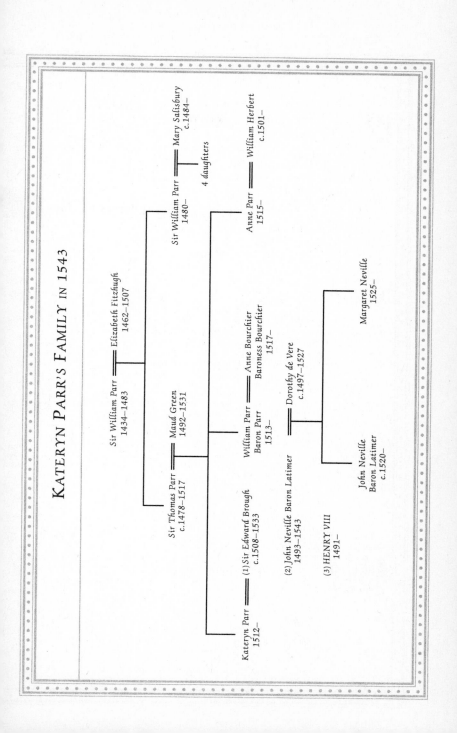

KATERYN PARR'S FAMILY IN 1543

Sir William Parr
1434–1483
═══ Elizabeth Fitzhugh
1462–1507

Sir Thomas Parr
c.1478–1517
═══ Maud Green
1492–1531

Sir William Parr
1480–
═══ Mary Salisbury
c.1484–

4 daughters

Anne Parr
1515–
═══ William Herbert
c.1501–

William Parr
Baron Parr
1513–
═══ Anne Bourchier
Baroness Bourchier
1517–

Dorothy de Vere
c.1497–1527
═══

Margaret Neville
1525–

John Neville
Baron Latimer
c.1520–

Kateryn Parr
1512–
═══ (1) Sir Edward Brough
c.1508–1533

(2) John Neville Baron Latimer
1493–1543

(3) HENRY VIII
1491–

Saint James's Palace

River Thames

Hampton Court Palace

River Thames

Whitehall Palace

Baynard's Castle

The Tower

London Bridge

Westminster Palace

Greenwich Palace

LONDON
1543

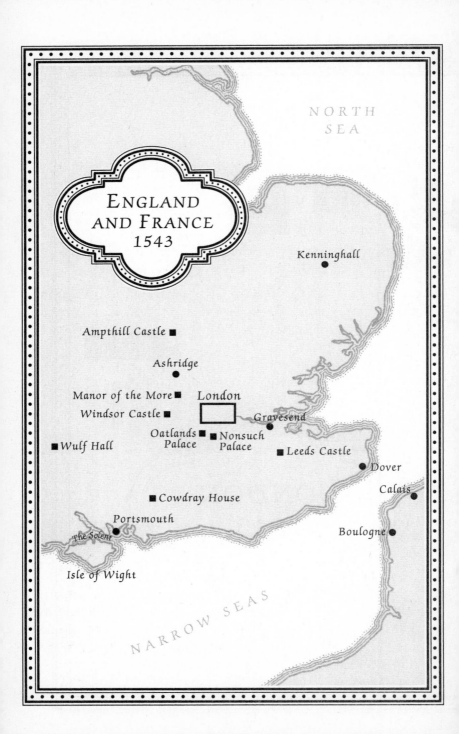

ENGLAND
AND FRANCE
1543

NORTH
SEA

Kenninghall

Ampthill Castle ■

Ashridge ●

Manor of the More ■   London

Windsor Castle ■   Gravesend ●

Oatlands ■ ■ Nonsuch
Palace   Palace

■ Wulf Hall   ■ Leeds Castle

■ Cowdray House   Dover ●

                          Calais ●

Portsmouth ●

The Solent   Boulogne ●

Isle of Wight

NARROW SEAS

HAMPTON COURT PALACE, SPRING 1543

KP

He stands before me, as broad as an ancient oak, his face like a full moon caught high in the topmost branches, the rolls of creased flesh upturned with goodwill. He leans, and it is as if the tree might topple on me. I stand my ground but I think—surely he's not going to kneel, as another man knelt at my feet, just yesterday, and covered my hands with kisses? But if this mountain of a man ever got down, he would have to be hauled up with ropes, like an ox stuck in a ditch; and besides, he kneels to no one.

I think, he can't kiss me on the mouth, not here in the long room with musicians at one end and everyone passing by. Surely that can't happen in this mannered court, surely this big moon face will not come down on mine. I stare up at the man who my mother and all her friends once adored as the handsomest in England, the king who every girl dreamed of, and I whisper a prayer that he did not say the words he just said. Absurdly, I pray that I misheard him.

In confident silence, he waits for my assent.

I realize: this is how it will be from now until death us do part; he will wait for my assent or continue without it. I will have to marry this man who looms larger and stands higher than anyone else. He is above mortals, a heavenly body just below angels: the King of England.

"I am so surprised by the honor," I stammer.

The pursed pout of his little mouth widens into a smile. I can see the yellowing teeth and smell his old-dog breath.

"I don't deserve it."

"I will show you how to deserve it," he assures me.

A coy smile on his wet lips reminds me, horribly, that he is a sensualist trapped in a rotting body and that I will be his wife in every sense of the word; he will bed me while I am aching for another man.

"May I pray and think on this great proposal?" I ask, stumbling for courtly words. "I'm taken aback, I really am. And so recently widowed . . ."

His sprouting sandy eyebrows twitch together; this displeases him. "You want time? Weren't you hoping for this?"

"Every woman hopes for it," I assure him swiftly. "There is not one lady at court who does not hope for it, not one in the country who does not dream of it. I among all the others. But I am unworthy!"

This is better, he is soothed.

"I can't believe that my dreams have come true," I embellish. "I need time to realize my good fortune. It's like a fairy story!"

He nods. He loves fairy stories, disguising and playacting, and any sort of fanciful pretense.

"I have rescued you," he declares. "I will raise you from nothing to the greatest place in the world." His voice, rich and confident, lubricated for all his life with the finest of wines and the fattest of cuts, is indulgent; but the sharp little gaze is interrogating me.

I force myself to meet his gimlet eyes, hooded under his fat eyelids. He doesn't raise me from nothing, I don't come from nowhere: I was born a Parr of Kendal, my late husband was a Neville, these are great families in the far North of England, not that he has ever been there. "I need a little time," I bargain. "To accustom myself to joy."

He makes a little gesture with his pudgy hand to say that I can take all the time I like. I curtsey and walk backwards from the card table where he suddenly demanded the greatest stake that a woman can wager: a gamble with her life. It is against the law to turn a back to him: some people secretly joke that it is safer to keep an eye on him. Six paces backwards down the long gallery, the spring sunshine beating through the tall windows onto my modestly bowed head, and then I curtsey again, lowering my eyes. When I come up, he is still beaming at me, and everyone is still watching. I make myself smile and step backwards to the closed doors that lead to his presence chamber. Behind me, the guards swing them open for me to pass, I hear the murmur as the people outside, excluded from the honor of the royal presence, watch me curtsey again on the threshold, the great king watching me leave. I continue backwards as the guards close the double doors to hide me from his sight, and I hear the thud as they ground their halberds.

I stand for a moment, facing the carved wooden panels, quite unable to turn and face the curious stares in the crowded room. Now the thick doors are between us, I find I am shaking—not just my hands, not just trembling in my knees, but shuddering in every sinew of my body as if I have a fever, shivering like a leveret tucked down in a wheat field hearing the swish of the blades of the reaping gang coming closer and closer.

It is long past midnight before everyone is asleep, and I put a blue cloak over my night robe of black satin and dark as a shadow in the colors of the night sky, go quietly out of the women's rooms and down the great stairs. No one sees me pass, I have the hood pulled over my face, and, anyway, this is a court that has bought and sold love for years. No one has much curiosity in a woman going to the wrong room after midnight.

There are no sentries posted at my lover's door; it is unlocked as he promised. I turn the handle and slip in, and he is there, waiting for me at the fireside, the room empty, lit only by a few candles. He is tall and lean, dark-haired, dark-eyed. When he hears me, he turns, and desire illuminates his grave face. He grabs me, my head against his hard chest, his arms tightening around my back. Without saying a word, I am rubbing my forehead against him as if I would drive myself under his skin, into his very body. We sway together for a moment, our bodies craving the scent, the touch of the other. His hands clutch at my buttocks, he lifts me up and I wrap my legs around him. I am desperate for him. He kicks open the door of his bedroom with his booted foot, and carries me in, slamming it behind him as he turns and lays me down on his bed. He strips off his breeches, he throws his shirt to the floor as I open my cloak and robe and he presses down upon me and enters me without a single word said, with only a deep sigh, as if he has been holding his breath all day for this moment.

Only then do I gasp against his naked shoulder: "Thomas, swive me all night; I don't want to think."

He rears above me so that he can see my pale face and my auburn hair spilling over the pillow. "Christ, I am desperate for you," he exclaims, and then his face grows intent and his dark eyes widen and are blinded by desire as he starts to move inside me. I open my legs wider and hear my breath coming short, and know that I am with the only lover who has ever given me pleasure, in the only place in the world where I want to be, the only place that I feel safe—in Thomas Seymour's warm bed.

Sometime before dawn, he pours wine for me from a flagon on the sideboard and offers me dried plums and some little cakes. I take a glass of wine and nibble on a pastry, catching the crumbs in my cupped hand.

"He's proposed marriage," I say shortly.

Briefly, he puts his hand over his eyes, as if he cannot bear to see me, sitting in his bed, my hair tumbled around my shoulders, his sheets wrapped around my breasts, my neck rubbed red with his biting kisses, my mouth a little swollen.

"God save us. Oh, God spare us this."

"I couldn't believe it."

"He spoke to your brother? To your uncle?"

"No, to me, yesterday."

"Have you told anyone else?"

I shake my head. "Not yet. I'd tell no one before you."

"So what will you do?"

"What can I do? I'll obey," I say grimly.

"You can't," he says with sudden impatience. He reaches for me and snatches my hands, crumbling the pastry. He kneels on the bed and kisses my fingertips, as he did when he first told me that he loved me, that he would be my lover, that he would be my husband, that no one should ever part us, that I was the only woman he had ever desired—ever!—in a long life of lovers and whores and servant girls and so many wenches that he cannot even remember. "Kateryn, I swear that you can't. I can't bear it. I won't allow it."

"I don't see how to refuse."

"What have you said?"

"That I need time. That I have to pray and think."

He puts my hand on his flat belly. I can feel the warm damp sweat, and the soft curls of his dark hair, the wall of hard muscle beneath the firm skin. "Is this what you've been doing, tonight? Praying?"

"I've been worshipping," I whisper.

He bends and kisses the top of my head. "Heretic. What if you told him you're already promised? That you were already secretly married?"

"To you?" I say bluntly.

He takes the challenge because he is a daredevil; any risk, any danger, and Thomas runs towards it as if it were a May game, as if he is only truly alive at a sword's length from death.

"Yes, to me," he says boldly. "Of course, to me. Of course we must marry. We can say that we are already married!"

I wanted to hear him say it, but I don't dare. "I can't defy him." I lose my voice at the thought of leaving Thomas. I feel hot tears on my cheek. I lift the sheet and mop my face. "Oh, God help me, I won't be able to even see you."

He looks aghast. He sits back on his heels, the ropes of the bed creaking under his weight. "This can't be happening. You're only just free—we've been together no more than half a dozen times—I was going to ask his permission to marry you! I only waited out of respect to your widowhood!"

"I should have read the signs. He sent me those beautiful sleeves, he insisted I break my mourning and come to court. He's always coming to find me in Lady Mary's rooms, and he's always watching me."

"I thought he was just flirting. You're not the only one. There's you, and Catherine Brandon, and Mary Howard . . . I never thought he was serious."

"He has favored my brother far beyond his deserts. God knows William wasn't appointed Warden of the Marches on his ability."

"He's old enough to be your father!"

I smile bitterly. "What man objects to a younger bride? You know, I think he had me in mind even before the death of my husband, God rest his soul."

"I knew it!" He slams his palm against the carved post of the bed. "I knew it! I've seen the way his eyes follow you around the room. I've seen him send you a little dish of this or a little piece of that at dinner, and lick his own spoon with his big fat tongue when you taste it. I can't bear the thought of you in his bed and his old hands pulling you this way and that."

I strain my throat and swallow down my fear. "I know. I know. The marriage will be far worse than the courting, and the courting is like a play with mismatched actors and I don't know my lines. I'm so afraid. Dear God, Thomas, I cannot tell you how very afraid I am. The last queen . . ." I lose my voice; I cannot say her name. Katherine Howard died, beheaded for adultery, just a year ago.

"Don't be afraid of that," Thomas reassures me. "You weren't here, you don't know what she was like. Kitty Howard ruined herself. He would never have hurt her but for her own fault. She was a complete whore."

"And what d'you think he'd call me, if he saw me like this?"

There is a bleak silence. He looks at my hands, clutched around my knees. I have started to tremble. He puts his hands on my shoulders, and feels me shudder. He looks aghast, as if we have just heard our death sentences.

"He must never ever suspect you of this," he says, gesturing to the warm fire, the candlelit room, the rumpled sheets, the heady, betraying smell of lovemaking. "If he ever asks you—deny it. I will always deny it, I swear. He must never hear even a whisper. I swear that he will never hear one word from me. We must agree it together. We will never ever speak of it. Not to anyone. We will never give him cause to suspect, and we will swear an oath of secrecy."

"I swear it. They could rack me and I wouldn't betray you."

His smile is warm. "They don't rack gentry," he says, and gathers me into his arms, with a deep gentle tenderness. He lays me down and wraps the fur rug around me, and he stretches out beside me, leaning over me, his head resting on his hand so that he can see me. He runs his hand from my wet cheek down my neck, over the curve of my breasts, my belly, my hips as if he is learning the shape of my body, as if he would read my skin with his fingers, the paragraphs, the punctuation, and remember it forever. Then he buries his face against my neck and inhales the perfume of my hair.

"This is good-bye, isn't it?" he says, his lips against my warm skin. "You've decided already, you tough little northerner. You made up your mind, all on your own, and you came to say good-bye to me."

Of course it is good-bye.

"I think I will die if you leave me," he warns me.

"For sure, we will both die if I don't," I say dryly.

"Always straight to the point, Kat."

"I don't want to lie to you tonight. I'm going to spend the rest of my life telling lies."

He scrutinizes my face. "You're beautiful when you cry," he remarks. "Especially when you cry."

I put my hands against his chest. I feel the curve of his muscle and his dark hair under my palms. He has an old scar on one shoulder from a sword cut. I touch it gently, thinking I must remember this, I must remember every moment of this.

"Don't ever let him see you cry," he says. "He would like it."

I trace the line of his collarbone, map the sinew of his shoulder. His warm skin under my hands and the scent of our lovemaking distracts me from sorrow.

"I've got to leave before dawn," I say, glancing at the shuttered window. "We don't have long."

He knows exactly what I am thinking. "Is this the way you want to say good-bye?" Gently he presses his thigh between mine so that the hard muscle rests against the folds of soft flesh and pleasure rises slowly through my body like a blush. "Like this?"

"Country ways," I whisper to make him laugh.

He rolls us both over so that he is on his back and I am lying along the warm lean length of him, on top of him so that I command this last act of love. I stretch out and feel him shudder with desire, I sit astride him, my hands against his chest, so that I can look into his dark eyes as I lower myself gently down to the entrancing point where he will enter me and then I hesitate until he pleads: "Kateryn." Only then do I ease onward. He gasps and closes his eyes, stretching out his arms, as if he were crucified on pleasure. I move, slowly at first, thinking of his delight, wanting to make this last for a long time, but then I feel the heat growing in me, and the wonderful familiar impatience rising, until I cannot hesitate or stop but I have to go on, thinking of nothing at all, until I call on him in pleasure, calling his name in joy and at the end weeping and weeping for lust, for love, and for the terrible loss that will come with the morning.

At chapel for Prime, I kneel beside my sister, Nan, the ladies of the king's daughter, Lady Mary, all around us. Lady Mary herself, silently praying at her own richly furnished prie-dieu, is out of earshot.

"Nan, I have to tell you something," I mutter.

"Has the king spoken?" is all she says.

"Yes."

She gives a little gasp and then puts her hand over mine and squeezes it. Her eyes close in a prayer. We kneel side by side, just as we used to do when we were little girls at home in Kendal in Westmorland and our mother read the prayers in Latin and we gabbled the responses. When the long service ends, Lady Mary rises to her feet, and we follow her from the chapel.

It is a fine spring day. If I were at home we would start plowing on a day like this and the sound of the curlews would ring out as loud as the plowboy's whistle.

"Let's walk in the garden before breakfast," Lady Mary proposes, and we follow her down the stairs to the privy garden and past the yeomen of the guard, who present arms and then stand back. My sister, Nan, raised at court, sees the opportunity to take my arm and slide us behind the backs of the ladies who are walking with our mistress. Discreetly, we sidestep to another path and when we are alone and cannot be overheard, she turns to look at me. Her pale tense face is like my own: auburn hair swept back under a hood, gray eyes like mine, and—just now—her cheeks are flushed red with excitement.

"God bless you, my sister. God bless us all. This is a great day for the Parrs. What did you say?"

"I asked for time to realize my joy," I say dryly.

"How long d'you think you've got?"

9

"Weeks?"

"He's always impatient," she warns me.

"I know."

"Better accept at once."

I shrug. "I will. I know I've got to marry him. I know there's no choice."

"As his wife, you'll be Queen of England; you'll command a fortune!" she crows. "We'll all get our fortunes."

"Yes—the family's prize heifer is on the market once again. This is the third sale."

"Oh Kat! This isn't just any old marriage arranged for you; this is the greatest chance you'll have in your life! It's the greatest marriage in England, probably in the world!"

"For as long as it lasts."

She looks behind her, then puts her arm through mine so that we can walk, head to head, and speak in whispers. "You're anxious; but it might not last so very long. He's very sick. He's very old. And then you have the title and the inheritance but not the husband."

The husband I have just buried was forty-nine, the king is fifty-one, an old man, but he could last till sixty. He has the best of physicians and the finest apothecaries, and he guards himself against disease as if he were a precious babe. He sends his armies to war without him, he gave up jousting years ago. He has buried four wives—why not another?

"I might outlive him," I concede, my mouth to her ear. "But how long did Katherine Howard last?"

Nan shakes her head at the comparison. "That slut! She betrayed him, and was foolish enough to be caught. You won't do that."

"It doesn't matter," I say, suddenly weary of these calculations. "Because I've no choice anyway. It's the wheel of fortune."

"Don't say that; it's God's will," she says with sudden enthusiasm. "Think of what you might do as Queen of England. Think of what you could do for us!"

My sister is a passionate advocate for the reform of the Church in England from the state it is in—a popeless papacy—to a true communion based on the Bible. Like many in the country—who knows how many?—she wants the king's reform of the church to go further and further until we are free from all superstition.

"Oh, Nan, you know I have no convictions . . . and anyway, why would he listen to me?"

"Because he always listens to his wives at first. And we need someone to speak for us. The court is terrified of Bishop Gardiner, he's even questioned Lady Mary's household. I've had to hide my own books. We need a queen who will defend the reformers."

"Not me," I say flatly. "I've no interest and I won't pretend to it. I was cured of faith when the papists threatened to burn down my castle."

"Yes, that's what they're like. They threw hot coals on Richard Champion's coffin to show that they thought he should have been burned. They keep the people in ignorance and fear. That's why we think the Bible should be in English, everyone should understand it for themselves and not be misled by priests."

"Oh, you're all as bad as each other," I say roundly. "I don't know anything about the new learning—not many books came my way in Richmondshire, and I didn't have any time to sit around reading. Lord Latimer wouldn't have had them in the house. So I don't know what all the fuss is about, and I certainly don't have any influence with the king."

"But Kat, there are four men, who only wanted to read the Bible in English, accused of heresy in Windsor prison right now. You must save them."

"Not if they are heretics, I won't! If they're heretics, they'll have to burn. That's the law. Who am I to say it's wrong?"

"But you will learn," Nan persists. "Of course you were cut off from all the new thinking when you were married to old Latimer and buried alive in the North, but when you hear the London preachers and listen to the scholars explaining the Bible in English, you'll understand why I think as I do. There is nothing in the world more important than bringing God's Word to the people and pushing back the power of the old church."

"I do think that everyone should be allowed to read the Bible in English," I concede.

"That's all you need to believe for now. The rest follows. You'll see. And I will be with you," she says. "Always. Whither thou goest, I will go. God bless me, I'll be sister to the Queen of England!"

I forget the gravity of my position and I laugh. "You'll puff up like a cock sparrow! And wouldn't Mother have been pleased! Can you imagine?"

Nan laughs out loud and claps her hand over her mouth. "Lord! Lord! Can you imagine it? After marrying you off and setting me to work so hard, and all for brother William's benefit? After teaching us that he must come first and we had to serve the family and never think of ourselves? Teaching us all our lives that the only person who mattered was William and the only country in the world was England, and the only place was court, and the only king was Henry?"

"And the heirloom!" I crow. "The precious heirloom that she left me! Her greatest treasure was her portrait of the king."

"Oh, she adored him. He was always the handsomest prince in Christendom to her."

"She would think me honored to marry what remains."

"Well, you are," Nan points out. "He will make you the wealthiest woman in England; nobody will come near you for power. You'll be able to do exactly as you please, you'll like that. Everyone—even Edward Seymour's wife—will have to curtsey to you. I'll enjoy seeing that, the woman is unbearable."

At the mention of Thomas's brother I lose my smile. "You know, I was thinking of Thomas Seymour, for my next husband."

"But you haven't said anything directly to him? You never mentioned him to anyone? You've not spoken to him?"

Bright as a portrait I can see Thomas naked in the candlelight, his knowing smile, my hand on his warm belly, tracing the line of dark hair downward. I can smell the scent of him as I kneel before him and put my forehead against his belly, as my lips part. "I've said nothing. I've done nothing."

"He doesn't know that you were considering him?" Nan presses. "You were thinking of marriage for the good of the family, not for desire, Kat?"

I think of him lying on the bed, arching his back to thrust inside me, his outflung arms, the dark lashes on his brown cheeks as his eyes close in abandonment. "He has no idea. I only thought his fortune and kin would suit us."

She nods. "He would have been a very good match. They're a family on the rise. But we must never mention him again. Nobody can ever say that you were thinking of him."

"I wasn't. I would have had to marry someone who would benefit the family, him as well as any other."

"It has to be as if he is dead to you," she insists.

"I've put aside all thought of him. I never even spoke to him, I never asked our brother to speak to him. I never mentioned him to anyone, not to our uncle. Forget him; I have."

"This is important, Kat."

"I'm not a fool."

She nods. "We'll never speak of him again."

"Never."

That night I dream of Tryphine. I dream that I am the saint, married against my will to my father's enemy, climbing a darkened stair in his castle. There is a bad smell coming from the chamber at the head of the stairs. It catches me in the back of my throat and makes me cough as I climb upwards, one hand on the damp curving stone wall, one hand holding my candle, the light bobbing and guttering in the pestilential breeze that blows down from the chamber. It is the smell of death, the scent of something dead and rotting coming from beyond the locked door, and I have to enter the door and face my greatest fear, for I am Tryphine, married against my will to my father's enemy, and climbing a darkened stair in his castle. There is a bad smell coming from the chamber at the head of the stairs. It catches me in the back of my throat and makes me cough as I climb upwards, one hand on the damp curving stone wall, one hand holding my candle, the light bobbing and guttering in the pestilential breeze that blows down from the chamber. It is the smell of death, the scent of something dead and rotting coming from beyond the locked door, and I have to enter the door and face my greatest fear, for I am Tryphine, married against my will to my father's enemy, and climbing a darkened stair in his castle . . . And so the dream repeats itself, over and over again, as I climb up and up the stair, which grows into another stair, which grows into another stair, up and up while the candlelight glitters on the dark wall and the smell from the locked room becomes stronger and stronger until finally I choke so hard on the stench that the bed shakes and Mary-Clare, another lady-in-waiting, who shares the bed with me, wakes me and says: "God bless you, Kateryn, you were dreaming and coughing and crying out! What's the matter with you?"

I say, "It's nothing. God bless me, I was so afraid! I had a dream, a bad dream."

The king comes to Lady Mary's rooms every day, leaning heavily on the arm of one of his friends, trying to hide that his bad leg is rotting away beneath him. Edward Seymour his brother-in-law supports him, talking pleasantly, charming as any Seymour. Often Thomas Howard, the old Duke of Norfolk, is holding up the other arm, his face locked in a wary courtier's smile, and broad-faced, broad-shouldered Stephen Gardiner, the Bishop of Winchester, trails behind them, quick to step forward and intervene. They all laugh loudly at the king's jokes and praise the insight of his statements; nobody ever contradicts him. I doubt anyone has argued with him since Anne Boleyn.

"Gardiner again," Nan remarks, and Catherine Brandon leans towards her and whispers urgently. I see Nan go pale as Catherine nods her pretty head.

"What's the matter?" I ask her. "Why shouldn't Stephen Gardiner attend the king?"

"The papists are hoping to entrap Thomas Cranmer, the finest, most Christian archbishop the court has ever had," Nan mutters in a rapid gabble. "Catherine's husband has told her that they plan to accuse Cranmer of heresy today, this afternoon. They think they have enough on him to send him to the stake."

I am so shocked I can hardly respond. "You can't kill a bishop!" I exclaim.

"You can," Catherine says sharply. "This king did: Bishop Fisher."

"That was years ago! What has Thomas Cranmer done?"

"He has offended against the king's Six Articles of Faith," Catherine Brandon explains rapidly. "The king has named six things that every Christian must believe, or face a charge of heresy."

"But how can he offend? He can't be against the teaching of the church; he's the archbishop: he is the church!"

The king is coming towards us.

"Beg for the archbishop's pardon!" Nan says to me urgently. "Save him, Kat."

"How can I?" I demand and then break off to smile as the king limps towards me, merely nodding to his daughter.

I catch Lady Mary's quizzical glance; but if she thinks my behavior is unsuitable for a thirty-year-old widow, there is nothing she can say. Lady Mary is only three years younger than me but she learned caution in a cruelly painful childhood. She saw her friends, her tutor, even her lady governess, disappear from her service into the Tower of London and from there to the scaffold. They warned her that her father would have her beheaded for her stubborn faith. Sometimes when she is praying in silence her eyes fill with tears, and I think she is sick with grief for those she lost and could not save. I imagine that she wakes every day to guilt, knowing that she denied her faith to save her life; and her friends did not.

Now she stands as the king lowers himself into his chair placed beside mine, and sits only when he waves his hand. She does not speak until he addresses her, but remains silent, her head obediently bowed. She is never going to complain that he flirts with her ladies-in-waiting. She will swallow her sorrow until it poisons her.

The king gestures that we may all sit down, leans towards me, and in an intimate whisper asks what I am reading. I show him the title page at once. It is a book of French stories, nothing that might be forbidden.

"You read French?"

"I speak it too. Not as fluently as Your Majesty, of course."

"Do you read other languages?"

"A little Latin, and I plan to study, now that I have more time," I say. "Now that I live at a learned court."

He smiles. "I have been a scholar all my life; I'm afraid you'll never catch up, but you should learn enough to read to me."

"Your Majesty's poetry in English is equal to anything in Latin," one of the courtiers says enthusiastically.

"All poetry is better in Latin," Stephen Gardiner contradicts him. "English is the language of the market. Latin is the language of the Bible."

Henry smiles and waves a fat hand, the great rings sparkling as he dismisses the argument. "I shall write a poem for you in Latin and you shall translate it," he promises me. "You can judge which is the best language for words of love. A woman's mind can be her greatest ornament. You shall show me the beauty of your intelligence as well as the beauty of your face."

His little eyes drift down from my face to the neck of my gown and rest on the curves of my breasts pressed against the tight stomacher. He licks his pursed lips. "Isn't she the fairest lady at court?" he asks the Duke of Norfolk.

The old man produces a thin smile, his dark eyes weighing me up as if I were sirloin. "She is indeed the fairest of many blooms," he says, glancing around for his daughter, Mary.

I see Nan looking urgently at me, and I remark: "You seem a little weary. Is there anything that troubles Your Majesty?"

He shakes his head as the Duke of Norfolk leans in to listen. "Nothing that need trouble you." He takes my hand and draws me a little closer. "You're a good Christian, aren't you, my dear?"

"Of course," I say.

"Read your Bible, pray to the saints and so on?"

"Yes, Your Majesty, every day."

"Then you know that I gave the Bible in English to my people and that I am the head of the church in England?"

"Of course, Your Majesty. I took the oath myself. I called in every one of my household at Snape Castle and made them swear that you are the head of the church and the pope is just the Bishop of Rome, and has no command in England."

"There are some who would have the English Church turn to Lutheran ways, changing everything. And there are some who think quite the opposite and would turn everything back to how it was before, restoring the power of the pope. Which do you think?"

I am very sure that I don't want to express an opinion either way. "I think I should be guided by Your Majesty."

He laughs out loud and so everyone has to laugh with him. He chucks me under the chin. "You are very right," he says. "As a subject and as a sweetheart. I tell you, I am publishing my ruling on this, calling it *The King's Book* so that people can know what to think. I will tell them. I am finding a middle wafy between Stephen Gardiner here—who would like all the rituals and the powers of the church to be restored once again—and my friend Thomas Cranmer—who is *not* here—who would like it pared back to the bone of the Bible. Cranmer would have no monasteries, no abbeys, no chantries, no priests even—just preachers and the Word of God."

"But why is your friend Thomas Cranmer not here?" I ask nervously. It is one thing to promise to save a man, but quite another to set about doing it. I don't know how I am supposed to prompt the king to mercy.

Henry's little eyes twinkle. "I expect he is fearfully awaiting to hear if he is to be charged with heresy and treason." He chuckles. "I expect he is listening for the tramp of soldiers coming to take him to the Tower."

"But if he is your friend?"

"Then his terror will be tempered by hope of mercy."

"But Your Majesty is so gracious—you will forgive him?" I prompt.

Gardiner steps forward and lifts a gentle hand as if he would silence me.

"It is for God to forgive," the king rules. "It is for me to impose justice."

Henry does not give me a week to come to terms with my great joy. He speaks to me again only two days later, on Sunday evening, after chapel. I am surprised that he combines piety with business, but since his will is God's will, the Sabbath can be holy and satisfactory, both at once. The court is processing from chapel to the great hall for dinner, the bright sunshine pouring in the great windows, when the king halts everyone and nods to summon me from the middle of the ladies to the head of them all. His velvet cap is pulled low over his thinning hair and the bobbing pearls encrusting the brim wink at me. He smiles as if he is joyful but his eyes are as blank as his jewels.

He takes my hand in greeting and folds it under the great heft of his arm. "Do you have an answer ready for me, Lady Latimer?"

"I have," I say. Now that there is no escape for me I find that my voice is clear and my hand, crushed between the bulge of his great belly and the thick padding of his sleeve, is steady. I'm not a girl, afraid of the unknown, I am a woman; I can face fear, I can walk towards it. "I have prayed for guidance, and I have my answer." I glance around. "Shall I speak it here and now?"

He nods; he has no sense of privacy. This is a man who is attended every moment of the day. Even when he strains in constipated agony on the closestool, there are men standing beside him ready to hand him linen to wipe, water to wash, a hand to grip when the pain is too great for him. He sleeps with a page at the foot of his bed; he urinates beside his favorites, when he vomits from overeating someone holds the bowl. Of course he has no hesitation in speaking of his marriage while everyone tries to hear—there is no risk of humiliation for him: he knows that he cannot be refused.

"I know I am blessed above all other women." I curtsey very low. "I shall be deeply honored to be your wife."

He takes my hand and brings it to his lips. He never had any doubts, but he is pleased to hear me describe myself as blessed. "You shall sit beside me at dinner," he promises. "And the herald shall announce it."

He walks with my hand squeezed under his arm, and so we lead everyone through the double doors to the great hall. Lady Mary walks on the other side of him. I cannot see her beyond the spread of his great chest, and she does not try to peep round at me. I imagine her face frozen and expressionless, and know that I must look the same. We must look like two pale sisters marched in to dinner by an enormous father.

I see the high table with the throne and a chair on either side, the head of the servery must have ordered the chairs to be set in place. Even he knew that the king would demand my answer as we walked in to dinner, and that I would have to say yes.

The three of us mount the dais and take our places. The great canopy of state covers the king's throne but stops short of my chair. Only when I am queen will I dine under cloth of gold. I look down the hall at the hundreds of people staring up at me. They nudge and point as they realize that I am to be their new queen, the trumpets scream and the herald steps forward.

I see Edward Seymour's carefully composed expression as he notes the arrival of a new wife who will bring her own advisors, a new royal family, new royal friends, new royal servants. He will be measuring the threat that I pose to his position as the king's brother-in-law, brother to the queen who tragically died in childbirth. I don't see his brother, Thomas, and I don't look to see if he is here, watching me. I gaze blindly down the long hall and hope that he is dining somewhere else tonight. I don't look for him. I must never look for him again as long as I live.

I pray for guidance, for God's will, not my own, for the bending of my own obstinate desires to His purpose and not mine. I don't know where God is to be found—in the old church of rituals and saints' images, miracles, and pilgrimages, or in the new ways of prayers in English and Bible readings—but I have to find Him. I have to find Him to crush my passion, to rein in my own ambitions. If I am to stand before His altar and swear myself to yet another loveless marriage, He has to bear me up. I cannot—I know I cannot—marry the king without the help of God. I cannot give up Thomas unless I believe it is for a great cause. I cannot give up my my first love, my only love, my tender yearning passionate love for him—this unique, irresistible man— unless I have God's love overwhelming me in its place.

I pray like a novice, ardently. I pray kneeling beside Archbishop Cranmer, who has returned to court without a word said against him, almost as if a charge of heresy was a step in a dance, forwards and backwards and turn around. It is incomprehensible to me but it seems that the king tricked his own council into charging the archbishop, and then turned on them and commanded the archbishop to inquire into those who brought the charges. So

Stephen Gardiner's affinity are now the ones filled with fear and Thomas Cranmer returns confidently to court, secure in the king's favor, and kneels beside me, his old lined face turned upwards as I silently pray, trying to hammer my desire for Thomas into a love of God. But even now—fool that I am—even in the most fervent prayer, when I think of the crucifixion, it is Thomas's dark face that I see: eyes closed, exalted in his climax. Then I have to squeeze my eyes shut and pray some more.

I pray kneeling beside Lady Mary, who says not one word about my elevation other than a quiet commendation to me and formal congratulations to her father. There have been too many stepmothers between the martyrdom of her mother and my arrival for her to resent me aspiring to Katherine of Aragon's place, too many for her to greet me with any hope. The last stepmother lasted less than two years, the one before that, six months. I could swear that Lady Mary kneels beside me in silent prayer and secretly thinks that I will need God's help to rise to her mother's position, and God's help to stay there. The way she bows her head and crosses herself at the end of her prayers and glances at me with brief pity tells me that she does not think God's help will be enough. She looks at me as if I were a woman walking into darkness with only the light of one small candle against the damp shadows—and then she gives a little shrug and turns away.

I pray like a nun, constantly, on the hour, every hour, anguished on my knees in my bedchamber, silently in chapel, or even desperately whenever I am alone for a moment. In the dark hours before the early summer dawn, when I am feverish and sleepless, I think that I have conquered my desire for Thomas, but when I wake in the morning I am aching for his touch. I never pray that he will come for me. I know that he cannot. I know that he must not. But still, every time the door of the chapel opens behind me, my heart leaps because I think it is him. I can almost see him, standing in the bright doorway, I can almost hear him saying: "Come, Kateryn, come away!" That's when I twist the beads of the rosary in my hands and pray that God will send me some accident, some terrible catastrophe, to stop my wedding day.

"But what could that be but the death of the king?" Nan demands.

I look blankly at her.

"It's treason to think of it," she reminds me, her voice low under the hum of the liturgy from the choir stalls. "And treason to say it. You cannot pray for his death, Kateryn. He has asked you to be his wife and you have consented. It's disloyal as a subject and as a wife."

I bow my head against her reproach; but she is right. It must be a sin to pray for the death of another, even of your worst enemy. An army going into battle should pray for as few deaths as possible even while they prepare themselves to do their duty. Like them, I must prepare myself to do my duty, risking myself. And besides, he is not my worst enemy. He is constantly kind and indulgent, he tells me that he is in love with me, that I will be everything to him. He is my king, the greatest king that England has ever had. I used to dream about him when I was a girl and my mother would tell me of the handsome young king and his horses and his suits of cloth of gold, and his daring. I cannot wish him ill. I should be praying for his health, for his happiness, for a long life for him. I should be praying for many years of married life with him, I should be praying that I can make him happy.

"You look terrible," Nan says bluntly. "Can't you sleep?"

"No." I have been getting up all through the night to pray that I shall be spared.

"You have to sleep," she rules. "And eat. You're the most beautiful woman at court, there's nobody even comes near you. Mary Howard and Catherine Brandon are nothing beside you. God gave you the gift of great beauty: don't throw it away. And don't think that if you lose your looks, he'll desert you. Once he decides on something he never changes his mind, even when half of England is against him . . ." She breaks off and corrects herself with a little laugh, "Unless of course—suddenly—he does, and everything is upside down and he is determined on the opposite course and no one can persuade him otherwise."

"But when does he change his mind?" I ask her. "Why?"

"In a moment," she says. "In a heartbeat. But never that you could predict."

I shake my head. "But how does anyone manage? With a changeable king? With a slippery king?"

"Some don't," she says shortly.

"If I can't pray to be spared, what can I pray for?" I ask. "Resignation?"

She shakes her head. "I was talking to my husband, Herbert. He said to me that he thinks that you have been sent by God."

At once I giggle. Nan's husband, William, has never troubled much about me before. I measure my growing importance in the world if now he realizes that I am a heavenly messenger.

But Nan is not laughing. "Truly he does. You have come at the very moment that we need a devout queen. You will save the king from sliding back to Rome. The old churchmen have the king's ear. They warn him that the country is not just demanding reform but becoming Lutheran, completely heretical. They are frightening him back to Rome, and turning him against his own people. They are taking the Bible from the churches of England so that people cannot read the Word of God for themselves. Now they have arrested half a dozen men at Windsor, the choirmaster among them, and they will burn them in the marshland below the castle. For nothing more than wanting to read a Bible in English!"

"Nan, I can't save them! I was not sent by God to save them."

"You have to save the reformed church, and save the king, and save us all. This is godly work that we think you can do. The reformers want you to advise the king in his private moments. Only you can do it. You have to rise to it, Kat. God will guide you."

"It's easy for you to say. Doesn't your husband understand that I don't know what people are talking about? I don't know who's on which side? I am not the person for this. I know nothing about it, and I have little interest."

"God has chosen you. And it's easy enough to understand. The court is divided into two parties, each of them convinced that they are in the right, guided by God. On the one hand are those who would have the king make an agreement with Rome and restore the monasteries, the abbeys, and all the ritual of the papist church. Bishop Stephen Gardiner and the men who work with him: Bishop Bonner, Sir Richard Rich, Sir Thomas Wriothesley, men like that. The Howards are papists and would have the church restored if they could, but they'll always do the king's bidding, whatever it is. Then there's us, who would see the church go onwards with reform, leave the superstition of the Roman practices, read the Bible in English, pray in English, worship in English, and never take another penny from a poor man for promising him remission of his sin, never cheat another poor man with a statue that bleeds on command, never order another poor man on a costly pilgrimage. We're for the truth in the Word of God—nothing else."

"Of course you think you're in the right," I remark. "You always did. And who speaks for you?"

"Nobody. That's the problem. There are more and more people in the country, more and more people at court who think as we do. Almost all of London. But we have no one of importance on our side but Thomas Cranmer. None of us has the king's ear. That's why it has to be you."

"To hold the king to reform?"

"Only that. Nothing more. Just to hold him to the reforms that he himself started. Our brother, William, is sure of it too. This is the greatest work that could be done, not just in England but in the world. This is a great opportunity for you, Kat. It is your chance to be a great woman, a leader."

"I don't want it. I want to be rich and comfortable and safe. Like any woman of any sense. All the rest is too much for me. It's beyond me."

"It's too much for you unless God holds you up," she says. "Then you will be triumphant. I will pray for that. We're all praying for that."

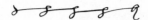

The king comes to Lady Mary's rooms and greets her first, as he will do until our wedding day, when I shall become the first lady of the kingdom and have my own rooms. Then he will greet me first, and she and every woman in the kingdom will follow in my train. When I review the ladies who looked down their noses at mere Kateryn Parr but will have to bow to the floor to Queen Kateryn, I have to hide my smug delight. He takes a seat between the two of us, which creaks under his weight as two squires lower him down. They bring him a footstool, and a page bends over and gently lifts the heavy leg onto it. The king wipes the grimace of pain from his face and turns to me with a smile.

"Sir Thomas Seymour has left us. He would not stay even a day, not even for the wedding. Why d'you think that is?"

I raise my eyebrows in calm surprise. "I don't know, Your Majesty. Where has he gone?"

"Don't you know? Have you not heard?"

"No, Your Majesty."

"Why, he's gone to do my bidding," he says. "He is my brother-in-law and my servant. He does just what I command him, whatever I command him. He is my dog and my slave." He bursts out in a sudden wheezy laugh and Edward Seymour, the other royal brother-in-law, laughs loudly too, as if he would have no objection to being described as a dog and a slave.

"His Majesty has trusted my brother with a great mission," Edward tells me. He appears to be pleased, but all courtiers are liars. "My brother, Thomas, has gone as ambassador to Queen Mary Regent of Flanders."

"We'll make an alliance," the king says. "Against France. And this time it will be unbreakable, and this time we will destroy France and win back our English lands, and more, eh, Seymour?"

"My brother will get an alliance for you and for England that will last forever," Edward promises rashly. "That's why he left in haste, to start the work at once."

I turn my head from one man to the other, like one of the little automata that the clockmakers forge. Ticktock: one man speaks and then the other. Tocktick: it goes the other way. So I am startled when the king turns to me sharply, out of order, and says: "Shall you miss Sir Thomas? Shall you miss him, Lady Latimer? He's a great favorite with you ladies, is he not?"

Hotly, I am about to deny it, but then I see the trap. "I am sure we shall all miss him," I say indifferently. "He's merry company for the younger ones. I am glad that his wit can do good service to Your Majesty, even though it was wasted on me."

"You don't like a courtly suitor?" He is watching me narrowly.

"I am a straightforward northern woman," I say. "I don't like a lot of lipwash."

"Enchanting!" Edward Seymour loudly proclaims as the king laughs at my country speech and snaps his fingers for the page, who lifts his leg off the stool, and then two of them haul him to his feet and steady him when he staggers. "We'll go in to dinner," he rules. "I am so hungry I could eat an ox! And you must get your strength up, Lady Latimer. You will have service to do also! I want a bonny bride!"

I curtsey as he hobbles past, his great weight bearing down on his frail legs, one calf bulked large with the thick bandage that is wrapped around the oozing wound. I rise up and walk beside Lady Mary. She gives me a cool little smile and says nothing.

I am to choose a motto. Nan and I are in my bedroom with the door barred to everyone, sprawled on my bed, the candles burning low.

"D'you remember them all?" I ask her curiously.

"Course I do. I saw each one's initials carved on every wooden beam and every stone boss in every palace. And then I saw them chipped off stone and adzed off wood and new initials put on again. I sewed every motto into flags for their weddings. I saw every emblem freshly painted. I saw their shields carved on and then burned off the royal barge. Of course I remember each one. Why wouldn't I? I was there when each one was announced, I was there when she was taken away. Mother put me into service to the Queen of England, Katherine of Aragon, and made me promise to always be loyal to the queen. She never dreamed there would be six of them. She never dreamed one of them would be you. Ask me any one's motto. I know them all!"

"Anne Boleyn," I say at random.

"*The Most Happy*," Nan says with a harsh laugh.

"Anne of Cleves?"

"*God Send Me Well to Keep*."

"Katherine Howard?"

Nan makes a face as if the memory is a bitter one: "*No Other Will but His*, poor little liar," she says.

"Katherine of Aragon?" We both know this one. Katherine was my mother's beloved friend, a martyr to her faith and to her husband's terrible infidelity.

"*Humble and Loyal*, God bless her. Never was a woman more humbled. Never was one more loyal."

"What was Jane's?" Jane Seymour will always be the favorite wife, whatever I say or do. She gave him his son and she died before he tired of her. Now he remembers a perfect woman, more saint than wife, and even manages to squeeze out a few hot little tears for her. But my sister, Nan, remembers that Jane died terrified and alone, asking for her husband, and nobody had the courage to tell her that he had ridden away.

"*Bound to Obey and Serve*," Nan says. "Bound hand and foot, if the truth be told."

"Bound? Who bound her?"

"Like a dog, like a slave. Those brothers of hers sold her to him as if she were a trussed chicken. Drove her to market, put her on sale right under Queen Anne's nose. Trussed her and stuffed her and put her into the oven heat of the queen's rooms, certain that the king would want a taste."

"Don't."

Both of my former husbands lived far from court, far from the gossip of London. When I got any London news, it was weeks late and through the rosy glow of distance, as told by the traveling pedlars, or in a rare hurried note from Nan. The rumors of royal wives who came and went over the years were like fairy stories told of imaginary beings: the pretty young whore, the fat German duchess, the angelic mother dead in childbirth. I don't have Nan's clear-eyed cynicism about the king and his court, I don't know half what she knows. Nobody knows all the secrets that she has heard. I came to court only in the last months of my husband Latimer's life to find a complete wall of silence around any mention of the last queen, and no happy recollections of any of them.

"Your motto had better be a promise of loyalty and humility," Nan says. "He is raising you to a great position. You have to declare publicly that you're grateful, that you will serve him."

"I'm not naturally a humble woman," I say with a little smile.

"You have to be grateful."

"I want something about grace," I agree. "Knowing that this is the will of God is the only thing that will carry me through."

"No, you can't say anything like that," she cautions me. "It has to be God in your husband, God in the king."

"I want God to use me. He has to help me. I want something like *All that I Do Is for God*."

"*All that I Do Is for Him*?" she suggests. "Then it sounds as if you're thinking only of the king."

"But it's a lie," I say flatly. "I don't want to use clever words to mean two things at once, like a courtier or a crooked priest. I want my motto to be something clear and truthful."

"Oh, don't be all blunt and northern!"

"Just honest, Nan. I just want to be true."

"What about: *To Be Useful in All that I Do*? It doesn't say useful to who—you know that it's for God and for the reformed religion, but you don't have to say that."

"*To Be Useful in All That I Do*," I repeat without much enthusiasm. "It's not very inspiring."

"*The Most Happy* was dead in three and a half years," Nan says harshly. "*No Other Will but His* had her lover in the jakes. These are mottoes: they aren't predictions."

Lady Elizabeth, the daughter of Anne Boleyn, is brought from her little court at Hatfield to be presented to me, her new stepmother—her fourth in seven years—and the king decides that this meeting shall be formal and public, so the nine-year-old child has to walk into the huge presence chamber at Hampton Court, the place crowded with hundreds of people, her back like a poker, her face as white as the muslin at the top of her gown. She looks like a player's brat, born to walk on a stage made from carts, lonely in a crowd, all show and no solid ground. Anxiety makes her plain, poor little thing, her copper hair scraped back under her hood, mouth pinched, her dark eyes goggling. She walks as her governess has taught her, back stiff, her head rigidly high. As soon as I see her I feel such pity for her, poor little child—her mother beheaded on her father's orders before she was three years old, her own safety always uncertain as she tumbled overnight from royal heir to royal bastard. Her very name was changed from Princess Elizabeth to Lady Elizabeth, and nobody curtseyed anymore when they served her bread and milk.

I don't see a threat in this little mite. I see instead a little girl who never knew her mother, who was not even sure of her name, who rarely saw her father, and who has been loved only by servants who cling to their posts by luck and work for nothing when the royal exchequer forgets to pay them.

She hides her terror behind a rigid formality—she has a veneer of royalty like a shell—but I am sure that inside, the soft little creature is cringing like a Whitstable oyster squirted with lemon juice. She curtseys low to her father and then she turns and curtseys to me. She speaks to us in French, expressing her gratitude that her father should allow her into his presence, and her joy in greeting her new honored mother. I find I am watching her almost as if she is a poor little beast from the menagerie at the Tower, ordered by the king to do tricks.

Then I see a swift glance between Elizabeth and Lady Mary and I realize that they are sisters indeed, both of them afraid of their father, completely dependent on his whim, uncertain of their position in the world and instructed never to put a foot wrong on a most uncertain path. Lady Mary was forced to wait on Elizabeth when she was a baby princess, but this failed to breed enmity. Lady Mary came to love her half sister, and now she nods encouragingly as the little voice trembles over the French words.

I rise from my seat and step quickly down from the dais. I take Elizabeth's cold hands and I kiss her forehead. "You're very welcome to court," I say to her in English—for who speaks a foreign language to their daughter? "And I shall be very glad to be your mother and care for you, Elizabeth. I hope you will see me as a mother indeed, and that we will be a family together. I hope that you will learn to love me and trust that I will love you as my own."

The color floods into her pale cheeks, up to her sandy eyebrows, her thin lips tremble. She has no words for a natural act of affection though she had speeches prepared in French.

I turn to the king. "Your Majesty, of all the treasures that you have given me, this—your daughter—is the one that gives me most delight." I glance at Lady Mary, who is blanched with shock at my sudden informality. "Lady Mary I love already," I say. "And now I will love Lady Elizabeth. When I meet your son, my joy will be complete."

The favorites, Anthony Denny and Edward Seymour, look

from me to the king to see if I have forgotten my place and embarrassed him—his commoner wife. But the king is beaming. It seems that this time he wants a wife who is as loving to his children as she is loving to him.

"You speak to her in English" is all he remarks, "but she is fluent in French and Latin. My daughter is a scholar like her father."

"I speak from my heart," I say, and I am rewarded by the warmth of his smile.

HAMPTON COURT PALACE, SUMMER 1543

KP

They tell me I must put aside mourning for my wedding day and wear a gown from the royal wardrobe. The groom of the wardrobe brings one sandalwood chest after another from the great store in London, and Nan and I spend a happy afternoon pulling out gowns, looking them over, and taking our pick as Lady Mary and a few other ladies advise. The robes are powdered and stored in linen bags and the sleeves are stuffed with lavender heads to keep away the moth. They smell like wealth: the cool soft velvets and the sleek satin panels have an odor of luxury that I have never known in my life before. I take my choice from the queens' gowns, in cloth of silver and cloth of gold, and I look at all the many sleeves and hoods, and the underskirts. By the time I have made my choice, of a richly embroidered gown in dark colors, it is nearly time for dinner. The ladies pack the spare gowns away, Nan closes the door on everyone and we are alone.

"I have to talk to you about your wedding night," she says.

I look at her grave face, and at once I fear that she somehow knows my secret. She knows I love Thomas and we are lost. I can do nothing but brazen it out. "Oh, what is it, Nan? You look very serious? I'm not a virgin bride, you need not warn me of what's to come. I don't expect to see anything new," I laugh.

"It is serious. I have to ask you a question. Kat—do you think you are barren?"

"What a thing to ask me! I'm only thirty-one!"

"But you never got a child from Lord Latimer?"

"God didn't bless us, and he was away from home, and in his later years he wasn't . . ." I make a dismissive gesture. "Anyway. Why do you ask?"

"Just this," she says grimly. "The king cannot bear to lose another baby. So you can't conceive one. It's not worth the risk."

I am touched. "He would be so grieved?"

She tuts with impatience. Sometimes I irritate my London-bred sister with my ignorance. I am a country lady—worse even than that—a lady from the North of England, far from all the gossip, innocent as the northern skies, blunt as a farmer.

"No, of course not. It's not grief, for him. He never feels grief." She glances at the bolted door and draws me farther into the room so that no one, not even someone with their ear pressed to the wooden panels, could hear us.

"I don't believe that he can give you a baby that can stay in the womb. I don't think he can make a healthy child."

I step closer so that we are mouth to ear. "This is treason, Nan. Even I know it. You're mad to say such a thing to me, just before my wedding day."

"I'd be mad if I didn't. Kateryn, I swear to you that he can't make anything but miscarriages and stillbirths."

I lean back to see her grave face. "This is bad," I say.

"I know."

"You think I will miscarry?"

"Or worse."

"What on earth could be worse?"

"If you were to birth a child, it might be a monster."

"A what?"

She is as close as if we were confessing, her eyes on my face.

"It's the truth. We were told never to speak of it. It's a deep secret. No one who was there has ever spoken of it."

"You'd better speak now," I say grimly.

"Queen Anne Boleyn—her death sentence was not the gossip and slander and lies they collected against her: all that nonsense about dozens of lovers. Anne Boleyn gave birth to her own fate. Her death sentence was the little monster."

"She had a little monster?"

"She miscarried something malformed, and the midwives were hired spies."

"Spies?"

"They went at once to the king with what they had seen, what had been birthed into their waiting hands. It was not a child born before its time, not a normal child. It was half fish, half beast. It was a monster with a face cleaved in two and a spine flayed open like something they might show pickled in a jar at a village fair."

I tear my hands from hers and cover my ears. "My God, Nan . . . I don't want to know. I don't want to hear this."

She pulls my hands away and shakes me. "As soon as they told the king, he took it as proof that she had used witchcraft to conceive, that she had lain with her brother to get a hell-born child."

I look at her blankly.

"And Cromwell got him the evidence to prove it," she said. "Cromwell could have proved that Our Lady was a drunk; that man had a sworn witness for anything. But he was commanded by the king. The king would not let anyone think that he could give a woman a monster." She looks at my horrified face and presses on: "So you think on this: if you miscarry, or if you give him a damaged babe, he will say the same about you and send you to your death."

"He can't say such a thing," I say flatly. "I'm not another Queen Anne. I'm not going to lie with my brother and dozens of others. We heard of her even in Richmondshire. We knew what she did. Nobody could say such a thing of me."

"He would rather believe that he was cuckolded ten times over than admit that there is anything wrong with him. What you heard in Richmondshire—the king's cuckolding—was announced by the king himself. You knew it, because he made sure that everyone knew it. He made sure the country knew that she was at fault. You don't understand, Kateryn. He has to be perfect, in every way. He cannot bear that anyone should think, even for a moment, that he is in the wrong. He cannot be seen as less than perfect. His wife has to be perfect too."

I look as blank as I feel. "This is hog swill."

"It is true," Nan exclaims. "When Queen Katherine miscarried, he blamed it on God and said it was a false marriage. When Queen Anne gave birth to the monster, he blamed it on witchcraft. If Jane had lost her baby, he would have blamed it on her, she knew it, we all knew it. And if you miscarry, it will be your fault, not his. And you will be punished."

"But what can I do?" I ask fiercely. "I don't know what I can do? How can I possibly prevent it?"

In answer she brings a little purse from the pocket of her gown and shows it to me.

"What's that?"

"This is fresh rue," she says. "You drink a tea made from it after he has had you. Every time. It prevents a child before it is even formed."

I don't take the little purse she holds out to me. I put out one finger and poke it.

"This is a sin," I say uncertainly. "It must be a sin. This is the sort of rubbish that the old women peddle behind the hiring fair. It probably doesn't even work."

"It's a sin to walk knowingly towards your own destruction," she corrects me. "And you will do that if you don't prevent a conception. If you give birth to a monster, as Queen Anne did, he will name you as a witch and kill you for it. His pride won't allow him another dead baby. Everyone would know it was a fault in him if another wife, his sixth healthy wife, birthed a monster or lost a baby. Think! It would be his ninth loss."

"Eight dead babies?" I can see a family of ghosts, a nursery of corpses.

She nods in silence and holds out the purse of rue. In silence, I take it.

"They say it smells awful. We'll get the maid to bring you a jug of hot water in the morning, and brew it ourselves, alone."

"This is terrible," I say quietly. "I've given up my own desires"—I have a pulse like a stab of lust in the belly when I think of my own desires—"and now you—my own sister—give me poison to drink."

She lays her warm cheek to mine. "You have to live," she says with quiet passion. "Sometimes, at court, a woman has to do anything to survive. Anything. You have to survive."

There is plague in the City of London and the king rules that our wedding shall be small and private with no crowds of common people that might bring infections. It will not take place in a great ceremony in the abbey, the fountains are not going to flow with wine, the people are not to roast oxen and dance in the streets. They are to take physic and stay in their homes, and nobody is allowed to come from the pestilential city to the clean river and the green meadows of the countryside around Hampton Court.

This, my third wedding, is to take place in the queen's oratory, a small, beautifully decorated room off the queen's chambers. I remind myself that this will be my private chapel, just off my closet, where I will be able to meditate and pray alone when this is all over. Once I have said my vows this very room—and all the others on the queen's side—will be mine, for my exclusive use.

The room is crowded, and the courtiers shuffle back as I enter in my new gown, and walk slowly towards the king. He stands, a man mountain, as broad as he is tall, before the altar, which is a blaze of light: hot white wax candles in branching golden candelabra on a jewel-encrusted altar cloth, gold and silver jugs, bowls, pyxes, plates, and, towering over it all, a great golden crucifix studded with diamonds. All the treasures looted from the greatest religious houses of the kingdom have silently found their way into the king's keeping and now blaze, like pagan sacrifices, on the altar, overwhelming the open pages of the English Bible, choking the simplicity of the chapel till the little room is more like a treasure hoard than a place of worship.

My hand is lost in the king's big sweating palm. Before us, Bishop Stephen Gardiner holds out the book of service and reads the marriage vows in the steady voice of a man who has seen queens come and go and quietly improved his own position. The bishop was a friend of my second husband, Lord Latimer, and shared his belief that the monasteries should serve their communities, that the church should be unchanged but for the head, that the wealth of the chantries and the abbeys should never have been stolen by greedy new men, and that the country now is poorer for throwing priests and nuns into the marketplaces and breaking the sacred shrines.

The service is in simple English, but the oration is in Latin, as if the king and his bishop want to remind everyone that God speaks Latin, and the poor and the uneducated, and almost all women, will never understand Him.

Behind the king, in a smiling crowd, are his most personal friends and courtiers. Edward Seymour, Thomas's older brother—who will never know that I sometimes search his dark eyes for a family resemblance to the man that I love—Nan's husband, William Herbert, standing with Anthony Browne, and Thomas Heneage. Behind me are the ladies of the court. First among them are the king's daughters, Lady Mary and Lady Elizabeth, and his niece Lady Margaret Douglas. Behind the three of them come my sister, Nan, Catherine Brandon, and Jane Dudley. Other faces swim together; it is hot and the room is overcrowded.

The king bellows his oath as if he were the herald announcing a triumph. I speak my words clearly, my voice steady, and then it is done and he turns to me, and his sweating face is beaming. He bends down to me, and now, amid a ripple of applause, he kisses the bride.

His mouth is like a little limpet, wet and inquisitive, his saliva tainted from his decaying teeth. He smells of rotting food. He releases me, and his sharp little eyes interrogate my face to see how I respond. I look downwards as if I am overcome by desire and I find a smile and peep up at him coyly, like a girl. It is no worse than I thought it would be, and anyway I will have to get used to it.

Bishop Gardiner kisses my hands, bows low to the king, offers congratulations, and everyone surges forward, filled with joy that it is done. Catherine Brandon, whose roguish prettiness keeps her dangerously high in the king's favor, is especially warm in her praise of the wedding and the happiness we are certain to enjoy. Her husband, Charles Brandon, stands behind his exquisite young wife and winks at the king—one old dog to another. The king waves them all aside and offers me his arm, so that we can lead the way out of the room and to dinner.

There is to be a feast. The smell of roasting meats has been seeping up through the floorboards from the kitchen immediately beneath these rooms for hours. Everyone falls into line behind us in the strict order of precedence, depending on title and status. I see Edward Seymour's wife, the sharp-featured, sharp-tongued aristocrat, roll her eyes and step back as she has to give way for me. I hide a smile at my triumph. Anne Seymour can learn to curtsey to me. I was born a Parr, a respectable family in the North of England, then I was the young wife of a Neville—a good family, but far from court and fame, and now Anne Seymour has to step back to me as the new Queen of England, the greatest woman in England.

As we enter the great hall, the courtiers rise to their feet and applaud, while the king beams to right and left. He hands me to my seat. Now my chair is a little lower than his, but higher than that of Lady Mary, who sits in turn higher than little Lady Elizabeth. I am the most important and wealthiest woman in England until death or disgrace—whichever comes first. I look across the room of cheering people, smiling faces, until I see my sister, Nan, walking composedly to the head of the table for the queen's ladies. She gives me a reassuring nod as if to say that she is here, she is watching over me, her friends will report on what the king says in private, her husband will praise me to him. I am under the protection of my family, ranged against all the other families. They expect me to persuade the king to the reform of the church, and to gain them wealth and position, to find places and fees for their children. In return, they protect my reputation, praise me above all others, and defend me against enemies.

I don't look for anyone else; I don't look for Thomas. I know he is already far away. Nobody will ever be able to say that I looked for his dark head, the quick glance of his brown eyes, a hidden smile. Nobody will ever be able to say that I sought him out, for I never will. In my long nights of prayer I have taught myself to know that he will never be here again: a perfect silhouette in a doorway, or bending over a gambling table and laughing, always the first on his feet to dance, the last to go to bed, his laughter ringing out, his quick attentive glance to me. I have surrendered my plan to marry him as I have surrendered my desire for him. I have hammered my soul into resignation. I may never see him again, and I shall never look for him.

Women before me have done this, and women who come after me will know this gutting of a heart's desire. It is the first task of a woman who loves one man but marries another, and I know I am not the first woman in the world who has had to cut out love, and then pretend that she is not wounded. A wife guided by God often has to surrender the love of her life, and I have done no more and no less. I have given him up. I think my heart has broken, but I have offered the fragments to God.

This is not my first wedding day, not even my second, but even so, I am dreading the night as if I were a virgin creeping up the dark stairs of a castle with a bobbing candle in my hand. The feast goes on forever, as the king calls for more dishes and the servants come running from the kitchen with great golden trays laden with food held high at shoulder level. They bring in a pride of peacocks, roasted and returned to their skins so the gorgeous feathers shimmer in the candlelight on the table before us. The server peels back the bloodstained inner skin, the blue iridescent neck flops over to one side as if it were a beheaded beauty, and the dead eyes, replaced with black raisins, gleam as if they are still looking for mercy. The carcass is revealed, the king impatiently crooks his finger and receives a great chunk of dark breast meat on his golden plate. They bring a tray of larks, the tiny bodies piled like a heap of victims from the Pilgrimage of Grace, numberless, nameless, stewed in their own juice. They bring plates with long slices of the breasts of snared herons, jugged hare drowned in deep bowls, rabbits trapped in pies under golden crusts. They serve the king one dish after another and he takes a great portion and waves the rest around the hall to his favored friends.

He laughs at me, that I eat so sparely. I smile as I hear his teeth crunch on the bones of little birds. They bring him more wine, more and more wine, and then there is a blast of a trumpet and in comes the great head of a boar, his tusks gilded, golden cloves of garlic bulging in his eye sockets, rosemary twigs piercing his face for bristles. The king applauds and they carve him a cheek glistening with fat, and the beast is paraded around the room by the servers, who dispense slices from his face, from his ears, from his stumpy neck.

I glance towards Lady Mary, who is pale with nausea, and I pinch my cheeks so that I look rosy beside her. I take a portion of everything that the king offers me and I make myself eat.

Mouthful after mouthful of thick meat in rich sauce is piled on my plate and I chew and smile and force it down my throat with a swallow of wine. I feel myself become faint and I start to sweat. I can feel my gown dampen at my armpits and down my spine. The king, beside me, is sprawled almost supine in his chair, felled by food, groaning as he beckons for another serving and another.

Finally, as if it is an ordeal that we cannot escape, they blow a blast of trumpets to announce that we have achieved the halfway point, and the meats go out, and the puddings and sweetmeats come in. There is a cheer for a marchpane model of Hampton Court with two little figures made from spun sugar standing before it. The sugar cooks are artists: their Henry looks like a boy of twenty, standing tall and holding the reins of a charger. They have me in widow's white and they have captured the interrogative tilt of my head as the little sugar Kateryn looks up inquiringly at the sparkling boy-prince Henry. Everyone exclaims at the artistry of the figures. It could be Holbein in the kitchen, they say. I have to keep the delighted smile on my face and swallow a sudden rush of tears. This is a little tragedy, crystallized in sugar. If Henry were still a boy-prince like this, we might have had a chance of happiness. But the Katherine who married the boy was Katherine of Aragon, my mother's friend, not Kateryn Parr—twenty-one years his junior.

The figures have little crowns of real gold and Henry gestures that I am to have both. He laughs when I put them on my fingers like rings, and then he takes the little sugar Kateryn and puts her whole in his mouth, breaking her legs to cram her in, as he eats her in one sucking gulp.

I am glad when he calls for more wine and more music, and slumps back in his throne. The choir from his chapel sings a pretty anthem and the dancers enter with a rattle of tambourines and perform a wedding masque. One of them, dressed as an Italian prince, bows low to me to invite me to join them. I glance to the king and he waves me to go out. I know that I dance well, the wide skirts of the rich gown billow as I turn and lead out the

Lady Mary, and even little Lady Elizabeth hops behind me. I can tell that Mary is in pain; her hand rests lightly on her hip; her fingers are digging into her side. She holds up her head and smiles with gritted teeth. I cannot excuse her from dancing just because she is sick. We all have to dance at my wedding, whatever we feel.

I dance with my ladies, one dance after another. I would dance all night for him if it would keep him from nodding to the gentlemen of the bedchamber that the evening is over and the court is closing for the night. But midnight comes as I am seated on my throne, applauding the musicians, and the king turns his great bulk towards me, heaving himself sideways so that he can lean over and say to me with a smile: "Shall we go to bed, wife?"

I remember what I thought when I first heard his proposal. I thought, this is how it will be, from now till death parts us: he will wait for my assent, or he will continue without it. It really doesn't matter what I say, I will never be able to refuse him anything. I smile and rise to my feet, and wait for them to haul him up, and then he struggles down the steps of the dais and waddles through the court. I go slowly beside him, fitting my stride to his rolling gait. The court cheers us as we go through them all, and I make sure that I keep my eyes forwards and meet no one's gaze. I can bear anything but a look of pity as I lead my ladies to my new bedchamber: the queen's bedchamber, to undress and wait for my master, the king.

It is late, but I don't allow myself to hope that he is too tired to come to my rooms. My ladies dress me in black satin, and I don't hold the sleeve to my cheek and remember another night when I wore a night robe of black and threw a blue cloak on top and went in the colors of the night sky to a man who loved me. That night was only a little while ago and I am obliged to forget it. The doors open, and in comes His Majesty, borne up on either side by the grooms of the bedchamber. They help him into the high bed:

as if they are wrestling a bull into a press. He swears loudly when someone knocks his bad leg. "Fool!" he snaps.

"Only one Fool here," the king's Fool, Will Somers, says briskly. "And I'll thank you to remember that I am keeping my place!"

Clever as always, he breaks the tension; the king laughs and everyone joins in. Somers winks at me as he goes by, his kind brown eyes twinkling. No one else even looks at me. As they bow and leave they keep their eyes on the ground. I think that they fear for me, left alone with him at last, as the fumes of the wine seep from his head and the food curdles in his belly and his mood sours. My ladies dash to get out of the room. Nan is the last to leave and she gives me a little nod as if to remind me that I am doing God's work as much as if I were a saint about to lie down on the rack.

The door closes behind them and I am kneeling at the foot of the bed in silence.

"You can come closer," he says gruffly. "I won't bite. Get into bed."

"I was saying my prayers," I say. "Shall I pray aloud for you, Your Majesty?"

"You can call me Henry now," he says. "When we're alone."

I take that as a refusal of the prayers, and I lift up the covers and slip into bed beside him. I don't know what he is going to do. Since he cannot even roll on his side unaided, he certainly cannot mount me. I lie beside him perfectly still and wait for him to tell me what he wants.

"You'll have to sit on my lap," he says eventually, as if he has been puzzling at this too. "You're not a foolish girl, you're a woman. You've been wedded and bedded more than once. You know what to do, eh?"

This is worse than I had imagined. I lift the hem of my nightgown out of the way, and creep towards him on my hands and knees. Unbidden, the vision of Thomas Seymour, outstretched and naked, his back arched, his dark eyelashes sweeping his brown cheeks, comes into my mind. I can see the muscles of his hard belly ripple with pleasure at my touch as he thrusts upwards.

"Latimer was no great lover, I take it?" the king inquires.

"He was not a man of great strength like you, Your . . . Henry," I say. "And of course, he was unwell."

"So how did he do?"

"His health?"

"How did he do the act? How did he bed you?"

"Very rarely."

He grunts in approval at that, and I see that he is aroused. The thought that he is more potent than my former husband excites him.

"That must have made him angry," he says with pleasure. "Taking a woman like you to wife and not being able to do the act." He laughs. "Come on," he says. "You're very lovely. I can't wait."

He takes hold of my right wrist and tugs me towards him. Obediently I kneel up and try to straddle his body. But his fleshy hips are so wide that I cannot get across, and he pulls me down so that I squat on him as if I were astride a fat horse. I have to hold my face rigid so that I don't grimace. I must not tremble, I must not cry.

"There," he says, excited at his own potency. "Feel that? Not bad for a man just over fifty, is it? You won't have got that from old Latimer."

I murmur a wordless response. He pulls me towards him and struggles to push upwards against me. He is soft, a half-formed thing, and now I am disgusted as well as embarrassed.

"There!" he says again more loudly. His face is becoming redder, the sweat is pouring off him with the effort of pulling me down with his hands and squirming his huge haunches upwards.

I put my hands over my face to block the sight of him laboring beneath me.

"You're not shy!" he exclaims, his voice loud in the room.

"No, no," I say. I must remember that I am doing this for God and for my family. I will be a good queen. This is part of my duty, my God-given duty. I put my hands to the neck of my nightgown and I untie the ribbons at the front. When he sees my naked breasts, he puts both fat hands over them and grasps at them, pinching the nipples. At last he penetrates me and I feel him try to thrust, then he gives a strangled shout, and falls back and lies still, completely still.

I wait, but nothing else happens. He says nothing. The brick red color drains from his face leaving his cheeks gray in the candlelight. His eyes are closed. His mouth sags open and he gives a long loud snore.

That seems to be it. Gently, I lift myself off his damp lap and carefully I slide off the bed. I gather my robe around me and I wrap it tightly, tying the sash around my waist and pulling it close. I sit at the fireside on the big chair that has been specially widened and strengthened for his weight, and I pull my knees to my chest and hug myself. I find I am shivering and I pour a glass of the mulled wedding ale that stands at my side on the table. It was supposed to give me courage and him potency. It warms me a little and I wrap my hands around the silver cup.

After a bleak time of staring blankly at the fire I creep into bed beside him. The mattress is deeply bowed under his weight, the blankets and the expensive coverlet heaped high over his great bulk. I am like a little child lying beside him. I close my eyes. I am thinking of nothing. I am absolutely determined to think of nothing at all. I close my eyes and I fall asleep.

Almost at once, I am dreaming that I am Tryphine, married against my will to a dangerous man, trapped in his castle and going up and up the spiral staircase, one hand on the damp wall, one holding the bobbing light of the candle. There is a terrible smell coming from the door at the top of the stairs. I go to the heavy brass ring of the door latch and slowly turn it. The door creaks open, but I cannot bear to go into the room, into that miasma of stink. I am so afraid that I struggle in the dream and struggle in my sleep, turning in the bed, and waking myself up. Even though I am awake, fighting sleep and feeling the fear of the dream, the smell still floods over me as if it were pouring out of my dream into the waking world, and I choke and struggle for breath as I wake. The smell of the nightmare is in my bed, it is stifling me, it has come from the dark night into my own bedroom, it is real and I am gagging on it. The nightmare is here, now.

I cry out for help and then I am awake and I realize it is not a dream: it is real. The suppurating wound on his leg is leaking, and yellow and orange pus is oozing through the bandages, staining my gown as if he had pissed the fine linen sheets, making the best bedroom in England smell like a charnel house.

The room is dark but I know that he is awake. The rumbling bubbling snores have stopped. I can hear his stertorous breathing, but it does not fool me: I know that he is awake, listening and looking for me. I imagine his eyes, wide open in the dark, staring blindly towards me. I lie completely still, my breathing steady and slight, but I am afraid that he knows, like a wild beast always knows, that I am afraid of him. He knows by some animal cunning that I am awake, and afraid of him.

"Are you awake, Kateryn?" he says very softly.

I stretch and give a little false yawn. "Ah . . . yes, my lord. I am awake."

"And did you sleep well?" The words are pleasant but there is an edge to his voice.

I sit up, tucking my hair under my nightcap, and turn towards him at once. "I did, my lord, thanks be to God. I hope that you slept well?"

"I felt sick; I tasted vomit in my throat. I was not propped up high enough on the pillows. It's terrible to feel like that in sleep. I could have choked. They have to prop me so that I am sitting up, or I choke on bile. They know that. You must make sure that they do that when I am in your bed as well as my own. There must have been something tainted in the dinner that made me sick. They have all but poisoned me. I shall send for the cooks in the morning and punish them. They must have used some bad meat. I need to vomit."

At once I am out of the bed, my soiled gown slick against my legs, fetching a bowl from the cupboard, a flask of ale. "Will you take a drink of small ale now? Shall I send for the doctors?"

"I shall see the doctor later. I was quite dizzy in the night."

"Ah, my dear," I say tenderly, as if I am a mother speaking to a sickly boy. "Perhaps you can take a drink of ale and sleep again?"

"No, I can't sleep," he complains peevishly. "I never sleep. The whole court sleeps, the whole country sleeps, but I am wakeful. I keep watch all night while lazy pages and slothful women sleep. I keep watch and ward over my country, over my church. D'you know how many men I will burn in Windsor next week?"

"No," I say, shrinking.

"Three," he says, pleased. "They'll burn them in the marshes and their ashes will float away. For questioning my holy church. Good riddance."

I think of Nan asking me to speak for them. "My lord husband . . ."

He has drained his cup of ale in three great gulps, and he gestures for more. I serve him again.

"More," he says.

"They left some pastries for us in the cupboard too, if you might want one," I offer doubtfully.

"I think one might steady my stomach."

I pass him the plate and watch as, absentmindedly, he folds one after another over and over and posts them into his little mouth and they disappear. He licks his finger and dabs at the crumbs on the plate and passes it back to me. He smiles. He is soothed by the food and the attention. It is as if sugar can sweeten him.

"That's better," he says. "I was hungry after our pleasures."

His mood is almost miraculously improved by ale and pastries. I think that he must carry a monstrous hunger with him all the time. He suffers with a hunger so great that he eats beyond nausea, a hunger so great that he mistakes it for nausea. I manage a smile.

"Can't you pardon those poor men?" I ask very quietly.

"No," he says. "What o'clock is it?"

I look around. I don't know: there is no clock in the room. I cross to the window and pull back the hangings, open the windowpane inwards, crack open the outer shutter and swing it to see the sky.

"Don't let the night air in," he says crossly. "God knows what pestilence might be on it. Close the window! Close it tight!"

I slam the window closed on the fresh cool air and peer through the thick glass. There is not a glimmer of light in the east though I blink my eyes to rid them of candlelight and wish it into being. "It must be early still," I say, longing for the sunrise. "I can't see any dawn."

He looks at me like an expectant child wanting to be entertained. "I can't sleep," he says. "And that ale is resting on my belly. It was too cold. It will give me colic. You should have mulled it." He moves a little and belches. At the same time a sour smell comes from the bed where he has farted.

"Shall I send to the kitchens for something else? A warm drink?"

He shakes his head. "No. But stir up the fire and tell me that you are glad to be queen."

"Oh! I am so very glad!" I smile as I bend and put on some kindling and then some great logs from the basket by the fireplace. The embers glow. I stir them with a poker, raising the logs so they rest one against another and flicker into life. "I am glad to be queen, and I am glad to be a wife," I say. "Your wife."

"You are a housewife," the king exclaims, pleased with my success at fire making. "Could you cook my breakfast?"

"I have never cooked," I say, a little on my dignity. "I have always had a cook, and kitchen maids too. But I know how to command a kitchen and a brew house and a dairy. I used to make my own physic from herbs, and perfumes and soaps."

"You know how to run a household?"

"I commanded Snape Castle and all our lands in the North when my husband was away from home," I tell him.

"Held it in a siege, didn't you?" he asks. "Against those traitors. That must have been hard. You must have been brave."

I nod modestly. "Yes, my lord. I did my duty."

"Faced down the rebels, didn't you? Didn't they threaten to burn down your castle and you inside it?"

I remember the days and the nights very well when the desperately poor men in rags came against the castle and begged for a return to the good days, the old days when the churches were free with charity and the king was guided by the lords. They wanted the church restored and the monasteries back in their former glory. They demanded that my husband Lord Latimer speak for them to the king, they knew that he agreed with them. "I knew they would not prevail against you," I say, faithless to them and their cause. "I knew that I had to hold on and that you would send my lord home to relieve us."

I am making the best of a bad story, hoping that he doesn't remember the truth of it. The king and his council rightly suspected my husband of siding with the rebels, and when the rebellion was brutally crushed, my husband had to side with reform: he betrayed his faith and his tenants for his own safety. How glad he would be now to see that it is all changed again. The churchmen have the upper hand and are busy restoring the abbeys. My husband would have delighted in his friend Stephen Gardiner's new authority. He would have been all for the burning of reformers in the marshes of Windsor. He would have agreed that the ashes of heretics should blow away into the mud and that they should never rise from the dead.

"And how old were you when you first went from your mother?"

The king settles back against the pillow like a child wanting a story.

"You want to know about my girlhood?"

He nods. "Tell me all about it."

"Well, I was a good age when I left home, more than sixteen.

My mother had been trying to marry me off from the age of eleven. But it didn't take."

He nods. "Why ever not? Surely you were the prettiest little girl? With that hair and those eyes, you could have had your pick."

I laugh. "I was pretty enough, but I had no more dowry than a tinker. My father left almost nothing—he died when I was only five. We all knew that Nan, my sister, and I would have to marry to oblige the family."

"How many of you?"

"Three, just three. I'm the oldest and then William, my brother, and then Nan. You will remember my mother? She was a lady-in-waiting, and then she got Nan a place with—" I break off. Nan served Katherine of Aragon and every queen since. The king has seen her walk in to dinner behind every single one of his six wives. "My mother got Nan a place at court," I amend. "And then she got my brother, William, married to Anne Bourchier. It was the very pinnacle of her ambition; but you know how badly that went. It's been a costly mistake for us all. Both Nan and I were put aside so that William could marry well. There was only money for William, and once my mother had got Anne Bourchier there was no money left for a dowry for me."

"Poor little girl," he says sleepily. "If only I had seen you then."

He did see me then. I came to court once with my mother and Nan. I remember the young king of those days: golden-haired, strong in the legs, chest broad but lean. I remember him on horseback; he was always on horseback like a young centaur. He rode past me once and I looked up at him, high on his horse, and he was dazzling. He looked directly at me, a little girl of six jumping up and down, waving at the twenty-seven-year-old king. He smiled at me and raised his hand. I stood stock-still and stared up at him in wonderment. He was as beautiful as an angel. They called him the handsomest king in the world, and there was not a woman in England who did not dream of him. I used to imagine him riding into our little home and asking for my hand in marriage. I thought that if he came for me, everything would be all right, for the rest of my life, for always. If the king fell in love with me, what more could I want? What more could anyone want?

"And so I was married to my first husband, Edward Brough, the eldest son of Baron Brough of Gainsborough."

"Mad, wasn't he?" comes sleepily from the richly embroidered pillows. His eyes are closed. His hands, clasped over the mound of his chest, rise and fall with each wheezy breath.

"That was his grandfather," I say very quietly. "But it was still a fearsome house. His lordship had a terrible temper and my husband shook like a child when he raged."

"He was no match for you," he says with sleepy satisfaction. "They were fools to match you to a boy. Even then, you must have been a girl who needed a man you could admire, someone older, someone who could command."

"He was no husband for me," I confirm. I understand now how he wants this bedtime story to go. There are only half a dozen tales in the world, after all, and this one is to be about the girl who never found happiness until she met her prince. "He was no match for me at all, and he died, God bless him, when I was just twenty."

As if the denigration of poor, long-dead Edward has lulled him, a long rumbling snore is my reply. I wait for a moment as he suddenly stops breathing. For one frightening moment there is no sound in the quiet room at all, then he catches his breath and loudly exhales. He does this over and over again until I learn not to flinch. I sit back in my chair by the fireside and watch the flames lick around the logs and flicker, making the shadows jump forward and then recede around me as the thick snorting goes on and on, like a boar in a sty.

I wonder, what is the time. Surely it must be dawn soon. I wonder when the servants will come. Surely they must make up the fires at dawn? I wish I knew the time. I would give a fortune for a clock to tell me how much longer I have to wait for this endless night to be over. It's so odd that the nights with Thomas passed in a moment, as if the moon flung itself to set and the sun hurried into the sky. Not now. Perhaps never again. Now I have to wait for a lifetime till dawn, and hours and hours go by as I wait for the first light.

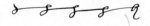

"How was it?" Nan whispers. Behind her, the servants take the golden washing bowl and ewer from my room, as the maids-in-waiting sprinkle my linen with rosewater and hold it to the fire to make sure that it is completely dry.

Nan has the purse of dried rue. With her back to the room she takes up the mulling poker from the red embers of the fire, seethes a mug of small ale, and stirs in the herb. Nobody notices as I drink it down. I turn my face away so no one can see my grimace.

I go with her to my prie-dieu and the two of us face the crucifix and kneel side by side so closely that no one can hear a word but will think that we are muttering our prayers in Latin.

"Is he potent?"

The question alone is a capital offense. Anne Boleyn's brother was beheaded for asking this very thing.

"Just about," I tell her tersely.

She puts a hand over mine. "He didn't hurt you?"

I shake my head. "He can hardly move. I'm in no danger from him."

"Was it . . . ?" She breaks off. A well-loved wife herself, she cannot imagine my revulsion.

"It was no worse than I thought it would be," I say, my head bowed over my beads. "And now I have some pity for him." I glance up at the crucifix. "I'm not the only one suffering. These are hard years for him. Think of what he was, and what he is now."

She closes her eyes in a silent prayer. "My husband, Herbert, says that God's hand is over you," she says.

"You must perfume my room," I decide. "Send to the apothecary for some dried herbs and perfume. Rose oil, lavender, strong perfumes. I can't stand the smell. The one thing I cannot stand is the smell. I really can't sleep with it. You've got to get this done. It's the only thing I really can't bear."

She nods. "Is it his leg?"

"His leg and his wind," I say. "My bed smells of death and shit."

She looks at me, as if I have surprised her. "Of death?"

"Of the corruption of the body. Of a corrupting body. Of the plague. I dream of death," I say shortly.

"Of course, the queen died here."

I cry out in horror, and as my ladies turn to look, I try to turn it into a cough. At once someone brings me a glass of small ale to sip. When they have stepped back, I turn on Nan. "Which queen?" I demand, thinking wildly of the child Katherine Howard. "Why didn't you tell me?"

"Queen Jane, of course," she says.

I knew that she died after giving birth to the prince, but I had not thought it was in these rooms, in my rooms. "Not here?"

"Of course," she says simply. "In this bedroom." When she sees my aghast face, she adds: "In this bed."

I shrink back, clutching my rosary. "In my bed? That bed? Where we slept last night?"

"But, Kateryn, there's no need to take on. It was over five years ago."

I shiver and find that I cannot stop. "Nan, I can't do this. I can't sleep in his dead wife's bed."

"Dead wives," she corrects me. "Katherine Howard slept here. It was her bed too."

I don't cry out this time. "I can't bear it."

She takes hold of my shaking hands. "Be steady. It is God's will," she says. "God's calling. You have to do this, you can do this. I will help you and God will bear you up."

"I can't sleep in the dead queen's bed and mount her husband."

52

"You have to. God will help you. I pray to Him, I pray every day—*God help and guide my sister.*"

I nod convulsively: "Amen, amen. God keep me, amen."

It is time for me to be dressed. I turn to let them take the night robe from my shoulders and wash me with the scented oils and pat me dry, and then I step into my beautifully embroidered linen shift. I stand like a doll while they tie the ribbons at my throat and at my shoulders. The ladies-in-waiting bring gowns and a choice of sleeves and hoods, and hold them before me in attentive silence. I choose a gown in dark green, sleeves of black and a hood of black.

"Very modest," my sister remarks critically. "You're out of black now. You're a bride, not a widow. You should wear gowns of brighter colors. We'll order some for you to choose."

I love fine clothes, she knows that.

"And shoes," she says temptingly. "We'll have the cobblers come to you. You can have all the shoes you want now." She sees my face and she laughs. "Now, you have much to do. You'll have to arrange your household. I have half of England wanting to send their daughters to serve you. I've got a list of names. We can go through them after Mass."

One of my ladies steps forward. "If you will forgive me, I have a favor to ask. If I may."

"We'll look at all the requests together, after chapel," my sister rules.

I step into the gown and stand still while they tie the skirt, the bodice, and then hold the sleeves in place and thread the laces through the holes.

"I'll send for our brother, William," I say quietly to Nan. "I'll want him here. And our uncle Parr."

"Apparently we have family we never knew before. From all over England. Everyone wants to claim kinship to the new Queen of England."

"I don't have to give them all places, do I?" I ask.

"You'll need people who depend on you around you," she says.

53

"Of course you would reward your own family. And I assume you'll send for the Latimer girl, your stepdaughter?"

"Margaret is very dear to me," I say, suddenly hopeful. "Can I have her with me? And Elizabeth my stepdaughter? And Lucy Somerset, my stepson's betrothed? And my Brough cousin, Elizabeth Tyrwhit?"

"Of course, and I thought you'd appoint Uncle Parr to something in your household, and his wife, Aunt Mary, will come too, and our cousin Lane."

"Oh, yes!" I exclaim. "I would want Maud with me."

Nan smiles. "You can have whoever you want. Whatever you want. You should ask for everything you want now, in the early days, when everything will be granted you. You need people who are yours, heart and soul, around you to guard you."

"Against what?" I challenge her as they put my hood on my head, as heavy as a crown.

"Against all the other families," she whispers as she smooths my auburn hair in the golden net. "Against all the previous families who enjoyed their kinswoman's patronage, and don't want to be excluded now by a new queen: families like the Howards and Seymours. And you will need protection against the king's new advisors, men like William Paget and Richard Rich and Thomas Wriothesley, men who have risen from nowhere and don't want a new queen advising the king instead of them."

Nan nods towards Catherine Brandon, who comes into the room carrying my small chest of jewels for me to make my choice. She lowers her voice. "And against women like her, wives of his friends, and any pretty lady-in-waiting who might be the next favorite."

"Not now!" I exclaim. "We were married only yesterday!"

She nods. "He's greedy," she says simply, as if it were a question of numbers of dishes at dinner. "He always wants more. He always needs more. He cannot get enough admiration."

"But he married me!" I exclaim. "He insisted on marrying me."

She shrugs. He married all my predecessors; it didn't stop him wanting the next one.

At chapel, on the second story, in the queen's box, looking down at the priest going about God's work, creating the miracle of the Mass and turning his back on the congregation as if they are not fit even to see it, I pray for God's help in this marriage. I think of the other queens who have knelt here, on this footstool embroidered with the royal coat of arms and the pied rose, and prayed here, too. Some of them will have prayed with increasing anguish for live Tudor sons, some of them will have mourned the loss of their previous lives, some will have been homesick for their childhood home and the family who loved them for themselves, not for what they could provide. One, at least, had a heartache like mine, had to wake each day and put away the thought of the man she loved. I can almost feel them around me as I rest my face in my hands. I can almost smell their fear in the wood of the book rest. I imagine that if I licked the polished grain I would taste the salt of their tears.

"Not merry?" The king meets me in the gallery outside the chapel. He with his friends behind him—Queen Jane's brother, Queen Anne's uncle, Queen Katherine's cousin—I with my ladies behind me. "Not merry on your wedding morning?"

At once I beam. "Very merry," I say determinedly. "And you, Your Majesty?"

"You can call me 'my lord husband,'" he says, and takes my hand and crushes it between the curve of his thickly padded waistcoat and the embroidered sleeve. "Come with me to my privy chamber," he says informally. "I need to talk with you on our own."

He releases me so that he can lean on a page and slowly limp forward. I follow him through his great waiting chamber, where there are hundreds of men and women gathered to see us pass, through the presence chamber, where scores more are waiting with petitions and requests, and into his privy chamber, where only the court is admitted. At each doorway more people fall away, excluded from the room within, until it is just the king and Anthony Denny, a couple of clerks, his two pages, his Fool, Will Somers, two of my ladies, and me. This is what he means by being alone with his wife.

They lower him into his great chair, which creaks a little under his weight, they put a footstool under his leg, then drape it with a cloth. He gestures that I may sit near him, and waves them all away. Denny goes to the back of the room and pretends to be talking to his wife, my lady-in-waiting Joan. I am sure that they are both ears pricked, to hear every word.

"So you are merry this morning?" Henry confirms. "Though I was watching you in chapel and you seemed grave. I can see you through the lattice of my box, you know. I can keep you under watch and ward all the time. Be very sure that I am always mindful of you."

"I was praying, my lord."

"That's good," he approves. "I like it that you are truly devout; but I want you to be happy. The Queen of England should be the happiest woman in Christendom as well as the most blessed. You must show the world that you are merry on your wedding morning."

"I am," I assure him. "I truly am."

"Visibly happy," he prompts me.

I show him my most dazzling smile.

He nods his approval. "And now you have work to do. And you must do everything that I say. I am your husband now, and you have promised obedience." His indulgent tone tells me that this is a joke.

I peep up at him. "I shall try to be a very good wife."

He chuckles. "These are my commands: you have to order the tailors and the seamstresses to bring beautiful clothes and fabrics, and you have to order a great many gowns," he says. "I want to see you dressed like a queen, not like the poor widow Latimer."

I give a little affected gasp and I press my hands together.

"They tell me you like birds?" he asks. "Colorful birds and singing birds."

"I do," I say. "But I could never afford to buy them."

"Well, now you can," he says. "I shall tell the captains of the ships that go far afield that they are to bring home little birds for you." He smiles. "It can be a new tax on shipping—little birds for the queen. And I have something for you now." He turns and snaps his fingers and Anthony Denny steps forward and puts a fat purse on the table and a small box. Henry passes me the box first. "Open it."

It is a magnificent ruby, table-cut like a block, on a simple gold band. It is too big for my fingers, but the king slides it on my thumb and admires the red glow. "Do you like it?"

"I love it."

"And there are more, of course. I have had them sent to your rooms."

"More?"

He warms to my naïvety. "More jewels, my dear. You are the queen. You have a treasury of jewels. You can pick out new ones to wear for every day of the year."

I don't have to feign my delight. "I do love pretty things."

"They're a tribute to your own beauty," he says gently. "I have wanted you draped in the royal treasures ever since I first saw you."

"Thank you, husband. Thank you so much."

He chuckles. "I am going to love giving you things. You blush like a little rose. This purse of gold is for you, too. Spend it on whatever you like and then come to me for another. You will have lands and rents and income of your own soon. Your steward will show you a list of all that you will own. You will be a wealthy woman in your own right. You will have all the queen consort lands and Baynard's Castle in London. You will command a fortune in your own name. This is just to tide you over."

"I should like to be tided over," Will Somers observes. "For some reason it is low tide with me, all the time."

The men laugh as, unobserved, I weigh the purse in my hand. It is heavy. If they are gold nobles, and I imagine that they are, this is a small fortune.

The king looks at his page. "Give me the list," he says.

The young man bows and hands him a rolled piece of paper. "These are men and women who want to serve in your household," the king says. "I have marked the ones that I wish you to take. But you can please yourself for most of the posts. I want you to be happy in your rooms and choose your own playmates."

It is the right of the queen to choose her own ladies. They are with her night and day. It is only fair that they should be her friends, family and favorites. The king should not be making out the list.

"I daresay I will approve your choices," he says. "I am sure there will be none that I do not approve. You have such beautiful taste, you are certain to choose ladies who will be an ornament to your court and to mine."

I bow my head.

"But they must be pretty," he specifies. "Make sure of that. I don't want an eyesore."

I say nothing to his plan that I should choose as my companions the women who will please him, and at once, he squeezes my hand. "Ah, Kate, we shall deal well together. We'll go hunting this afternoon and you shall sit with me."

"I would love that," I say. I long to be on my horse and ride with the hunt. I want the sense of freedom of riding behind the hounds, following where the scent takes them, going fast and riding far from the great palace, but I know it will not be like this. I shall have to sit in the royal shelter beside the king and watch the deer driven towards us so that Henry can shoot his loaded bow from his seat. Before him the huntsmen will herd and chivy the deer forward. Behind him, a page will take the sharpened bolt and load it into the crossbow. The king will do nothing but point and shoot. He makes a hunt, with all the chance and hazard of field and woodland, into a farmyard killing, a butcher's yard. The king's hunt, which was once a pageant of excitement, has become a shambles where animals are driven and slaughtered. But this is all he can do now. The man whom I remember as a centaur, as a huntsman, who rode three horses one after another in a single day till they foundered, is diminished to a murderer, slumped in a chair, defeated by old age and ill health, with a younger man loading his bow.

"I shall be so happy to sit beside you," I lie.

"And you shall learn to shoot," he promises me. "I will give you a little crossbow of your own. You must share in the sport. You must have the pleasure of the kill."

He intends to be kind to me. "Thank you," I say again.

He nods that I am to leave. I rise to my feet and hesitate as he beckons me towards him and lifts up his big moon face. He is like a little child, trustingly offering a kiss. I put one hand on his massive shoulder and I bend down. His breath is terribly rank—it is like letting a hound pant in my face—but I don't flinch. I kiss him on the mouth and I meet his eyes and smile.

"Dearest," he says quietly. "You are my dearest. You will be my last and dearest wife."

I am so touched that I bend down again and put my cheek to his.

"Go and buy some pretty things," he commands me. "I want you to look like a beloved wife and the finest queen that England has ever known."

I leave the room a little dazed. If I look like a beloved wife, it will be for the first time. To my second husband, Lord Latimer, I was a partner and a helpmeet, someone to guard his lands and educate his children. He taught me the things that he needed me to know and he was glad to have me alongside him. But he never petted me, or gave things to me, or imagined how I would appear to others. He rode away and left me in terrible danger, expecting me to serve him as the captain of Snape Castle, confident I would command his men in his absence. I was his deputy, not his love. Now I am married to a man who calls me his beloved and plans treats for me.

Nan is waiting with Joan at the door, which opens before us. "Come on," I say to her. "I think there are some things you'll want to see in my chambers."

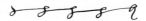

My own presence chamber is already filled with people come to congratulate me on my wedding and hoping to ask me for a place or a favor or an audience or a fee. I walk through them with a smile to one side and the other, without pausing. I will start my work as queen today. But right now, I want to see my husband's gifts.

"Oh, my," Nan says as the guards throw open the double doors to my private rooms and my ladies rise to their feet and gesture, rather helplessly, to the half a dozen boxes that the king's men have put all around the room, the great keys ready in the locks.

It is a sin to feel this leap of cupidity. I laugh at myself. "Stand back!" I say jokingly. "Stand back, for I am about to dive into treasure."

Nan turns the key to the first chest and we together lift the heavy lid. It is a traveling chest and it holds the gold plates and goblets for the queen's private tables. I nod to two of the maids-in-waiting to come forward. They unpack one glorious plate after another and tip the reflections so the golden lights dance around the room like mad angels. "More!" I say, and now everyone holds a plate and shines it into each other's eyes and flashes discs of light into every corner of the room until the room is dappled with shifting reflections. I laugh with delight and we shine the gold plates on one another, rise up, dance, and the whole room is dancing with us, filled with dazzling light.

"What's next?" I demand breathlessly, and Nan opens the next chest. This is filled with necklaces and belts. She draws out ropes of pearls and belts embroidered and encrusted with sapphires, rubies, emeralds, diamonds, and stones that I cannot even name, sparkling dark beauties set in thick blocks of silver or gold. She spreads chains of gold on the arms of chairs, necklaces of silver and diamonds in the laps of the maids so that they dazzle against rich fabric. There are opals with their soft milky light gleaming in green and peach, there is amber in great chunks of dark orange, and there are handfuls of uncut stones in purses looking like pebbles, hiding the flash of precious light within their rocky depths.

Nan opens another chest that has been carefully packed with rolls of the softest leather. Out come rings heavy with precious stones, and single stones on long chains. Without comment, she lays before me Katherine of Aragon's famous necklace of plaited gold. Another purse is undone and there are Anne Boleyn's rubies. The royal jewels of Spain come from one great box, the dowry of Anne of Cleves is spread on the floor at my feet. The treasure that the king showered on Katherine Howard comes in a chest all to itself, untouched since she was stripped of everything and went out to take the axe on her bare neck.

"Look at these earrings!" someone exclaims, but instead I turn away and go to the window to look down on the formal gardens and the glimpse of the silvery river through the trees. I am suddenly sickened. "Those are dead women's goods," I say unsteadily as Nan comes to my side. "They are the favorite treasures of dead queens. Those necklaces have been around the necks of the wife before me, some of them have been worn by every one of them who has gone before me. The pearls were warmed by their dead skins, the silver is tarnished by their old sweat."

Nan is as pale as me. She wrapped Katherine Howard's emeralds in their leather folders and put them in that very jewel box on the day of her arrest. She fastened Jane Seymour's sapphires around her neck on her wedding day. She handed

Katherine of Aragon her earrings and here they are now, on the table in my privy chamber for my use.

"You are the queen, you get the queen's treasures," she rules, but her voice trembles. "Of course. It's how it has to be."

There is a rap on the door and the guard swings it open. William Herbert, Nan's husband, comes into the room and smiles to see us all surrounded by jewels like children amazed in the pastry kitchen, spoiled for choice. "His Majesty sent this," he says. "It was overlooked. He says I am to put it on your beloved head."

As I rise to my feet and come towards my brother-in-law, I see he cannot meet my eyes. He looks at the window behind me, at the sky scudding with clouds; he does not look at the treasures at my feet as I step carefully around Katherine of Aragon's hoods, Katherine Howard's glossy black sables. In his hand is a small heavy box.

"What's this?" I ask him. I think at once—I don't want it.

In reply he bows, and unlocks the metal hasp. He lifts the lid and it falls back on its bronze hinges. There is a small ugly crown inside. The ladies behind me gasp. I see Nan make a little movement as if she would prevent what must come next.

William puts down the box and lifts out the elaborately worked crown, encrusted with pearls and sapphires. Mounted at the pinnacle, as if it were a domed church, is a plain gold cross.

"The king wants you to try it on."

Obediently, I bend my head for Nan to remove my hood, and her husband gives her the crown. It is the right size, it settles on my forehead like a headache.

"Is it new?" I ask faintly. I long for it to be newly made for me. He shakes his head.

"Whose was it?"

Nan makes a little gesture with her hand as if to warn him to be silent.

"It was Anne Boleyn's crown," he tells me. I feel it pressing down on my head as if I might sink beneath the weight of it.

"Surely he doesn't want me to wear it today," I say awkwardly.

"He'll tell you when," he says. "Important feast days or when you are meeting foreign ambassadors."

I nod, my neck stiff, and Nan takes it off for me and puts it back in the box. She closes the lid as if she does not want to see it. Anne Boleyn's crown? How can it be anything but cursed?

"But I'm to take back the pearls," William says, embarrassed. "They were brought in error."

"Which pearls?" Nan asks her husband.

He looks at her, still carefully not looking at me. "The Seymour pearls," he says quietly. "They're to be kept in the treasure room."

Nan bends down and picks up the ropes and ropes of pearls, milky and glowing in her hands, and piles them back in their long box, the strands running up and down the length of it like a quiescent snake. She hands them to William and smiles at me. "It's not as if we didn't have a fortune in pearls already," she says, trying to cover the awkward moment.

I walk with William to the doorway. "Why is he taking them back?" I ask him in an undertone.

"For remembrance of her," William tells me. "She gave him his son. He wants to keep them for the prince's future wife. He doesn't want anyone else wearing them."

"Of course, of course," I say quickly. "Tell him how pleased I am with everything else. I know that her pearls were special."

"He is at prayer," my brother-in-law says. "He is hearing a Mass for her now."

Carefully, I maintain my expression of sympathy and interest. The belief that God will shorten the days that a soul waits to enter heaven if He is offered a hundred Masses, a thousand prayers, bonfires of incense, was dismissed by this king, and the chantries closed. Even the chapel that he dedicated to pray for Jane's soul was abolished; I didn't know that he still clung to a belief that he has forbidden to the rest of us—the hope of praying someone out of purgatory.

"Stephen Gardiner is holding a special Mass for Queen Jane," William tells me. "In Latin."

Surely it's a little odd to be praying for the dead queen on the first day of the king's honeymoon? "God bless her," I say awkwardly, knowing that William will report this to his royal master. "Take her pearls and keep them safe. I will pray for her soul myself."

Just as the king promised, the word goes out that the new queen has a liking for pretty birds. One of the rooms off my presence chamber is emptied of furniture and filled with perches and cages. At the windows are little aviaries for the singing birds from the Canary Islands. When the sun pours in through the thick glass, they chrip and preen and flutter their little wings. I keep them according to color, the golds and yellows together, the greens next door to them, while the blues flit their little wings against a sky that mirrors their color. I hope that they will breed true. Every morning, after chapel, I visit my bird room and feed them all by hand, loving the feeling of their scratchy light little feet as they perch and peck for seed.

To my delight one day, a dark-skinned lascar sailor with a silver ring in his ear and his face tattooed, more like a painted devil than a man, comes to my presence chamber with a huge bird, as blue as indigo and as big as a buzzard, sitting on his clenched fist. He sells it to me for a ridiculously high price and now I am the very proud owner of a parrot with black knowing eyes. I name him Don Pepe, since he speaks nothing but the most obscene Spanish. I will have to put a cover over his cage when the Spanish ambassador, Eustace Chapuys, comes to pay his respects, but Nan assures me that he's a hard man to shock: after years at the court he has heard far worse.

The king gives me a new horse for riding, a beautiful bay mare, and a puppy, an adorable spaniel with a shining tan coat. I take him with me everywhere and he sits at my feet even when I go to chapel in the morning. I've never owned a dog that was not a working dog before, only the hounds for hunting in the stables at Snape, or the sheepdogs with their quick dashes here and there.

"You are the most idle thing," I tell him. "How can you live with yourself when all you have to be is ornamental?"

"He's very sweet," Nan agrees.

"Purkoy was a darling," Catherine Brandon remarks.

"Oh, what was Purkoy?" I ask.

"Anne Boleyn's dog." Nan frowns at Catherine. "Nothing like little Rig, here."

"Is there anything new?" I ask irritably. "Is there anything that I do that one of them hasn't already done?"

Catherine looks embarrassed.

"Your clocks," Nan says with a small smile at me. "You're the first queen to love clocks. All the goldsmiths and clockmakers in London are in heaven."

The court is to go on progress, as it does every summer. I cannot imagine how we are to pack up everything and move, every week, sometimes after only a few days, from one house to another, where all our servants will be expected to unload furniture, tapestries, and silverware and make a court in a new house. How am I to know what clothes to pack? How am I to know what jewels I should take? I don't even know how they take enough linen for the beds.

"It's nothing for you to trouble yourself about," Nan says. "Really, nothing. All the servants have moved the queen's household a score of times, a hundred times. All you have to do is to ride beside the king and look happy."

"But all the bedding! And all the clothes!" I exclaim.

"Everyone knows their part," she repeats. "You need do nothing but go where you are sent."

"My birds?"

"The falconers will take care of them. They'll go in their own cart behind the falcons and hawks."

"My jewels?" I ask.

"I take care of them," she says. "I've done this for years, Kat, honestly. All you have to do is to ride beside the king if he wants you there, and look beautiful."

"And if he doesn't want me?"

"Then you ride with your companions and your master of horse."

"I don't even have a master of horse yet, I haven't filled all my household posts."

"We'll appoint them as we travel. It's not for lack of applicants! All the clerks will travel with us, and most of the court. The Privy Council meets wherever the king happens to be; it's not like we are leaving court, we take everything with us."

"Where are we going?"

"Oatlands first," she says with satisfaction. "I think it is one of the best palaces, on the river, newly built, as beautiful as any of them. You'll love it there, and the bedrooms aren't haunted!"

OATLANDS PALACE, SURREY, SUMMER 1543

KP

Nan is completely right: the court breaks itself up and re-forms with practiced ease, and I love my rooms in Oatlands Palace. It was built on the river near Weybridge to be a honeymoon palace for Anne of Cleves, so Nan cannot truly claim that it is not haunted. Anne of Cleves's sorrow and disappointment are in every courtyard. Her maid-in-waiting Katherine Howard was triumphantly married to the king, here in the chapel; I imagine he chased her, panting endearments, limping as fast as he could go through the beautiful gardens.

The palace was built with the stone of the abbey at Chertsey, every beautiful sandstone block pulled down from where it was dedicated to God to stand forever. The tears of the faithful must have fallen in the mortar; but nobody thinks of that now. It is a huge sunny palace, near to the river, designed like a castle with a tower at each corner and a huge courtyard inside. My rooms look towards the south and they are sunny and light. The king's rooms adjoin them, and he warns me that he can walk in at any time to see what I am doing.

Over the next few days Nan and I draw up the list of posts in my household and start to fill them with the king's choices, with our friends and family and then, when we have satisfied everyone who has a claim on me, with those whose careers we want to advance. I look at the list prepared by Nan and her friends who support the religious reforms. Giving them a place as my household officials at court and in my rooms as my companions strengthens their numbers at the very moment that they are losing the king's support.

He has approved the publication of a statement of doctrine called *The King's Book*, which tells people that they have to make confession and believe in the miracle of the Mass. The wine becomes blood, the bread becomes flesh—the king says it is so, and everyone must believe. He has taken away the great English Bible from every church in every parish and only the rich and the noble are allowed to read the Bible in English, and they can only do so at home. The poor and the uneducated are as far from the Word of God as if they were in Ethiop.

"I want some scholarly ladies," I say to Nan, almost shyly. "I always felt that I should have read more and studied more. I want to improve my French and Latin. I want to have companions who will study with me."

"Certainly you can hire tutors," she says. "They're as easy to get as parakeets. And you could have an afternoon sermon preached every day, Katherine of Aragon did. You have a range of opinion in your rooms already. Catherine Brandon is a reformer, while Lady Mary is probably secretly faithful to Rome. Of course she would never deny that her father is Supreme Head of the Church." Nan lifts a warning finger to me. "Everyone has to be very, very careful what they say. But now that the king is restoring the rituals that he banned, and taking away the English Bible that he gave to his people, Lady Mary hopes that he will go further and reconcile with the pope."

"I have to understand this," I say. "We lived so far from London, we heard almost nothing, and I couldn't get hold of books. And anyway, my husband Lord Latimer believed in the old ways."

"There are many who still do," Nan warns me. "A frightening number still do, and they are rising in favor. But we have to fight them and win this argument. We have to get the Bible back into the churches for the people. We cannot let the bishops take the Word of God from the people. It is to condemn people to ignorance. Even you will have to study discreetly, with an eye on the law of heresy. We don't want Stephen Gardiner sticking his ugly nose into your rooms, like he does everywhere else."

The king comes to me almost every night, but often wants nothing more from me than conversation, or to share a glass of wine before he goes to his own bed. We sit together like an old loving couple, he in a glorious embroidered nightgown strained across his massive chest and belly, with his sore leg propped on a footstool, me in my black satin with my hair in a plait.

His physician comes with him to give him his evening doses: drugs to ease the pain of his leg, for his headaches as his eyes are failing, to make his bowels move, to clear his urine, which is dangerously dark and sticky. Henry winks when he tells me that his physician has given him something to help with vigor. "Perhaps we will make a son," he suggests. "What about a little Duke of York to follow my prince?"

"In that case I'll have some of that physic?" Will Somers takes the liberties allowed to an official Fool. "I could do with a bit of vigor at nighttime. I would be a bull, but I am a little lamb; truly, I am a little lamb."

"Do you skip and prance?" the king smiles as the physician hands him another draft.

"I gambol. I gamble away my fortune!" Will clinches the joke with a pun, making the king laugh as he drinks, so that Will thumps him familiarly on the back. "Choke up, Nuncle. Don't cough up your own vigor!"

I smile and say nothing while the physician is measuring out the series of little drafts, but when everyone has gone from the room, I say: "My lord husband, you have not forgotten that I had no child from two previous marriages?"

"But you had precious little joy in them, didn't you?" he asks bluntly.

I give a little embarrassed laugh. "Well, yes, I wasn't married for my own joy."

"Your first husband was little more than a boy, afraid to say boo to a goose, probably unmanned, and your second was a dotard, probably impotent," the king declares inaccurately. "How should you have got a child from either of them? I have studied these things, and I know. A woman needs pleasure in order to take a child. She has to have a crisis of pleasure, just as her husband does. This is ordained by God. So at last, dearest wife, you have a chance of becoming a mother. Because I know how to please a woman till she weeps for joy, till she cries out for more."

I am silent, remembering the involuntary cry that I used to make when Thomas was moving inside me, his breath coming fast and my pleasure mounting. Afterwards I would find that my throat was sore and I would know that I had screamed with my face against his naked chest.

"I give you my word," the king says.

I push away my thoughts and smile at him. I know that there can be no pleasure for me in a dead woman's bed. It can't be possible that his damp fumblings can give me a child, and the rue should prevent a monster birth. But since two earlier wives were divorced for lack of a son I would be a fool to say that I don't think we'll get one—whatever sensual pleasures he promises.

Besides, oddly, I find that I don't want to hurt his feelings. I'm not going to tell Henry that I cannot feel desire for him, not when he is smiling at me and promising me ecstasy. At the very least I owe him kindness, I can give him affection, I can show him respect.

He beckons me towards him as he sits on his great chair at the fireside. "Come and sit on my lap, dearest."

I go readily enough and perch on the breadth of his good thigh. He puts his arms around me, he kisses my hair, he puts his hand under my chin and turns my face towards him so that he can kiss me on the mouth.

"And are you glad to be a very rich woman?" he asks me. "Am I kissing a great personage? Did you like the jewels? Did you bring them all with you?"

"I love them," I assure him. "And I take such a pleasure in the wardrobe and the furs. You are very good to me."

"I want to be good to you," he says. He pushes a strand of hair away from my face and tucks it behind my ear. His touch is gentle, assured. "I want you to be happy, Kate. I married you to make you happy, not just for myself. I am not thinking just of myself, I am thinking of my children, I am thinking of my country, I am thinking of you."

"Thank you," I say quietly.

"Is there anything else you would like?" he asks. "If you command me, you command all of England. You can have samphire from the cliffs of Dover, you can have oysters from Whitstable. You can have gold from the Tower and cannonballs from the Minories. What would you like? Anything. You can have anything."

I hesitate.

At once he takes my hand. "Don't be afraid of me," he says tenderly. "I imagine that people will have told you all sorts of things about me. You will think yourself a Saint Tryphine, married to a monster."

I give a little choke as he names my dream.

He is watching me closely. "My love," he says. "My last and only love. Please know this. What people will tell you about my marriages is completely wrong. I'll tell you the truth. Only I know the truth, and I never speak of it. But I will tell you. I was married when I was a boy to a woman who was not free to marry me. I didn't know it till God harrowed me with grief. Baby after baby was taken from us. It nearly killed her, it broke my heart. I had to let her go to spare her further pain. I had to release her from a marriage that was cursed. It was the hardest thing I ever did. But if I were to have a son for England I had to let her go. I sent Katherine of Aragon away, the finest princess that Spain ever raised, and it broke my heart to do so. But I had to do it.

"And then, God forgive me, I was seduced by a woman whose only desire was ambition. She was a poisoner, a witch, and a seductress. I should have known better, but I was a young man, longing for love. I learned my lesson late. Thank God I saved my children from her. She would have killed us all. I had to put a stop to her and I found the courage to do so.

"Jane Seymour—my choice, the only wife I freely chose for myself—was my only true wife, and she gave me a son. She was like an angel, an angel, you know? And God took her back. I cannot complain for she left me with a son and His wisdom is infinite. The Cleves woman was an arranged marriage brought to me against my wishes by bad advisors. The Howard girl . . ." His face crumples into rolls of fat. "God forgive the Howards for putting a whore in my bed," he gulps. "They deceived me, she deceived them, we were all blinded by her whorish prettiness. Kate, I swear, you will be a good wife to me indeed if you can make me forget the pain that she caused me."

"I will if I can," I say quickly. "Please don't distress yourself."

"I have been heartbroken," he says honestly. "More than once. I have been betrayed—more than once. And I have been blessed by the true love of a good woman." He carries my hand to his lips. "Twice, I hope. I hope you will be my second and my last good angel. I hope you will love me as Jane did. I know that I love you."

"If I can," I say softly. I am genuinely moved to tenderness. "If I can, I will."

"So you can command me," he says gently. "I will do anything that you want. You just have to say."

I trust him. I think that I will dare to name the favor that I want. "It's my rooms at Hampton Court," I start. "Please don't think me ungrateful, I know they are the finest rooms and Hampton Court is—"

He waves away my words. "It's the most beautiful palace in England, but it is nothing to me if you don't like it. I shall demolish it if you wish. What displeases you? I will have it altered at once."

It is the ghosts in every corner, it is the initials of dead women on the stone bosses, it is the flags where their feet walked. "The smell," I say. "From the kitchens below."

"Of course!" he exclaims. "You're so right! I have often thought it myself. We should rebuild, we should change. The place was planned by Wolsey. He looked after himself, you can be sure of that. He planned his own apartments perfectly but he did not think what the other wing would be like. He never cared for anyone but himself, that man. But I care for you, beloved. Tomorrow you shall come to me and we shall get a builder to draw up new rooms for you, a queen's side that will suit you completely."

Truly, this is a rare husband. I've never known anyone so quick to understand, and so eager for the happiness of a wife. "Lord husband, you're very good to me."

"I love your smile," he replies. "You know, I watch for your smile. I think I would give all the treasures of England for that smile."

"My lord . . ."

"You shall be my wife and my partner, my friend and my lover."

"I will," I say earnestly. "I promise it, husband, I will."

"I need a friend," he says confidingly. "These days, I need a friend more than ever. The court is like a pit for dogfighting. They turn on one another and everyone wants my agreement and everyone wants my favor, but I can't trust anyone."

"They seem so friendly—"

"They are all liars and dissemblers," he overrules me. "Some of them are for the reform of religion and would make England Lutheran; some of them would have us return to Rome and put the pope at the head of our church again; and they all think that the way ahead is to trick me and entice me, step by step, down their way. They know that all the power is in my two hands. I alone decide everything, so they know that the way ahead is to persuade me."

"Surely, it would be a great shame to go back on your godly reforms," I say tentatively.

"It's worse now than ever. Now they look beyond me to Edward. I can see them trying to calculate how long I might live and how they can win Edward to their will and against mine. If I were to die soon, they would fight over my boy like dogs over a bone. They would tear him apart. They wouldn't see him as their master, they would see him as their road to greatness. I have to save him from that."

"But you are well," I reply gently. "Surely, you will live for years yet? Long enough to see him grow into a man and into his power?"

"I have to. I owe it to him. My boy, my only boy. His mother died for him, I have to live for him."

Jane again. I nod sympathetically and say nothing.

"You will guard him with me," the king rules. "You will be as a mother to him, in place of the mother whom he has lost. I can trust you as my wife in a way that I can trust no councillor. Only you are my partner and my helpmeet. You are my second self, we are as one. You will care for my power and for my son—no one else can love and guard him. And if we go to war with France and I ride with the army you shall be regent here, and his protector."

This is the greatest trust, proof of love beyond anything I ever expected. This is far more than I could have dreamed, better than birds or jewels, better than new rooms. This is the chance to be a queen indeed. I have a moment of vaulting ambition succeeded by fear. "You would make me regent?"

The only woman to be regent in the absence of the king was Katherine of Aragon, a princess raised to rule a kingdom. If the next were to be me, then I would be honored higher than anyone but a royal in her own right, born and bred. And if I were Regent of England and protector of the heir, then I would be expected to guide the people and the church in the way of God. I would have to become a defender of the faith, just as the king named himself. I would have to sponsor the faith of the people. I would have to learn the wisdom to steer the church towards truth. I am breathless at the prospect. "My lord, I would be so proud, I would work so hard. I would not fail you. I wouldn't fail the country. I don't know enough, I don't understand enough, but I will study, I will learn."

"I know it," he says. "I know you will be a devoted wife. And I trust you. I hear from everyone that you were Lord Latimer's friend and his helpmeet, that you cared for his children as if they were your own, that you saved his castle from the ungodly. You shall do the same for me and mine. You are above faction, you are above taking sides." He smiles. "You shall be *Useful in All That You Do*. I was so moved when they told me that was your motto. For I want you to be useful and to take pleasure, too, my dear. I want you to be happy—happier than you have ever been in your life."

He takes my hands and kisses one, then the other. "You will come to love me and understand me," he predicts. "I know you would tell me that you love me now, but that is to flatter an old fool. These are early days for us, honeymoon days; you have to speak of love, I know that. But you will come to love me in your heart, even when you are alone and no one is watching. I know it. You have a loving heart and a clever mind, and I want them both devoted to me. I want them both turned to me and to England. You will watch me at work and at play, at bed and board and at prayer, and you will understand the man that I am, and the king that I am. You will see my greatness, and my faults and my tender parts. You will fall in love with me. I hope you will fall in love with me completely."

I give a little nervous laugh but he is completely convinced. He is quite certain that he is irresistible, and in the face of his smiling determination I think he may be right. Perhaps I will learn from him and love him. He is very persuasive. I want to believe him. It is God's will that I married him, there can be no doubt of that. Perhaps it is His will that I will come to love my husband fully, as a wife should do. And who could not love a man who trusts a wife with his kingdom? With his children? Who pours treasure at her feet? Who offers his love so sweetly?

"You need never say one word of a lie to me," he promises me. "There shall never be anything but honesty between us. I don't need you to say that you love me now. I don't want any early promises, easy words. I need only to know that you care for me now, that you are glad to be my wife, and that you accept that you might love me in the future. I know that you will."

"I will," I say. I did not know that he would be like this as a husband. I never dreamed it. I have never had a husband who cared for me. It is an extraordinary sensation to have the devotion of a powerful man. It is extraordinary to feel this tremendous will, this burning concentration turned on me. "And love will grow, as you say, my lord."

"Love will grow, Henry," he prompts.

I kiss him, unasked. "Love will grow, Henry," I repeat.

I know that I have to understand more about the changes that my husband has brought to the Church in England. I ask both Thomas Cranmer and Stephen Gardiner to recommend preachers who can come to my rooms and expound their views to me and to my ladies. By listening to both sides of the debate—the reformers and the traditionalists—I hope that I will understand the cause that divides the court and the country, and the careful route that Henry has so brilliantly traced between the two.

Every afternoon, as we sew, one of the priests attached to the king's chapel, or a preacher from London, comes to my rooms and reads the Bible to us in English, and delivers a sermon explaining the passage. To my surprise, the task that I have undertaken as a duty becomes my favorite part of the day. I realize that I am a natural scholar. I have always loved to read, and for the first time in my life I have time to do so and I am able to study with the greatest thinkers in the kingdom. I take an almost sensual delight in their work. They take a text from the Bible—the Great Bible that the king commanded should be translated into English so that everyone could study it—and they examine it word by word. It is like reading poetry, like studying the philosophers. The shades of meaning that arise and dissolve with translation, with the juxtaposition of one word against another, fascinate me, and then the way that the truth of God shines through, layer after layer like a sun through strips of cloud, as one wrestles with the words.

My ladies, all drawn to the reform of the church, are in the habit of going directly to the Bible rather than to a priest for their learning, and we form a little group of scholars, interrogating the visiting preachers and offering our own suggestions. Archbishop Cranmer says that we should keep a note of our discussions so that we can share them with the colleges and with other theologians. I feel absurdly flattered that he thinks our studies are worthy to be read by others, but he persuades me that we are part of a body of thinkers, sharing what we study. Since I find the sermons so illuminating, will others?

Everything must be scrutinized, everything must be considered. Even the translation of the Bible is a powerful controversy. The king gave the Bible in English to his people, putting a translated Bible into every parish church in the country. But—as the traditionalists point out—people did not read it reverently, they started to discuss passages and dispute meanings. What should have been a gift from the king to his grateful people became the center of argument and so the king took the Bibles away, and now only noblemen may read them.

I cannot help but think this is wrong. *In the beginning was the Word, and the Word was with God, and the Word was God*—surely it is the work of the church to bring the Word to the people? Surely it is the work of the church not to bring pictures and stained glass and candles and robes to the people but first, before everything, to bring the Word?

Lady Mary often comes from her own set of rooms to listen to the daily sermon in mine. Sometimes, I know, she fears that the priests stray too far from the teachings of the church; but her love of languages and her devotion to the Bible mean that she always comes back, and sometimes she will offer her own translation of a phrase, or challenge the preacher's version. I admire her scholarship. She has had the best of teachers and her understanding of Latin and her subtlety of translation are quite beautiful. If she had not been frightened into silence, I think she might have been a poet. She laughs when I tell her this one day and says that we are so alike, we should be sisters rather than a stepmother and daughter—we are both women who love fine clothes and beautiful language.

"Almost as if they are the same thing!" she confesses. "I get so much pleasure from embroidery and from poetry. I think there should be beauty in the words of the church and in the church paintings, so the little prie-dieu in my room should be beautiful too, with a golden crucifix and a crystal monstrance. But then I think I am sliding towards vanity. Really, I cannot deny it. I have my books bound with fine leather and jewels, and I collect illuminated manuscripts and prayer books. Why not, if it is for the glory of God and the delight of our eyes?"

I laugh. "I know! I know! And I'm afraid that my love of study is the sin of pride. I find it quite thrilling to understand things, as if reading were a journey of discovery. I long to know more and more, and now I want to make translations and even compose prayers."

"Why should you not?" she demands. "If you take pride in reading the Word of God, that is surely a little sin? It's more a virtue of study than a pride of scholarship."

"It's a joy I never thought I would have."

"If you are a reader, you are already halfway to being a writer," she says. "For you have a love of words and pleasure from seeing them on a page. And if you are a writer, then you will find that you are driven to write. It is a gift that demands to be shared. You cannot be a silent singer. You are not an anchorite, a solitary saint, you are a preacher."

"Even though I am a woman and a wife?"

"Even though."

I am to meet my stepson, the Prince of Wales, Queen Jane's son. He comes in state from his own palace at Ashridge, where he lives at a safe distance from the plagues and illnesses of the city. I watch from the windows that overlook the river and the gardens, and see the royal barge approaching, the banks of oars cutting into the water and then lifting out, and pulling onwards again. I see the barge feather the oars to slow its stately progress and then steer smoothly to the pier. The oarsmen throw the ropes and moor up as the guns roar out to salute him. The richly carved gangplank is run ashore, and the men make a guard of honor with their green and white oars erect. Half of the court is already on the riverbank to greet the prince. I see Edward Seymour's dark head and Anthony Denny beside him, Thomas Howard trying to get in front. They look almost as if they are jostling to be first to greet him. These are the men who will want him to favor them, whose power will come only from him, whose futures depend on him. If my husband dies and this boy becomes a child-king, then one of them will be his governor, his protector. It may fall to me to defend him from them all, to raise him as his father would have it done, and keep him in the ways of the true religion.

I turn to my ladies and let them adjust my hood, settle my jewels at my neck, and pull out the hem of my gown. I am wearing a new gown in deep red, the king's huge ruby ring cut down to fit my finger, Queen Anne's rubies sitting heavily and coldly on my neck. With my ladies behind me and with Rig, my spaniel, trotting beside me in his red leather collar with silver rings, we walk to the king's presence chamber, through a whispering crowd of people who have come to witness this meeting.

His Majesty is there already, seated beneath the golden cloth of estate, his leg supported on a footstool. His face is dark with bad temper. I guess that he is in pain and I curtsey before him and take my place at his side without speaking. I have learned that it is better to be silent when he is ill; the least word angers him. He cannot hear a reference to his weakness, but he cannot bear that his suffering should be ignored. It is impossible to say the right thing, impossible to say anything at all. I feel nothing but pity for him, fighting the decay and collapse of his body with such dauntless courage. Anyone else in pain like this would be wild with temper.

"Good," is all he says as I sit beside him, and I see that however sour his mood, he is not displeased with me.

I turn my head to smile at him in silence and we exchange a little gleam of mutual understanding.

"Did you watch from the window?" he asks. "Were the jackals gathering around the young lion?"

I nod. "They were. So I came to the great lion," I say. "I cleave to the greatest lion there is."

Henry gives a little grunt of amusement. "The old lion still has his teeth and claws. You will see I can draw blood. You will see I can rip a throat."

The double doors are flung open, the herald bellows, "Edward Prince of Wales!" and the little boy of just five years old walks in, with half the court trailing sycophantically behind him. I could almost laugh aloud. All their shoulders are hunched, all their heads are stooped, everyone is trying to bend down to smile at the little boy, to lean towards him so that they can hear anything he might say. When they walk behind the king, they match his swagger, heads up and shoulders back, chests thrust out, pacing themselves to his limping stride. But to follow his son they have invented a new way of sidling along. What fools they are, I think to myself, and I glance at my husband and see his sardonic grin.

Prince Edward stops before the thrones and bows. His pale face is turned to his father with the dazzled expression of a child who hero-worships a distant parent, his lower lip trembles. He gives a small speech in Latin in a piping little voice that I assume expresses his honor and pleasure at coming to court. The king replies briefly in the same language. I can pick out a few words but I have no idea what he is saying. I guess that he had this speech prepared for him; he has little patience with study these days. Then Edward turns to me and speaks in French, a courtly language more appropriate for a woman without much learning.

As I did with Elizabeth, I rise to my feet and go towards him, but he looks anxious as I approach and this makes me cautious. He bows, I curtsey, I extend my hand and he kisses it. I dare not embrace him as I did Elizabeth; I cannot fold him into my arms. He is only a little boy, but he is a unique being, as rare as a unicorn, sighted only in tapestries. This is the only Tudor prince in the whole world. After a lifetime of marriages and couplings, this is the only surviving boy who Henry could get.

"I am so pleased to meet you, Your Highness," I say to him. "And I look forward to knowing and loving you, as I should."

"I too am honored," he says carefully. I imagine he has been coached in every possible response. This is a boy whose speech was scripted from the first words he ever learned. His first word was not "Mama"; they will have taught him to say something else. "It will be a comfort and joy to me to have a mother in you."

"And I'll learn Latin," I say.

No one could have prepared him for this surprising promise

and I see the leap of amusement of a normal boy. "You'll find it awfully hard," he warns me in English, and for a moment I see the child that he is, under the carapace of the prince that he has to be.

"I'll get a tutor," I say. "I love to learn and study. I have wanted all my life to have a good education. Now I can start, and then I can write to you in Latin and you can correct me."

He gives a funny little formal bow. "I shall be honored," he says, and looks up fearfully to see if his father approves.

But Henry, the king, somber in his own thoughts and besieged with pain, does not smile at his little son. "Very well," is all he grudgingly says.

MANOR OF THE MORE, HERTFORDSHIRE, SUMMER 1543

KP

The plague is worsening in London, it is going to be one of the deadly years. Left behind us, hundreds are dying in the filthy streets as we ride farther and farther away from the city, making our way north, hunting and feasting. Guards are posted along the road from London to prevent anyone following the court, and the gates to every palace are bolted shut as soon as we are inside.

In a plague year at my home at Snape Castle I used to order the nursing of sick people in the village, send out tisanes and herbs to prevent the spread of the disease, and pay the burial parties for the pauper graves. I would have the newly orphaned children to eat in the castle kitchens, and ban travelers from visiting. It's odd to me that now I am Queen of England and all the people are my people, I act as if I don't care for any of them, and they can't even beg food at the kitchen doors.

The king decides to order a Rogation, a day of processions with prayers. Everyone must call on the help of God to save England, at this time of her need. There are to be nationwide pilgrimages of faith, and a service in every church in the land. The day is made known from every pulpit, and every congregation is commanded to process around their parish, praying and singing psalms. Only if every parish in England prays for all the people of England will the plague leave us. But instead of an outpouring of faith and hope, the occasion is a complete failure. Hardly anyone attends and nobody gives alms. It's not like it used to be. There are no monks and no choirs to lead the processions, no one has any sacred relics to parade, the gold and silver holy vessels have been taken away and melted down, the abbeys and monasteries are all closed, their hospitals closed too. As a demonstration of national faith all it shows is that nobody cares anymore.

"The people won't pray for their own country?" Henry demands of Stephen Gardiner Bishop of Winchester, as if it is all his fault. We are on the royal barge, taking the air on the river, when Bishop Gardiner remarks that he would have to walk on water to convince the people of Watford to say their prayers. "Have they run mad? Do they think they can get eternal life by arguing for it?"

He shrugs. "They have lost their faith," he says. "All they want to do now is dispute the Bible. I would have them sing the old psalms, observe the old ways, and leave understanding to their betters. After we took the English Bible from the churches I thought that they would pray in the words we allowed them."

"It is those very words that fail to speak to them," Thomas Cranmer disagrees. "They don't understand what they mean. They can't read Latin. Sometimes they can't even hear the priest. People don't want empty ritual anymore. They don't want to process singing a hymn that they can't understand. If they could pray in English, they would do so. You gave them an English Bible, Your Majesty, and then took it away again. Restore it to them, let them have a reason for their faith. Let us do more! Let us give them an English liturgy too."

The king is silent and glances towards me to show that I can speak. "You think that people don't like the Latin prayers anymore?" I ask Archbishop Cranmer. "Do you really think they would be devout if they were allowed to pray in their own language?"

"The language of the sewers," Bishop Gardiner remarks quietly to Henry. "Shall every potboy write his own Ave Maria? Shall the street sweepers compose their own blessings?"

"Row faster," Henry remarks to the rowers, hardly attending to this. "Steer us into the middle of the river where we can catch the current."

The barge master alters the rhythm of the drum that keeps the rowers to time, and the steersman directs us into the center of the river, where there is a cool breeze over the deeper current. "No one may enter into our palace from the city," Henry tells me. "People may wave from the bank, they can pay their respects, but they may not come on board. I don't want them anywhere near me. No one from the city can come even into the gardens. They bring disease. I cannot risk it."

"No, no, certainly not," I say soothingly. "My household knows this as well as yours, my lord. I have told them. Nobody will even take a delivery from London."

"Not even books," he says suspiciously. "And no visiting preachers or scholars, Kate. No one coming from the city churches. I won't have it."

"They are all carrying diseases," Gardiner asserts. "All of these heretic Lutheran preachers are blasted with illness and half of them crazed with misunderstanding. They come from Germany and Switzerland, sick and mad."

The face I turn up to Henry, as he sits on the raised throne above me, is completely serene. "Of course, my lord," I say, though I am lying. As I promised Prince Edward, I am now studying Latin with a scholar from Cambridge, and I take deliveries of books from the London printers. Some come to me from the Protestant printers of Germany, too, the so-called heretic printers, publishing books of scholarship and theology in Flanders. Christendom is alive as it has never been before, with study and thought about the Bible, about the form that services should take, even about the nature of the Mass. The king himself, when he was younger, joined these discussions and wrote his own documents. Now, under the influence of the Howards and Stephen Gardiner, disappointed in the country's response to the changes he has made, fearful of the excited movements spreading across Europe, he does not want discussion, he does not want to press on with reform.

When the North rose against him, demanding that the abbeys be reopened and the chantries sing for the dead again, that the old lords take their power and the Plantagenets be honored, the king decided that he wanted no arguments at all: not of his rule, not of his church, not of his heirs. The king hates thinking as much as he hates illness, and now he says that books carry both.

"Surely Her Majesty can have no interest in books from London, or hedgerow preachers," Stephen Gardiner prompts sweetly. "Why would a lady so perfect in so many ways want to study like a dirty old clerk?"

"So that I can talk with His Majesty," I say simply. "So that I can write in Latin to his son the prince. So that such a great scholar-king does not have a wife who is a fool."

Will Somers, sitting on the edge of the barge, dangling his long legs towards the water, turns at this. "Only one Fool here!" he reminds us. "And I can't admit an amateur foolish woman in my guild. How big would such a guild have to be? I should recruit thousands."

The king smiles. "You are no fool, Kateryn, and you may read what you wish, but I will have no deliveries or visitors from London until the city is free from illness."

I bow my head. "Of course."

"I trust that Your Majesty is not reading books of folly," Stephen Gardiner suggests spitefully.

I can feel myself bristle at the patronizing tone. "Oh, I hope not," I say with false sweetness. "For it is your sermons that I have been reading, my lord."

"I do this to protect you as well as the court," Henry points out.

"I know that you do, and I am grateful for your care of us all," I say, and it is true. He guards against disease as if it were our worst enemy. He will keep me safe if he possibly can. Nobody has ever thought of my health before. Nobody has ever devised ways to keep me safe. Until I was married to Henry there was no one who cared enough to guard me.

We listen to the musicians who are following in their barge behind us. They are playing a pretty air. "Hear this?" the king says, beating the time on the arm of his chair. "I wrote this."

"It's lovely," I say. "How clever of you, my lord."

"Perhaps I shall write some more music," he says. "I think you have inspired me. I shall write a little song for you." He pauses, listening to his own tune with admiration. "Anyway, it is better that no one comes from London," he continues. "It's pleasant to have little business to do in the summer. They never stop with their demands and their requests, urging me to rule for one against another, to favor one against another, to cut a tax or pay a fee. I get tired of them. I am sick of them all."

I nod as if I think that the burden of showing a shifting favoritism is very heavy.

"You shall help me," he says. "When we open the court again and all the requests come in. You shall read them and judge with me. I shall trust you to sit beside me and be my only advisor."

"So there are two fools here, after all," Will remarks. "Myself, a guaranteed and apprenticed Fool, and here is a new Fool, a fool for love."

Henry chuckles. "Just as you say, Will," he agrees. "I am a fool for love."

AMPTHILL CASTLE, BEDFORDSHIRE, AUTUMN 1543

KP

The argument on the barge between the bishops, Stephen Gardiner, who wants the restoration of the old church to the old ways, and Thomas Cranmer, who believes that the church should reform, comes to a head when we are staying at Ampthill Castle, Katherine of Aragon's old home. We are kept indoors by a week of cold and foggy weather: the leaves on the trees drip water all day long, the ground is sodden, and the lanes are deep with mud. The king takes a slight fever that makes his eyes and nose run, he aches in every bone and cannot go out. Trapped indoors with the courtiers using every moment to persuade him, he agrees that the reformers have gone too far, become heretical, and authorizes a wave of arrests that reach from London into the court itself. The heresies, one by one, are traced back to Thomas Cranmer, and once again the Privy Council scents triumph and calls him in to face an inquiry.

"They thought they had him this time," Nan whispers to me as we are kneeling on the chancel steps of the little chapel, the king seated at the back with a writing desk, surrounded by advisors, signing papers, as the priest mumbles the words of the Mass hidden behind the rood screen. "He went in like Thomas More, expecting martyrdom."

"Not him!" Catherine Brandon hisses from the other side. "He knew he was safe. It was all a play, a game."

"The king himself said it was a masque," Anne Seymour leans forward on the other side of Nan to tell me. "He said it was a masque called *The Taming of the Archbishop*."

"What did he mean?"

"The king let Stephen Gardiner arrest Thomas Cranmer. But he had already warned Cranmer that his enemies had evidence against him, months ago. He called him the greatest heretic in Kent and laughed as he said it. The Privy Council sent for Cranmer, thinking he would shake with fear. They called him in to accuse him and take him to the Tower. They had the guards ready, the barge was waiting for him. Stephen Gardiner and Thomas Howard Duke of Norfolk were triumphant. They thought they would silence the archbishop and halt reform forever."

"Gardiner didn't even bring him in at once. He made him wait. He took his time over it," Catherine interpolates.

"He was savoring his moment," Anne agrees. "But just as they were about to grab him and tear his hat from his head, Thomas Cranmer pulls out a ring, the king's own ring, and says that he has His Majesty's friendship and trust, and that there is to be a new inquiry into heresy: *he* is now going to inquire into *them*— and that charges will follow."

I am astounded. "He triumphed? Again? And everything is turned around in a moment?"

"In a frightened heartbeat," Nan says. "That is how this king keeps his power for year after year."

"So what happens now?" I ask.

"Stephen Gardiner and Thomas Howard will have to humble their pride and beg pardon of the archbishop and of the king. They have fallen from favor."

I shake my head in wonderment. It is like a traveler's tale, a fairy tale, filled with sudden reverses of fortune and magical triumphs.

"And Thomas Cranmer will hold an inquiry into all the people who thought they were going to arrest and execute him, and if there are letters that reveal treason or heresy, they will find themselves in the Tower waiting for the scaffold, in his place."

"And now we are on the rise," Nan crows. "And reform will go on. We'll get the Bible back into the churches, we will be allowed to read books on reform, we'll get the Word of God to the people and the dogs of Rome can go back to hell."

The king is planning a great Christmas feast. "Everyone will attend," he says exuberantly. The pain in his leg has eased, the wound is still open but it is not weeping so copiously. I think that it smells less. I mask the stink with pockets of perfumes and spices scattered around my rooms, even tucked into my bed, the scent of roses overlaying the haunting odor of decay. The summer of riding and traveling has rested him, he hunts every day, all day—even if he is only standing in a hide as they drive the beasts towards him. We have a lighter dinner than when he is in his great hall twice a day with twenty, thirty different dishes being brought in, and he is even drinking less wine.

"Everyone," he says, "every ambassador in Christendom will come to Hampton Court. They all want to see my beautiful new wife."

I smile and shake my head. "I shall be shy," I say. "I don't like to feel that all eyes are on me."

"You have to endure it," he says. "Better still, learn to enjoy it. You are the greatest woman in the kingdom: learn to revel in it. There are plenty who would take it from you if they could."

"Oh, I'm not so shy that I would rather stand aside," I confess.

"Good," he says, catching up my hand and kissing it. "For I am not disposed to let you go. I want no pretty new girl pushed into your place." He laughs. "They dangle papist poppets before me, did you know? All this summer on progress they have been introducing pretty daughters with crucifixes at their necks and rosaries at their belts and missals in Latin in their pockets. Did you not notice?"

I try to remember. Now that he points it out to me I do think there were a lot of noticeably devout young women among the many that we met on progress. I give a little giggle. "My lord husband, this is—"

"Ridiculous," he finishes for me. "But they think I am old and restless. They think I am whimsical, and that I would change my wife and change my church in the morning and change it back again in the evening. But you know," he kisses my hand again, "you know better than anyone that I am faithful, to you and to the church that I am making."

"You will hold to your reforms," I confirm.

"I will do what I think right," he says. "We shall have your family at court for Christmas. You must be pleased that I am going to honor them? I will give your uncle a title—he shall be Lord Parr—and I will make your brother an earl."

"I am so grateful, my lord. And I know they will serve you loyally in their new positions. I shall be so pleased to see them at court. And—dear husband—may the children come for Christmas, too?"

He is surprised at the suggestion. "My children?"

"Yes, my lord."

"They usually stay at their own houses," he says uncertainly. "They always celebrate Christmas with their people."

Will Somers, who is at the king's side, cracks two walnuts together in his hands, picks out the shells, and offers the nut to his royal master. "Who are their people—if not us?" he demands. "Lord, Lord, King! See what a good woman will do to you? You've only been married for five months and already she is giving you three children! This is the most fertile wife of all! It's like keeping a cony!"

I laugh. "Only if Your Majesty would wish it?"

Henry's jowls are trembling with his emotion, his face flushes, his eyes fill with tears. "Of course I wish it, and Will is right. You are a good woman and you are bringing my children home to me. You will make us into a family of England, a true family. Everyone shall see us together: the father—and the son who will come after him. And I shall have Christmas with my children around me. I've never done such a thing before."

HAMPTON COURT PALACE, CHRISTMAS 1543

KP

The oars of the royal barge, muffled by the cold mist that lies in heavy ribbons on the river, dip in and out of the water with one splashy movement. The boat surges forward with each stroke and then seems to rest before going forward again as if it were breathing on a living river: leaping and then stilling. Coots and moorhens scurry away from us ahead of the barge, lifting out of the water with their long legs trailing. A broad-winged heron rises silently from the reeds at the riverbank, flapping on huge slow wings; overhead the seagulls cry. To approach Hampton Court in the royal barge on the river, with the bright winter sunlight breaking through the swirls of cold mist, is to see a magical palace emerge, as if it, too, is floating on the cold water.

I snuggle deep into my thick furs. I have rich glossy black sables delivered from the wardrobe of my London house of Baynard's Castle. I know these belonged to my predecessor, Katherine Howard. I don't have to ask: I have become familiar with her perfume, a memorable musky smell—she must have drenched everything in it. The moment they bring me a new gown I can smell her, as if she is haunting me in scent as she haunts me in life. I cannot help but wonder if she was drowning out the stink of his rotting leg, as I do with rose oil. At least I refuse to wear her shoes. They brought me a pair with golden heels and velvet toes, fit for a tiny child. She must have been like a little girl beside my husband, more than thirty years younger than him. She must have looked like his granddaughter when she danced with the young people of the court and glanced around at his squires, seeking her boyish lover. I wear her gowns, which are so beautifully made and so richly embroidered, but I will not walk in her shoes. I order new ones, dozens and dozens of pairs, hundreds of them. I pray that I will not dream of her as I follow her footsteps into Hampton Court, wearing her furs, her—and all the others. I sail in Katherine of Aragon's barge. I wrap Kitty Howard's sables around me and think that the cold wind blowing down the river will blow away her presence, will blow all the ghosts away, and soon her furs, so soft and luxurious, will be my furs and, brushing constantly against my throat and shoulders, will pick up my perfume of orange blossom and rose.

"Isn't it beautiful? Nan asks me, looking ahead to where the palace shines in the morning sunlight. "Isn't it the best of them all?"

All of Henry's many houses are places of wonder. This palace he took from Cardinal Thomas Wolsey, who built it in deep rosy-red brick, with high ornamental chimneys, broad courtyards, and exquisitely planned gardens. They have completed the changes that Henry promised me, and now there is a new queen's side overlooking the gardens and away from the kitchens. These will be my rooms; no ghosts will walk the newly waxed floorboards. There is a broad stone quay that runs along the riverbank, and as our barge and all the accompanying ships come into sight, all the standards are unfurled at all the flagpoles, and there is a great roar of cannon fire to welcome the king home.

I jump at the noise and Nan laughs. "You should have heard it the day that we brought Anne of Cleves to London," she says. "They had barges on the river shooting off guns, and the sky was lit like a thunderstorm with the fireworks."

The barge comes smoothly in to the stone pier and the rowers ship their oars. There is another bellow of ordnance and the gangplank is run ashore. The yeomen of the guard, in their green and white livery, hammer down the shallow stone stairs to line the quay. The trumpeters blast out a shout of sound, and all the royal servants come out before the doors of the palace and stand, stiffly, heads uncovered in the wintry air. The king, who was resting his leg on an embroidered footstool under an awning in the stern, hauls himself to his feet and goes first, as he needs a man on either side to support him on the gently rocking deck. I follow him, and when he is steady on the white marble paving stone of the quay, he turns and takes my hand. The trumpeters are playing a processional anthem, the servants are bowing low, and the people held back from the quay are cheering Henry's name—and my own. I realize that our marriage is popular not just in our court and the foreign courts, but here, in the countryside too. Who could believe that the king could marry again? Yet again? Who could believe that he would take a beautiful widow and restore her to wealth and happiness? Who could believe that he would take an Englishwoman, a countrywoman, a woman from the despised and feared North of England, and put her in the very heart of the smart southern court, and that she would outshine everyone? They cheer and shout my name, wave documents that they want me to see, requests that they want me to grant, and I smile and wave back. The steward of my household goes among them and gathers up their letters for me to read later.

"It's good that you are looking well," Henry remarks shortly as we go slowly through the wide open doors. He gives a little grimace as each step pains him. "It is not enough to be a queen, you have to look like one. When the people come out to see us, they want to see a couple set far above them, larger than life, grander than anything they have ever dreamed. They want to be awed. Seeing us should be like seeing beings far above them, like angels, like gods."

"I understand."

"I am the greatest man in the kingdom," Henry says simply. "Perhaps the greatest in the world. People have to see that the minute that they see me."

The whole court is waiting to greet us inside the great hall. I smile at my uncle, soon to be a peer of the realm, and my brother, who will be the Earl of Essex, thanks to me. All my friends and family, newly enriched by my patronage, are here for Christmas, and the greater lords of the realm, the Howards, the Seymours, the Dudleys; the rising men like Thomas Wriothesley, his friend and colleague Richard Rich, the other courtiers and the churchmen in their crimson and purple robes. Stephen Gardiner is here, smoothly untouched by Archbishop Cranmer's inquiry. He bows to me and his smile is confident.

"I am going to teach you to be Queen of England," Henry says quietly into my ear. "You shall look at these wealthy and powerful men and know that you command each and every one of them; I have set you above them. You are my wife and my helpmeet, Kateryn. I am going to make you into a great and powerful woman, a true wife to me, the greatest woman in England, as I am the greatest man."

I don't modestly disclaim, I meet the cold determination in his eyes. They may be loving words but his face is hard.

"I will be your wife in every way," I promise. "This is what I have undertaken and I will keep my word. And I will be queen of this country and mother to your children."

"I'll make you regent," he confirms. "You shall be their master. You shall command everyone that you see here. You will put your heel on their necks."

"I will rule," I promise him. "I will learn to rule as you do."

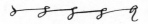

The court welcomes me and acknowledges me as queen. I could almost think that there had never been another. In turn, I welcome the two youngest children, Prince Edward and Lady Elizabeth,

PHILIPPA GREGORY

and weld them into a royal family where they have never truly belonged before. I add royal nieces: Lady Margaret, the daughter of the king's sister the Scots' queen, and little Lady Jane Grey, the granddaughter of his sister the French queen. Prince Edward is an endearing mixture of formality and shyness. He has been schooled since the day of his birth in the knowledge that he is a Tudor son and heir, and everything is expected of him. In contrast, Elizabeth has never been sure of her position: her name and even her safety are completely uncertain. At the execution of her mother she fell, almost overnight, from the grandeur of being a tiny beloved princess addressed as "Your Grace" in her own palace, to being a neglected bastard named "Lady Elizabeth." If anyone could prove the rumors that still swirl around her paternity, she would be an orphan "Miss Smeaton" in a moment.

The Howards ought to love and support her as their girl, the daughter of the Boleyn queen, their kin. But when the king is counting his injuries, and brooding over the wrongs done to him, the last thing the duke and his son want him to remember is that they have put several Howard girls in his bed and two on the throne, and that both queens ended in heartbreak, disgrace, and death. Alternately, they support or neglect the little girl, as serves their purpose.

She cannot be betrothed to any foreign prince while nobody knows if she is a princess or a bastard. She cannot even be properly served while no one knows if she is to be called Princess or Lady Elizabeth. Nobody but her governess and Lady Mary have loved this little girl, and her only refuge from her fear and loneliness is in books.

My heart goes out to her. I too was once a girl too poor to attract a good marriage, a girl who turned to books for company and comfort. As soon as she comes to court I see that she is given a bedroom near to mine. I hold her hand as we go together to the chapel every morning, and we spend the day together. She responds with relief, as if she has been waiting all her life for a mother, and finally I have arrived. She reads with me, and when the preachers come from London she listens to them and even joins in the discussion of their sermons. She loves music, as we all do; she loves fine clothes and dancing. I am able to teach her and, after a few days, joke with her, pet her, reprimand her, and pray with her. In a very little while, I kiss her forehead in the morning and give her a mother's blessing at night almost without thinking.

Lady Mary takes to this Christmas family as a young woman who has tiptoed through the world since the exile of her mother. It is as if she has been holding her breath in fear and she can breathe out at last. At last she knows where she should be: and she lives in a court where she has an honored place. I would not dream of trying to mother her—it would be ridiculous: we are nearly the same age—but we can be like sisters together, making a home for the two younger ones, diverting and comforting the king, and keeping the country in alliance with Spain: Mary's kinsmen. I support the religious reforms that her father has judged are right; naturally she would want the church to return to the rule of Rome; but I think that the more she hears of the philosophers who want to restore the church to its earliest purity, the more she will question the history of the papacy that has brought the church into corruption and disrepute. I believe that the Word of God must mean more to her than the empty symbols that decorated the churches and monasteries, the pointless ritual that was used to dazzle people who cannot read and think for themselves. When she thinks of this, as I am thinking about it, she will surely turn to reform as I am doing.

Though we may differ over points of doctrine she comes every day to my rooms and listens to the readings. This Christmas season I have chosen the favorite psalms of the late Bishop Fisher. It is an interesting example of the delicate path I tread: inside inquiry, outside challenge. The bishop, a sainted man, a wonderful writer, died for the Church of Rome in defiance of the king. He was confessor to Katherine of Aragon, Mary's mother, so it is natural and daughterly that she should think well of him.

Many who secretly thought as he did are now the king's favored advisors, so it is allowed to read the bishop's writings once again.

My almoner, Bishop George Day, served as Fisher's chaplain and loved his master. He reads from his collection of Latin psalms every day, and no one can deny that these words of God have been beautifully rendered by the old bishop from the original Greek. It's like a precious inheritance: from Greek to Latin and now, the ladies of my rooms, my churchmen, the Lady Mary, and even little Elizabeth and I work on an English translation. The language is so fine that it seems wrong to me that only those who can understand Latin should be able to read what this holy man composed. Mary agrees with me, and her care for the work and the beauty of her vocabulary make every morning a time of great interest—not just to me but to all my ladies.

My stepson Edward is my sweetheart, the darling of the court. He speaks with ridiculous formality, he is stiff with etiquette, and yet he longs to be loved and petted, teased, and tickled like a normal boy. Slowly, gradually, through sports, games, and silly jokes, with shared study and shared amusement, he comes to be easy with me, and I treat him as I treated my two Latimer stepchildren when they were under my care—with affection and respect, never trying to replace the mother whom they had lost, but loving them as she might have done. To this day, Margaret Latimer still calls me "Lady Mother," and I write often to my stepson Latimer. I am confident that here too I can give these royal children a mother's love. My best judgment, I think, is to treat Edward with familiarity—as if we are a loving, carefree family, as if he might trust me, and I might be easy with him.

Having struggled for my own place in the world—first in the house of a bad-tempered father-in-law, and then as a young wife to a cold and distant husband, before coming into a court as an insignificant widow—I have learned that the most precious thing is a place where you can be as you are, where someone can see you as your true self. Edward comes to my presence chamber where I am hearing petitions, and is greeted both as a prince and a little boy. I pull him up to my great throne to sit beside me, to listen and to talk quietly to me, to be the child who he is, and not a little manikin whom everyone secretly eyes, wondering what he can do for their prospects.

"Kate, you are everything that I hoped you would be," the king says, coming to my rooms late one night. I had thought that he was sleeping in his own bed and my maid-in-waiting, who had been settled for the night on the truckle bed, scuttles quickly away, bobbing a curtsey and closing the door behind her.

"Thank you," I say, a little startled.

"I shall trust you further," he tells me, easing his great bulk into my bed. "No, I can manage," he says, raising his hand and heaving himself up into a half-sitting position. "You shall have the care of the kingdom while I am away. Tom Seymour has done his job: we have an alliance with the Netherlands, we have a treaty with Spain, we are ready to go to war with France."

His name, suddenly dropped into the conversation as I sit in my bed, naked but for my thin linen nightgown, gives me a shock that is almost physical, as if someone has violently shaken me, shouting his name aloud in the quiet room. I realize that the king is watching me closely.

"You are alarmed?" he asks. "What's the matter? You've gone white!"

"At the thought of war," I say unsteadily. "Only at the thought of danger."

"I will go myself," he announces. "I. Myself. Into the very heart of danger. I shall not send my armies without me. I shall lead them."

I close my eyes briefly. Thomas will almost certainly be coming home. If he has agreed the treaty, he will have to come to court to receive his orders. He will meet with his brother and together they will muster their tenants and soldiers. It is certain that I will see him. It is impossible for him to stay away or for me to avoid him. He will have to bow before me and congratulate me on my happiness. I will have to nod and look indifferent.

I shudder at the thought of it. Everything that I have achieved—with the children, with the court, with the king—has been in the certainty that I will never feel Thomas's dark eyes on me, that I will never glance up and see him looking at me. I don't know that I can even sleep if he is under the same roof. I can't imagine lying quietly in my bed if he is somewhere in the palace, naked but for a sheet, waiting for my soft tap on his door. I won't know how to dance if he is watching. What if we are in the same set and there is a moment when we go hand to hand? How shall I feel his touch and not turn to him? And when he puts his warm hand on my waist? How shall I land on my feet if he lifts me in the *haute danse* and I feel his breath on my cheek? When he helps me down from my horse I will have to put my hands on his shoulders; when he puts me on the ground, will he take the chance to hold me close?

I have no idea how I can hide my utter need for him. I cannot imagine how it should be done. I am on show all the time; everyone watches me. I cannot trust myself; I cannot trust my hand not to shake when I hold it out for the polite brush of his warm lips. This is a court schooled in the bad habit of watching Henry's queens. I succeed Katherine Howard: a byword for immorality. Everyone will always be watching me to see if I am a fool like her.

"I shall lead them myself," Henry repeats.

"Oh, no," I say weakly. "My lord . . ."

"I shall," he says.

"But your health?"

"I am strong enough. I would not send an army to France without their king at the head. I would not ask them to face death without me."

I know very well what I am to say, but I feel too slow and stupid to form the words. All I can think is that Thomas Seymour will be coming home to England and I will see him again. I wonder if he still thinks of me, if his desire is unchanged, if he still wants me as he did. I wonder if he has put me out of his mind, if—like a man—he has cut off love and severed desire, put it away and forgotten it. Or, does he, like me, still ache? I wonder if I will be able to ask him.

"Surely, one of your lords can go?" I say. "You don't need to be at the forefront."

"Oh, they will all go!" the king says. "Be very sure of that! The Seymours, the Howards, the Dudleys, every single one of them. Your brother will earn his new title and ride at my side. But I shall be at the head of the army. They shall see my standard go out and they will see it enter Paris. We will reclaim our lands in France. I shall be King of France in truth."

I clasp my hands together to keep them from trembling at the thought of Thomas Seymour going to war. "I'm afraid for you."

He takes my hands. "Why, you're icy! Are you so fearful?" He smiles. "Don't be afraid, Kateryn. I shall come home safe. I shall ride to victory and come home triumphant. And you shall rule England in my absence. You will be regent, and should God require of me the greatest sacrifice"—he pauses and his voice quavers a little at the thought of my loss, of England's loss—"should I be taken from you and from my army and from my country, then you will rule England for me until Edward is a man."

God forgive me, the first thing I think is that if England loses its king then I will be free to marry, and Thomas will be free, and there is no one who could stop us. Then I think: I will be queen regent. Then I think: I will be the most powerful woman in the world.

"Don't even say it." I put my cold fingers to his little mouth. "I can't think of it." It is true. I really must not. I cannot allow myself to think of another man, as my husband leans back on the heaped pillows, the bed ropes creaking, and beckons me to come to him, his big pink face gleaming with sweat and anticipation.

He kisses my fingertips. "You shall see me return in triumph," he promises me. "And I shall know that you are my faithful wife and helpmeet in every way."

WHITEHALL PALACE, LONDON, SPRING 1544

KP

Bishop George Day comes to find me in my rooms, a roll of manuscript in his hand. "My clerk has completed the copying," he says with triumph in his voice. "It's done. It's fair."

He gives me the pages. For a moment I simply hold them, as if they were my newborn baby and I wanted to feel his weight. I have never borne a child, but I imagine I feel something of a mother's pride. This is a new joy for me. This is the joy of scholarship. For long moments I don't unfurl the pages; I know well enough what they are, I have waited for them.

"The psalms," I whisper. "Bishop Fisher's psalms."

"Just as you translated them," he confirms. "The Latin psalms set into English. They read very beautifully. They read as if the first psalmist spoke the finest English. As they should. They are an honor to God and an honor to you. They are an honor to John Fisher, God bless him. I congratulate you."

Slowly, I spread the pages out and start to read them. It is like reading a chorus through time: the old, old voice of the original psalmist in Hebrew translated to Greek, the sonorous wise voice of the martyred bishop rendering the Greek into Latin, and then it is my voice which sounds through the English lines. I read one psalm:

Thou art our Defender, our refuge, and our God and in Thee we trust. Thou shalt deliver me from the snares of the hunters, and from the perils of my persecutors. Thou shalt make a shadow for me under Thy shoulders; and under Thy wings I shall be harmless. Thy truth shall be my shield and buckler; and no evil shall approach near unto me.

"Should it be *harmless*?" I ask myself.

George Day knows better than to answer. He waits.

"*Without harm* is clumsy," I say. "*Safe* is too strong. But *harmless* has the merit of meaning without harm and without being able to do harm. It feels a little odd perhaps, but the oddness draws attention to the word." I hesitate.

"My clerk can copy any changes you want into fair script for the printer," he offers.

"*Under Thy wings I shall be harmless*," I whisper to myself. "It's like poetry. It carries a sense that is greater than the words, greater than the simple meaning of the words. I think it's right. I don't think I should change it. And I love how it sounds—*under Thy wings*—you can almost feel the feathers of the great wings, can't you?"

George smiles. He can't. But it doesn't matter.

"I don't want to change it," I say. "Not this, not anything."

I glance up at George Day, nodding his head at the steady rhythm of the words. "Clear as plainsong," he says. "Clear as a bell. It is open and honest."

Clarity means more to him than poetry, and so it should. He wants Englishmen and -women to understand the psalms that Bishop Fisher loved. I want to do something more. I want to make these verses sing as they once did in the Holy Land. I want boys in Yorkshire, girls in Cumberland to hear the music of Jerusalem.

"I shall publish these." I shudder at my own daring. No other woman has ever published in English under her own name. I can hardly believe that I can find the courage: to stand up, to speak aloud, to publish to the world. "I really will. George—you do think that I should? You don't advise against it?"

"I took the liberty of showing them to Nicholas Ridley," he remarks, naming the great reformer and friend of Thomas Cranmer. "He was deeply moved. He said that this is as great a gift to the faithful Christians of England as the Bible that your husband the king gave them. He said that these will be spoken and sung in every church in England where the priest wants the people to understand the beauty of God as well as His wisdom. He said that if you will lead the court and the country to a true understanding you will be a new saint."

"But not a martyr!" I say, cracking a weak joke. "So it can't be known that I am the translator. My name, and the names of my ladies, especially Lady Mary and Lady Elizabeth, cannot be attached to it. The king's daughters must never be mentioned. I will make many enemies at court if people know that I believe that psalms should be read in English."

"I agree," he says. "The papists would be quick to criticize, and you cannot risk Stephen Gardiner turning against you. So these will be known only as the bishop's psalms. Nobody need know that it is your study and scholarship that has brought them into English. I have a very discreet printer. He knows that the manuscript comes from me, and that I serve you at court, but I have not told him the name of the author. He thinks highly of me—I must say, he thinks far too highly of me—for he imagines that I could have done this translation. I have denied it, but not so strongly that he is searching for another candidate. I think we can publish and you not own it. Except . . ."

"Except what?"

"I think it's a pity," he says frankly. "These are fine translations with the ear of a musician, the heart of a true believer, and the language of a serious writer. Anyone—I mean any man—would be proud to publish them under his own name. He would boast of them. It seems unfair that you have to deny that you have such a gift. The king's grandmother collected translations and published them."

I have a wry smile on my face. "Ah, George," I say. "You would lure me with vanity, but neither the king nor any man in England wants to be taught by a woman, not even a queen. And the king's grandmother was above criticism. I will publish these as you suggest, and I shall get great happiness from knowing that the bishop's psalms translated by me and my ladies into English may guide men and women to the king's church. But it must be for the glory of the bishop and the glory of the king. I think it better for all of us if they come without my name emblazoned on the cover, like a boast. We are all safer if we don't advertise our beliefs."

"The king loves you. Surely he would be proud . . ." George starts to argue when there is a tap on the door. At once he shuffles the pages out of the way as Catherine Brandon comes in, drops me a curtsey, smiles at George, and says: "The king is asking for you, Your Majesty."

I get to my feet. "He is coming here?"

She shakes her head but does not answer. George at once understands that she does not want to explain before him. He gathers up the papers. "I shall take these, as we agreed," he says, and I nod as he leaves.

"His leg has gone bad," Catherine says quietly, as soon as the door is closed behind my almoner. "My lord husband warned me, and then sent a messenger to say that the king would see you this morning in his private rooms."

"Am I to go to him without being seen?" I ask. There are interconnecting rooms between the king's and the queen's sides at Whitehall. I can either process through the great hall with everyone observing that I am visiting my husband, or I can go through to his wing by our shared gallery with only a lady in attendance.

"Discreetly." She nods. "He doesn't want anyone to know that he has taken to his bed."

She leads the way. Catherine has been in and out of the royal palaces since childhood. She was the daughter of Katherine of Aragon's most favored lady-in-waiting, María de Salinas, and is the wife of Henry's great friend Charles Brandon. She was brought up as an expert way finder around palaces, avoiding wrong turnings and malicious courtiers alike. It is not the first time that I feel like a provincial nobody trailing behind one of the exclusive few, born and bred to this court.

"Are his physicians with him?"

"Doctor Butts and Doctor Owen, and his apothecary is making up a draft to ease the pain. But it is very bad this time. I don't think I have seen him worse."

"Did he knock it? Has it broken open?"

She shakes her head. "It's just the same as it always is," she says. "He has to keep the wound open or the poison will mount to his head and kill him, but often when they pull the wound apart with wires, or grind gold chips into it, it seems worse than before. Now it was healing up and so they have torn it open and the poison is oozing out as it should, but this time it has gone very red inside. It's swollen up very hot and puffy, and the ulcer seems to be deepening into his leg. Charles told me it is eating its way to the bone. It's causing him terrible pain, and nothing eases it."

I can't help but be apprehensive. The king in pain is as dangerous as a wounded boar. His temper is as inflamed as his pulsing wound.

She gives me a gentle touch on my back as she steps aside for me to go first through the adjoining double doors. "Go on," she says very quietly. "You can manage him when no one else can."

Henry is in his privy chamber. He looks up as the private door opens and I come into the room. "Ah, thank God, and here is the queen," he says. "The rest of you can hold your tongues and step back and let me speak privately with her."

He is surrounded by men. I see Edward Seymour looking flushed and angry and Bishop Gardiner looking smug. I guess they have been bickering, jostling for a place before the king, even as the doctors put a drain into his leg to draw off poison from the wound, thrusting a sharp metal spoon deep into the raw flesh. No wonder my husband is red as a Lancaster rose, his eyes squeezed into tearstained slits in the ferocious grimace of his face. Charles Brandon, Catherine's husband, keeps a cautious distance.

"I am sure that Her Majesty the Queen herself will agree . . ." Bishop Gardiner starts smoothly, and I see Wriothesley nod and come a little closer as if to reinforce a viewpoint.

"The queen will say nothing," Henry spits out. "She will stand by me and hold my hand and hold her tongue as a good wife should. You will not suggest that she does other. And you will all leave."

Promptly, Charles Brandon bows to the king, bows hand on heart to me, nods farewell to his wife and melts away from the king's brooding presence.

"Of course," Edward Seymour says quickly. He looks at me. "I am glad that Her Majesty is here to bring comfort and peace. His Majesty should not be troubled at such a time. Especially when matters are perfectly well as they are."

"Nothing will bring peace to the king but when matters are made perfectly well," Bishop Gardiner cannot resist saying. "How can His Majesty be at peace when he knows that his Privy Council is constantly disturbed by new men coming and bringing in even newer men with them? When there are constant inquiries into heresy because people keep redefining what heresy is? Because they are allowed to wrangle and dispute without check?"

"I'll take them out." Thomas Howard speaks over the other councillors, directly to the king as if he is his only friend. "God knows they will never fall silent even when they are ordered to be quiet. They will plague you forever." He gives him a wolfish grin. "You should behead them all."

The king laughs shortly and nods his assent, so Thomas Howard wins the upper hand, ushering the others from the room. He even turns in the doorway and gives the king a friendly wink, as if to assure him that only a Howard can manage such troublesome upstarts. As the door shuts behind them there is a sudden silence. Catherine Brandon curtseys to the king and goes to sit in the window seat, her pretty head turned towards the gardens. Anthony Denny lounges over to stand beside her. There are still half a dozen people in the room but they are quiet and talking amongst themselves or playing a game of cards. By the standards of the overcrowded court, we are alone.

"Dear husband, are you in great pain?" I ask him.

He nods. "They can do nothing," he says furiously. "They know nothing."

Doctor Butts looks up from a worried consultation with the apothecary as if he knows he will have to take the blame.

"Is it the same trouble? The old wound?" I ask cautiously.

The king nods. "They say they may have to cauterize it." He looks at me as if I can save him. "I pray to be spared that."

If they cauterize the wound they will put a red-hot brand against it to burn out infection. It is an agony worse than branding a criminal with a *T* for *thief*. It is a merciless cruelty to an innocent man.

"Surely that won't be necessary?" I demand of Doctor Butts.

He shakes his head; he does not know. "If we can drain the wound and make sure that it does not close up, then the king may be well again," he says. "We have always managed before to cleanse it without cauterizing. I would not undertake it lightly. His heart . . ." His voice trails away. I imagine he is terrified at the thought of giving such a shock to Henry's massive poisoned bulk.

I take Henry's hand, and feel his grip tighten. "I am afraid of nothing," he says defiantly.

"I know," I say reassuringly. "You are naturally courageous."

"And this is not caused by age or infirmity. It's not sickness."

"It was a wound from jousting, wasn't it? Years ago?"

"Yes, yes, it was. An injury from sport. A young man's wound. Reckless, I was reckless. Fearless."

"And I don't doubt that you'll be riding again within a month— still reckless and fearless," I say with a smile.

He draws me closer. "You know I have to be able to ride. I have to lead my men to France. I have to get well. I have to get up."

"I am sure you will," I say, the easy lie quickly in my mouth. I am not at all sure that he will. I can see the drain from the wound dripping the vile pus into a bowl on the floor, the stink of it worse than carrion. I can see a great glass jar with black hungry leeches crawling up the sides. I can see the table spread with flagons and bottles and pestles and mortars, and the apothecary desperately stirring drafts, and the worried faces of the two greatest doctors in England. I have nursed a dying husband before, and his bedroom looked like this, but God knows I have never smelled a stink like this before. It is a fog of rotting flesh, like a charnel house.

"Sit," the king commands me. "Sit beside me."

I swallow down disgust as a page brings a chair to me. The king is on his great strengthened seat, his wounded leg supported on a footstool, draped in sheets to try to contain the smell, to try to hide that the King of England is slowly rotting away.

"I am going to name my heirs," he says quietly. "Before I go to France."

Now I understand what the councillors were arguing about. It is essential that I betray neither hope nor fear for Lady Mary and Lady Elizabeth. It is essential that I do not show my own interest. I don't doubt that the courtiers who just left the room were advocating their own candidates—Edward Seymour reminding everyone of the primacy of his nephew the prince, Thomas Howard advocating for the inheritance of Lady Elizabeth, Bishop Gardiner and Thomas Wriothesley pushing for the elevation of Lady Mary to be heir after Edward.

They don't know how moderate she is in her religion, how interested in open and thoughtful discussion. They don't know that she is a scholar and that we are talking about a new translation of the Gospels. They don't know that Lady Elizabeth has now read every single one of Bishop Fisher's psalms and even translated lines under my supervision. They don't think of either young woman as anything but an empty figurehead for their supporters. They don't realize that we are all women with minds of our own. Bishop Gardiner thinks that if Lady Mary ever comes to the throne she will take the country back to Rome at his bidding. Thomas Howard thinks that a Howard girl will deliver the ruling of the country to his family. None of them believes I am a serious power at court. They don't consider me to be a thinking woman. Yet I may be regent, and then it will be I who will rule whether the country will hear Mass in English or Latin, and I shall determine what the priests say in their sermons.

"My lord? What is your wish?"

"What d'you think would be right?" he asks me.

"I think that there is no need for a king as strong and as young as you to trouble himself at all," I flatter him.

He gestures to his leg. "I am half a man," he says bitterly.

"You will get better. You will be riding again. You have the health and strength of a man half your age. You always recover. You have this terrible wound and you live with it, you defeat it. I see you conquer it like an enemy, day after day."

He is pleased. "They don't think that." He nods irritably towards the door. "They are thinking of my death."

"They think only of themselves," I say, condemning them generally in order to maintain my own position. "What do they want?"

"They want their own kin to have preference," he says shortly. "Or their candidate. And they all hope to rule the kingdom by ruling Edward."

Slowly I nod, as if the naked ambition of the courtiers is a sad revelation to me. "And what do you think, my lord? Nothing matters more than what you think is right."

He shifts his seat and winces with the pain. He leans a little closer. "I have been watching you," he says.

His words ring in my head like a warning bell. He has been watching me. What has he seen? The rolled manuscript of psalms going to the copyist? The mornings of study with the two princesses? My recurring nightmare of closed doors at the top of a damp stair? My erotic daydreams of Thomas? Can I have spoken in my sleep? Can I have said his name? Have I been such a fool as to lie beside the king and breathe the name of another man?

I swallow on a dry throat. "Have you, my lord?"

He nods. "I have been watching how you spend time with Lady Elizabeth, how you are always a good friend to Lady Mary. I see how they enjoy each other's company, how you have brought them both into your rooms and how they are blooming under your care."

I nod, but I don't dare to speak. I don't yet know what he is thinking.

"I have seen you with my son, Edward. I am told that you send each other notes in Latin in which he says he is your schoolmaster."

"It is a jest," I say, still smiling. "Nothing more." I cannot tell from his grim expression whether he is pleased with this intimacy or whether he suspects me of deploying his children to further my own ends, like the courtiers. I don't know what to say.

"You have made a family out of three children with three very different mothers," he says. Still, I cannot be sure if this is a good or a bad thing to have done. "You have taken the son of an angel and the daughter of a whore and the daughter of a Spanish princess and brought them together."

"They are all the children of one great father," I remind him faintly.

His hand shoots out as if he is slapping a fly and grabs my wrist too quickly for me to flinch. "You are certain?" he asks. "You are certain of Elizabeth?"

I can almost smell my fear over the stink of the wound. I think of her mother, Anne Boleyn, sweating at the May Day joust, knowing her danger but not knowing what form it would take. "Certain?"

"You don't think I was cuckolded?" he demands. "You don't think she is another man's child? Do you deny her mother's guilt? I had her mother beheaded for that guilt."

She is the spit of him. Her brassy hair, her white skin, her stubborn little pout of a mouth. But if I deny her mother's guilt I accuse him of being a wife killer, a jealous fool who put an innocent woman to death on the gossip of old midwives. "Whatever Anne

Boleyn did in later years, I believe that Elizabeth is yours," I say carefully. "She is a little copy of you. She is Tudor through and through."

He nods, greedy for reassurance.

"Whatever her dam, nobody could deny her sire," I continue.

"You see me in her?"

"Her scholarship alone," I say, denying Anne Boleyn's powerful intelligence and commitment to reform, in order to secure the safety of her daughter. "Her love of books and languages—that's all you."

"And you say that, who see my children altogether, as no one else has ever done?"

"Lord husband, I brought them together as I thought it would be your wish."

"It is," he says finally. His stomach churns—I can hear it gurgle—and then he belches noisily. "It is."

I can smell the sourness of his breath. "I am glad to have done the right thing for love of you and for love of your children," I say cautiously. "I wanted the whole country to see the beautiful royal family that you have made."

He nods. "I am going to restore the girls to their place," he announces. "I am going to name them both as princesses. Mary will follow Prince Edward to the throne if she should survive him and he has no heir—God forbid it. After her: Elizabeth, and after her: my niece, Lady Margaret Douglas, and my Scots sister's line."

It is against the will of God and against tradition that the king shall name who comes after him. It is God who chooses kings, just as he chose this one—a second son—by taking all other heirs to Himself. God calls a king to his throne, God creates the order of birth and the survival of his chosen. But since the king rules the church in England and he holds the throne in England, who is going to stop him naming his heirs? Certainly not those men whom he bundled from the room for arguing with him. Certainly not I.

"Prince Edward will be king," I confirm. "And his children as yet unborn, who come after him."

"God bless them," he says mistily. He pauses. "I have always feared for him," he continues very quietly. "The child of a sainted mother, you know."

"I know," I say. Jane again. "God bless her."

"I think of her all the time. I think of her sweet nature and her early death. She died to give me an heir; she died in my service."

I nod as if I am overwhelmed at the thought of her sacrifice.

"When I am ill, when I fear I may never get well, I think that at least I will be with her."

"Don't say it," I murmur, and I really mean it.

"And people say terrible things. They say there is a curse, they speak of a curse, they say such things—a curse on Tudor boys, on our line."

"I've never heard it," I say stoutly. Of course I have. The rebels in the North were certain that the Tudor line would die out for its sins against the church and against the Plantagenets. They called him the Mouldwarp—a beast who was undermining his own kingdom.

"You haven't?" he says hopefully.

I shake my head. Everyone said that the Tudors were cursed for killing the York princes in the Tower. How should a prince killer be blessed? But if the king thought this, how could he dare to plan a future, he who killed the Plantagenet heirs: Lady Margaret Pole, and her innocent son and grandson? He, who beheaded two wives on suspicion?

"I have heard nothing like that."

"Good. Good. But it's why I keep him so safe. I guard him against murderers, against disease, against ill fortune. I guard him as my only treasure."

"I will guard him too," I promise.

"So we will trust to God for Edward, pray that he gets strong sons, and in the meantime I shall put an act through Parliament to name the girls as coming after him."

England has never had a reigning queen, but I am not going to point this out either. I don't know how to raise the question of who will be Lord Protector during Edward's minority. That is to suggest the king might die within the next eleven years, and he won't want to hear that.

I smile. "This is generous of you, my lord. The girls will be glad to know that they have your favor. That will mean more to them than being listed to succeed. To know that their father loves and acknowledges them is all that your girls want. They are blessed with such a father."

"I know," he says. "You have shown me that. I have been surprised."

"Surprised?" I repeat.

He looks awkward. It makes him, for a moment, endearingly vulnerable, a weak father: not a cursed tyrant. "I have had to think of them always as heirs or usurpers," he says, fumbling for the words. "D'you see? I've had always to consider whether I accept them as my daughters or put them aside. I have had to think of their mothers, and my terrible wars with their mothers, and not think of them. I have had to suspect them as if they were my enemies. I've never before had them at court, together, with their brother, and just seen them, all three, as my children. Just seen them as themselves."

I am enormously, absurdly touched. "Each one of them is a child to be proud of," I tell him. "You can love each one as your own."

"You have shown me that," he says. "Because you deal with Edward like a little boy, and Elizabeth as a little girl, and Mary as a young woman. I see them through your eyes. I see the girls without thinking of their poisonous dams, almost for the first time."

He takes my hand and kisses it. "I thank you for this," he says very quietly. "Truly, I do, Kateryn."

"My dear," comes easily from my lips.

"I love you," he says.

And I reply easily, without thought, "I love you, too."

We are hand-clasped for a moment, united in tenderness, and then I see his eyes narrow as a pulse of pain grips his whole body. He grits his teeth, determined not to cry out.

"Should I leave you to rest now?" I ask.

He nods. Anthony Denny is on his feet at once, to show me from the room, and I see in the way that he glances at the king without curiosity that he knew all of this, before it was explained to me. Denny is the king's confidant and friend, one of the closest of the circle. His quiet confidence reminds me that I should remember that just as I hint that the Howards and Wriothesley and Gardiner are self-serving fools, there are those, close to the king, who could do just the same to me. And that Denny is one of several men whose fortunes have been made in royal service, who have the king's ear in his most private moments, and whisper to him alone, just as I do.

I allow myself the pleasure of telling the king's daughters that they are to be princesses again. I speak to them separately. I am aware that this makes them rivals once more, and that they can only succeed to the throne on the death of their brother, that Elizabeth can only succeed through the unlikely combination of the death of her younger brother and her older sister.

I find her at her studies in my privy chamber with her cousin little Lady Jane Grey and Richard Cox, their tutor, and I call her aside to tell her that this is a symbol of her father's favor. Of course, she jumps at once to the idea of her inheritance.

"Do you think a woman can rule a kingdom?" she asks me. "The word would suggest not. It's not called a queendom, is it?"

The cleverness of the ten-year-old girl makes me smile. "If you are ever called to rule this kingdom or any other you will take on the courage and wit of a man. You will call yourself a prince," I assure her. "You will learn what every clever woman has to learn: how to adopt the power and courage of a man and yet to know that you are a woman. Your education can be that of a prince, your mind can be that of a king, you can have the body of a weak and feeble woman and the stomach of a king."

"When is it to happen? When do I get my title back?"

"It has to go through the Parliament," I warn her.

She nods. "Have you told Lady Mary?"

What a Tudor she is, this little girl; these are a statesman's questions: When is it official? And which daughter was told first?

"I'm going to tell her now," I say. "Wait here."

Lady Mary is in my presence chamber, embroidering a part of an altar cloth that we are making. She has delegated the boring blue sky to one of the ladies and she herself is working on the more interesting flowers that will form the border. They all rise and curtsey as I come in from the privy chamber and I gesture that they may sit and continue with their work. Joan, Anthony Denny's wife, is reading from the manuscript of our translation of Fisher's psalms, and I beckon Lady Mary into the oriel window so we can speak privately. We sit on the window bench, our knees touching, her earnest gaze on my face.

"I have some very good news for you," I say. "You will learn it from the Privy Council, but I wanted to tell you before the announcement. The king has decided to name the succession, and you are to be called Princess Mary and inherit the throne after Edward."

She looks down, veiling her dark eyes with her eyelashes, and I see her lips move in a prayer of thanksgiving. Only her rising blush tells me that she is deeply moved. But it is not for a chance at the throne. She has not Elizabeth's ambition. "So, finally, he accepts my mother's purity," she says. "He withdraws his claim that they were not married in the sight of God. My mother was a widow to his brother and then a true wife to him."

I put my hand on her knee to silence her. "He said no word of that, nor do I, nor should you. He names you as princess, and Elizabeth as princess also. Elizabeth comes after you in the succession, Lady Margaret Douglas and her line after her. He said nothing about the old matter of your mother's marriage and him putting her aside."

She opens her mouth to argue for only a moment, and then she nods. Anyone of any intelligence can see that if the king names his daughters as legitimate, then he must, logically, accept his marriage to their mothers as valid. But—as this highly intelligent daughter realizes—this is not a logical man. This is a king who can command reality. The king has ruled that they are princesses again, just as once he ruled that they were both bastards, on a whim, with no good reason.

"Then he will arrange a marriage for me," she says. "And for Elizabeth. If we are princesses, then we can be married to kings."

"You can," I say smiling. "I hadn't thought of that. It will be the next step. But I don't know that I can bear to spare either of you."

She puts her hand on top of mine. "I don't want to leave you," she says. "But it is time I was married. I need my own court and I want to have a child of my own to love."

We sit hand-clasped for a moment. "Princess Mary," I say, trying out her new title, "I cannot tell you how glad I am that you are come to your own again, and that I can call you aloud what I have always called you in my heart. My mother never spoke of you as anything but a princess, and never thought of your mother as anything but a great queen."

She blinks the tears from her dark eyes. "My mother would have been glad to see this day," she says wistfully.

"She would," I say. "But her legacy to you is your descent and your education. Nobody can take either, and she gave you them both."

A Spanish duke, Don Manriquez de Lara, is to come to court though the king is still unwell.

"You'll have to entertain him," Henry snaps. "I can't."

I am a little aghast. "What should I do?"

"He'll come in and see me, I'll receive him in my privy chamber, but I can't stand it for more than a moment. Understand?"

I nod. Henry is speaking in a tone of tight fury. I know that he is frustrated by his pain and bitter at his disability. In a mood like this he can lash out at anyone. I glance around the room: the pages are standing with their backs against the wall, the Fool sitting quietly at the king's side. The two secretaries are bent over documents as if they dare not raise their eyes. "He can dine with your brother, and with Henry Howard. That's the flower of the court, the handsome young men. Should be good enough for him. Agreed?"

"Yes, sire," I say. Henry Howard is the eldest son of the Duke of Norfolk, born to a great position and never doing anything to earn it. He is proud, vain, a troublemaker, a self-proclaimed golden youth. But he will be invaluable here where we will need someone handsome and young and proud as a peewit.

"Then the Spanish duke can go to your rooms and you can have music and dancing and supper and any entertainment you wish. You can do that?"

"Yes, I can."

Anthony Denny glances up from his place behind a table at the window where he is copying the king's orders to be sent to the various councillors and heads of household. I look away so that I don't see the sympathy in his face.

"Princess Mary will be with you; she speaks Spanish and they love her for the sake of her mother. The Spanish ambassador, that old fox Chapuys, will bring the duke and make sure that everything goes smoothly. You needn't worry about Spanish. You can speak in French and English to them."

"I can."

"He's not to whisper with her. You're to show him every courtesy but you're not to put her forward."

I nod.

"And you're to dress very fine and be very queenly. Wear your crown. Speak with authority. If you don't know something, say nothing. There's nothing wrong with a woman being silent. You have to impress them. Make sure you do."

"I am sure that we can show them that the English court is as elegant and learned as any in Europe," I say calmly.

At last the king looks at me and the pained furrow between his sandy eyebrows melts away and I see a glimmer of his old, charming smile. "With the most beautiful queen," he says, suddenly warm. "Whatever broken-down bad-tempered old warhorse you have for a husband."

I go to his side and take his hand. "Nay, not so old," I say softly. "And not so broken-down either. Shall I come and show you my gown before I go in to the ambassador? Shall you want to see me in all the finery you have given me?"

"Yes, come to me. And make sure that you are utterly drowned in diamonds."

I laugh, and Denny, seeing that I have charmed the king back into good humor, looks up and smiles at us both.

"I want you to frighten them with my wealth," Henry says. He is smiling now but completely serious. "Everything that you do, every chain that you wear, will be noted and reported back to Spain. I want them to know that we are rich beyond anything they could imagine, quite rich enough to make war with France, rich enough to bend Scotland to our will."

"And are we?" I ask so quietly that not even Denny at the table, bent over the scratching of his quill, can hear me.

"No," Henry says. "But we have to be like masquers, like troubadours. We have to have dazzling rags. Kingship and warfare are mostly appearance."

I put on a great show. "Magpie queen," Nan remarks as I let them load chain after chain on my waist and put diamonds and rubies on my fingers and at my neck.

"Too rory?" I ask, looking in the mirror and smiling at her horrified face.

"Speak English!" she commands me. "Not your rough country tongue! No, it's not too much. Not if he told you to load on the jewels. He'll want an alliance with Spain so that he can go to war with France. Your task is to make it look as if England can afford a war with France. You've got an army's pay on your fingers alone."

She steps back and scans me from head to foot. "Beautiful," she says. "The most beautiful of all the queens."

My stepdaughter Margaret Latimer comes towards me with the little box in her hands. "The crown," she says, awed.

I nerve myself to be unmoved as Nan opens it up, takes out the Boleyn crown, and turns to me. I straighten up to take the weight of it and look at myself in the mirror. The beaten silver looking-glass shows me a gray-eyed beauty with bronze hair and a long neck, with diamonds at her ears and rubies at her throat, and this ugly heavy sparkling little crown making her taller still. I think I look like a ghost queen, a queen in darkness, a queen at the top of a dark tower. I could be any one of my predecessors, favored like one of them, doomed like them all.

"You could wear your golden hood," Nan offers.

I stand, my head poised. "Of course I'll wear the crown," I say flatly. "I'm queen. At any rate, I'm today's queen."

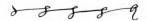

I wear it all evening. I take it off only when the dazzled duke begs us to dance and then Nan fetches my hood. It is a successful evening; everything goes just as the king commanded. The young men are charming and loud and cheerful; the ladies are reserved and beautiful. Lady Mary speaks Spanish to the duke and to her ambassador but is every inch an English princess, and I feel that I have taken another step closer to being the wife that the king needs—one who can deputize for him, one who can rule.

The king requires that I move my bed to be nearer to him while he is sleepless with pain at night, and my household transfers my beautiful bed with the four great posts and the embroidered canopy to a withdrawing room off the king's own bedroom. With it go my table and chair, and my prie-dieu. With a silent gesture I command that my box of books and my writing box with my manuscripts, my studies, and my translation of the Fisher psalms stay in the queen's apartments. Although I read nothing but what is approved by the king and his Privy Council, I don't really want to draw attention to my growing library of theological books or have everyone know that my principal interest is the teachings of the early church, and the call for reform of the abuses of recent years. This seems to me the one thing that a scholar of our time should study; it is the central question of our days. All the great men are reviewing how the church has strayed from its early simplicity and piety, all the discussions and writings are about finding the true way, the authentic way to Christ, whether that is inside the Church of Rome or alongside it. They are translating the documents that tell us how the earliest church was organized, and they keep finding histories and gospels that suggest ways that a holy life can be lived in the world, that show how earthly powers should sit alongside the church. I believe that the king was completely right when he transferred the leadership of the church in England to himself. It must be right that a king rules his lands, church buildings and all. There cannot be one law for the people and one for the clergy. Surely, the church must command the spiritual realm, the holy things of God; the king must command the earthly things. Who could argue against that?

"Many," Catherine Brandon, the greatest reformer of my ladies, explains. "And many of them have the ear of the king. They are growing in strength again. They were set back when the king sided with Archbishop Cranmer, but Stephen Gardiner has regained the king's ear and his influence is growing all the time. Naming Princess Mary with her title will please Rome, and we are extending friendship to Spain, honoring their ambassador. Many of the king's advisors have been bribed by Rome to try to persuade him to return the ownership of the English Church to Rome—back to where we were before—telling him that we will be in accord with all the other great countries. And then, in the towns and villages, there are thousands of people who understand nothing of this but just want to see the shrines restored at the roadsides and the icons and statues back in the churches. Poor fools, they understand nothing and don't want to have to think for themselves. They want the monks and nuns to come back to look after them and tell them what to think."

"Well, I don't want anyone to know what I think," I say bluntly. "So keep my books in my rooms and locked in the chest, Catherine, and you keep the key."

She laughs and shows me the key on the chain at her belt.

"We're not all as carefree as you," I say, as she whistles for her little dog, named after the bishop.

"Puppy Gardiner is a fool who comes for a whistle and sits at a command," she says.

"Well, don't call him or command him by name in my rooms," I say. "I don't need enemies, certainly not Stephen Gardiner. The king already favors him. You will have to rename your dog if my lord bishop continues to rise."

"I'm afraid he's unstoppable," she says frankly. "He and the traditionalists are overwhelming us. I hear that Thomas Wriothesley is not satisfied by being the king's Secretary and Lord Privy Seal, but is to be Lord Chancellor too."

"Did your husband tell you?"

She nods. "He said that Wriothesley is the most ambitious man in the king's rooms since Cromwell. He said he is a dangerous man—just like Cromwell."

"Does Charles not advise the king in favor of reform?"

She smiles at me. "Not he! You don't stay a favorite for thirty years by telling the king what you think."

"So why does your husband not try to contain you," I ask curiously, "as you name your spaniel for a bishop in order to tease him?"

She laughs. "Because you don't survive four wives by trying to contain them!" she says merrily. "I am his fourth and he lets me think what I like, and do what I like, as long as it does not disturb him."

"He knows that you read and think? He allows it?"

"Why not?" She asks the most challenging questions that a woman can ask. "Why should I not read? Why should I not think? Why should I not speak?"

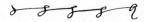

The king cannot sleep for pain in the long dark nights of spring. He feels very low when he wakes long before dawn. I have commissioned a pretty clock to help me get through the hours, and I watch the minute hand move quietly over the brass face in the flickering light of a little candle that I leave beside it on the table. When the king wakes, fretful and bad-tempered at about five in the morning, I get up and light all the candles, stir the fire, and often send a page for some ale and pastries from the kitchen. Then the king likes me to sit beside him and read to him as the candles gutter and slowly, so very slowly, the light comes in at the window, first as a grayer darkness, then as a dark gray, then only finally, after what seems like hours, can I see daylight and say to the king: "Morning is coming."

I feel tender towards him as he endures the long nights in pain. I don't begrudge waking and sitting with him though I know I will be tired when dawn finally comes. Then he can sleep but I have to attend to the duties of the court for us both—leading everyone to Mass, breakfasting in public before a hundred watching eyes, reading with Princess Mary, watching the court ride to hounds, dining with them at midday, listening to the councillors in the afternoon and dining, watching the revels and dancing all evening, and often dancing myself. This is sometimes a pleasure but it is always a duty. A court has to have a focus and a head. If the king is not well it is my task to take his place—and to conceal how very ill he is. He can rest during the day if I am there, smiling on the throne and assuring everyone that he is a little tired but better every day.

Stephen Gardiner supplies all the books for the king's nighttime reading, it is a most limited library; but I am not allowed to read anything else, and so I find myself having to recite pious arguments for the unity of the church under the pope, or fanciful histories of the earliest church that stress the importance of the patriarchs and the Holy Father. If I believed these orthodox writings, I would think that there were no women in the world at all, certainly no women saints in the early church laying down their lives for their faith. Bishop Gardiner is now a great enthusiast for the Eastern Church, which is a full member of the Catholic communion but not subservient to the pope. The Greek Church is to be our model and I read long sermons that suggest the fine level of purity that can be achieved in a Catholic church in partnership with Rome. I have to declare that people should be kept in sanctified ignorance and that it is best that they say their prayers and have no idea what the words mean. Knowingly, I recite nonsense, and I despise Bishop Gardiner for dictating lies.

Henry listens; sometimes his eyes close and I see that I have read him to sleep, sometimes the pain keeps him alert. He never comments on my reading, except to ask me to repeat a sentence. He never asks me if I agree with the plodding arguments against reform, and I take care to make no comment. In the quietness of the nighttime room I can hear the little gurgle as the pus drains from his leg and drips into the bowl. He is shamed by the stink, and struggles with the pain. I cannot help him with either, except to offer him the draft that the physicians leave to drug him into sleep, and to assure him that I hardly smell anything. The rooms are laden with dried rose petals and the sharp scent of lavender heads, and in every corner there are bowls filled with the oil of roses, but still the stench of death seeps like a fog into everything.

Some nights he hardly sleeps at all. Some days he does not get up, but hears Mass in his bed, and his advisors and councillors meet in the chamber that adjoins his bedroom, with the door open so that he can hear them speak.

I sit beside his bed and listen as they plan the future union of England with Scotland through the marriage of Lady Margaret Douglas, the king's niece, and Matthew Stuart, a Scottish nobleman. When the Scots reject this, I listen to the advisors plan an expedition to be led by Edward Seymour and John Dudley to lay waste the border country and teach the Scots to respect their masters. I am horrified by this plan. Having lived in the North of England for so many years I know how hard life is in those hills. The balance between harvest and hunger is so carefully weighed that an invading army will cause starvation just by marching through. This cannot be the way to bring about unity with the Scots. Are we to destroy our new kingdom before we gain it?

But, silently listening from the king's room, I begin to see how the Privy Council works, how the country reports to the lords, who report to the council, who debate before the king. Then the king decides—quite whimsically—what shall be done and the council considers how it shall be drafted into law, put before the Parliament for their consent, and imposed on the country.

The king's advisors, those who filter all the news that he hears and draft the laws that he demands, have enormous power in this system, which depends on the judgment of one man—and that is a man in too much pain to rise out of his bed, who is frequently dazed and stupid with drugs. It is easy for them to withhold information that he should have, or cast the law in a way that suits themselves. This should give us all concern for the well-being of the country, whose destiny sits in Henry's sweating hands. But it also gives me confidence to be regent, as I see that with good advisors I could judge just as well as the king. Almost certainly I could judge better, for Henry will suddenly bellow from his bed, "Move on! Move on!" when something bores him, or a disagreement irritates him, and he favors one policy or another depending on who presents it.

I also learn how he plays one party against another. Stephen Gardiner is his preferred advisor, always pointing out that there should be more and more restrictions on the English Bible, that it must be strictly limited to the nobility and the learned, locked-up in their private chapels, that the poor must be prosecuted if they try to read it. He never misses an opportunity to complain that men everywhere are debating the sacred Word of God as if they could understand it, as if they are equal to educated men. But just as Stephen Gardiner thinks he has won and that the Bible will never be restored to the churches, stolen forever from the very people that need it most, the king tells Anthony Denny to send for Thomas Cranmer.

"You'll never guess what task I am going to give him," he says, slyly smiling at me as he lies back on his great heap of pillows and I sit beside his enormous bed, his fat damp hand in mine. "You'll never guess!"

"I am sure I never will," I say. I like Thomas Cranmer, a constant believer in the reform of the church, whose sermon was published at the front of the Great Bible in English, and who has always urged that the king should rule the English Church and that the sermons, psalms, and prayers should be in English. The quiet courage that he showed when he faced the plot against him has confirmed my liking for him, and he often comes to my rooms as an honored friend, to see what I am writing and to join our discussion.

"This is the way to play them," Henry confides in me. "This is the way to rule a kingdom, Kateryn. Watch and learn. First you appoint one man, then you appoint another, his rival. You give one a task—you praise him to the skies, then you give an opposite task, a complete contradiction, to his greatest enemy. While they fight one against the other, they can't conspire to plot against you. When they are divided to death, they are yours to command. D'you see?"

What I see is a zigzag confusion of policy so that no one knows what the king believes or truly wants, a muddle in which the loudest voice or the most pleasing person can triumph. "I am sure Your Majesty is wise," I say carefully. "And cunning. But Thomas Cranmer would serve you in anything; surely you don't have to trap him into obedience?"

"He is my balance," the king says. "I balance him against Gardiner."

"Then he will have to drag us to Germany," Will Somers suddenly intervenes. I had not realized he was listening. He has been sitting so quietly on the floor, his back against the great pillars of the bed, throwing a little golden ball from one hand to the other.

"Why so?" Henry asks, always tolerant of his Fool. "Jump up, Will. I can't see you down there."

The Fool springs up, tosses the golden ball high in the air and catches it, half singing:

> *Thomas must pull us all the way*
> *Over the mountains to Germany,*
> *For Stephen is dragging us up and down*
> *Over the Alps to Rome.*

Henry laughs. "I have my counterpoise to Gardiner," he tells me. "I am going to get Cranmer to write an exhortation and litany in English."

I am stunned. "An English prayer book? In English?"

"Yes, so that when people come to church they can hear the prayers in their own language and understand them. How are they to make a true confession in a language they don't understand?

How are they to truly pray if the words mean nothing to them? They stand at the back and say 'yammer yammer yammer—amen.'"

This is exactly what I thought when I translated Bishop Fisher's psalms from Latin to English. "What a gift to the people of England it would be!" I am almost stammering in excitement. "A prayer book in their own tongue! What a saving of souls! I should be so pleased if I were to be allowed to work on it, too!"

"And I say good morning to the queen," Will Somers says suddenly. "Good morning to the morning queen."

"Good morning to you, Will," I reply. "Is this a joke?"

"It is a morning joke. And the king's idea is the plan for this morning. After dinner you will find it quite different. This morning we send for Cranmer, tonight—heigh-ho—it will be my lord Gardiner who is the fount of all knowledge, and you will be the morning queen and quite out of your time."

"Hush, Fool," Henry says. "What do you think, Kateryn?"

Despite Will's warning, I cannot resist speaking. "I think it is an opportunity to write something both true and beautiful," I say enthusiastically. "And something that is beautifully written must lead people to God."

"But it cannot be ornamental," Henry insists. "It cannot be a false god. It has to be a true translation from the Latin, not a poem grafted on it."

"It must be the Word," I say. "The Lord spoke in simple language to simple people. Our church must do the same. But I think there is great beauty in simple language."

"Why don't you write some new prayers yourself?" Henry asks suddenly. "Write in your own hand?"

For a moment I wonder if he knows of my book of translated psalms published without a name on the cover. I wonder if his spies have told him that I have already translated prayers and discussed them with the archbishop. I stammer. "No, no, I could not presume . . ."

But he is sincere in his interest. "I know that Cranmer thinks highly of you. Why not write some original prayers? And why don't you translate some prayers from the Latin Mass and show your version to him? Bring one to me to read. And Princess Mary works with you, doesn't she? And Elizabeth?"

"With her tutor," I say cautiously. "As part of Elizabeth's study, with her cousin Jane Grey."

"I believe that women should study," he says kindly. "It is not part of the duty of woman to remain ignorant. And you have a learned and scholarly husband; there is no chance of you outpacing me, after all!" He laughs at the thought of it and I laugh with him.

I don't even look at the Fool, though I know he is listening for my reply. "Whatever you think best, my lord," I say levelly. "I should enjoy to do the work and it would be an education for the princesses also. But you will judge how far it should go."

"It can go far," the king rules. "It can go as far as Cranmer can compose it. Because I will send my dog Gardiner after it to bring it back if it goes too far."

"Is it possible to find a middle way in this?" I wonder aloud. "Cranmer either writes the prayers of the Mass in English and publishes in English or he does not."

"We'll find my way," Henry replies. "My way is inspired by God Himself to me, His ruler on earth. He speaks to me. I hear Him."

"You see," Will suddenly bounds to the fireside and addresses the sleeping hound, lifting his big head and putting it on his knee, "if she said that, or I said that, they would beg us as a madwoman and a Fool. But if the king says that, everyone thinks it is nothing but true since he is descended from God, and has the holy oil on his chest so he can never be wrong."

The king narrows his eyes at his favorite. "I can never be wrong for I am king," he says. "I can never be wrong because a king is above a mortal man, seated just below the angels. I can never be wrong because God speaks to me, in words that no one else can hear. Just as you can never be wise for you are my Fool." He glances towards me. "And she can never have an opinion that is not mine, for she is my wife."

I pray that night for discretion. All my life I have been an obedient wife, first to a young, fearful and foolish boy, then to a powerful, cold man. To both of them I showed complete obedience for that is the duty of a wife, laid down by God and taught to every woman. Now I am married to the King of England and owe him three sorts of duty: as a wife, as a subject, and as a member of the church over which he sits as Supreme Head. That I should read books that he would not like, and think of opinions that he does not hold, is disloyalty or worse. I should think as he does, morning and evening. But I cannot see that God would give me a brain and not want me to think for myself. The words ring in my head: *I cannot see that God would give me a brain and not want me to think for myself.* And with them comes the couplet: *And God has given me a heart, He must want me to love.* I know that the pairing of the two sentences is not the logic of a philosopher: but that of a poet. It comes from having a writer's ear; it is the words that persuade me as well as the idea. *God has given me a brain—He must want me to think. God has given me a heart—He must want me to love.* I hear them in my mind. I don't say them out loud, not even here, in the deserted chapel. But when I look up from my place at the chancel rail at the painting of the crucified Christ, all I see is Thomas Seymour's dark smile.

Nan marches into my bird room where I am sitting in the window seat with a pair of yellow canaries on one hand pecking at a speck of manchet bread that I hold in the other. I am reveling in their bright little eyes, the cock of their heads, the brilliance of their color, the intricate detail of feather upon feather and their warm, scratchy little feet. They are like a miracle of intense life, sitting in the palm of my hand. "Sshh," I say without raising my head.

"You need to hear this," Nan says in a tone of muted fury. "Put the birds away."

I glance up to refuse, but then I see her grim face. Behind her Catherine Brandon is pale. Beside her is Anne Seymour looking grave.

Gently, so as not to startle them, I put my hand into the pretty cage and the pair hop to their perches, and one of them begins to preen and tidy his feathers as if he was an important ambassador, returned from a visit, and must straighten his cloak.

"What is it?"

"It's the new Act of Succession," Nan says. "The king is naming his heirs before he goes to war with France. Charles Brandon and Edward Seymour were with him when he was taking advice, and Wriothesley—Wriothesley!—was there with the lawyers drawing it up."

"I know all about this," I say calmly. "He discussed it with me."

"Did he tell you that he is naming the heirs of your body to follow Prince Edward?" she demands.

I wheel round and the little birds in the cage flutter at my sudden movement.

"My heirs?" I demand.

"We have to take care what is said." Anne Seymour glances anxiously around as if the parrot might report to Bishop Gardiner any words of treason.

"Of course, of course," I nod. "I was just surprised."

"And any other heirs," Catherine Brandon says, her voice very quiet, her face carefully expressionless. "That's the point, really."

"Other heirs?"

"From any future queen."

"Any future queen?" I repeat. I look at Nan, not at Catherine or Anne. "He is planning for a future queen?"

"Not really," Anne Seymour reassures me. "He is just drawing up an Act of Succession that would still apply even if he were to outlive you. Say you died before him . . ."

Nan gives a little choke. "From what? She's young enough to be his daughter!"

"It has to be provided for!" Anne Seymour insists. "Say you were to be so unlucky as to become unwell and die . . ."

Catherine and Nan exchange blank glances. Clearly Henry has a habit of outliving his queens and none of them has ever become unwell.

"Then he would be obliged to marry again and to get a son if he could," Anne Seymour concludes. "It is not to say he is planning it. It is not to say it is his intention. It is not to say that he has anyone in mind."

"No," Nan snarls. "He did not have it in mind; someone has put it into his mind. They have put it into his mind now. And your husbands were there when they did so."

"It may just be the proper way to draw up the Act of Succession." Catherine suggests.

"No, it isn't." Nan insists. "If she were to die and he remarried and had a son, then the boy would become heir after Edward by right of birth and sex. There's no need for the king to provide for this. If she were to die, then a new marriage and a new heir would mean a new Act of Succession. It does not need to be provided for here and now. This is just to put the idea of another marriage into our minds."

"Our minds?" I ask. "He wants me to consider that he might put me aside and marry again?"

"Or he wants the country to be prepared for it," Catherine Brandon says very quietly.

"Or his advisors are thinking of a new queen. A new queen who favors the old ways," Nan replies. "You have disappointed them."

We are all silent for a moment.

"Did Charles say who added the clause?" Anne Seymour asks Catherine.

She gives a little shrug. "I think it was Gardiner. I don't know for sure. Who else would want to prepare for a new queen, a seventh queen?"

"A seventh queen?" I repeat.

"The thing is," Nan concludes, "as King of England and head of the church, he can do what he likes."

"I know that," I say coldly. "I know that he can do exactly as he likes."

WHITEHALL PALACE, LONDON, SUMMER 1544

KP

Thomas Cranmer has worked constantly on his liturgy; he brings it to the king, prayer by prayer, and the three of us read it and reread it. Cranmer and I study the original Latin, and rephrase it, and read it again to the king, who listens, beating his hand on the chair as if he were listening to music. Sometimes he nods his head approvingly at the archbishop or at me and says: "Hear it! It's like a miracle to hear the Word of God in our own language!" and sometimes he frowns and says: "That's an awkward phrase, Kateryn. That sticks on the tongue like old bread. No one will ever say that smoothly. Rework it, what d'you think?" And I take the line and try it one way and then another to make it sing.

He says nothing about the Act of Succession and neither do I. It goes before the Houses of Parliament and is passed into law without my remarking to my husband that he is providing for my death, though I am young enough to be his daughter, that he is providing for a queen to follow me, though he has made no complaint of me. Gardiner is away from court, Cranmer is a frequent companion, and the king loves to work with us both.

Clearly, he is serious about this translation being made and offered to the churches. Sometimes he says to Cranmer: "Yes, but this has got to be heard up in the gallery, where the poor people stand. It's got to be clear. It's got to be audible even when an old priest is muttering away."

"The old priests won't read it at all unless you force it on them," Cranmer warns him. "There are many who think that it cannot be the Mass unless it's Latin."

"They will do as I command," the king replies. "This is the Word of God in English, and I am giving it to my people whatever the old priests and the old fools like Gardiner want. And the queen is going to translate the old prayers, and write some new ones."

"Are you?" Cranmer asks me with a gentle smile.

"I am thinking about it," I say cautiously. "The king is so kind as to encourage me."

"He is right," Cranmer says with a bow. "What a church we will make with the Mass in English and prayers written by the faithful! By the Queen of England herself!"

The warmer weather brings an improvement to the king's leg, which has been drained of the worst of the pus and is now only weeping gently, and this improves his temper. Working with me and his archbishop, he seems to regain some of his old joy in study, and it even deepens his love of God. He likes us to come to him when he is alone before dinner, perhaps with only a page to serve him some pastries, or one of his clerks in attendance. He has to wear his spectacles for reading now, and he does not like the court to see him with the gold-rimmed glasses tied on his nose. He is shamed by the blurring of his sight and fearful that he will go blind, but he laughs when one day I take his fat face in my hands and kiss it and tell him he looks like a wise owl and that he is handsome in his spectacles and should wear them everywhere.

I go to my own rooms in the day and I am able to work on the liturgy with my ladies. In the afternoons Thomas Cranmer often comes in, and we work together. It is not a long piece, of course, but it is intense. It feels as if every word must be weighted with holiness. There is not a spare line or a false note from beginning to end.

In May, the archbishop brings me the first printed copy, bows, and lays it in my lap.

"This is it?" I say almost wonderingly, my finger on the smooth leather cover.

"This is it," he replies. "My work and yours, perhaps the greatest work that I will ever do. Perhaps the greatest gift that you will ever be able to give to the English people. Now they can pray in their own language. Now they can speak and trust that God hears them. They can be the people of God, indeed."

I cannot lift my hand from the cover; it is as if I am touching the hand of God. "My lord, this is a work that will last for generations."

"And you have done your part in it," he says generously. "Here is a woman's voice as well as a man's, and men and women will say these prayers, perhaps they will even kneel side by side, equals in the sight of God."

SAINT JAMES'S PALACE, LONDON, SUMMER 1544

KP

We have days of sunshine and the king gets stronger. He is pleased with his campaign against Scotland, and in June we go to the rebuilt Saint James's Palace for the wedding of his niece, my lady-in-waiting and friend Margaret Douglas, to a Scots nobleman, Matthew Stuart, the Earl of Lennox. Here the king can walk in the garden and he starts to move more easily and even takes up archery, though he'll never play tennis again. He watches the young men of the court and I know that he eyes them as if they were still his rivals though he is far older than they are, older than their fathers, and he will never strip off his jacket and dance in his lawn shirt again. Especially, he watches the handsome young bridegroom Matthew Stuart.

"He'll win Scotland over for me," Henry says in my ear as the bride and groom walk handclasped down the aisle. Henry's niece throws me a naughty wink as she goes by. She is a most unruly bride, openly relieved at finally being allowed to marry aged nearly thirty years old, after two scandals, both of them involving young men from the Howard house. "He'll win Scotland for me and then Prince Edward shall marry the little Queen of Scots— Mary—and I shall see Scotland and England united."

"That would be wonderful if it can be done."

"Of course it can be done."

The king heaves himself to his feet and leans on the arm of a page as we process down the aisle. I walk by his side and we go slowly, an ungainly trio, towards the open chapel doors. There is to be a great feast in honor of this wedding, which promises so much for the safety of England.

"With the Scots on my side it leaves me safe to take France," Henry says.

"My lord husband, are you really well enough to go yourself?"

The smile he shows me is as bright as any young captain in his army. "I can ride," he says. "However weak my leg is beneath me when I am walking, at least I can sit on a horse. And if I can ride at the head of my army, I can lead them to Paris. You'll see."

I look up to protest—half the Privy Council have come to me and begged me to support their appeal to the king that he does not go to war himself; even the Spanish ambassador says that the emperor advises against it—when I see, among the hundreds crowding into the chapel, the turn of a dark head, a profile, a jewel in a hat, and, from under the brim of the hat, a quick glance at me, and at once, in a moment, I know my lover, Thomas Seymour.

I would know him anywhere. I recognized him by the back of his head. The king has stumbled and is cursing the page for failing to support him, and I step back and grab Nan's arm and grip it tightly as the dimly lit chapel swims around me and I think that I am going to faint.

"What is it?" she demands.

"A gripe," I say at random. "In my belly. Just my monthly course."

"Steady," she says, watching me, so she does not notice Thomas and he has the sense to step back, out of sight. I take a few dizzy steps, blinking. I cannot see him but I can feel his eyes on me, I can feel his presence in the little chapel, I can almost smell the haunting scent of his clean sweat. I feel as if the print of his naked chest is on my cheek like a brand. I feel as if anyone looking at me could know that I am his lover, I am his whore. One night I lay beneath him and begged him to swive me all night, as if I were his field and he a plow.

I dig my fingernails into the palms of my hands as if I would draw blood. The king has commanded another page to help him and he has one on either side as we walk on. He jarred his leg and is fighting his pain and unsteadiness and not looking at me. No one has observed my moment of faintness. People are watching him, remarking that he is stronger than he was but still needs help. Henry glowers from right to left. He does not want to hear anyone suggest that he is still not well enough to ride at the head of his own army.

He nods for me to come beside him. "Fools," he remarks.

I twist my face into a smile and I nod, but I don't hear him.

The trumpets sound a great brassy shout as we come into the great hall, and I remember the taste of Thomas's mouth, the way he bites my lips in a kiss. I have a sudden memory, as sharp as if it were happening right now, of his taking my lower lip in his teeth and nibbling it till my knees go weak and he has to lift me to the bed. Henry and I walk in state through the bowing court to the raised dais. I can see nothing but Thomas's face in candlelight.

Two men come either side of the king to heave his great bulk up the two shallow steps and then seat him on his throne, his leg propped. I take my seat beside him and turn and look over the heads of the court, through the wide-open entrance door to the inner courtyard, where the afternoon is shining rosy on the new red bricks.

I take a breath. I wait for the moment, which must come, which must be now, when Thomas Seymour comes forward to make his bow.

There is a movement at my side. Princess Mary takes her seat beside me. "Are you all right, Your Majesty?" she asks me.

"Why?"

"You're so white . . ."

"Just a little gripe," I say. "You know."

She nods. She is seldom free of pain herself and she knows that I cannot be excused from this feast or even show any discomfort. "I have a tincture of raspberry leaves in my room," she offers. "I can send someone to get it for you."

"Yes, yes, please," I say at random.

My gaze rakes the room. He has to step forward and greet the king before the servers come in with the endless parade of courses that make up the bridal feast. He has to come and bow and then take his seat at the table for the noble lords of the court. And everyone will watch him bow to the king, and then everyone will see him bow to me, and nobody must remark that I look pale. Nobody must know that my heart is pounding so fast that I think Princess Mary will hear it over the clatter of the court pulling up the benches and stools to the trestle tables and taking their seats.

I wonder if his nerve will fail. I wonder if his reckless laughing courage will fail him this once, and he won't come in to dinner at all. Or is he outside now, nerving himself to walk forward? Perhaps he cannot greet me as a courteous acquaintance, perhaps he cannot bring himself to congratulate me on my wedding and my rise to greatness? But he knows that he will have to do it, so surely now would be better than later?

Just when I think he is taking so long that he must have given some excuse and gone away, I see him, weaving his way between the tables, ahead of the servers, a smile to one man at one side and a touch on the shoulder of another, moving through the crowd with people calling his name and greeting him.

He stands before the dais, and the king looks down at him. "Tom Seymour!" he exclaims. "I'm very glad you're back. You must have ridden hard. You had far to come."

Thomas bows. He does not look at me. He smiles up at the king, his easy, familiar smile. "I rode like a horse thief," he confesses. "I was so afraid that I would be too late and you would be armed and mounted and gone without me."

"You're just in time," the king says. "For I will be armed and mounted and gone within the month."

"I knew it!" Thomas exclaims. "I knew you would wait for nothing," and the king beams back at him. "Say I am to come with you?"

"I'd have no one else. You're to be marshal of the army. I am trusting you, Tom. Your brother is away thrashing the Scots into peace. I am counting on you to bring glory to your name and defend your royal nephew's inheritance in France."

Thomas puts his hand on his heart and bows. "I would die rather than fail you," he says. He still has not looked at me.

"And you may greet your queen," Henry says.

Thomas turns to me and bows very low, a Burgundy bow, the most graceful gesture in the world, one long-fingered hand sweeping the floor with his embroidered hat. "It is a joy to see Your Majesty," he says, his voice completely steady and cool.

"You are welcome back to court, Sir Thomas," I say carefully. I can hear the words as if I were a little girl reciting them in a schoolroom, the correct way to greet a returning councillor: "You are welcome back to court, Sir Thomas."

"And he has done great work for us!" Henry turns to me and pats my hand as it rests on the arm of my throne. He leaves his damp palm over mine, as if to show that he owns my hand, my arm, my body. "Sir Thomas has a treaty with the Netherlands that will keep us safe as we advance on France. He persuaded Queen Mary, the governor. He's a charmer, this one. Did you find her very beautiful, Tom?"

I can tell from Thomas's hesitation that this is an unkind jest against the queen's plain looks. "She is a thoughtful and gracious lady," he says. "And she would prefer peace with France to war."

"An oddity on two counts!" Will Somers bobs up to observe. "A thoughtful woman who wants peace. What will you tell us of next, Tom Seymour? An honest Frenchman? A witty German?"

The court breaks into laughter.

"Well, you're welcome home in time for war; the time for peace is over!" Henry exclaims, and holds up his great goblet in a toast. Everyone stands and holds their tankards and their glasses and drinks to war. There is a clatter and scrape of the benches on the wooden floor as everyone sits again and Thomas bows and steps back to the table for the first noblemen of the court. He takes his seat, someone pours him wine, and someone slaps him on the back. He still has not looked at me.

WHITEHALL PALACE, LONDON, SUMMER 1544

KP

He does not look at me. He does not look at me, ever. When I am dancing in a circle and my gaze goes from one smiling face to another I never see him. He is talking with the king, or in a corner laughing with a friend; he is at a gaming table, or looking out of the window. When the court goes hunting, he is high on a big black horse, his face turned down, tightening the girth or patting its neck. When there is archery, his dark narrowed gaze is directed only along the shaft of the arrow to the target; when he plays tennis, a white linen scarf around his neck, his shirt open at the throat, his attention is entirely on the game. When he comes to Mass in the morning, with the king's hand resting on his shoulder, he does not look up to my gallery where the ladies and I are kneeling, heads bowed in prayer. During the long service, when I peep between my fingers, I see that he is not praying with his eyes closed; he is gazing at the monstrance, his face illuminated by the light falling from the window above the altar, as beautiful as a carved saint himself. I close my eyes then and I whisper in my mind: "God help me, God take this desire from me, God make me as blind to him as he is to me."

"Thomas Seymour never says one word to me," I remark to Nan when we are alone before dinner one evening, to see if she has noticed.

"Doesn't he? He's as vain as a puppy and always flirting with someone. But his brother never makes much of you, either. They're a family who think very highly of themselves, and of course they won't want a Parr stepmother to make people forget the Seymour mother of the prince. He is always perfectly polite to me."

"Sir Thomas speaks to you?"

"In passing only. For politeness only. I don't have much time for him."

"Does he ask you how I am?"

"Why should he?" she demands. "He can see how you are. He can ask you himself, if he has any interest."

I shrug as if I don't care. "It's just that since he has come home from the Netherlands he seems to have no time for any of the ladies, whereas before he was such a flirt. Perhaps he has left his heart behind."

"Perhaps," she says. Something in my face makes her remind me: "Not that you care."

"I don't care at all," I agree.

Seeing Thomas every day makes me stumble in my confident progress to love and respect the king, and throws me back into the feelings that I had before my wedding, as if the year between had never been. I am angry with myself: one year into a good marriage, and as breathless as a girl in love again. I have to get down on my knees once more and beg God to cool my blood, to keep my eyes off Thomas and my thoughts on my duty and my love for my husband. I have to remind myself that Thomas is not playing with me, nor is he torturing me; he is doing as we agreed—keeping as far from me as possible. I have to remember that before, when I loved him and reveled in the knowledge that he loved me, I was a widow and free. Now I am a wife, and it is a sin against my vows and against my husband to feel as I do.

I pray to God to keep me in the state of peaceful loving tenderness that I have established with the king, to keep me a wife in my dreams as well as in my daily life. But as the presence of Thomas churns my thoughts, I start to dream again, not of a happy marriage and the duties of an obedient wife, but of climbing up damp stairs, a candle in my hand, and the stink of rotting flesh all around me. In the dream I go towards a door that is locked, and try the handle as the smell of death grows stronger. I have to know what is behind it. I have to know. I am terrified of what I might find but, dreamlike, I cannot stop myself going forward. Now the key is in my hand and I listen at the keyhole for any sound of life from the room that smells of death. I insert the key, I turn it, silently the lock yields, and I put my hand on the door and it swings horribly open.

I am frightened into wakefulness. I sit bolt upright in my bed, gasping, the king fast asleep in his bedroom next door, the open door between our bedchambers admitting the roaring snore and snuffle and the terrible stench of his leg. It is so dark, it must be long hours from dawn. Wearily, I get out of my bed and go to the table to look at my new clock. The golden pendulum swings backwards and forwards, beautifully balanced, emitting a tiny click like a constant heartbeat. I feel my pounding heart steady to its rhythm. It is half past one, hours yet before I can look for light. I wrap myself in a robe and I sit beside the dying fire. I wonder how I am to get through the night, how I am to get through the next day. Wearily, I get down on my knees and pray again that God will take this passion from me. I did not seek love with Thomas, but I did not resist it. And now I am trapped in desire like a butterfly with its feet in honey, and the more I struggle, the deeper I sink. I think I cannot bear to live my life trying to do my duty to a good man, a gentle and generous husband who cries out for attentive care and a loving heart, while all I do is long for a man who does not need me at all but sets my skin on fire.

And then, though I am trapped in the sin of fear, and a slave to a passion, something very strange happens. Though it is nowhere near dawn, though it is the darkest time of the night, I feel the room lighten, the ashes of the fire grow a little brighter. I raise my head, and my forehead no longer throbs and my fearful sweat has cooled. I feel well, as if I had slept well and I am waking to a bright morning. The smell from the king's room is diminished and I know once again my deep pity for him in his pain and illness. His rumbling snore has grown quieter and I am glad that he is sleeping well. Hardly believing my own sense of being uplifted, I feel as if I can hear the voice of God, as if He is with me, as if He has come to me in this night of my trial, as if His mercy can look on me, a sinner, a woman who has sinned and has longed for sin, who still longs for sin, and that, even seeing all this, He can forgive me.

I stay, kneeling on the hearthstone, till the clock on the table strikes four with its silvery little chime and I realize that I have been in a trance of prayer for hours. I have prayed and I believe that I have been heard. I have spoken and I believe I have been answered. No priest took my confession or gave me absolution, no church took my fee, no pilgrim badges or miracle cures or little pieces of trumpery helped me to come into the presence of God. I simply asked for His great mercy and I received it, as He promised in the Bible that it should be granted.

I rise up from the floor and I get into my bed, shivering a little. I think, with a sense of great wonderment, that I have been blessed, as God promised I would be blessed. I think He has come to me, a sinner, and that I have, by His grace, been granted forgiveness and the remission of my sins.

WHITEHALL PALACE, LONDON, SUMMER 1544

KP

The army is setting sail for France; Thomas Howard has already gone with the vanguard but still the king delays.

"I have summoned my astronomer," he says to me as we leave Mass one morning. "Come with me and see what he advises."

The king's astronomer is as skilled as any of the European scientists in understanding the movement of the stars and the planets, and he can also identify a favorable date for any venture depending on which planet is in the ascendancy. He treads a difficult course between describing the known and observable movement of the heavens, which is philosophy, and the art of fortune-telling, which is illegal. To suggest that the king might be ill or injured is treason, so anything he sees or foresees has to be described with extreme caution. But Nicholas Kratzer has drawn charts for the king many times before, and knows how to phrase his warnings and advice to stay inside the law.

Henry tucks my hand under his elbow and leans on his page on the other side as we walk to his privy chamber. Behind us come the rest of the court, the king's noblemen and my ladies. Somewhere among them is Thomas Seymour; I don't glance round. I think that God will hold me to my resolution. I will not glance round.

We walk through the presence chamber and most of the court

waits here, only a few of us going inwards to the privy chamber, where a great table has been pulled into the center of the room, spread with charts weighted down with little astrological symbols made of gold. Nicholas Kratzer, his blue eyes twinkling, is waiting for us, holding a long pointer in one hand and rolling a couple of the little gold figures in the other. He bows low when he sees us and then waits for the king to command him.

"Good, I see you are prepared. I am come to listen to you. Tell me what you think." The king approaches the table and leans heavily on it.

"Am I right in thinking that you are in alliance with Spain for this war against France?" the astronomer asks.

Henry nods.

"Even I know that!" Will Somers interrupts from under the table. "If that's a prediction, I could have done it myself. And I could have found it in the bottom of a mug of ale in any taproom outside the Tower. I don't need to look at stars. Just give me the price of a jug of ale and I'll make another prediction."

The astronomer smiles at the king, not at all disturbed by the Fool .Behind us I see that a few of the courtiers have come in. Thomas is not among them. The door shuts. Perhaps he is waiting outside in the presence chamber, perhaps he has gone to his own rooms or to the stables to see his horses. I suppose that he is avoiding me for our safety. I wish I could be sure of that. I cannot help but fear that he has lost his desire for me, and that he is keeping out of my way to spare us both the embarrassment of a love that is dead and gone.

"So I shall show you first the chart of the Emperor of Spain, your ally," Nicholas Kratzer says. He draws one chart forward and shows how the emperor's fortune is coming into the ascendancy this autumn.

"And here is the chart for the French king."

There is a murmur of interest as the chart shows clearly that Francis of France is moving into a time of weakness and disorganization.

"This is promising," Henry says, pleased. He glances at me. "Don't you think so?"

I was not listening, but now I look alert and interested. "Oh, yes."

"And this is a chart for Your Majesty." Nicholas Kratzer points to the most complex chart of them all. The signs for Mars: the dogs of war, the spear, the arrow, the tower, are all drawn and beautifully colored around the king's chart.

"See that?" The king nudges me. "Warlike, isn't it?"

"Mars is rising in your house," the astronomer says. "I have seldom seen more puissance in any man."

"Yes, yes." The king approves. "I knew it. You see it in the stars?"

"Absolutely. But therein lies the danger—"

"What danger?"

"The symbol for Mars is also the symbol for pain, for heat in the blood, pain in the legs. I fear for Your Majesty's health."

There is a muted murmur of agreement. We all fear for the king's health. He thinks he can ride to war like a boy when he cannot even walk to dinner without support on either side.

"I'm better," the king says flatly.

The astronomer nods. "Certainly the auguries are good for you," he says. "If the physicians can keep the heat from your old wound. But, Your Majesty, remember it was a weapon's wound, and like a war wound it waxes and wanes with Mars."

"Then it is bound to trouble me a little when I go to war," the king says stoutly. "By your own reading, Astronomer. By your own signs."

I give him a little smile. The king's stubborn courage is one of the finest things about him.

The astronomer bows. "That would certainly be my reading of the chart."

"And shall we get as far as Paris?"

This is a dangerous question. The court, the whole country,

is anxious that the king shall not attempt to go too deep into France. But nobody dares to tell him so.

"You shall go as far as you wish," the astronomer says cleverly. "A general such as yourself, who has fought over this very ground before, shall be the best one to judge what should be attempted when you see the opposition, the ground, the weather, the temper of your men. I would advise that you don't overreach what your army can do. But what might a king such as you do with them? Not even the stars can answer that."

The king is pleased. He nods to his page, who gives Master Kratzer a heavy purse. Everyone tries not to look at it and estimate its worth.

"And what of Venus?" the king asks with heavy humor. "What of my love for the queen?"

I am so glad that Thomas is not in the room, hearing this. Whatever he thinks of me now I would not have him see the king rest his heavy hand on my shoulder, and stroke my neck as if I am his mare, his hound. I would not want Thomas Seymour to see the king lick his little lips and my tolerant smile.

"The queen was born for happiness," Kratzer states.

I turn to him in surprise. I've never thought such a thing. I was raised to assist my family to greatness, perhaps God has called me to help England stay true to the reformed faith, but I never thought I was born for happiness. My life was never planned with my happiness as its goal. "D'you think so?"

He nods. "I looked at the stars at the time of your birth," he says. "And it was clear to me that you would marry several times and find happiness at the end."

"You saw that?"

"He saw true happiness in your third marriage," the king explains.

I show him my prettiest smile. "Anyone can see happiness in it."

"Again," Will intones wearily from under the table, "I could have predicted all of this, and then I could have had that heavy purse. Are we now to observe that the divine Katerina is happy?"

"Kick him," Henry advises me, and the court laughs when I pretend to swing a foot and Will bounds out, howling like a dog and holding his buttocks.

"The queen was destined to marry for love," Kratzer says as Will limps to the side of the room. "In spirit, and in person, she is formed and destined to love deeply and well." He looks solemn. "And alas, I think she will pay a great price for her love."

"You mean that she has had to take great office, she has to undertake great duties for her love?" the king asks gently.

The astronomer frowns slightly. "I am afraid that love may lead her into grave danger."

"She is Queen of England for love of her husband," Henry says. "That is the greatest and the most dangerous place for any woman in the country. Everyone envies her, and our enemies would see her humbled. But my love for her, and my power, will defend her."

There is a silence as many people are genuinely moved by the king's words of devotion. He takes my hand to his mouth and kisses it, and I too am deeply touched that he should love me, and declare it so publicly. Then some sycophantic courtier exclaims, "Hurrah!" and the moment is broken. The king opens his arms to me and I step into his warm embrace, and as his big fat head comes down I press my lips to his damp cheek. He lets me go and I turn away from the table and the astronomer. Nan is at my side.

"Ask the king's astronomer to draw my chart and bring it when I send for him," I say to her. "Tell him to keep it private and discuss it with no one but me."

"Are you interested in the love or the danger?" she asks sharply.

I look at her blandly. "Oh, in both, I suppose."

WHITEHALL PALACE, LONDON, SUMMER 1544

KP

The astronomer's predictions convince the king that he should start for France while Mars is high in his chart. The physicians strap up his wound and give him drugs that ease the pain and keep him as elated as a young man drunk at his first joust. The Privy Council surrenders to the king's enthusiasm and comes to Whitehall Palace to see him set sail in the royal barge to go downriver to Gravesend, and from there to ride to Dover. He will cross the Narrow Seas to meet the Spanish emperor and decide on the pincer attack of their two armies on Paris.

The king's rooms at Whitehall are filled with maps and lists of equipment that need to be assembled and the goods that must be sent out after him. Already, the army in France is complaining that they have not enough powder and shot; already we are robbing the Scots border forces to supply the invasion of France. Once a day, every day without fail, the king remarks that the only man who could organize a war was Cardinal Wolsey and that the people who tormented that great almoner should go down to hell themselves for robbing England of such a treasure. Sometimes he stumbles on the name and curses everyone for robbing him of Thomas Cromwell. It makes us all oddly uneasy, as if the red-robed cardinal might be summoned from the grave by his old master's need, the fur-robed councillor come quietly behind him;

as if the king can recall the beheaded and press them into service once again.

My ladies and I are all sewing standards and rolling strips of linen for bandages. I am embroidering the king's thick jacket with Tudor roses and gold fleurs-de-lys when the door opens and half a dozen noblemen walk in with Thomas Seymour at their head, his handsome face quite impassive.

I realize that I am staring at him completely aghast, my needle suspended. He has not looked at me since we parted as lovers, at dawn more than a year ago, and we swore then that we would never again speak to each other, nor seek each other out. My sense of being called by God has failed to dilute my passion for him though I prayed that it would. I never enter a room without searching for his face. I never see him dance with one of my ladies without hating her for his hand on her waist, for the attentive tilt of his head, for her sluttish flushed face. I never look for him at dinner but somehow he is always at the corner of my eye. Outwardly I am pale and grave; inside, I burn up for him. I wait to see him every day, at Mass, at breakfast, at the hunt. I make sure that no one ever sees me notice him. No one can ever tell that I am acutely, passionately aware when he is in the room, bowing to me, or walking across the chamber, or that he has thrown himself casually onto a bench at the window and is talking quietly with Mary Howard. Morning and evening, breakfast and dinner, I keep my face completely impassive as my eyes glide over his dark head and then I look away as if I have not seen him at all.

And now, suddenly, he is here, walking into my rooms as if he could ever be an invited guest, bowing to me, and to the princesses, his hand on his heart, his dark eyes veiled and secretive, as if I have summoned him with the passionate thudding of my pulses, as if he can feel the heat of my skin burning his own, as if I had shouted aloud that he must come to me, that I will die if he does not come to me.

"I have come, Your Majesty, at the command of the king, who

asked me to bring you to him, through the privy garden, on your own."

I am already on my feet, the precious royal jacket fallen to the floor, the thread whipping out of the needle's eye as I walk away from it, the needle still in my hand.

"I'll bring the princesses," I say. I can hardly speak. I cannot breathe.

"His Majesty said you were to come alone," he replies. The tone is courteous, his mouth smiles, but his eyes are cold. "I think he has a surprise for you."

"I'll come at once then," I say.

I can hardly see the smiling faces of my ladies as Nan silently takes the needle from my hand; Thomas Seymour presents his arm to me, and I put my hand on his and let him draw me from the room and down the broad stone stairs to where the doors to the sunlit gardens stand open.

"It must be a trap," I say in a hushed monotone. "Is this a trap?"

He shakes his head at my question, then nods to the guards, who raise their pikes and let us out into the sunshine. "No. Just walk."

"He means to trap me by sending you to me. He will see . . . I shouldn't go with you."

"The only thing to do is to behave as if nothing is out of the ordinary. You should come, and we should go without delay, taking exactly the time that it always takes to walk through the gardens. Your ladies are watching from your windows, the noblemen will be watching from the king's windows. We are going to walk along together without pausing, and without looking at each other."

"But you never look at me!" I burst out.

A sharp pinch of my fingers reminds me to keep steadily walking. I think this is like some sort of purgatory. I have to walk beside the man that I adore, match my steps to his, and take no pleasure in it, while my heart hammers against my ribs with all the things that I want to say.

"Of course I don't," he says.

"Because you have stopped loving me." My voice is very low, strained with pain as I accuse him.

"Oh, no," he says lightly, and turns to me with a smile. He glances up to the king's rooms and nods to an acquaintance at the oriel window. "Because I love you desperately. Because I can't sleep for thinking of you. Because I burn up with desire for you. Because I dare not look at you, because if I did, every man and woman at court would see all that in my eyes."

I almost stumble as my knees go weak and I feel a pulse deep in my belly at his words.

"Walk on!" he raps out.

"I thought—"

"I know what you thought. You thought wrong," he says abruptly. "Keep walking. Here is His Majesty."

The king is seated on a great chair they have brought out to the sunny garden, his foot propped on a stool.

"I can't tell you . . ." I whisper.

"I know," he says. "We can't speak."

"Can we meet?"

He presents me to the king and bows low. "No," he says as he steps backwards.

I am to be honored. The king's beaming smile tells me that I am to be trusted with a greater post than any queen has held before, except for the greatest: Katherine of Aragon. The king tells me privately in the garden, and then announces to the country, that I am to serve as Regent General. Half of the council are to go with him to France, the other half to stay with me as advisors. Archbishop Thomas Cranmer is to be my principal councillor, and I see how the king balances the advice I shall hear:

the next greatest man in my service will be the Lord Chancellor, Thomas Wriothesley, Cranmer's natural enemy and an increasingly doubtful friend of mine. When he returns from laying waste to Scotland to teach them to welcome our proposals, Edward Seymour will advise me, and Sir William Petre, the quiet softspoken king's Secretary, will serve me too.

This is an extraordinary step to greatness for me. I feel the eyes of the two princesses on me when they learn the news. They will see a woman rule a country, they will see that it is possible. It is one thing to tell them that a woman is capable of judgment and holding power, it is another for them to see their stepmother, a woman of thirty-two years, actually running the kingdom. I fear that I cannot do it, and yet I know that I can. I have watched the king day after day and deplored his changeable opinions and whimsical commands. Even without advisors from both sides of the religious argument, I would choose a moderate middle course. The kingdom must be held to reform but I will have no persecutions. Never will I do as Henry does: suddenly investigate one man, let him tremble with fear and put him under arrest, secretly knowing all the time that he will not be tried. I think there is a sort of madness in the way that my husband exercises power and—though I would never criticize him—I can at least rule in a way that I think has more sense and humanity.

Half of the court are going to war with the king. They all have posts and titles and duties. They are all equipped. The king has a new suit of armor. He has barely worn so much as a breastplate since he fell and injured his leg, but for this campaign his old suit was brought out and hammered into his new broader shape. They had to rivet in extra pieces, they had to strengthen it all round; then he swore it did not suit him and he commissioned an entirely new suit from the armory at the Tower, where the blacksmiths and armorers are hammering out metal from dawn till midnight, the forges blazing long into the night. As soon as the new suit is completed, in the new huge dimensions necessary to get a breastplate around his massive frame, with widened cuisses to fit his gross thighs, he wants another set. His final choice is Italian designed, trimmed with gilt, etched in black, an enormous amount of beautifully worked metal, a clanking shout of power and wealth.

The grooms have been exercising his horse with great weights strapped to its saddle for weeks so that it can bear up beneath him and carry him safely. It is a horse new to royal service, a heavy courser, with hooves like trenchers and legs like tree trunks. It too has massive armor plates strapped to its neck, head, and body. It does not seem possible that this massive king can ride, or that his overloaded horse can bear him, but its great broad hooves make the gangplank shiver as it stamps up the ramp to his barge and Henry kisses my hand on the quayside.

"Good-bye," he says. "Just for a little while, beloved. I shall come back to you. Don't fear for me."

"I will fear for you," I insist. "Promise that you will write to me often to tell me how you are and how you are doing?"

"I promise," he says. "I know that I leave the country in safe hands with you as regent."

It is a great responsibility, the greatest that an Englishman could accept. And to give it to an Englishwoman is greater still. "I won't fail you," I say.

He bows his head for my blessing and then, leaning on a page for support and hauling himself upward, he goes up the gangplank. He turns into the royal cabin, I see the door closed on his bulky silhouette, and the guards take up their posts.

At the stern of the barge, standing behind the steersman, I see Thomas Seymour. He, too, is going to war, and, I know, into far greater danger. As the drum starts to beat and they cast off the ropes, as the oars dip in the water and the barge yields to the pull and glides away from the quayside, the man that I adore exchanges one dark glance with me and then he turns away. I don't even mouth "God bless you" or "Keep safe." I hold up my hand to wave to the king and then I turn away too.

HAMPTON COURT PALACE, SUMMER 1544

KP

It is the most beautiful weather, sunny and bright and hot every day, and I wake alone in my own bed every morning in my rebuilt rooms on the southeast corner of the base court, overlooking the pond gardens facing south, far from ghosts, reveling in the satisfaction of my own company.

I have the three royal children with me, and every morning I wake to such pleasure in knowing that they are all three under the same roof, that we will pray in the same chapel, that we will eat breakfast in the great hall, and spend the day together in study and in play. Edward is living with his sisters for the first time in his lonely little life. I have gathered all three of them around me as no queen has been allowed to do before. I have everything that could make a woman happy, and I am Regent General of England. Everything shall be as I decide, nobody can even argue with me. The children are with me because I say that it shall be so. There is nobody who can take Edward away from this: his family; from me: his stepmother. We will stay here, in the most beautiful of all the English palaces, because it is my choice, and later—when I choose and not before—we will go on a progress of pleasure, hunting and sailing and riding up the Thames valley, myself and the children and those of the court that I want with me.

I take my seat at the great table in the presence chamber every day and have the Privy Council report to me that the kingdom is at peace and that we are taking in taxes and fines, and we are making enough weapons and armor to keep the king's army supplied in France. I make it a priority to supply our forces, to make sure that wages, weapons, ammunition, armor, food, even arrowheads, are shipped in the amounts that are needed. I have been compared, to my detriment, to the saintly Jane Seymour ever since I was married; I don't want to suffer from a comparison to Thomas Wolsey too. I don't want anyone to say that Katherine of Aragon was a better regent than Kateryn Parr.

Every morning, after breakfast and before I take the children out hunting, I have a brief meeting of my council to read any dispatches that have come in overnight, either from the king in France or from the troubled northern lands. If there is work to do, or something that I want to make sure of, I will call them to meet with me again before dinner.

We gather in one of the grand rooms at Hampton Court, and I have had a table set in the middle, chairs around for the councillors, and a great map of France and the sea roads pinned on the wall. On the opposite wall there is as much of a map of the border lands of the North and of Scotland as can be drawn from the little knowledge that we have of the countryside. I sit at the head of the table and William Petre, the king's Secretary, reads whatever dispatches have arrived from our armies, and whatever letters or appeals from other parts of the kingdom. As the king is at war with the French there is trouble in most of the towns where Frenchmen have settled, and I have to write to the local lords or even the justices of the peace and command them to be sure that their districts are quiet. A country at war is as nervous as one of my little birds. We have constant reports of spies and invasions, which I judge to be false, and I send the proclamations out to the whole kingdom.

Next to me, on my right hand, sits Archbishop Thomas Cranmer, a steady and patient advisor and a calm voice, while Lord Thomas Wriothesley tends to be more dramatic and loud.

He has good reason for worry. It was Wriothesley who was ordered by the king to declare what funds would be needed for an invasion of France and a march on Paris. After much calculation and many sheets of close-written estimates, he thought it would be about a quarter of a million pounds: a fortune. We have raised that through loans and taxes and by scraping every last gold coin from the royal treasuries, but now we are burning through these funds and it is clear that Wriothesley has underestimated.

William Petre is a newly made man, risen on his abilities, the sort that old families like the Howards hate, the son of Devon cattle farmers. His quiet good sense keeps the meeting steady when some of the other councillors argue for their own causes, or for taxes to be lifted from their home towns. It is Petre who suggests that we make up the shortfall of funds by stripping the lead from all the roofs of the monasteries and selling it. This will make them leak when it rains, and it will complete the ruination of the Roman Catholic church in England. I see that this is good for reform as well as for raising money for the king, but a part of me mourns the loss of the beautiful buildings and the charity and the scholarship that they extended to their communities.

Often Princess Mary attends a meeting with me, and sometimes I think that it is well that she does, for one day—who knows?—she might have a kingdom of her own to rule. Princess Elizabeth never misses one. She sits a little behind me, her sharp chin on her clenched fists, her dark eyes going from one man to another, observing everything, her cousin Jane Grey beside her.

We have finished the business for the morning and the councillors have bowed to me and are gathering up their papers and leaving the room, each with a task to perform, when Elizabeth touches my sleeve and looks up at me.

"What is it?" I ask.

"I want to know how you learned to do this," she says shyly.

"How I learned to do what?"

"How you learned what you should do. You were not born a princess, and yet you know when you should listen, and when you should command, how to make sure that they understand you, how to make sure that they do as they are told. I didn't know that a woman could do it. I didn't know that a woman could rule."

I hesitate before I answer. This is the daughter of a woman who turned England upside down by letting a young king pet her breasts, parlaying lust into influence until she commanded the country. "A woman can rule," I say quietly. "But she has to do it with the guidance of God and using all her sense and wisdom. It's not enough for a woman to want power, to seek power for its own sake. She has to take the responsibility that comes with it. She has to prepare herself for power and judge wisely. If your father marries you to a king, then you may be a queen one day, and you may find that you have to rule. When you do, I hope that you will remember me telling you this—the victory is not to get a woman on the throne, the victory is to get a woman to think like a king, for her to aspire to more than her own greatness, for her to humble herself to serve. Getting a woman into power is not the point—it's getting a good woman into power who thinks and cares about what she does."

Gravely, the little girl nods. "But you'll be there," she says. "You will advise me."

I smile. "Oh, I hope so! I shall be an irritating old lady at your court, who always knows better than everyone else. I shall sit in a corner and complain about your extravagance!"

She laughs at the thought of it and I send her to my ladies to tell them I will come in a moment and we can go hunting.

I don't tell Elizabeth how much I relish the work of ruling the kingdom. The king's manner of command is one of sudden ideas, dramatic favors and reversals, sudden countermands. He likes to surprise and keep his Privy Council unsteady with fear of change. He likes to set one man against another, encourage reform and then hint at a return to papacy. He likes to divide the church and the council, to disrupt the Parliament.

Without his turbulence, the wheels of the trade of the country, the laws of the country, the laws of the church, go on steadily and well. Even the accusations of heresy among ordinary people against both papists and Lutherans are fewer. It is generally known that I am not interested in twisting justice to serve one side or the other. Without the sudden issuing of repressive laws or the banning of books there are no protests, and the preachers who come from London to talk to my ladies while the children listen every morning are moderate and thoughtful. All the talk is about the careful definition of words, not the great passion of loyalty torn between Rome and the king.

I make sure that I write to the king almost daily: bright and cheerful letters in which I praise his valor and courage and ask him for reports of the siege of Boulogne, and tell him that I am certain it must fall soon. I tell him that the children are well and that they miss him, as I do. I write to him as if I were a loving wife, a little heart-sore to be without him, but proud of the courage of her husband, as a great general's wife should be. It is easy for me to write convincingly. I have discovered that I have a talent for writing, a love of writing.

My book of psalms, beautifully bound, is tucked deep in my locked box of books. I think of it as my treasure, my greatest treasure, one that I have to keep secret. But seeing those words that were first written, and scratched out, and rewritten again in print and bound into a book, I know that I love the process of writing and publishing. To take a thought and work on it, to render it into the clearest form possible, and then to send it out into the world—this is work so precious and so joyful that I am not surprised that men have kept it to themselves.

So now I practice my letter writing to my husband. I compose it as I would translate a psalm, by imagining the state of mind of the author that I want to be. When I am writing a translation of a prayer, I always imagine the first author—a man miserably conscious of his own sin. I think myself into his mind and then I write the most beautiful sonorous version of what I think might come from his mouth. Then I bring myself into the work, powerfully aware that I am a woman, not a man. The sins that grieve a man are often those of pride, or greed, or a lust for power for its own sake. But these are not the sins of a woman, I think. These are not my first sins. My worst sin is a failure of obedience: I find it so hard to bend my will. My other great fault is a passion: an adoration as if I were setting up an idol, a false God.

So writing a love letter to the king is the same as writing a prayer. I create a character to say the words. I pull the page towards me and I think how I would be if I were deeply in love with a man who is setting siege to the town of Boulogne in France. I think, what would his wife say? How would she tell him that she loves him and misses him and that she is glad that he is doing his duty? I think, how would I write to a man whom I cannot see, who is so very far from me, who is so careful of my safety that he will not even breathe a kiss to me in farewell, so proud and independent and yet loves me, and wishes he had not left me, would never leave me?

In my mind, as bright as if it were real, I see Thomas Seymour before the walls of Boulogne and his dark smile as he faces danger and feels no fear. And so I take that sense of love and longing and I write to the king, tenderly and obediently, asking sincerely for his health, promising him truly that I am thinking of him. But running in my mind, at the same time, there is another letter—a shadow letter of words that are never written on paper. I never even scribble his name to clean the nib of ink; I never sketch his crest. I never say the words aloud. I only allow myself, last thing at night before I go to sleep in my empty bed, to think of the letter that I would write to him if I could.

I would tell him that I love him with a passion that leaves me sleepless. I would tell him that some nights I cannot bear the touch of the sheet on my shoulders, on my breasts, because the cool linen makes me yearn for his skilled, warm hand. I would write that I put my palm against my mouth and imagine that I am kissing him. I would write that I lay the flat of my hand against my most private parts and press down, and that the leaping sensation of joy is all his. I would write that without him I am a shell, a hollow crown, that all my true life is stolen away. I would write that my life is like a beautifully carved tomb, an empty space, that I have everything a woman could desire—I am Queen of England—but a beggar woman with her legs and arms wrapped around her husband, and his mouth pressing down on hers, is richer than me.

I will never write this. I am an author and a queen. I can write only words that everyone can read, that the king's clerks can read aloud to him before all his courtiers. I write words that can go to London and be published even if no one knows who wrote them. I will never write, like poor little Queen Kitty: *When I think that you shall depart from me again it makes my heart die.* The king beheaded her for that silly little love letter. She wrote her own death warrant. I shall never write such a thing.

The king replies to me, telling me of their progress. He is by turns boastful and wistful, missing his home. The plan to march on Paris was abandoned as soon as he arrived in Calais and was discouraged by the Spanish emperor. They decided that first they should lay siege to the nearby towns. Charles Brandon and Henry take on Boulogne. Thomas Howard Duke of Norfolk continues in his dogged siege of nearby Montreuil. They all demand more powder, more cannon, more shot, and I am to send some miners from Cornwall to dig under the walls of the French towns. I send to the magistrates in Cornwall and demand volunteers, I order cannon to be cast, I have them make powder, I press more and more masons into carving stones for round shot. I summon the Lord Treasurer and ensure that we have enough money coming in to keep the army supplied, and caution him that he may have to go back to Parliament to demand another grant. He warns me that the price of lead is falling as we put more and more on the market, and nobody will buy. I receive petitions from everyone who would normally apply to me, and then I meet with everyone who would normally apply to the king. I sit in the king's presence chamber every day and the steward of my household indicates who may come forward and speak to me. I answer every letter the day that I receive it, I allow no neglected business to overwhelm my household, I draft in clerks from the Privy Council to work alongside my own people, and, without fail, I report every single thing that I do to the king.

He must know that I am Regent General in every way, neglecting nothing, but I make it clear that he rules through me. He must never think that I have taken power and am ruling for myself. I have to rule like a king and report like a wife. I have to walk this careful line in every word I put on paper, in everything I say that will be reported to him, in every meeting I have with the Privy Council, who are partly men of my household and affinity and partly there in their own interests. None of them can be wholly trusted not to sneak a report that I am greedy for power and doing too much, that I am the worst thing in the world: a woman with the heart and stomach of a man.

The king writes that he is in good health. They have built a platform for him to survey the siege of Boulogne, and he can climb the steps unaided and walk around without support. His leg has dried up, and the surgeons are keeping the wound safely open, and so he has less pain. He rides out every day on his great horse, with a massive musket laid over the pommel of the saddle, ready to fire on any Frenchman he sees. He goes all around the town and the siege camp to show himself to the men and assure them that he is leading them to victory. He is living the life that he loves, the imaginary life of his fairy-tale youth—his company are all handsome young men, invoking the chivalric dream of the Knights of the Round Table. He is reliving the campaign that he won as a young man at the Battle of the Spurs, the tents of his household are as beautiful as those that were raised on the Field of the Cloth of Gold. It is as if in his old age he has been given the chance to enjoy the delights of his youth once more: comradeship, token danger, victory.

They give great dinners every night in which they report skirmishes during the day, drink celebratory toasts, and plan the advance on Paris. Henry is at the heart of the campaign, arm in arm with his reckless friends, and he swears that he will be King of France in name and in deed.

The king and his minions do not put themselves at risk—the viewing stage is well out of range of Boulogne's guns. Of course, there is the hazard of illness in the army; but at the first sign of disease Henry will run away and his court will leave with him. While he is strong enough to ride and walk and dine as he is doing I don't fear for his health or safety. And every single man in his train knows that he must lay down his life rather than let the king be in danger while his son and heir is a boy of only six in the nursery. The last boy king to take the throne lost our lands in France and his own throne in England. The kingdom cannot be abandoned to a boy with a woman regent.

So I don't fear for Henry, nor do I fear for my brother, who is safely at the king's side. The only one of them, the only man in the whole army who makes me drop my head in desperate prayer, is Thomas Seymour. Now the king has appointed him to the navy and he is commanding the ships that supply the army, constantly at sea in the treacherous Narrow Seas while the French ships mount a blockade, and the Scottish ships harry our fleet, and pirates of every nation cruise under black flags, hopeful of easy pickings. Thomas is on these stormy waters, in these dangerous seas, with the ships of two nations against him, and nobody thinks to tell me—for why would they?—if he is safe, if he is in harbor, or if his ship is at sea. Once a week I insist that the Privy Council are shown on the great map exactly where our army is in France, where the king is camped, where Howard is established, and where our ships are. It's the only way I can learn if he is safe. But the map is muddled, the king's army never moves anywhere, nobody is very interested in the ships and the news is old. I have to pretend that I am interested in Boulogne when I am so fearful of the sea.

The king commands me to consult the royal astronomer as to

when the stars are best aligned for his march on Paris. Nicholas Kratzer attends me in my new privy chamber with only my stepdaughter Margaret and Princess Mary and Princess Elizabeth at my side. He bows low to the three of us, and I wonder what he thinks when he sees me, little Kateryn Parr as Regent General of England flanked by two royal princesses.

"You have the best date for an advance on Paris?" I ask him.

He bows again and produces a roll of manuscript from his sleeve. "The stars suggest the first week in September," he says. "I have drawn the alignments for you to study. I know that you take an interest in such work."

"I do." He puts the papers on the table at my side. "And what do you think when you see these princesses?" I ask him. "You see them here with their little coronels on their heads, as Tudor princesses."

"I think they can have nothing but glory ahead of them," he says tactfully. He smiles at Elizabeth's dazzled face. "Who can doubt but that you will both reign over a great country?"

Mary smiles; of course she hopes for an alliance with Spain. But Elizabeth has ambitions in her own right. She watches me command the Privy Council, she watches me take reports from all around England. She is learning that a woman can educate herself, follow her own determination, command others. "Will I?" she whispers.

I wonder what he really thinks, what he can really see. I nod to Elizabeth and Mary, and they withdraw from the table as Nicholas Kratzer produces another roll from his satchel.

"I have drawn up your chart," he says. "I am honored that you show such a gracious interest in my poor work."

I rise from my chair as he spreads the document on the table and anchors it, as before, with the little gold models of the planets. "These are pretty things," I say, as if I am not longing to see what he has drawn for me.

"They are paperweights," he says. "Not charms, of course. But they please me."

"And what do you see for me?" I ask him quietly. "Between the two of us, and speaking to no other—what do you see for me?"

He points to the sign for my house, the feathered helmet. "I see you were married as a young woman to a young man." He shows me the markings that indicate the early years of my life. "The stars say you were a child, as innocent as they."

I smile. "Yes, it was like that, perhaps."

"Then before you were much more than twenty years old, you were married again, to a man old enough to be your father, and you faced great danger."

"The Pilgrimage of Grace," I confirm. "The rebels came to our castle and put it under siege. They took me and his children hostage."

"You must have known they would never hurt you," he says.

I knew it then. But the king justified his cruelty to the North on the basis of wild reports of savagery. "They were treasonous," I say, rather than answering him honestly. "At any rate, they were hanged for treason."

"You were married for nearly ten years," he says, showing me the barred lines on the chart. "And no child ever born to you."

I bow my head. "It was a sorrow," I say. "But my lord had his heir and his daughter; he never reproached me."

"And then His Majesty honored you with his favor."

It is such a bleak story told like this that I feel a sudden rush of self-pitying tears and I turn away from the table and the papers before I start to weep, which would be sheer folly.

"And now we see that your spiritual life begins," the old astronomer says gently. "Here we see the sign of Pallas—wisdom, and scholarship. You are studying and writing?"

I hide a gasp. "I am studying," I admit.

"You will write," he says. "And your words will be of value. A woman writer—a novelty indeed. Nurture your talent, Your Majesty. It is rare. It is precious. Where you lead other women will follow, and that is a great thing. Perhaps your books will be your children, your legacy, your descendants."

I nod. "Perhaps."

"But it is not just study for you," he says. "Here"—he points to the recognizable symbol of Venus—"here is love."

I look in silence. I dare not ask him what I want to know.

"I think the love of your life will come home to you," he says.

I grip my hands tightly, and I make sure that my face is blank. "The love of my life?"

He nods. "I can't say more."

Indeed, I dare not ask more. "He will be safe?"

"I think you will marry again," he says very softly. With his ivory pointer, like a wand, he shows the later years, my fourth decade. "Venus," he remarks quietly. "Love, and fertility, and death."

"You can see my death?" I ask boldly.

Quickly he shakes his head. "No, no. It is forbidden. See your chart, it is just like the king's, it goes on and on, it never ends."

"But you see love?"

"I think that you will live with the love of your life. He will come home to you."

"Of course, you mean the king, home from the war," I say quickly.

"He will come home safe from the war," he repeats. He does not say who.

The astronomer is accurate at least in his predictions about my studies. Archbishop Cranmer attends on me every day to discuss the work of the Privy Council and how I should respond to any requests or reports from the country, but as soon as the work of the world is done we turn to the world of the spirit. He is a most inspirational scholar and each day he brings a sermon or a pamphlet, sometimes written by hand, sometimes newly published, for me to consider; and the following day we discuss it together. My ladies listen, and often make a contribution. Princess

Mary tends always to defend the traditional church but even she acknowledges the archbishop's logic and his spirituality. My rooms become a center of debate, a little university for women, as the archbishop brings his chaplains and invites preachers from London to come and share their vision of the church and its future. They are all great students of the Bible in Latin, Greek, and in the modern translations. We often find ourselves turning from one version to another to reach the true meaning of a word, and while I revel in my increasing understanding of Latin I know that I am going to have to learn Greek.

One morning Thomas Cranmer comes into my rooms, bows to me, and whispers: "May I have a word with you, Majesty?"

I step to one side and to my surprise he tucks my hand under his arm and leads me out of the room to the long gallery where we are out of earshot. "I wanted to show you this," he says, his dark eyes twinkling under his gray eyebrows.

From his sleeve he produces a book bound in leather. Inside is the title page with the one-word title: it says *Psalms*. With a little start I see that he has my book, my first published book. "There is no author," Cranmer says, "but I recognized the voice at once."

"It is printed anonymously," I say quickly. "There is no acknowledged author."

"And that is wise. There are many people who would deny the right of common people to understand the Bible or the psalms, and there are many who would be quick to criticize a man brave enough to translate Bishop Fisher's Latin psalms." He pauses, his smile warm. "I don't think it would occur to anyone that a woman might have done it."

"It had better stay that way," I say.

"I agree. I just wanted you to know that I received this little book from someone who had no idea of the author, but who thought that it was an exceptional translation; and I was glad to have it. Whoever the author, he should be proud of his work. It is very good, very good indeed."

I find I am blushing furiously, like an embarrassed clerk. "You are kind . . ."

"I give praise where it is due. This is the work of a linguist and a poet."

"Thank you," I whisper.

Encouraged by the publication and the success of the book of psalms, I suggest to the archbishop that I might dare to start a great project—the translation of the four Gospels of the New Testament, the key documents of the life of Christ. I am afraid that he will say it is too great a task, but he is enthusiastic. We will start with the Latin translation of the scholar Erasmus, and try to render it into English, in beautiful but simple words that anyone can read.

And if they read of the life of Christ in simple language and understand it, can they not follow Him? The more that I study, the more certain I am that men—and equally women—can take charge of their own souls, can work for their own salvation, and can pray directly to God.

Of course, once I think this, the more I come to believe that the tricks and trades and treats of the Church of Rome are a shameful battening on ignorant people. To sell a woman a pilgrim badge and tell her that it shows that she has been on pilgrimage and her sins are forgiven is surely a sin itself. To assure someone that if enough nuns sing enough Masses, then her dead child will go to heaven is trickery as low as passing a false coin as good. To buy a pardon from the pope, to force the pope to annul a marriage, to make him set aside kinship laws, to watch as he fleeces his cardinals, who charge the bishops, who rent to the priests, who seek their tithes from the poor—all these abuses would have to fall away if we agreed that a soul can come to God without any intervention. The crucifixion is the work of God. The church is the work of man.

I think of the night when I prayed and I knew that God came to me. I heard him, I truly did. I think of the simplicity and beauty of the sacrifice of Christ, and I know in every way—from reading and from revelation—that the rituals of the old church must fall away and the people come to Christ one by one as He calls them. There shall be no blind obedience, there shall be no mumbling in a foreign tongue. The people will learn to read and will have a Bible so that they can learn their own way. This is what I believe now, and this is what I will achieve as Regent General and as queen. It is my holy duty. It is my calling.

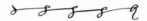

In September the town of Boulogne falls to the English siege, and the king prepares to come home to a hero's welcome. Indeed, he writes from France to command a hero's welcome and it is my task to make sure that he has one. The king's victory procession will march from Dover to London and the whole court will ride down to greet him at Leeds Castle, in Kent. I must commission the royal glazier to make special windows for the banqueting hall, bedrooms, and chapel at Leeds Castle, and Master Glazier Hone comes to my rooms and shows me his design of the doomed castle of Boulogne and the king and his army before it.

"The sun will stream through the glass and the walls of Boulogne will seem to glow with pride as they face the sunset for the last time before they fall into rubble," Galyon Hone tells me. "The glass is with the painters and the cutters now."

"It will be ready in time?"

"We are working all day and into the night, and we can get the banqueting hall windows made in time for the feast. The others will follow later."

"You must get the chapel window finished too," I say. "The king will want it ready. We are to have a celebration Mass; the windows must be there. I have to insist, Master Glazier."

He nods. He is a busy little man, his hands as rough as old

leather from a lifetime of cuts. "Very well, Your Majesty, you are a hard taskmaster. But look at the designs! See how I have shown the king and his nobles before the walls of Boulogne!" He shows me another drawing. "See, here is the Duke of Norfolk, the Duke of Suffolk Charles Brandon, Sir Thomas Seymour. See, Your Majesty, here is your noble brother."

He has made quick clever sketches of the nobles of the court around the king; some are in armor, their standards flying. In the background, miniature horses wait loaded with armor, cannons recoil with little puffs of cloud above them.

My eyes rest on the clear profile of Thomas Seymour. "You have them to the life," I say unsteadily. "May I have a copy of this?"

"It is a very good likeness of the king." He is pleased. "Take it, take this one, Your Majesty. I have another made fair for the glass cutter. And here is the moment when the walls fall. It's a great moment. Like Jericho for Joshua."

"Yes," I say. I wonder if I am safe to keep the picture of Thomas. The king is at the very center of the design, Thomas's beloved profile half hidden at the back. Nobody looking at the picture could guess that I wanted it for the tiny glimpse of him. I could keep it safely hidden away, with my study books, with the manuscript of the psalms that I have translated. I could keep it tucked inside my Bible. Nobody would know that I long to see his face when I open the page.

Hone shows me the other designs he has made. They will be a sequence, telling the story of the invasion of France, the alliance with Spain, and the triumphant siege. The window for the chapel is one of thanksgiving and celebration. An angel blesses the campaign, the king rides home under an arch of laurel leaves, angels look down on him.

"I'll have it ready for when the king arrives," he promises me. "I go to Kent tomorrow with the pieces of glass and we will lead them in place there, for fear of breakages. We will be ready. The lead will be cooling as he enters, but we will be ready."

I let him gather up his papers and prepare to bow. I push back the portrait of Thomas Seymour with the other designs.

"Did you not want this, Your Majesty? Shall I get it framed for you?"

"It's of no matter. I'll wait till I can see the real thing in glass," I say indifferently. Katherine Howard went to the gallows on the evidence of one note that she wrote to Thomas Culpepper in her silly childish little hand, misspelled, with a tear blot, asking if he was well. I don't dare to have anything that could ever be cited against me. I don't even dare to keep a charcoal sketch of his profile half hidden at the back of a crowd. Not even that.

LEEDS CASTLE, KENT, AUTUMN 1544

KP

The king's arrival at his castle is staged like a masque. It is all for show. The steward of his household and the master of horse have arranged all the details with my stewards and we have our places as precisely as if we were learning a dance. At eight o'clock the grateful people of Kent start to assemble on either side of the road leading to the castle and the first yeomen of the guard take their posts along the road to hold back the wildly excited crowd, or, in the case of their not being wildly excited, to lead the cheers and command applause.

The gardeners and builders have erected triumphal arches with boughs of bay and laurel, the trumpeters are positioned on the turrets of the castle and the musicians ready at the entrance. We can hear the hammering hooves of the outliers and then those in the first rank, and now I can see, from where I stand at the gateway of the castle with Mary and Elizabeth on one side, Edward on the other, the rippling standards of the royal party and the great flag of England coming on.

It is impossible to miss the king. He looks magnificent in his black Italian armor, his enormous warhorse in matching metal, the biggest horse in the rank, the rider towering above the rest: bigger, brighter, higher than any other on the road. People do cheer, quite spontaneously, and the king turns his head and smiles to one side and another, and behind him his almoner throws coins to encourage the enthusiasm.

I am nervous. The procession with ambassadors, noblemen, supporters, and the cream of the army comes slowly forward, the beautiful horses tossing their heads and blowing, the archers with their bows across their backs, the infantry in newly clean jackets, some sporting battered helmets, and at the head of them, always drawing the eye, the great king.

He pulls up his horse and four men run to their appointed places to get him out of the saddle. A wheeled platform is brought to the side of the horse, he is helped down and steadied where he stands. He turns, and waves to me. The crowd cheer, the soldiers leading the applause, and then the four men guide him down the steps to the ground.

His squires come forward and unstrap his cuisses and the rerebrace from his arms, but he keeps on his breastplate and holds his helmet under his arm for the warlike look of it. I keep my eyes fixed adoringly on him. Somewhere, Thomas is on his horse, watching me.

One page gets one side of him and one the other, but he does not lean on them to walk. Even now, at the moment of our greeting I know that I must not approach him; he will come to me. He walks towards me and I see that the men are lined up so that they can see our greeting. The king comes closer and closer, and I and all my household sink into low deferential curtseys. His children bow almost to the ground. At once I feel his hand under my elbow, raising me up and he turns and, in sight of everyone, kisses me passionately on the mouth.

I guard my expression. There must not be the smallest flinch from this stale wet kiss. The king turns his back to me to face his army. "I have led you out, and I have led you home!" he bellows. "I have brought you back in honor. We have come back in triumph."

There is a roar of approval from his men and, peeping around him, I find I am smiling at their excitement. It is impossible not to be caught up in their joy in their victory. It is a triumph, a great triumph, that they have reclaimed English lands in France; they have shown the power and might of our King Henry, and they have come home with a victory.

We sit, side by side, before the altar at Leeds Castle chapel in special low chairs which give the appearance of our devoutly kneeling. Behind us the children have their heads reverently bowed. The king prays earnestly for a few moments and then gently touches my hand to get my attention. "And Edward is well?" he says.

Before us, the priest faces the altar and blesses the bread and the wine, the choir's voices soar into their celebratory anthem. I turn my attention from my prayers to my husband; from the sacred to the profane. Not for the first time I wonder if Henry can really believe that a miracle is taking place: the wine becoming holy blood, the bread becoming the body of Christ, since he turns his head and talks to his friends while the sacred act is taking place. Does he really think that a true miracle happens before him every day? And if so, why would he ignore it?

"As you see. He is well. And your daughters."

"You said there was plague?"

"We went on progress and avoided all signs of it. It's over now."

"I have secured his inheritance in France. Another city under English control. And we will gain more. This is just our foothold."

"It has been a wonderful campaign," I say enthusiastically.

He nods. He closes his eyes as the priest approaches and folds his big hands together like a child at prayer. His rosebud mouth opens, his big tongue rolls out as he takes the sacred bread into his mouth and swallows it in one great gulp. The server comes with the goblet and whispers: "*Sanguis autem Christi.*"

"Amen," the king confirms, and takes the goblet and tips it and drinks deep.

They come to me. In the sacred silence as the priest holds up the wafer before me, I whisper in my heart: "Thank you, Lord, for preserving the king from the many dangers of war." The holy wafer is heavy and thick in my mouth. I swallow as the priest comes towards me with the goblet of wine. "And keep Thomas Seymour under your protection and in your grace," I finish my secret prayer. "God bless Thomas."

The royal kitchens excel themselves with the victory feast. We sit down to dinner after Mass at ten in the morning and I think we will never stop eating. One great dish after another marches out of the kitchens, carried shoulder-high through the court: great golden platters piled high with meat or fish or fowl, golden bowls of stews and sauces, trays with pastries, massive constructions of pies. The centerpiece of the feast is a roast within a roast, a bird stuffed and packed into another bird: lark into mistle thrush into chicken. Chicken into goose, goose into peacock, peacock into swan, and the whole thing encased in a castle of pastry wondrously made into a model of Boulogne. The court cheers and everyone hammers their knives on the tables as four men bear the pie on a massive tray through the hall to the king, and set it on a trestle before him. The choir in the gallery above the great hall sing an anthem of victory, and the king, sweating and exhausted by the marathon feast, beams with pleasure.

My clockmaker has made a miniature cannon of clockwork, and now Will Somers, prancing and leaping under the standard of Saint George, wheels it into the hall on its own little carriage. With enormous comedy, while people cheer and shout encouragement, Will approaches the tiny gold cannon with a little candle, pretends to shrink from it in terror, and finally enacts the lighting of the fuse.

Skilfully he touches a hidden button, and the little cannon spits a flame and ejects a ball with a bang towards the pastry walls of the pie castle. It is weighted, it is well aimed: the tower crumbles under the attack, and there is a roar of applause.

The king is delighted. He hauls himself to his feet. "*Henricus vincit!*" he bellows, and the whole court shouts back at him, "Hail! Caesar! Hail! Caesar!"

I smile and applaud. I dare not look across to the table of the lords, where Thomas will be observing this ecstatic greeting of a meat pie. Unseen, I pinch my fingertips to remind myself not to sneer. The court is right to celebrate, the king is right to revel in his triumph. It is my place to show delight, and besides, in my heart I am proud of him. I rise to my feet and raise my glass in a toast to the king. The whole court follows me. Henry stands, swaying slightly, taking in the adulation of his wife, of his daughters, of his people. I don't look at Thomas.

Dinner goes on and on. After everyone has had a slice of the pie castle and eaten all the rest of the meat and the fish, in come the sweetmeats and the puddings, serving after serving of sugar maps of France and marchpane models of the king's war courser. Fruit, dried and stewed, comes in pies and sugar baskets and great bowls. The voider course of dried fruits and nuts is placed on every table and sweet wines from Portugal are brought in for those who can bear to go on drinking and eating.

The king's appetite is prodigious. He eats as if he has not had a meal since he left England. He eats and eats as his face grows redder and redder, and he sweats so much that a page stands at his side with a clean linen napkin and mops his brow and damp neck. He calls for more wine to be poured into his huge glass, he beckons dish after dish to come back to him. I sit beside him and nibble on little things so that we are dining together, but this is an ordeal that lasts all day.

I am afraid he is going to make himself ill. I glance across at the royal physicians and wonder if they dare to suggest that he finish this giant meal. All of the court have pushed back their plates, some have dropped their heads on the table, too drunk to stay awake. Only the king goes on eating with relish, and sending out the best dishes to his favorites, who bow and smile and thank him, and have to serve themselves and mime their delight at yet another dish.

Finally, as the sun is setting, he pushes back his plate and waves the servers away. "No, no, I have had enough. Enough!" He glances towards me and wipes the glistening fat from his mouth. "What a feast!" he says. "What a celebration."

I try to smile. "Welcome home, lord husband. I am glad you have dined well."

"Well? I am choked with food, my belly aches with it."

"Did you overeat?"

"No, no. A man of my stature likes a good dinner. I need a good dinner after what I have endured."

"Then I am glad that you had one."

He nods. "Are there masquers? Will there be dancing?"

Of course, now that he has finished gorging himself he wants something else to happen, and he wants it to happen immediately. I think for a moment that Edward, aged only six, dining quietly in his rooms, has more patience than his father, who has to eat to the point of nausea and then wants to know what will happen next, immediately next.

"There will be dancing," I reassure him. "And there is a special masque to celebrate your victory."

"Will you dance?"

I gesture to Anne Boleyn's crown that sits heavily on my head. "I'm not dressed for dancing," I say. "I thought I would sit and watch the dancers with you."

"You must dance!" he says instantly. "There is no more

beautiful woman at court than you. I want to see my wife dance. I haven't come home to see you sit on a chair. It will be no celebration for me if you don't dance, Kateryn."

"Shall I go and change into my headdress?"

"Yes, go," he says. "And come quickly back."

I nod to Nan, who summons two maids-in-waiting with a snap of her fingers, and I go out through the door behind our thrones into the little lobby. "He wants me to change my crown for a headdress so that I can dance," I say wearily. "I have to dance."

"Girls, run and get Her Majesty's golden hood from her dressing room," Nan says. The girls run off, and Nan tuts. "I should have told them to bring a comb and a net," she says. "I'll get one from my room. Wait here."

She bustles off and I go to the window and look out. The cool air drifts in; the buzz of the court behind the closed door seems far away. Leeds Castle is surrounded by a moat of still water, and the swallows are flying low, dipping into their silvery reflections, round and round as I watch them, and the sky turns peach and golden. It is a wonderful sunset, almost scarlet along the horizon and then paler and paler pink till the underside of the clouds are gilded and the sky above them the palest blue. For a moment I feel aware of myself—I have a sense of myself as I do when I pray alone. A woman, still young, looking out of the window at the birds and the water, positioned in time and in a place, the stars of my destiny unseen in the sky above me, the will of God before me, knowing so little and longing so much, a sun setting as if to mark the ending of a day.

"Don't say a word."

I recognize Thomas's quiet voice at once—who else do I hear in my dreams every night?—I turn, and he is standing before the closed door, looking a little more tired and a little thinner than when I last saw him in the stern of the king's barge, going away from me without a gesture of farewell.

I am silent, waiting for him to speak.

"It was not a great victory." He speaks with a low-toned fury.

"It was a shambles. It was a mess. We didn't have the weaponry we needed, we didn't have the equipment for the army. We couldn't even feed them. The men lay without cover or tents in mud and they died in their hundreds from disease. We should have marched on Paris as we agreed. Instead we wasted English lives on a city of no value that we will never be able to keep, so that he could say that he had won a city and come home."

"Hush," I say. "At least you're home safe. At least he wasn't ill."

"He had no idea what to do, he had no idea what should be done. He does not know how to time a march, how to allow an army time to move, to prepare to rest. He doesn't even know enough to give orders. He says one thing and then another and then flies into a fury because nobody understands him. He orders the horses to charge in one direction and the archers in another and then he sends after them to bring them back and blames them for the mistake. And when it was falling apart around us—the men sickening, the French holding firm—he could not see that we were in trouble. He did not care that the men were in danger. He would declare that war was costly and that he was not afraid of a gamble. He has no idea of the value of life. He has no idea of the value of anything."

I want to interrupt him; but he will not be silenced.

"When we finally won, it was a massacre. Two thousand townsmen and women and their children trailed out of the town past him as he sat high on his horse, in his Italian armor. They went out in the wind and rain with nothing, not even a bag of food. He swore that they must walk all the way to the French lines at Abbeville; but they lay down and died on the road as his troops looted their homes. He is a killer, Kateryn, he is a merciless killer.

"And now it is over he calls it a great victory; has no idea that it was a mess. Howard's army was on the brink of mutiny. Boulogne will never be held. It is all vanity, a vain conquest. He has no idea that it isn't a great victory. He knows only what he wants to know. He believes only what he wants to think. He hears only what he orders. Nobody tells him the truth and he would not know it if it were spelled out for him in the blood of his victims."

"He's king," I say simply. "Isn't it always like this for kings?"

"No!" Thomas exclaims. "I've been at the court of the King of Hungary, I have spoken with the emperor himself. They are great men who are obeyed without question but they can question themselves! They have doubts! They ask for true reports. They take advice. This is not the same. This king is blind to his own failings, deaf to counsel."

"Hush, hush," I say anxiously, glancing at the closed door.

"Every year it gets worse," he insists. "All his honest advisors are dead or disgraced; he has killed all the friends of his childhood. Nobody around him dares to tell him the truth. His temper is completely out of control."

"You shouldn't say—"

"I should say! I must say—because I am warning you."

"Warning me of what?"

He comes a step closer; but he puts out his hands to prevent me reaching for him. "Don't. I cannot be near you. I came only to tell you: he is dangerous. You have to be careful."

"I am unendingly careful!" I exclaim. "I dream of you but I never speak of you. I never write to you, we never meet! I have given you up; I have completely given you up for him. I have broken my heart to do my duty."

"He will tire of you," he says bitterly, "and if you give him no cause to divorce you, he will kill you to be rid of you."

It is such a deadly prediction that I am stunned into silence for a moment. "No, Thomas, you are wrong. He loves me. He made me regent. He trusts me like no other. I have brought his children to court. I am their mother. I am an exception. He has never loved a wife as he loves me."

"It is you who are wrong, you little fool. He made Katherine of Aragon regent. He ordered a nationwide service of thanksgiving for Katherine Howard. He can turn in a moment and kill within the week."

"Not so! Not so!" I am shaking my head like one of the little figures on my clocks. "I swear to you that he loves me."

"He threw Queen Katherine into a cold damp castle and she died of neglect, if not poison," he lists. "Anne, he beheaded on false evidence. My sister would have been abandoned within the year if she had not got a child, and even then he left her to die alone. He would have executed Anne of Cleves for treason if she hadn't agreed to a divorce. His marriage to Katherine Howard was invalid because she was married already, so he could have abandoned her to her shame, but he chose to execute her. He wanted her dead. When he is tired of you, he will kill you. He kills his family, his friends, and his wives."

"Traitors must be executed," I whisper.

"Thomas More was no traitor. Margaret Pole, the king's cousin, was no traitor, she was an old lady of sixty-seven! Bishop John Fisher was a saint, Thomas Cromwell was a loyal servant, Robert Aske and all the Pilgrims of Grace held a royal pardon. Katherine Howard was a child, Jane Rochford was mad: he changed the law so he could behead a madwoman."

I am trembling as if I have an ague. I clamp my jaw to stop my teeth chattering. "What are you saying? Thomas, what are you saying to me?"

"I am saying what you know already, what we all know but none of us dares to say. He is a madman. Kateryn, he has been mad for years. We have sworn loyalty to a madman. And every year he is blinder and more dangerous. None of us is safe from his whims. I saw it. I finally saw it in France, for I have been blind too. He is a murderer without cause. And you will be his next victim."

"I've done nothing wrong."

"That is why he will kill you. He cannot bear excellence."

I lean back against the cold stone wall. "Thomas, oh, Thomas, this is a terrible thing to say to me!"

"I know. This is the man who let my sister die."

He crosses the little hall in two swift strides and he wraps his arm around me and kisses me savagely, as if he would bite me, as if he would devour me. "You are the only person I would say this to!" he says urgently in my ear. "You have to keep yourself safe from him. I won't speak to you again. I may not be seen with you, for both of our sakes. Guard yourself, Kateryn! God keep you. Good-bye."

I cling to him. "It can't be good-bye again! I will see you. Surely, now you are home, now we are at peace, I will at least see you every day?"

"I am the new admiral of the king's navy," he says. "I shall be at sea."

"You're going back into danger! Not now, when the whole court is safely home?"

"I swear to you, I will be safer at sea than you with that killer in your bed," he says grimly, and he wrenches himself from me, and goes.

WHITEHALL PALACE, LONDON, AUTUMN 1544

KP

A new painter, Nicholas de Vent, has been commanded to come from Flanders to paint a picture, a massive near-life-size portrait of the royal family in the style of the late Hans Holbein. I am so proud that there is to be a family portrait of us all. I have triumphed in bringing this family together, in persuading the king to acknowledge his daughters publicly as princesses and heirs, in bringing father and son under the same roof. I may not be able to help them to understand and love each other, but at least they have met. The father is not an entirely imaginary being to this lonely little boy. The child is not the phantom son of a sainted mother but a real boy, deserving attention in his own right.

The king and I spend a happy afternoon discussing how the portrait shall look, and how it must fit on the wall at Whitehall Palace, where it is to be placed forever. People hundreds of years from now will see it as if they were standing before us, as if they were being presented to us. We decide that it is to be almost like an altarpiece, with the king center stage and I beside him, Edward leaning against the throne, his heir. On either side, almost in side panels defined with some frame we can't yet decide, will be the two girls, Elizabeth and Mary. I want to see a lot of color in the picture, on the walls and on the ceiling. The girls and I are keen embroiderers and love strong colors and patterns, and I want the portrait to reflect this. I want it to be as beautiful as the things that we make. The king suggests a ruined Boulogne glimpsed behind the throne on the skyline with his standard flying from the crumbling turret, and the painter says that he will sketch it and show it to us.

The work will start with preliminary sketches done of each of us, individually. The princesses are to go first. I help Elizabeth and Mary pick out their gowns and their jewels for their sittings with the artist. He is to draw them in chalk and charcoal and then copy their images onto the rich background, which the apprentices will paint in his studio.

Henry comes to watch Master de Vent make his first sketches of Mary. She is wearing a skirt of deep scarlet and an overgown with sleeves of brocade. She has a golden French hood on her auburn hair and she looks beautiful. She is standing a little stiffly and she bobs a curtsey, afraid to move, as the king comes in. Henry blows her a kiss, as if he were a courtier.

"We have to show ourselves to the people," he tells me. "They have to see us, even when we are not here, even when we are away on progress or traveling or hunting. People have to be able to see the king and all the royal family. They have to recognize us, as they would their own brothers and sisters. D'you see? We have to be as distant as gods and as familiar as their own painted saints in the parish church."

Mary stands looking proud and fragile. I think she looks both like a woman ready to fight for her rights, and a girl who fears that no one will love her. She is such a contradiction of fierceness and vulnerability that I don't know if the painter can capture all the aspects of her, if he can understand that here is a daughter accustomed to being denied, and a young woman longing to be loved. Posed with her hands clasped before her in her gown of deep crimson, I see her pale stern face and think how dear she is to me, this staunch, intractable young woman.

Elizabeth will come next and she will raise her dark eyes and smile at the artist. She is pleasing while Mary is defiant, but under the veneer of Elizabeth's coquetry is the same passionate need for love and the same anxiety to be acknowledged.

The painter has shown me the first drafts, and now there is to be an outside rim of the portrait showing two beautiful archways into the gardens beyond, and in the doorways he is going to paint the two Fools: Will Somers with his little monkey, and Mary's female Fool. This is an improvement on the ruins of Boulogne, but I am not sure that I want a pair of Fools in a portrait of the royal family. The painter explains their purpose: they are there to signify that we have not grown overly great. We still have people who challenge us, who speak to our human failings, who laugh at us as sinners.

"And the king knows this?" I ask.

The painter nods.

"He agreed?"

"His Majesty liked the idea."

I am glad. It shows that the king does not think of himself beyond challenge, as Thomas wrongly claimed. The king does indeed feel doubts, and he listens to the Fool Will, whose God-given gift is to voice these doubts.

The wall between the two glowing doorways is to be ornate, like a jewel box, with a ceiling of red roses and four golden pillars, a fitting background to this family that own everything. On the right will be Elizabeth, on the left will be Mary, and center stage, also in deep Lancaster red, will be the prince, darling Edward, standing beside his father the king, seated square on his throne, and me beside him. The picture will be copied and engraved and will spread through the kingdom, through Christendom. It will proclaim the triumph of Tudor ambition. Here is Henry, broad and handsome, strong and virile, with his son, a healthy boy, growing into manhood beside him, me his wife still in her fertile years seated at his side, his two beautiful daughters adjacent to us, and the people of England—a pair of Fools—looking in at our glory.

"She looks well," Henry says quietly behind me, glancing approvingly at Princess Mary.

"She suffers very badly from pain in her belly, but I think she is improving," I say. "I think she is better all the time. I make sure that her diet is regular and that she takes exercise and rest by turns."

He nods. "Perhaps she should be married," he says, as if the idea has just occurred to him.

I shoot him a small, sideways smile. "My lord husband," I say teasingly, "who do you have in mind? For I know, as well as I know you, that you will have someone in mind for her. And probably an ambassador is already speaking of it in some great court."

He takes my hand and draws me away from the artist and from Princess Mary, whose dark eyes follow us as if she would know what her father is planning for her.

"I fear she won't like it at first, but with France against us, and Spain such an unreliable ally, with the enmity of the pope, I was thinking of a new alliance—perhaps Germany, perhaps Denmark or Sweden."

"She would have to be free to practice her faith. Aren't they Lutheran?"

"She would have to obey her husband," he corrects me.

I hesitate. Mary is intelligent and thoughtful. Perhaps if she were to have the chance of discussing religion with a husband of intelligence, she might become converted to my view that God speaks to us individually, each and every one of us, that we need neither pope nor priest, nor bleeding statue, to find our way to faith. God is calling and we only have to listen. There are no clever tricks to forgiveness. There is only one way and there is only one Bible, and a woman can study it as well as a man. Mary has listened to Cranmer, she has talked to the visiting preachers. She has worked on the Erasmus New Testament with me and is making a beautiful translation of the Gospel of Saint John, working almost entirely on her own. When she has to bend her will to a husband, she might find that the taming of her spirit leads her to God. I think that I heard the voice of God when I knew I had to stop listening to my own will. Perhaps it will be the same for my stepdaughter.

"I think it would be a great opportunity for her," I say truly. "It would be very good for her to marry. But she could not go against her faith."

"Aha? You think she should be married?"

"I think a good man might give her an opportunity to think and study and serve him and her country," I say. "And to love him, and their children."

"You could prepare her for this change in her circumstances? You could recommend it to her?"

I bow my head. "I would be honored to talk with her and tell her that it is your intention," I say.

"Leave it for now," he says cautiously. "Say nothing for now. But it is my intention. If I am to hold Boulogne and force France into peace, I shall need some help. Mary will make an alliance with the Germans unbreakable. She is a princess; she knows that is her life's work."

This autumn, with the king back in my bed and my room filled once more with the sickly odor of rotting flesh, I start to dream again. It is always the same dream. I walk up a damp circular stair, one hand on the clammy stone wall, one hand holding the flickering candle. A cold draft swirling up from the floor below warns me that I am not alone, there is someone coming up the stairs after me. The fear of whoever is silently following me drives me upwards, stepping quickly on the stairs so my candle flame bobs in the breeze and threatens to go out. At the top I am faced by six doors arranged in a circle around the landing, as small as the entrances to cells. I think that they will be locked but when I go to the first door and take hold of the ring, it turns easily, silently in my hand. I think then that I will not enter. I don't know who is inside, and I can smell a miasma of putrefaction as if there is something bad behind the door, as if there is something rotting in the room. But then I hear a step on the stair behind me and I know I have to go onward and get away from whoever is following me. The door yields, and I go inwards, the door is snatched and locked behind me, I am captive, my candle flame blows out, and I am in darkness.

In the complete blackness of the enclosed silence of the room, I hear someone stealthily move.

The king's need for allies becomes acute as French attacks on our shipping increase. There is no doubt in anyone's mind that the French will raid our coastal towns and ports, perhaps even invade. The king has reports from his spy network, and from our merchants, that his lifelong rival and enemy King Francis of France is arming his fishermen and merchantmen, and building his own warships. It is a race to see who can muster the greatest fleet and we are lagging behind the French, who boast that they rule the Narrow and even the Northern Seas.

At this time of danger, Thomas is never at court. He is at Portsmouth, Plymouth or Dartmouth, Ipswich, Shoreham or Bristol, supervising the building of new ships, the refitting of old ones, and the muster and training of crews. Now he has his own ship of the line, he lives on board reviewing those ships that he has pressed into service, trying to find men to enlist as fighting soldiers on the unstable wooden castles that are built onto the decks of the merchantmen and little fishing ships.

As the sun sets earlier and earlier every day I imagine him, wrapped in a thick cloak, standing behind the steersman, scanning the darkening horizon for enemy sails, and I whisper a prayer to keep him safe. In their terror at the threat of the French invasion the court speak constantly of him, and I learn to be stony-faced when someone mentions the admiral and the fleet that he is mustering. I train myself to listen as if I am concerned for the ships and not for their commander.

It is in some of the worst weather of the autumn that Thomas plans an attack on the coast of Brittany, gathering his fleet off the Isle of Wight, hoping to catch the French navy sheltering in port and destroy them at their moorings. I hear of his plan from his sister-in-law, Anne Seymour, who has it from her husband, Edward. Thomas has sent his battle plan to the Privy Council for their approval. He says that the French must be destroyed in port before spring. He says that they have oared galleys that can fight in any weather, unlike our sailing ships, which depend on a favorable wind. He says that the only way to prevent an invasion is to destroy the French fleet before they even set sail. All the king's castles on the south coast cannot do as much damage to the enemy as one well-timed sea-borne raid, if he can catch them unawares, at anchor.

He writes about new ways of using our ships. They have always been used as transport—delivering the soldiers and weapons to the battle where they will fight—but Thomas writes to the king that if we can make the ships more maneuverable, if we can arm them with heavy cannon, then we can use them as weapons themselves. A ship could meet another at sea and bombard from a distance, conquer at sea with cannon, and not depend on getting close enough to board. He writes that the French galleys carry a terrifyingly heavy cannon that launches stone cannonballs at the target, and that they can hole an enemy vessel, ram it with the blade at their prow, and only then get alongside to allow the soldiers to board for hand-to-hand fighting on a vessel that is already wounded.

His brother, Edward, argues in council that Thomas has a great sense of the sea, has traveled far and seen the shipyards of Venice, has watched their galleys maneuver and fight; but even as he tells the king this, the brothers' rival for the king's attention, Thomas Howard and his son Henry laugh scornfully and say that ships will only ever serve the king by delivering his armies to France, or by blocking the English harbors from invading French ships. The idea of a naval campaign fought by sailors at sea is ludicrous. They say Thomas Seymour has been drinking sea water and courting mermaids. He is a dreamer, a fool.

Those in favor of a naval war are almost all reformers. Those who say that the ships must be used in the old way are those who want the old religion. The argument deteriorates into the usual division of the court. It is as if nothing can be decided without religion; and religion can never be decided, but lurches from one side to the other.

"And now it turns out that the Howards are right and Tom Seymour is a fool," Henry spits furiously at me as I come to his rooms before dinner. He is not dining in court tonight. His leg is giving him too much pain and now he is running a fever. I look at his red sweating face and I feel as sick with fear as a little child facing an angry parent. I feel as if there is nothing I can do to pacify him; I will be in the wrong whatever I say.

"Shall I dine with you, my dear?" I ask softly. "I can have a table set for us here. I don't need to go into the hall."

"Dine in the great hall!" he snaps. "They need to see the throne filled and, God knows, my daughters cannot take my place and my son is a motherless child. I am all but alone in the world, and my commanders are fools and Tom Seymour the worst of them all."

"I shall come to you when dinner is over," I say soothingly. "But can I send my musicians to play for you in the meantime? They have a new choral piece based on your own—"

"Tom has played ducks and drakes with my ships and now stands to lose them all! D'you think I can be cosseted by some fools twanging lutes? D'you think I am not in despair? Despair and nobody can help me!"

Anthony Denny looks up and exchanges a glance with Doctor William Butts. They all wait to see if I can calm the king. I am their only hope. I go very close to him and put my hand against his hot damp face.

"My love," I say. "You're not alone. I love you, the country adores you. This is terrible, I am so sorry."

"I have heard this very night from Portsmouth, from Portsmouth, madam. Tom Seymour set sail into the worst storm they have seen for years and is likely to be lost. And all my ships lost with him."

I don't flinch, I don't even close my eyes, though I feel a great pulse in the core of my body, as if I am wounded, actually bleeding inside; but I remain steadily smiling down at his furious face, my hand against his burning cheek. "God save them for England," I say. "God save all of them in peril on the sea."

"God save my ships!" he bellows. "D'you have any idea how much it costs me to build and equip a ship? And then Tom gets one of his brilliant ideas and throws away the fleet on a hopeless venture! Drowns himself in the process."

"He is drowned? The fleet is lost?" My voice is steady but I can feel my temples pulse with pain.

"No, no, Your Majesty, it's not that bad yet. We have no news for certain." Denny steps forward and addresses the king. "We know there is a storm and that some ships are missing, the admiral's ship among them, but we have no more news than that. It might all be well."

"How can it be well when they are sinking like stones?" Henry shouts.

We are all silent. Nobody can do anything with the king when he is in such a rage, and nobody dares to try. My hands are trembling but so too is Denny. I think: surely I would know if he were dead? Surely I would simply know it—if he were rolling with the tide, his dark hair floating from his white face, his boots slowly filling with water and taking him down to the seabed? Surely God would have more mercy than to let a sinner like me, a sinner like him, be parted without one word of love?

"The admiral's ship is lost?" I ask Denny quietly as Doctor Butts steps forward with a draft in a small glass. Wordlessly he presses it into the king's hand, which is clenched on the arm of his chair, and wordlessly we watch as Henry downs it in one great gulp. After silent moments we see his grip ease on the chair, the terrible scowl ironed from his forehead. He heaves a great sigh.

"I suppose you are not at fault," he says begrudgingly to me.

I manage a smile. "I think not," I say.

He rubs his damp face against my hand like a sick dog seeking a caress. I bend and kiss his cheek. He puts his hand on my tightly laced back and, out of sight of the court, slides it down to clench my buttock. "You are distressed," he states.

"For you," I say firmly. "Of course."

"Very good. So go to dinner and come back to me when you are in a quieter frame of mind. Come back when you have dined."

I curtsey and go to the doorway. Anthony Denny, now Sir Anthony Denny since his knighthood at Boulogne, steps out with me.

"Are many men lost?" I ask him quietly.

"They set out and got scattered, and then they had to run before a storm, but more than that we don't know," he says. "It's in God's hands."

"The admiral's ship?"

"We don't know. Pray God that we get news soon and that the king is not further distressed."

Of course, that is the most important thing to Sir Anthony. The lives of the sailors, the bright courage of Thomas, matter little—to him, to all of us—compared to the king's temper. I bow my head. "Amen."

I pray for him; it is all I can do. I pray for his safety and I listen to the king complain of his failure, of his stupidity, of his recklessness, while I pray that he is alive, that he has survived the storm, that somewhere out on the Narrow Seas he is scanning the horizon for a break in the dark clouds and watching the reefed-in sails for the slackening of the gale.

Then we get news from Portsmouth that the fleet has limped into port, one at a time, sails ripped and masts torn down, and that some vessels are still missing. The admiral's ship comes in with its mainmast broken but Thomas is standing, wrapped in his sea cape, in the stern. Thomas has returned, Thomas is safe. There is joy at court that he is alive—his brother, Edward, runs to the chapel to fall on his knees to thank God for sparing his most brilliant kinsman—but the king does not share it, and nobody dares to voice it before him. On the contrary, he repeats his complaints that Thomas is a fool, a fearless fool, and that he has destroyed the king's trust and been false to his appointment. The king mutters that it is probably treason, that it is a matter for a trial, a man so reckless with the king's fortune and forces is as bad as a traitor, worse than a traitor. That since God did not drown him it falls to the king to behead him.

I pray in silence. There can be no thanksgiving Mass from me for the survival of the admiral. I don't say one word in his defense. Only once do I think, madly, of asking his sister-in-law Anne to write in her own name, never mentioning me, and warn him to come to court at once, before the king argues himself into a greater rage, and arrests Thomas for the crime of bad weather. But I dare not. She may share my interest in the new religion, she may be sworn to my service, but she is no great friend of mine; her devotion to the Seymour family comes before everything else. She has never been a friend to Thomas for his own sake. Foolishly, her passionate devotion to her husband makes her jealous of everyone else in his life. She eyes Thomas with suspicion for his charm and his ease at court. She is afraid that people prefer him to her husband—and she is right. Her only praise for any single member of her husband's family is reserved for his dead sister Jane, Queen Jane, the mother of Prince Edward, and she mentions her before the king whenever she can: "my sister Jane," "sainted Jane," conveniently dead Jane.

So I dare say and do nothing, not even when the king limps painfully into my rooms to sit with me to watch my ladies dancing, or to listen to me read. Not even when he comes in with a chart of the south coast and the endangered ports under his arm as I am pouring water into a shallow dish for my favorite pair of canaries to take a bath, warmed by the sunshine that streams in the window.

"Take care! Will they fly away?"

"They come to my hand."

"Won't they drown themselves?" he asks irritably.

They duck their bright heads in the water and flutter their wings, I step back laughing as they splash. "No, they like to take a bath."

"They're not ducks," he observes.

"No, lord husband. But they seem to enjoy water."

He watches for a moment. "I suppose they are pretty things."

"I love them dearly, they are so bright and quick, you would almost think that they understand."

"Just like courtiers," he says grimly.

I laugh. "Do you have a map there, my lord?"

He gestures with it. "I am on my way to meet with the Privy Council," he says. "We have to repair every castle at every southern port. We will have to build new ones. The French are coming, and Thomas Seymour has failed to stop them."

He snaps his fingers for his page, who is waiting in the doorway. The youth comes forward and takes the king's weight on his shoulder. "I will leave you to your amusements. You did not have sunny mornings and little birds when you were married to old Latimer."

"Indeed, I did not." I am thinking desperately how to ask him about Thomas. "Are we in danger, lord husband?"

"Of course we are, and it's all his fault. I shall command the Privy Council to try Tom Seymour for treason for the reckless loss of my fleet."

The cock bird flutters to the top of one of the cages, alarmed by the king's rough tone, so I am able to turn my face away and say lightly: "Surely he cannot be guilty of treason? He has been such a good and loyal servant to you, and you have always loved him."

"I'll have that handsome head on a spike," he says with sudden cold violence. "Would you take a wager on it?" and he goes out of the door.

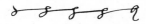

Silently, like a ghost, I make my way to the king's side of the old palace. Nobody is with me. I told my ladies that I had a headache and would lie down and sleep, then I slipped from my bedroom to make my way to the king's rooms, through the small winding galleries to the secret door into his bedroom, then through his deserted privy chambers to his inner presence chamber, where the Privy Council meet. It is like my dream, creeping about on my own, seen by no one. I could be climbing a dark stair, in a silent tower. It is like my dream in the quiet rooms with no one here. There is no guard on the door between the inner presence chamber and the empty rooms. I can stand outside the door and listen to what they say. I swear to myself that if I hear them say that they will arrest Thomas, I will send a message to warn him, whatever the risk. I cannot stand by, struck dumb with fear, when the king takes bets about putting his head on a spike on London Bridge.

His brother, Edward, speaks up for him. I can hear him reading aloud from a letter Thomas has sent defending himself. Edward's voice is clear and I can make out every word through the thick door.

"And look here," Edward says. "Let me read you this, Your Majesty. Thomas writes:

> *Call all the masters and captains that were in this journey and*
> *if any of them are able to say that we might lay longer in Dover*
> *Road, the Downes, or Bollen Rode as the wind did change,*
> *without putting ourselves and the king's ships in greater danger,*
> *then let me bear the blame, and if we have done but as the*
> *weather would serve I should desire your lordships to blame the*
> *weather and let me, with the rest in my company, be excused to*
> *encourage us to serve on the sea another time . . ."*

"Oh, he writes a good letter," Henry grumbles. "Nobody ever said he was lacking in charm. But how many ships are missing?"

"It is the mischance of war," Edward replies. I hear the crackle of the paper as he slides the letter across the table for the king to read. "Nobody knows better than Your Majesty the dangers a man may run when he goes to war. You, who have sailed to France in the most hazardous weather! Thomas is lucky to report to a king who knows better than any other in Christendom what dangers a brave man has to face. You have been in terrible danger, Your Majesty. You know how a man of courage has to throw the dice and hope that it falls his way. It is the very essence of chivalry—the chivalry that you love so well—that a man takes his life in his hands to serve you."

"He was reckless," the king says flatly.

"In a season of storms," I hear the old Duke of Norfolk Thomas Howard's rumbling complaint. "Madness to go out! Why could he not wait for spring, as we always do? Typical of a Seymour that he thought he could outrun an autumn wind."

"The coast has to be defended against the French," John

Dudley intervenes. "And the French are not waiting for fair weather. He couldn't risk leaving our fleet in port. What if they had attacked? He writes that their barges can bombard from a distance, they can go among moored ships with or without wind. They carry weapons, they are rowed by their crew and they can make war in any season in any water. He had to destroy them before they invaded us."

I hear the king's thick hacking cough and his juicy hawk and spit. "You all seem satisfied with his conduct," he says grudgingly.

I hear a protesting bark from Henry Howard.

"All except the Howards and their party," the king says grimly. "As usual."

"Certainly there was no deliberate attempt to risk the fleet," someone points out.

"Well, I am not satisfied," says Stephen Gardiner. "Clearly he has been reckless. Clearly, he should be punished."

"Easy to say from a warm fireside," Edward mutters.

I hold my breath. Thomas's popularity with the court is playing in his favor, and besides, everybody knows that he is risking his life at sea while they are dry-shod.

"He can keep his commission," Henry decides. "Make sure you tell him I am most displeased. He must come and report to me himself."

I hear the scrape of his chair and the rustle of the strewing herbs as he struggles to rise and the Privy Council jump to their feet and two of them go to help him. At once I tiptoe, silently in my leather slippers, away from the door, through the inner privy chamber, and I am about to run through the king's bedroom when I freeze in sudden terror.

There is someone in the room. I see a silent figure, seated in the window seat, knees folded up to his chin, in sunshine now where he was hidden in shadow before. A spy, a silent spy, who has been frozen like a statue, watching me. It is Will Somers, the king's Fool. He must have seen me creep in, he must have watched me listening at the door, and now he sees me hurrying back to my own rooms, a guilty wife tiptoeing through her husband's bedroom.

He raises his dark eyes to me and sees the naked guilt on my face.

"Will . . ."

He makes an exaggerated comical start as if he has seen me for the first time, a great Fool's leap of surprise that sends him bounding from his seat to tumble to the floor. If I were not so afraid, I would have laughed out loud.

"Will . . ." I whisper urgently. "Don't fool now."

"Is that you? I thought you were a ghost," he exclaims quietly. "A ghost of a queen."

"I was listening for plans. I am afraid for the Princess Mary," I say quickly. "I fear that she will be married against her will . . ."

He shakes his head, choosing to ignore the lie. "I have seen too many queens," he says. "And too many of them are ghosts now. I don't want to see a queen in danger; I don't want to see another ghost. Indeed, I swear that I won't see one. Not even one."

"You did not see me?" I ask, catching his meaning.

"I did not see you, nor Kitty Howard creeping down the stairs in her nightgown, nor Anne of Cleves, pretty as her portrait, crying at her bedroom door. I am a Fool, not a guard. I don't have to see things, and I am forbidden to understand them. There's no point in me reporting them. Who would listen to a Fool? And so God bless."

"God bless you, Will," I say fervently, and melt through the doorway into the king's bedroom and through the private corridor to the safety of my own rooms.

WHITEHALL PALACE, LONDON, SPRING 1545

KP

The cold wet days of this early spring seem to last forever, as if there never will be warm days of summer. The light gets brighter in the mornings and the daffodils flower coldly on the banks of the river, but the gardens are wet, and the city outside the great walls of the palace is awash: the ill-drained streets flooded with cold, dirty water. When we ride, there is no pleasure in it, for the horses labor in the mud, and the frozen rain comes in scuds into our faces. We come home early, hunched in the saddle, chilled and bedraggled.

Trapped indoors by days of rain, my ladies and I continue our studies, reading texts from the Bible and translating them, both as practice for our Latin and as a stimulus to thoughtful discussions on the meanings of the words. I notice that I have become more and more aware of the sonorous beauty of the Bible, the music of the language, the rhythm of the punctuation. I set myself the task of trying to write better English, so the beauty of my translation matches the importance of the words. Before I write a sentence, I listen to the sound in my head before I put it on the page. I start to think that words can be pitch-perfect just as a musical note can be, that there is a beat in prose, just as there is in poetry. I realize that I am undertaking an apprenticeship in writing and reading, and I am my own master and my own student. And I realize that I love the work.

We are studying one morning when there is a little knock at the narrow door that leads down a stone stair to the stable yard. My maid puts her head into the room. "The preacher is here," she says quietly.

She has waited at one of the many gates to bring the man directly to my rooms. It is not that they are instructed to come in secret—the king himself knows that I have preachers from his own chapel, from Saint Paul's Cathedral, and from the other churches. But I don't see why the court in general—those who do not attend our sermons and readings, others who criticize my interest—should know what we study and who we meet. If they want to learn, they can come and sit with us. If they simply want to know for the sake of gossip, they can do without. I don't need the Lord Chancellor to look down his long nose at me, or his household to whisper the names of the serious pious men who come to talk to me and my ladies, as if we were meeting gallants. I don't need Stephen Gardiner's men to keep a list of the names of everyone who comes to talk to me, and then send his clerks to follow them to their homes and question their neighbors.

"There's an odd thing, Your Majesty," the maid says tentatively.

I look up. "What odd thing?"

"The person who claims to be your preacher is a woman, Your Majesty. I didn't know if it was all right?"

I can feel a giggle starting, and I dare not look at Nan. "Why should it not be all right, Miss Mary?"

The girl shrugs. "I didn't know that a good woman could preach, Your Majesty. I thought a good woman had to be silent. It's what my father always told me."

"Your father thought, no doubt, that he was telling the truth," I say carefully, conscious of Nan's bright eyes and hidden smile. "But we know that God's Word comes equally to men and women and so men and women can equally speak of it."

She does not understand. I can see by her glazed eyes that she only wants to know if she should let this odd being—a woman preacher—into my rooms; or have the stable boys throw her back into the cobbled streets that circle the palace.

"Can you speak, Miss Mary?" I ask her.

She dips a curtsey. "Of course, Your Majesty."

"Can you read?"

"I can read a little, if it is writ plain."

"Then if the Bible is writ plain, you could read God's Word. And then you could tell others of it."

She drops her head. We make out from her embarrassed mutter that the Bible is not for the likes of her, she knows only what the priest tells her, and he only speaks loud enough for them to hear at the back at Christmas and Easter.

"It is for you," I insist. "The Bible is written into English for you to read. And Our Savior came from heaven for you and for everyone, as He makes it plain in the Bible that He gave us."

Slowly her head comes up. "I could read the Bible?" she asks me directly.

"You could," I promise her. "You should."

"And a woman could understand it?"

"She can."

"And so this woman can preach?"

"Why not?"

This silences her again. Centuries of male priests and men teachers, monk scholars and bullying fathers, have told her and me—told every woman in England—that a woman cannot preach. But under my hand I have the Bible in English, given by my husband to the people of England, which says that Jesus came for everyone—not just for male priests and men teachers, monk scholars and bullying fathers.

"Yes, she can," I say to conclude the lesson. "And you can show her in. What is her name?"

"Mistress Anne Askew."

She comes in and curtseys as low as if I am an empress, then she shoots a little smile at Catherine Brandon and curtseys again to the ladies. I see at once why Mary hesitated to allow her into my chamber. She is an outstandingly pretty young woman, dressed like a country lady, the young wife of a wealthy farmer or town merchant. She's not nobility, but one of those on the rise who probably have an old name and have used it to get a new fortune. Her white cap on her glossy brown hair is trimmed with expensive white lace. It frames an exquisite heart-shaped face with bright brown eyes and a ready smile. She is wearing a plain gown of wool in brown with a kirtle of red silk. Her sleeves are plain brown too, and round her neck she has a filet of good linen. She looks like a young woman whom we might meet on a progress, voted as Queen of the May for her pure beauty, shining among the other girls of the village. We might see her in a tableau, chosen to play the princess to a painted dragon in a prosperous town. She is so lovely that any mother would get her married young, any father would see that she married extremely well.

She is certainly not how I imagine a woman inspired by God. I was expecting someone older, with a scrubbed, plain face, engraved with benevolent lines. Someone more like one of the abbesses of my childhood, certainly someone more austere than this little beauty.

"Have we met before?" She seems oddly familiar, and I am sure that I recognize her dazzling smile.

"I did not dare to hope that Your Majesty would remember me," she says politely. I hear the rolling Lincolnshire accent. "My father, Sir William, served your father-in-law, Lord Brough, at Gainsborough, and I used to be invited to the hall when you held a feast and dancing. I always came to the hall for the Twelve Days of Christmas, and at Easter, too, and at Maytime. But I was a little girl. I didn't expect you to recognize me now."

"I thought I knew you."

"You were the most learned young lady I'd ever seen," she confesses. "We talked together once, and you told me that you were reading Latin with your brother. I understood then that a woman can study, a woman can learn. It set me on my path to learn and memorize the Bible. You were my inspiration."

"I'm glad that I talked to you, if this is the result. Your reputation as a gospeler goes before you. Do you think you can teach us?"

She bows her head. "I can only tell you what I have read and what I know," she replies.

"Have you read more than me and these learned ladies?"

She gives me a sweet respectful smile. "I doubt it, Your Majesty, for I had to learn from my Bible when I was blessed with it, and I had it snatched from my hands many a time. I had to fight for my understanding. But I expect that you all have been given a Bible and taught by the finest scholars."

"Her Majesty is writing her own book," Nan interrupts boastfully. "The king has asked her to translate prayers from the Latin to give to the people. She works with the king himself. She studies with the great scholar Thomas Cranmer. Together, they are working on an English missal."

"It is true then?" she demands of me. "We will hear the prayers in English in the churches? We will be allowed to know what the priest has been saying for all these years?"

"Yes."

"God be praised," she says simply. "You are blessed to be doing such work."

"It is the king who gives the liturgy to his people," I say. "And Thomas Cranmer who translates it. I have just helped."

"I shall be so glad to read the prayers," she says fervently. "And God will be glad to hear them, as He must hear the prayers of all of the people, in whatever language they speak, even when they are silent."

I cannot help but be intrigued. "Do you think that God, who gave us the Word, understands without words? Beyond words?"

"He must do," she says. "He understands my thoughts, even when they are in my mind before I have put words to them. He understands my prayers when they are nothing more than a wordless calling to Him, like a hen clucking back to a poultry woman." She corrects herself. "A sparrow does not fall but He knows it; He must understand what a sparrow feels. He must know what I mean when I go *chuck chuck chuck*. He must understand parables and simple stories since His own Son spoke in parables and simple stories, in whatever language they had in Bethlehem."

I smile but I am impressed. I had not thought of the language of God as the language before words, as the language spoken in the heart, and I like the thought of God understanding our prayers as if we were clucking hens, pecking at His feet. "And did you come to this understanding through private study?" I ask. "Were you taught at home?"

Anne Askew takes her stand, one hand resting gently on my table, her head raised. I realize that this is her sermon, speaking from the heart, speaking of her own personal experience and of the presence of the Word of God in her life. "I was taught with my brothers until they went to university," she begins. "It was an educated home but not a learned one. My father attended your husband the king, when he was a young man. When I was sixteen years old, he married me to a neighbor, Thomas Kyme, and we had two children together before he called me a heretic and threw me out of the house because I read the Bible that King Henry, in his wisdom, gave to all the people of England."

"It is only for noblemen and ladies now," Nan cautions her, with a glance at the closed door. "Not for women like you."

"It was put into our church, at the back of the church, where the poorest man and the humblest woman could go in and read, if they could read," the surprising young woman corrects her. "They told us that it was for the people to read, that the king had given it to his people. They may have taken it away again, but we remember that the king gave it to the people of England—all the people of England—for us to read. The lords took it back, the princes of the church who think themselves so great took it away from us; but the king gave it to us, God bless him."

"Where did you go?" I ask. "When your husband threw you out of your home?"

"I went to Lincoln," she says with a smile. "I sat at the back of the great cathedral and I took a Bible in my hands and I read it in the sight of the congregation and in the sight of the benighted pilgrims who come through the doors, kissing the floor and creeping on their knees. Poor souls, they chinked with the pilgrim badges they had pinned on their clothes but they thought it was a heresy that a woman should read God's Word in a church. Imagine that! To think it is a heresy for a believer to read a Bible in church!

"I read it aloud to everyone who came and went in that great building, buying and selling favors, trading pilgrim badges and relics, all the fools and hucksters. I read the Bible to teach them that the only way to God is not through chips of stone and bits of bone, flasks of holy water and prayers written backwards on scraps of paper and pinned to a coat. It is not through sacred rings and kissing the foot of a statue. I showed them that the only way to God is through His Holy Word, in His own holy words."

"You're a brave woman," I remark.

She smiles at me. "No, I am a simple woman," she corrects me. "When I understand something true, it goes to my heart. I have understood this: that we have to read and know the Word of God. This, and nothing else, will bring us to heaven. All the rest of it: the threat of purgatory, the promise of forgiveness in return for payment, the statues that bleed and the pictures that leak milk, all these things are the invention of a church that has gone far from the Word of God. It is for me, and for those who care about truth, to cling to the Word of God and turn our face from the masquing. The church does not put on mystery plays once a year anymore, it plays them every day all the year. It is all costume and show and pretense. But the Bible is the truth and there is nothing but the Bible."

I nod. She speaks simply, but she is absolutely right.

"So I came in the end to London, and spoke before the great men of this city. My brother helped me, and my sister is Mrs. Jane Saint Paul, whose husband serves the duchess." She curtseys to Catherine Brandon, who nods her head in reply. "I found a safe house with honest kinsmen who think as I do, and I listened to preachers and spoke with many learned men, far more learned than me. And a good man, a preacher that you know, I think, Your Majesty, John Lascelles, took me to meet other good men and speak with them."

An almost imperceptible breath from Nan tells me that she knows the name. I glance at her.

"He bore witness against Queen Katherine," she says.

"I have met a few people of your court," Anne goes on, looking around and smiling. "Lady Denny and Lady Hertford. And others listen to gospelers and believe in the reform of the church." She takes a breath. "And then I went to the church for a divorce," she says.

Nan gives a little scream of shock. "How? How could you?"

"I went to the church and I said that since my husband was a believer in the old ways and I am for the new, we never made vows that meant the same thing. We did not join hands in the same church, the true God can have nothing to do with the vows that they made me swear, in a language that I didn't understand, and so our marriage should be dissolved."

"Mistress Anne, a woman can't get her marriage dissolved at will," Catherine protests.

Nan and I exchange glances. Our own brother's wife ran away from him and he was awarded a divorce as a gift from the king. The king is head of the church; marriage and divorce are in his gift, they are not for a woman to take.

"Why should not a woman leave a marriage? If she can make it, surely she can unmake it," Anne Askew replies. "What was sworn can be unsworn. The king himself—"

"We don't speak of the king," Nan says swiftly.

"The law does not recognize a woman except when she is alone in the world," Anne Askew says authoritatively. "Only a woman without father or husband has any legal rights in this world. That, in itself, is unjust. But think of this: I am a woman alone, a *feme sole*. My father is dead and I deny my husband. The law must deal with me as an adult equal person as I am before God. I will go to heaven because I have read and accepted the Word of God. I demand justice because I have read and accepted the word of the law."

Nan exchanges a quick worried look with me. "I don't know the rights and the wrongs of this," she says. "But I know it is not a fit discourse for a queen's household." She glances at Princess Elizabeth, who is listening carefully. "Not for young ears."

I shake my head. I am married to a man who declares his own annulments. He is divorced when he says it is so. Anne Askew suggests that a woman might claim as much power as the king.

"You had better speak of your faith," I command her. "I have translated Psalm 145: *All things be under Thy dominion and rule.* Speak of that to us."

She bows her head as if to gather her thoughts for a moment, and then she speaks simply and eloquently, and in her voice I hear the ring of complete conviction, and in her face I see the shine of innocence.

She stays all the morning and I send her home with a purse of coins and an invitation to come again. I am fascinated by her, inspired by this woman who says that she can choose where she lives, choose or reject a husband, this woman who knows that God forgives her sins, because she confesses them to Him—not to a priest—she speaks to Him directly. I think this is the first woman I have ever met who strikes me as being one who makes her own life, who walks her own path, who is responsible for herself. This is a woman who has not been tamed to be as others want; she has not been cut down to fit her circumstances.

The portrait painter comes to finish his sketches of the two princesses. I think that Princess Mary stands straighter and taller than usual, as if she knows that this may be her likeness as an English princess, as if it is her last portrait before she is sent away. Perhaps she thinks that this portrait will be copied and sent to her proposed husbands.

I go to her side to pull her train a little straighter, to show off the beautiful brocade, and I whisper in her ear: "You're not posing as an icon, you know. You can smile," and am rewarded by her swift fugitive giggle.

"I do know," she says. "It's just that people will see this portrait years from now, perhaps hundreds of years from now."

Princess Elizabeth, blooming under the attention of the painter, is as pink as the inside of a little shell. She spent so long hidden from sight that she loves the male gaze.

I sit and watch the two girls as they stand at a distance but half facing each other. The painter has his sketches of their faces, and a careful note of the colors of their gowns. All of this will be transferred to the great work like a *tisserand* weaving flowers on a tapestry on the loom from pictures that she has sketched in the garden.

Then the painter turns to me. "Your Majesty?"

"I am not in my gown," I protest.

"For today, I just want to capture your likeness," he says. "The way that you hold yourself. Will you be so good as to sit as you will be seated? Perhaps you can imagine that the king is on your right. Would you tilt your head towards him? But I need you to look straight at me."

I sit as he directs, but I cannot lean towards the space where the king would be. The painter, de Vent, is very exact. Gently he moves the angle of my head this way and that until Mary laughingly takes the place where her father will be positioned, and I sit beside her and tip my head just slightly, as if I am listening.

"Exquisite, yes," de Vent says. "But it is too flat. The new fashions . . . Your Majesty, would you allow me?"

He come closer and turns my chair a little towards where the king will sit. "And will you let your eyes go this way?" He points to the window. "So."

He steps back to gaze at me. I look where he directs, and in my line of sight, outside the window, a blackbird lands on a branch of a tree and opens its yellow beak in a trill of song. At once I am transported to that spring when I ran through the palace to Thomas's rooms and heard a blackbird, drunk with joy and confused by torches, singing at night like a nightingale.

"*Mon Dieu!*" I hear de Vent whisper, and I am recalled to the present.

"What is it?"

"Your Majesty, if I could capture that light in your eyes and that beauty in your face I would be the greatest painter in the world. You are illuminated."

I shake my head. "I was daydreaming. It was nothing."

"I wish I could capture that radiance. You have shown me what I should do. Now I shall make some sketches."

I raise my head, and look out of the window, and watch the blackbird as it ruffles its wings in a little scud of rain and then flies away.

WHITEHALL PALACE, LONDON, SPRING 1545

KP

The king summons me, and Nan and Catherine Brandon follow me along the privy gallery to his rooms. All the windows are open to the spring sunshine and the birds are singing in the trees in the gardens below. We can hear the gulls crying over the River Thames and see the bright flicker of sunlight on their white wings.

Henry is in good humor, his thickly bandaged leg resting on a stool, a pile of papers before him, each dense with type.

"See this!" he says joyfully to me. "You who think you're such a great scholar. See this!"

I curtsey and step forward to kiss him. He takes my face in both his big hands and pulls me closer so that I kiss him on his mouth. He smells of some sort of spirits and sweets.

"I never call myself a scholar," I say at once. "I know I am an ignorant woman compared to you, my lord. But I am glad for the chance to study. What is this?"

"It is our pages back from the printer!" he exclaims. "The liturgy at last. Cranmer says that we will put a copy into every church in England and end their mumbling away in Latin that neither the congregation nor the priest can understand. That's not the Word of God; that's not what I want for my church."

"You're right."

"I know! And look, you can see the prayers that you have translated, and Cranmer's work is in here, too, and I have polished it and in some parts set it into better language, and translated some parts myself. And here it is! My book."

I take up the sheets and read the first few pages. It is beautiful, just as I hoped it would be. It is simple and clear, with a rhythm and a cadence like poetry, but there is nothing forced or overly worked about it. I look at a line that took me half a day to translate, changing one word for another, scratching it out and starting again. Now, in print, it looks as if it could never have been other, and it reads as if it has been the prayer of the English forever. I feel that deep joy of a writer seeing her work in print for the first time. The absorbing private work has become public, it has stepped out into the world. It will be judged and I am full of confidence that it is good work.

"My liturgy, in my church." For the king, it is ownership that gives him joy. "My church, in my kingdom. I have to be both king and pope in England. I have to guard the people from enemies outside and lead them to God within."

Nan and Catherine give a little impressed murmur of awe. They know every phrase and passage, having passed it from one hand to another, improving and polishing the phrasing, reading Thomas Cranmer's changes aloud for him, checking my words with me.

"You can take this," the king says grandly. "You can read these pages and check them for foolish mistakes by the printer's boys. And you can tell me what you think of this, my greatest work."

One of his pages steps forward and gathers up the pile of papers. "Mind," the king says, wagging a finger at me, "I want your real opinion, nothing designed to please me. All I ever want from you is the truth, Kateryn."

I curtsey as the guards hold the doors open for us. "I will read with attention and give you my true opinion," I promise. "This will be the hundredth time I have read these words and I hope to read them a thousand times. Indeed, all of England will read them a thousand times, they will be read every day in church."

"You must always speak honestly to me," he says warmly. "You are my helpmeet and my partner. You are my queen. We will go forward together, Kateryn, leading the people from darkness into light."

Nan, Catherine, and I say not a word until we are back in the safety of my rooms and the door is shut.

"How wonderful!" Catherine exclaims. "That the king should put his own name to the work. Stephen Gardiner can say nothing against it if it is under the king's own seal of approval. How you are leading him, Your Majesty! How far we are going towards true grace!"

Nan spreads the pages out on the table and I take up a

pen to mark any errors when a sudden quiet tap on the little door that leads directly from the stable stairs makes us look up. The preachers who wish to enter discreetly use this door by appointment; perhaps a bookseller with a book that one of Gardiner's spies would name as heretical. All other visitors, great and small, visitors of state and petitioners, come up the broad public stairs and are announced at my presence chamber, as the huge double doors swing open.

"See who it is," I say quietly, and Nan goes to the door and opens it. The guard who stands below, at the bottom of the stair, watches as a young man comes in and bows to me and to Joan Denny.

"Oh, this is Christopher, who serves my husband," Joan says, surprised. "What are you doing here, Christopher? You should have come in the main door. You gave us a fright."

"Sir Anthony said to come to you unobserved," he replies, and he turns to me. "Sir Anthony said to tell Your Majesty at once that Mistress Anne Askew has been arrested and questioned."

"No!"

He nods. "She was arrested and questioned by an inquisitor and then by the Lord Mayor of London himself. Now she is in the keeping of Bishop Bonner."

"She is charged?"

"Not yet. He is questioning her."

"On the very day that the king gives you the prayers in English?" Nan whispers to me incredulously. "On the very day that he promises that England will be freed from superstition? He has her arrested and questioned?"

"God help us and keep us; this is his dogfight," I say, my voice shaky with dread. "Set up one cur and then another. Let the two of them fight it out."

"What d'you mean?" Nan asks, frightened by my tone. "What are you saying?"

"What shall we do?" Catherine Brandon demands. "What can we do to help Anne?"

I turn to Christopher. "Go back," I say. "Take this purse." Nan goes to a drawer in my table and brings out a small purse of gold that I keep for my charitable giving. "See if there are men around Bishop Bonner that will take a bribe. Find out what the bishop requires of Mistress Askew, whether he needs an oath, or a recantation, or an apology. Find out what it is that he wants. And be sure that the bishop knows that I have heard Anne preach, that she is a kinswoman to George Saint Paul, who works for the Brandons, that I have never heard a word from her that is anything but devout, holy, and within the law, that this very day the king has his liturgy in English back from the printers. And that I expect her to be released."

He bows as Nan makes a little fearful noise. "Is it wise to confess acquaintance with her? To let yourself be identified with her?"

"Anyone can discover that she has preached here," I say. "Everyone knows that her sister works at court. What the bishop needs to know is that we, her friends, will stand by her. He needs to be aware that when he questions her, he is questioning one of my preachers, a friend to the Suffolk household. He must be told that she has important allies and we know where she is."

Christopher nods that he understands, and swiftly turns and goes out of the door.

"And send a message back as soon as she is released," I call after him. "And if they proceed against her, come back at once."

We have to wait. We wait all the day, and we try to pray for Anne Askew. I dine with the king and my ladies dance for him, and we smile until our cheeks ache. I glance at him sideways as he is listening to the music and beating time with his hand, and I think: do you know that a woman who thinks as I do, who has preached before me, who loved me when she was a little girl and whose gifts I admire, is being questioned for the offense of heresy, which might take her to the stake? Do you know this and are you waiting to see what I will do? Is it a test, to see if I will act for her? Or do you know nothing? Is this nothing more than the clockwork movements of the old church, set in motion like automata, the ambition of the Bishop of London, the bigotry of Stephen Gardiner, the endless conspiracy of the old churchmen grinding on and on and resisting change? Should I tell you of this and ask for your help? Am I sitting beside the man who would save Anne, or beside the king who is playing her as a piece in one of his games?

Henry turns and smiles at me. "I shall come to your rooms tonight, sweetheart," he says.

And I think: that proves it. He must know nothing. Not even a king as old and as duplicitous as this King of England could possibly smile and bed his wife while her friend was being interrogated on his orders.

I do not speak of Anne to my husband, though as he strives to reach his pleasure he groans: "You please me, ah, Kateryn, you do please me. You can have anything . . ."

When he is quiet and falling asleep he repeats: "You please me, Kateryn. You can have any favor."

"I want nothing," I say. I would feel like a whore if I named a favor now. Anne Askew prides herself on being a free woman; she defied her husband and her father. I should not buy her freedom with the sexual pleasure of a man old enough to be our father.

He understands this. He has a sly smile as he lies back on the heaped pillows, his eyes half closed, drowsy. "Ask me later then," he says, "if you would detach payment from the deed."

"The deed is a gift of love," I say pompously, and then I feel that I have earned his scoffing laugh.

"You make it gracious by naming it so," he says. "It is one of the things that I like about you, Kateryn: you do not see everything as a trade, you don't see everyone else as a rival or an enemy."

"No, I don't," I say. "But it must be a grim world if you see it like that. How would one bear to live in it?"

"By dominating it," he answers easily. "By being the greatest trader with the most to deal in; by being the master of everyone, whether they know it or not."

Two things save Anne Askew: her own keen intelligence, and my protection. She confesses to nothing but believing the scriptures, and when they try to trap her with details of the liturgy she says that she does not know, that she is a simple woman, that all she does is read her Bible, the king's own Bible, and try to follow its precepts. Anything else is too complex for a faithful God-fearing woman like herself. The Lord Mayor tries to trap her with questions of theology and she keeps her head and says that she cannot speak of such things. She irritates Edmund Bonner, the Bishop of London, almost beyond speaking, but he can do nothing against her when he hears from the people of his household that Anne Askew preaches to the queen and her ladies, and that the queen and her friends and companions—the greatest ladies in the land—heard no heresy. The queen—so high in favor with the king that he stayed all last night in her rooms—cannot be denied. She has not yet spoken to the king in favor of her court preacher, but clearly, she can do so. In a frightened hurry, they release Anne Askew, and send her home to her husband. As bullies and men this is the only way they can devise to control a woman. I laugh when they tell me. I believe it will be more of a punishment for him than for her.

KP

The Spanish ambassador, Eustace Chapuys, who clung to the doomed cause of Princess Mary's poor mother, Queen Katherine, who called Anne Boleyn "The Lady" with such a sneer that everyone knew he meant "the whore," has grown old in the service of Princess Mary and her mother and is going home to Spain. He is as lame as the king, crippled with gout, and can walk only if he leans on his sticks, his old face crumpled with pain. He comes to Whitehall Palace to say good-bye to the king on a fine day in early May, a day so warm, with winds carrying the scent of blossom from the apple orchards, that we go out into the garden to catch him before he goes in to his royal audience and I tell him that he should stay—England will be as hot as Spain come June.

He tries to bow and I gesture that he should sit in his chair.

"I need the Spanish sun on my old bones, Your Majesty," he says. "It has been a long, long time since I saw my home. I want to sit in the sun and write my memoirs."

"You will write your memoirs?"

He sees my sudden attention. "Yes. I love to write. And I have so much that I recall so clearly."

I clap my hands. "They will be worth reading, my lord! The things that you have seen! Whatever will you say?"

He does not laugh; his face is grave. "I will say that I have seen the birth of dark times," he says quietly.

I see Mary coming towards us, through the garden, her ladies behind her, and I can see by the way she holds the crucifix on the rosary at her belt that she is nerving herself to say good-bye to this man who has been like a father to her. Indeed, he has been more of a father than the king ever was. He loved and served her mother and he loved and served her. Perhaps she thought he would never leave.

"I will let you say good-bye to the princess alone," I say gently. "She will be so sad to see you go. She has trusted you for good advice since she was a very little girl. You are one of the few . . ." I mean to say that he is one of a very few faithful friends to her; but as I speak I am suddenly aware that she had many friends, and many of them have died. He is one of the few who has survived. Almost everyone who loved Mary was put to death by her father.

There are tears in his dark eyes. "You are generous to let us be alone together," he says, his old voice trembling. "I have loved her since she was a little girl. It has been an honor to advise her. I wish I could have—" He breaks off. "I could not serve her as I hoped," he says. "I did not keep her mother safe, nor her."

"They were difficult times," I say diplomatically. "But no one could doubt your devotion."

He hauls himself to his feet as Princess Mary comes near. "I shall pray for you, Your Majesty," he says quietly. "I shall pray for your safety."

It is such a strange remark from the ambassador who could not save his own queen that I hesitate before beckoning Mary forward. "Oh, but I'm safe, thank you, Ambassador," I say. "The king made me Regent General; he trusts me. You can have every confidence, Princess Mary is safe in my keeping. You can leave her without fear. I am Queen of England and her mother. I will keep her safe."

Ambassador Chapuys looks at me as if he pities me. He has

seen five queens take their place at the side of the king since his own Infanta from Spain. "It is you I am afraid for," he says shortly.

I give a little laugh. "I would do nothing to offend the king," I say. "And he loves me."

He bows. "My queen, Katherine of Aragon, did nothing to offend him," he says gently. I realize that for him Henry has only ever really had one queen: the first and only Queen Katherine. "And he loved her deeply and truly. Until the moment that he stopped loving her. And then nothing would ease his discomfort but her death."

Despite the sunshine in the garden I am suddenly cold. "But what could I do?" I ask.

I mean—what does he imagine can go wrong, what could I possibly do that would offend the king so badly that he would put me aside, as he put Katherine of Aragon aside, imprisoned her in a cold distant castle, and let her die of neglect? But the old man misunderstands me. He thinks I mean what could I do to escape, and his answer is chilling: "Majesty, when you lose his favor, when you get your first hint of it, I pray you leave the country at once," he says quietly. "He will not annul another marriage. He has outgrown that; he could not bear the shame of it. All of Christendom would laugh at him and he could not bear that. When he is tired of you, he will end it with your death."

"Ambassador!" I exclaim.

He nods his gray head. "These are the last words I will ever say to you, Your Majesty. They are a warning from an old man with nothing to lose. Death is the king's preference now. He is not driven to it. I have known kings forced to execute their friends or loved ones; but he is not one of them." He pauses. "He likes finality. He likes to turn against someone and know they are dead the next day. He likes to know that he has that power. If you lose his favor, Your Majesty, please make sure you get away."

I cannot reply.

He shakes his head. "My greatest regret, my greatest failure, was that we did not get my queen away," he says softly.

My ladies are watching me. I move my hand in a little gesture to invite Princess Mary to join us, and I step aside to allow them time to speak together in private. By her suddenly guarded expression I think he is warning her, as he just warned me. This is a man who has observed the king for sixteen years, who has studied him and seen him grow in his power, observed the advisors who disagreed with him dragged to the Tower and executed, watched the wives who displeased him exiled from court or executed, known the innocent men of small rebellions hanged in their thousands in chains. I feel a shudder down my spine, as if my tingling skin knows of a danger that I cannot name, and I shake my head, and walk away.

NONSUCH PALACE, SURREY, SUMMER 1545

KP

George Day, my almoner, comes to my privy chamber as I am reading with my ladies, with a wrapped parcel under his arm. I know at once what he has for me and I step to the bay of the window, with Rig trotting at my heels, so that he can unwrap the book and show it to me.

"*Prayers Stirring the Mind to Heavenly Meditations,*" I read, tracing the title on its inner page. "It is done."

"It is, Your Majesty. It looks very fair."

I open the first pages and there is my name as the editor, *Princess Katherine, Queen of England.* I draw a breath.

"The king himself approved the wording," George Day says quietly. "Thomas Cranmer took it to him and told him that it was a fine translation of the old prayers, that would be read alongside the Litany. You have given the English an English prayer book, Your Majesty."

"He does not object to my name being on it?"

"He does not."

I trace my name with a fingertip. "It feels almost too much for me."

"It is God's work," he assures me. "And also . . ."

I smile. "What?"

"It's good, Your Majesty. It is a good piece of work."

The king returns to health as the summer comes, looking forward to his annual progress down the beautiful valley of the Thames, and he walks from his room in Nonsuch Palace, through the private gallery to my rooms with only two pages and Doctor Butts to accompany him. Nan warns me that he is on his way, and I seat myself at the fireside reading, beautifully dressed in my best nightgown and with my hair in a plait under a dark net.

The pages tap on the door, the guards throw it open, Doctor Butts bows low at the threshold, and the king enters. I rise from my seat at the fireside and curtsey.

"I am so glad to see you, my lord husband."

"It's about time," he says shortly. "I did not marry you to spend my nights alone."

From the shuttered expression on Doctor Butts's face I guess that he advised the king against struggling through the passages to my room, and staying here. Without speaking he goes to the table before the fireplace and prepares a draft for the king.

"Is that a sleeping draft?" Henry demands irritably. "I don't want one. I haven't come here to sleep, you fool."

"Your Majesty should not overexert—"

"I'm not going to."

"This is just to keep your fever down," the doctor replies. "You are heated, Your Majesty. You will heat up the queen's bed."

He strikes just the right note. Henry chuckles. "Should you like me in your bed instead of a warming pan, Kateryn?"

"You are a much warmer bedfellow than Joan Denny," I smile. "She has cold feet. I shall be glad to have you in my bed, my lord."

"You see," Henry says triumphantly to William Butts. "I shall tell Sir Anthony I am a better bedfellow than his wife." He laughs. "Get me into bed," he says to the pages.

Together they push him up onto the footstool before the bed, and then, as he sits back, they go either side of the bed; one of them has to stand on the covers to heave him up to sit upright so that he can breathe, propped by the pillows and the bolster. Gently, they lift his thick wounded leg into bed and then the other beside it. Tenderly, they drape the sheets and the blankets over him, and step back to see that he is comfortable. I have the disturbing thought that they are admiring him as if he were the enormous wax effigy of his corpse which must one day be placed on his coffin.

"Good enough," he says shortly. "You can go."

Doctor Butts brings the little medicine glass to the king and he swallows it in one.

"Is there anything else you need to make you more comfortable?" the doctor asks.

"New legs," Henry says wryly.

"I wish to God I could give you them, Your Majesty."

"I know, I know, you can leave us."

They go out through my privy chamber, closing the door behind them. I hear the guard at the outer door of the presence chamber ground his pike on the stone floor in salute to the doctor, and then it is quiet, but for the crackle of the fire in the fireplace and the hoot of an owl, out in the dark trees of the garden. From somewhere, perhaps beyond the hawks' mews, I can hear the distant pipe of a flute for dancing.

"What are you listening for?" the king asks me.

"I heard an ullet."

"A what?"

I shake my head. "An owl. I meant an owl. We call them ullets in the North."

"D'you miss your home?"

"No, I am so happy here."

This is the right answer. He gestures that I am to come to bed beside him, and I kneel briefly before my prie-dieu, then take off my robe and slip between the sheets in my nightgown. Wordlessly, he tweaks at the fine lawn of my gown and gestures that I should straddle him. I make sure that I am smiling as I go astride him, and I lower myself gently onto him. There is nothing there. Feeling a little foolish I glance down to make sure that I am in the right place, but I can feel nothing. I make sure that my smile does not waver and, slowly, I undo the top ribbon of my nightgown. Always I have to balance my actions so that I do not seem wanton—like Kitty Howard—but I do enough to please him. He gets hold of my hips in an unkind grip and draws me downwards, grinding me against him, trying to thrust himself upwards. His legs are too weak to take his weight, he cannot arch his back, he can do nothing but flounder. I can see his color and his temper rising, and I make sure I am still smiling. I widen my eyes and I take little shallow breaths as if I am aroused. I start to pant.

"It's no good," he says shortly.

I pause, uncertainly.

"It's not my fault," he insists. "It's this fever. It has un-manned me."

I dismount with as much ease as I can manage, but I feel painfully awkward as if I were getting gracelessly off a fat cob. "I am sure it's nothing . . ."

"Yes, yes," he says. "It's the fault of that damned doctor. The physic he gives me would castrate a horse."

I giggle at the phrase, then I see his face and realize he is not joking. He really does think himself as strong as a stallion, only rendered impotent by a draft against fever.

"Get us something to eat," he says. "At least we can dine."

I slip from the bed and go to the cupboard. There are pastries and some fruit.

"For God's sake! More than that."

I ring the bell and Elizabeth Tyrwhit my cousin comes and curtseys low when she sees the king in my bed. "Your Majesty," she says.

"The king is hungry," I tell her. "Bring us some pastries and some wine, some meats and some cheeses and some sweet things."

She bows and goes, I hear her waking a page and sending him running to the kitchens. One of the cooks has to sleep there, in a truckle bed, waiting for a nighttime demand from the king's rooms. The king likes great meals in the middle of the night as well as the two big regular feasts of the day, and often stirs in his rest and wants a pudding to soothe him back to sleep again.

"We'll go to the coast next week," he tells me. "I have been waiting for months to be well enough to ride."

I exclaim in pleasure.

"I want to see what Tom Seymour has left of my navy," he says. "And they say the French are massing in their ports. They are likely to raid. I want to see my castles."

I am sure he will see the rapid pulse in the hollow of my bare neck at the thought of seeing Thomas. "Is it not dangerous?" I ask. "If the French are coming?"

"Yes," he says with pleasure. "We might even see some action."

"There might be a battle?" My voice is perfectly steady.

"I hope so. I did not refit the *Mary Rose* for her to sit in harbor. She is my great weapon, my secret weapon. D'you know how many guns I have on her now?"

"But you won't go on board, will you, my lord?"

"Twelve," he says, not answering me but pursuing his thoughts about his refitted ship. "She was always a mighty ship and now we're going to use her like a weapon, as Thomas says. He's quite right, she is like a floating castle. She has twelve port pieces, eight culverins and four cannon. She can stay far out at sea and bombard a land-based castle with guns as big as they have. She can shoot from one side and wheel around and shoot from the other while the first are reloading. Then she can grapple a ship and my soldiers can board them. I've put two fighting castles on her upper deck, fore and aft."

"But you won't sail in her with Sir Thomas?"

"I may." He is excited at the thought of a battle. "But I don't forget that I have to keep myself safe, my dear. I am the father of the nation, I don't forget it. And I would not leave you alone."

I wonder if there is a way that I can ask which ship Thomas will command. The king looks at me kindly. "I know you will want to see that all your pretty things are packed. My steward shall tell yours when we will leave. We should have a good journey; the weather should be fine."

"I love going on progress in the summer," I say. "Shall we take Prince Edward with us?"

"No, no, he can stay at Ashridge," he says. "But we can call on him as we come back to London. I know you will like that."

"I always like to see him."

"He is studying well? You hear from his tutors?"

"He writes to me himself. We write to each other in Latin now for practice."

"Well enough," he says, but I know that he is at once jealous that his son loves me. "But you must not distract him from his studies, Kateryn. And he must not forget his true mother. She must live in his heart before anyone else. She is his guardian angel in heaven, as she was his guardian angel on earth."

"Whatever you think, my lord," I say, a little stiff at this snub.

"He is born to be king," he says. "As I was. He has to be disciplined, and well taught and strictly raised. As I was. My mother was dead in my twelfth year. I had no one writing loving letters to me."

"No," I say. "You must have missed her very much. To lose her, when you were so young."

His face compresses with self-pity. "I was heartbroken," he says huskily. "The loss of her broke my heart. No woman has ever loved me as she did. And she left me so young!"

"Tragic," I say softly.

There is a knock at the door and the grooms of the servery come in with a table groaning with food. They place it at the side of the bed and heap a plate for the king as he points to one dish after another.

"Eat!" he commands me, his mouth full. "I can't dine alone."

I take a small plate and let them serve me. I sit by the fireside on my chair and nibble on a few pieces of pastry. The king is served wine. I take a glass of small ale. I cannot believe that I will see Thomas Seymour within the week.

It is a long two hours before the king has finished with the food and he is sweating and breathing heavily by the time he has eaten several slices of pie, some meats, and half of a lemon pudding.

"Take it away, I am weary," he announces.

Quickly and efficiently they load the table and carry it out of the room.

"Come to bed," he says thickly. "I will sleep here with you."

He tips his head back and belches loudly. I go to my side of the bed and climb in. Before I have the covers spread over us he has let out a loud snore and is fast asleep.

I think I will be wakeful but I lie in the darkness and feel such joy as I think of Thomas. Perhaps he is in Portsmouth, perhaps sleeping on board his ship in his low-ceilinged wooden admiral's cabin, with the candles rocking gently on their gimbals on the walls. I will see him next week, I think. I may not speak to him, I must not look for him, but at least I will see him, and he will see me.

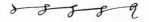

The dream is so like my waking life that I do not know I am dreaming. I am in my bed and the king is sleeping beside me, snoring, and there is a terrible smell, the smell of his rotting leg, in my bed, and in my room. I slip out of bed, careful not to wake him, and the smell is worse than ever. I think, I must get out of the room, I cannot breathe, I must find the apothecary and get some perfume, I must send the girls out to the garden to pick some herbs. I go as quietly as I can towards the door to the private galleries between his room and mine.

I open the little door and step out, but instead of the wooden floor and scattered rushes and the stone walls of the gallery I am at once on the narrow landing of a stone staircase, a circular staircase, perilously steep. I put one hand on the central column and start to climb upwards. I must get away from this terrible smell of death, but instead it is getting worse, as if there is a corpse or some rotting horror just around the curve of the stair above me.

I put a hand over my mouth and nose to shield me from the smell and then I give a little choke as I realize that it is my hand that smells. It is me that is rotting; and it is my own stink that I am trying to escape. I smell like a dead woman, left to rot. I pause on the stair as I think that all I can do is to fling myself down the stairs, headfirst down the stairs so that this decaying body can complete the task of dying and I am not locked in with death, twinned with death, mated with death, decay in my own body at my fingertips.

I am crying now, raging at the fate that has brought me to this, but as the tears run down my cheeks they are like dust. They are dry as sand when they run into my lips and they taste like dried blood. In my desperation and with all the courage I can find, I turn on the step and face down the steep stone stairs. Then I give one despairing scream as I dive downwards, down the stone staircase, headfirst.

"Hush, hush, you're safe!"

I think it is Thomas who has caught me up, and I cling to him, shuddering. I turn to his shoulder and press my face against his warm chest and throat. But it is the king holding me in his arms, and I recoil and cry out again for fear that I have said Thomas's name in my nightmare and now I am in real danger indeed.

"Hush, hush," he says. "Hush, my love. It was a dream. Nothing but a dream. You're safe now." He holds me gently against his fleshy comforting side, soft as a pillow.

"My God, what a dream! God help me, what a nightmare!"

"Nothing, it was nothing."

"I was so afraid. I dreamed I was dead."

"You are safe with me. You are safe with me, beloved."

"Did I talk in my sleep?" I whimper. I am so afraid that I said his name.

"No, you said no words, you just wept, poor girl. I woke you at once."

"It was so terrible!"

"Poor little love," Henry says tenderly, stroking my hair, my bare shoulder. "You are safe with me. Do you want something to eat?"

"No, no," I give a shaky laugh. "Nothing to eat. Nothing more to eat."

"You should have something, for comfort."

"No, no, really. I couldn't."

"You are awake now? You know yourself?"

"Yes, yes, I do."

"Was it a dream of foretelling?" he asks. "Did you dream of my ships?"

"No," I say firmly. Two of this man's wives were accused by him of witchcraft; I'm not going to claim any sort of second sight. "It was nothing, it meant nothing. Just a muddle of castle walls and feeling cold and afraid."

He lies back on the pillows. "Can you sleep now?"

"Yes, I can. Thank you for being so kind to me."

"I am your husband," he says with simple dignity. "Of course I guard your sleep and soothe your fears."

In a moment he is breathing heavily, his mouth lolling open. I put my head against his bulky shoulder and close my eyes. I know that my dream was the dream of Tryphine, the maid who was married to a man who killed his wives. I know it was the smell of dead wife on my own fingers.

SOUTHSEA CASTLE, PORTSMOUTH
HARBOUR, SUMMER 1545

KP

It is a most delightful day, like a painting of a summer day, the sun bright on the blue waters of the Solent, the brisk wind scuffing little white caps on the waves. We have climbed to the top of one of the defensive towers overlooking the harbor, and now that they have hauled the king up the stone stairs and he can see everything, he is delighted with the world, standing astride at the seawall, hands on his hips, as if he were an admiral on his own ship, the court around him abuzz with excitement and anxiety.

I cannot believe that everyone is joyous, as if we were about to watch a joust on a summer day, as if this were the legendary Field of the Cloth of Gold—a struggle between France and England to be the most glamorous, the most graceful, the most cultured and the most sporting. Surely everyone knows that it is nothing like that today? This is not playing at war but the hours before a real battle. There can be nothing to celebrate and everything to fear.

Looking behind me, over the open fields of Southsea Common, I see that though the court is putting a brave face on it, I am not the only one to be anxious. The yeomen of the guard are already prepared for the worst, their horses saddled and held on tight reins by their pages, ready for mounting and galloping away. The guardsmen are already in armor, with only their helmets to put on. Behind them, the great baggage train that always follows the royal court everywhere—petitioners, beggars, lawyers, thieves, and fools—is slowly dragging itself away—the baggage train always knows which side will win—and the people of Portsmouth are fleeing their own town, some of them walking under a burden of household goods, some riding, and some loading up carts. If the French defeat our fleet, they will sack Portsmouth and probably fire it as well. The king's court seem to be the only ones who expect triumph and are looking forward to a battle.

The many bells of the town churches are tolling as our ships get ready to sail out of the harbor, the hundreds of noisy peals scaring the gulls, who circle and cry over the sea. There are about eighty ships, the greatest fleet England has ever assembled, some on the far side loading crew and weapons, some ready to go. I can see them unfurling their sails to our right, deeper in the harbor, the rowing boats and the galleys busy about them, taking ropes and preparing to haul them out of port to the sea.

"The greatest navy ever mustered," the king declares to Anthony Browne at his side. "And ready to fight the French in the new way. It will be the greatest battle we have ever seen."

"Thank God we are here to see it!" replies Sir Anthony. "What a great chance. I have commissioned a picture to show our victory."

The painter, hurrying with his sketch book to record the sailing from the harbor, gives a low bow to the king and starts to outline the view before us, the tower where we are standing, the harbor to our right, the ships slowly emerging, the sea before us, the fluttering pennants, the cannon rolled out at the ready.

"I'm glad that my husband is not on board one of the ships," Catherine Brandon remarks quietly.

I look at her pale face and see a reflection of my own unease. This is not a masque, this is not one of the expensive spectacles that the court loves; this is going to be a genuine sea battle fought between our ships and the French in sight of land. I will see what Thomas faces. I will have to watch as his ship is bombarded.

"Do you know who is commanding which ship?" I ask her.

She shakes her head. "Some new admirals were named last night at dinner," she says. "The king has honored his friends with commands so that they can take part in the battle. My husband wasn't very happy at new men being put in command the night before they have to fight. But he is overall commander of land and sea, and, thank God, he stays on land."

"Why, are you afraid of the sea?"

"I am afraid of all deep water," she confesses. "I can't swim. But then nobody in armor can swim. Few sailors know how and none of the soldiers would be able to stay afloat in their heavy jackets."

I stop her with a small gesture. "Perhaps nobody will have to swim."

There is a ragged cheer from the quayside as the king's newly refitted ship *Mary Rose* spreads her beautiful square sails and throws out ropes to the galleys to drag her out to sea.

"Oh, there she goes. Who is her commander?"

"Tom Seymour, God bless him," Catherine says.

I nod and raise my hand to my forehead, as if to shield my eyes from the sunshine. I think, I can't bear to watch him sail out to battle, and chirrup like one of my songbirds, as meaningless and as stupid as they. "It's quite windy," I remark. "Is that good?"

"It's a benefit for us," Uncle Parr reassures me. He is standing with my ladies, his hands shading his eyes, staring out to sea. "They have fighting galleys that can get amongst our ships in flat calm. They can row wherever they like. But on a day like today, when we can cram on sail we can burst out of the harbor and bombard them. We can come down on them like the wind, with the wind behind us."

Everyone falls back as the king comes to stand beside me, his head high, gulping in the sea air. "It's certainly a beautiful sight," I remark as one by one his ships are dragged out of port, raising their sails and being set free, like flying doves, like seagulls out to sea. The court cheers as each ship, the *Peter*, and the *Henry Grace à Dieu*, and the ships we have stolen from the Scots, the *Salamander* and the *Unicorn*, go past our vantage point. Then suddenly, as if a cloud has passed over the sun, we fall silent.

"What is it?" I ask Henry.

For the first time he is not looking out to sea, his face bright; he is not striking a pose, hands on hips for the artist that is sketching him. He looks behind him, as if to see that his guard is ready to cover his retreat, and then he looks back to where the dark blue mass of the Isle of Wight looms on the horizon. Before the island, in the channel, the French fleet has suddenly silently appeared, sailing in, row upon row of them. If it were land, it would be a cavalry charge of huge coursers, ridden knee to knee, one row after another in a great bank of brute strength. But here there is no sound, and it is somehow more terrifying for this. The ships move easily through the water, their sails spread, all on the same tack, and there seem to be hundreds, thousands of them. I cannot see the sea, not between them nor beyond them. It is like a forest of sails on the move. They are like a wall of sail.

And before them, in their vanguard, is another fleet. These are galleys, each one moving with an aggressive thrust through the water, each one keeping time with the other, row after row leaping forward with each blow of the oars into the sea. Even from here, even from our brave pretty little turret on Southsea Common, I can see the dark mouth of the single cannon that is mounted in the prow of each low barge as it looks hungrily towards our ships, our few ships, our little ships, as they tumble out of the safety of harbor to defend our coast, and I know that on his flagship, the *Mary Rose*, Thomas Seymour will be beside the steersman, looking out and seeing that he is massively outnumbered.

"God help us," I whisper.

The king looks down at me, sees my white face, and pulls the hat off his thinning hair. He waves it in the air. "For God! For Harry! And for Saint George!" he bellows, and his court, and then the people all crowding around us, take up the cry so that they may even hear it over the sea: English sailors may even hear it as they look up and see death sailing towards them with thousands of sails spread wide.

The king is thrilled by the challenge. "We're outnumbered but

I think they are outgunned," he shouts. He takes Charles Brandon by the shoulder. "Don't you think so, Charles? I think so! Don't you think so?"

"They're outgunned," Charles says certainly. "But they're double our number."

"You've got Portsmouth fortified," the king confirms.

"I've got cannon on every point, including here," Charles says grimly. "If they come any closer, you can fire the gun yourself."

"They shan't come closer," the king declares. "I won't have them in English waters. I forbid them to come anywhere near English land. I am the king! Are they going to challenge me on my own land? In my own castle? I am afraid of nothing. I am always completely fearless."

I see that Charles Brandon does not look at me, as if it is better not to note the king's vainglorious boast. I look around for Doctor Butts and I find his pale face at the back of the court. I nod to him and he draws closer.

"His Majesty is overexcited," I observe.

He watches as Henry shouts for a page to help him limp painfully from one side of the tower to the other, as he leans out over the walls and claps a gunner on the back. He is acting like a man taking the battle to the heart of a weak enemy, certain of victory. He is shouting threats as if they can hear him, as if he can make any difference. He is acting as if his fury and his rage against the French can prevail against the silent approach of their thousands of ships and the steady beat—which now we can hear—of the drums from their galleys, keeping the time of the inexorable oars.

"There is no containing him now," Doctor Butts says.

I know that we are about to see something terrible. The French fleet comes on and onward, and the little English ships bob out of harbor and cannot get themselves into any formation, the harbor barges fruitlessly pulling them forward, trying to catch the wind. A few ships spread their sails and move swiftly away from shore, and some of them try to come about to get their guns trained on the low French galleys. Mercilessly the French come on, the galleys before, the great ships behind.

"Now you'll see it! Now you'll see something," the king predicts. He hobbles down to the outermost point on the castle wall, turns his head, and shouts back to me, but his words are drowned in the roar of cannon as the first English ships come within range of the French guns.

The English cannon respond. We can see the black squares open up on the sides of the ships as the gun doors open and the cannon are rolled out, then a puff of smoke as each cannon fires and rebounds into the ship for reloading.

"*Mary Rose!*" Henry yells, like a boy naming his favorite champion in a joust. "*Henry Grace à Dieu!*"

I can see the *Mary Rose* getting ready to engage, her gun doors wide open. It seems like there are hundreds of them, stacked in rows from her upper deck to the waterline. I can see men on the upper deck: the master of the ship and the boatswain at the wheel, and a figure—I suppose it is Thomas; I suppose that small still figure in the bold red cape is the man I adore—standing behind them.

"God keep him. Oh, God keep him," is all I whisper.

I can see the two fighting castles at prow and stern, built high, crowded with men. The sun is shining on their helmets and I see them raise their pikes as they wait for their chance to grapple and board the enemy ships. Thomas will lead them when the charge comes. He will have to jump from one ship to another and bellow for them to follow him. Below the fighting castles, over the middle of the open deck, there are nets stretched from side to side. They are the boarding nets, so that no one can jump on board in a rival attack, and take our precious ship. I can see the ranked soldiers underneath the nets. When they get close enough to a French ship, they will be released and swarm out.

"Fire!" Henry shouts, as if they can hear him from the castle. "Fire! Fire! I command it!"

A barge comes towards the beautiful wallowing English ship, the oars like the legs of an insect crawling through the water. A cloud of black smoke suddenly spits from the prow. Now we can smell the stink of gunpowder, drifting over the water.

The cannon of the *Mary Rose* roll forward to every open gun port so that she is bristling with weapons, all of them moving as one. She turns and fires from her left-hand guns and there is a simultaneous roar. It is beautifully done, and powerful as a move in a chess game. At once, we see one of the galleys struggling in the water, going down. The king's great plan, Thomas's strategy, is showing its power to the astounded enemy. Ship is engaging with ship, and the soldiers have nothing to do yet but cheer in their fighting castles and raise their swords in threat. The great ship is coming about, turning in the water, so that she can fire her starboard guns while the port guns reload.

A sudden gust makes all the standards snap with a noise like tearing silk. "Fire! Come about and fire!" Henry shouts, but the wind is too loud for anyone to hear him. I hold my hat and Anne Seymour loses her cap, which goes sailing from the walls of the castle and out to sea.

Someone laughs at her mishap and it is then that we realize something is going wrong. The *Mary Rose* was reefing her sails and turning against the wind to get her starboard guns to bear on the French just as the gust of wind caught her. She heels over in the sea, dangerously low, her sails dipping towards the waves, her beautiful square sails no longer proudly upright above her arched decks, but now at an angle, odd and ugly.

"What are you doing?" the king bellows, as if anyone can answer him. "What the hell are you doing?"

She is like a horse that has taken a curve too tight. You can see a horse with his legs going from under him, running harder and faster, and yet everything happens very slowly, but with a terrible inexorability.

"Right her!" Henry howls like a dog, and now everyone is beside him at the castle wall, leaning out as if they will ever hear us shouting instructions. Someone is screaming "No! No! No!" as the beautiful proud ship, her standards still rippling, goes farther and farther over on her side and then we see her slowly lie on her side like a fallen bird, half in, half out of the scudding waves.

We can't hear them scream. The sailors are trapped belowdecks as the water rushes in through the open gun ports, and they cannot climb up the narrow ladders in the waist of the ship. They drown in their own coffin as she takes them gently, softly down. We can hear the men on the upper deck. They are clinging to the boarding nets, which are now entrapping them, trying to slash them away. Some of the fighting men jump down from the ship's turrets and stab with their pikes at the ropes or hack with their swords at the thick net. But they can't get the men free, can't open the nets. Our soldiers and sailors die like netted mackerel, struggling to breathe against the mesh.

The free men on top tumble off the castles like so many toy soldiers, like the little lead men that Edward plays with, and their leather jackets drag them down in moments. Those who have helmets feel them fill with cold sea water before they can untie the straps. Thick boots drag their owners down, heavy plate armor strapped on knee and breast plunges men in a rush to the bottom. I can hear a voice crying: "No, no, no."

It feels like a long hour of agony, but perhaps it is only minutes. It feels timeless. The side of the ship seems to rest on the water like a sleepy bird, moving with the sea as a handful of men, no more, fling themselves from the rigging and disappear into the smoke-drenched waves. The roar of the cannon goes on, the battle itself goes on. Nobody but us has frozen in horror to watch as the keel rolls a little more to the sky, as the sails fill with water, not wind, and billow and swell in their strange submerged beauty, and then drag the ship down to the green depths.

I can hear someone weeping: "No, no, no."

COWDRAY HOUSE, MIDHURST, SUSSEX, SUMMER 1545

KP

The battle is inconclusive, they tell me, when the smoke finally clears and the fleets limp their different ways: the French back to France, the English ships into port. They report to the king that England was triumphant. We sent out a few tiny ships against a great French armada, and the French soldiers that landed on the coast of Sussex and the Isle of Wight burned a few barns but were driven off by the farmhands.

"Englishmen," Sir Anthony Denny whispers encouragingly to the king. "For God and for Harry!"

But the king is not stirred by the battle cry of an earlier, greater king. He is shocked, his great carcass beached in his bed like his great ship is beached on the seabed, underwater in the Solent. They come almost hourly to tell him that it is not as bad as it seems. They say that they will raise the *Mary Rose*, that it will be no more than a matter of days before they have hauled her to the surface and pumped out the water. But after a while they stop boasting that she can be reclaimed from the sea, and the beautiful ship and her sailors, and the fighting men—four hundred of them, five hundred, nobody knows how many were enlisted—will be left to the chantry of the tides and the singing of the sea.

As soon as the king can ride we go by stages to Cowdray House at Midhurst, hoping that one of the king's most boastful court-iers, Sir Anthony Browne, can raise his spirits and comfort him. The king sits on his horse in silence, looking around him, look-ing everywhere at green fields, strips of crops, flocks of sheep, herds of cows, as if he can see nothing but the heeling over of his proud ship and the terrible gurgle in the water as she sailed downward to drown. I am beside him and I know that my face is frozen like a stone angel on a tomb. The country that we ride through is quiet, the people resentful. They know that the French nearly landed, that the royal fleet cannot defend them. This is a countryside of inlets and tidal rivers, terribly exposed to an inva-sion. They are afraid that the French will refit and come again, and there are many people who whisper that if the French came and restored the abbeys and the churches and the holy shrines, then they would be a blessing to England.

I do not ask about Thomas Seymour. I do not dare to say his name. I think if I say so much as "Thomas," that I will cry out, and if I start, I will never be able to stop. I think there is a sea of tears in me as deep as the tides that sigh through the rigging of his ship.

"The king has granted Lady Carew a great pension," Nan says quietly to me as she is brushing my hair before putting on my gold net and my hood.

"Lady Carew?" I ask indifferently.

"Her husband went down on the ship," she says. Nobody says *"Mary Rose"* anymore. It is as if she is a ghost, another lost queen, a nameless woman missing from Henry's court.

"Poor lady," I say.

"The king made him vice admiral the very night before, and gave him the command," she says. "He replaced Thomas

Seymour, who was furious at the slight. He always had the luck of the devil, did Tom. He had to make another ship his flagship and he came through unscathed."

She looks up from the work of twisting my hair into ringlets and tucking them into the net and sees my face in the mirror. "What's the matter?" she asks. "Are you ill?"

I put my hand to my stomacher. I can feel my heart pound through the tightly laced silk. "I am sick," I whisper. "Nan, I am terribly sick. Let me lie down for a moment."

They all crowd round me and I close my eyes to blot out the sight of the anxious avid faces. Then someone lifts me at my shoulders and two of them bear up my feet and I feel them put me onto my bed. Someone cuts my laces and loosens my stomacher so I can breathe more easily. Nan slips off my silk slippers and chafes my icy feet.

Someone holds a cup of warm ale to my lips and I sip, and then lean back on the pillows and open my eyes.

"You don't feel hot," one of the ladies volunteers nervously. They are all terrified of the Sweat. It can kill a man in four hours, and there is no easy way to tell if he will die. He complains of heat at dinner and he sweats to death by nightfall. It is a Tudor plague; it came in with this king's father.

"I am sick in my belly," I say. "Something I ate."

Two of them exchange secret smiles. "Oh—do you feel sick in the mornings?" Anne Seymour says, suggestively, hopefully.

I shake my head. I don't want this sort of rumor starting. Even now, as I am struggling with the news that Thomas is alive, I have to watch what I say, what they say, what anyone says about me. "No," I insist, "and no one is to say such a thing. It is not that, and the king would be much displeased if you gossiped about me."

"I was just hoping for the best for you," Anne defends herself.

I close my eyes. "I need to sleep" is all I say.

I hear Nan chivy everyone from my room and then the shutting of my bedroom door and the rustle of her dress as she sits beside my bed. Without opening my eyes I reach out my hand and she takes it in her comforting grasp.

"Such a terrible day," I say. "I can't stop seeing it."

"I know," she says. "Try to sleep."

GREENWICH PALACE, SUMMER 1545

KP

We make our way back to London in slow stages. The journey, which set out as a summer's jaunt to see the fleet in triumph, crawls home with a king stunned by disappointment, through a fearful countryside. The fields of dark gold wheat and the springing green of the second growth in the hayfields bring us no pleasure as we look at the prosperous manor houses and the little villages and think they are impossible to defend.

We go to Greenwich, where the waves that slap at the stone pier before the palace remind us of the unforgiving waters of the Solent and the sinking of the king's pride to its dark depths. Thomas stays at his post in Portsmouth, repairing and rebuilding the houses that were fired by the invading French, overseeing the refitting of the ships that were damaged in battle, sending down swimmers to see if they can salvage anything from the warship as she settles into her last berth. He cannot come to court; I don't hope to see him. He writes privately to the king and Henry shows no one the letter.

People think that the king is ill again, that perhaps his leg has opened up or the fever that shakes him four times a year has come back. But I know what is wrong: he is sick to his heart. He has seen a defeat, an undeniable defeat, and he cannot bear it.

This is a man so sharp with pride that he cannot hear contradiction. This is a man who will play both sides at once to make sure that he wins. This is a man who from a boy has never been refused. And, in addition to all of this—here is a man who cannot see himself as anything but perfect. He has to be the very best. King Francis of France was his only rival; but now Francis and all of Europe are laughing at the English navy, which was supposed to be so mighty, and at our famous flagship, which sank as soon as she set sail. They are saying that the king piled so many guns on her that she was as fat and as clumsy as he is.

"It wasn't that," he says to me shortly. "Don't think that."

"No, of course," I say.

"Of course it was not."

He is like an animal in a trap, twisting and turning against his own pain. He grieves more for his hurt pride than for the drowned men. He has to rescue his self-regard. Nothing is more important than that; no one is more important than that. The ship can sink into the silt of the Solent as long as the king's pride can be salvaged.

"There was nothing wrong with the ship," he says another night. "It was the fools of the gunners. They left the gun ports open after firing."

"Oh, was that what happened?"

"Probably," he says. "I should have left Thomas Seymour in command. I am glad that fool Carew paid with his life."

I swallow a protest against this harsh judgment. "God save his soul," I say, thinking of his widow who saw her husband drown.

"God forgive him," Henry says heavily. "For I never will."

The king talks to me every night about his ship. He cannot sleep without persuading me that it was the fault of others, fools or villains. He can do no other work. Most of the Privy Council go back to Westminster ahead of us, and Charles Brandon, Henry's old friend, asks permission to go quietly home with his wife, Catherine.

"He should have warned me," Henry says. "Of all the people in the world Charles should have warned me."

"How could he know?" I ask.

"He should never have let her sail if she was overloaded with men," Henry bursts out in sudden anger, his face blazing, a vein in his temple bulging like a thick worm under his skin. "Why would he not know that she was overloaded? He must have been careless. I shall call him back to court to explain himself. He was commander on land and sea: he has to take responsibility. It was not my plans that were at fault, it was his failure to execute them. I have forgiven him everything, all my life, but I cannot forgive him this."

But before the messenger summoning Charles back has even left the palace, we hear from the Brandon household that he is ill, and then a horseman thunders up the London road from Guildford and says that he is dead. The king's greatest and longest-surviving friend is dead.

It is the last blow of a terrible summer. The king is inconsolable. He locks himself into his room and refuses all service. He even refuses to eat. "Is he sick?" I ask Doctor Butts when they tell me that the monstrous dinner has been sent back.

He shakes his head. "Not in his body, God keep him. But this is a great loss to him. Charles Brandon is the last of his old friends, the only friend from his childhood. It is like losing a brother."

That night, even though my bedroom is three rooms away from the king's chamber, I hear a terrible noise. It is a scream like a vixen makes at night, a howl so unearthly that I forget that I despise empty ritual, and I cross myself, and kiss my thumbnail and say, "God bless and keep me!" There is another and another, and I jump out of my bed, snap, "Stay there!" to my companion, and run into my empty presence chamber, through the king's presence chamber, his privy chamber, his inner chamber, to his bedroom door, where the guard stands impassive. But behind the door I can hear heartbroken sobbing.

I hesitate. I don't know whether to go forward or back. I don't even know if I should tell the guard to knock for me, or try the door to see if it is locked from the inside. I don't know if it is my duty to go to him and remind him that Charles Brandon will have died in his faith and will be waiting in purgatory, certain of his ascent to heaven on the uplifting vapor of expensive Masses, or whether I should leave the king to his monstrous grief. He is sobbing like a heartbroken child, like an orphan. The sound of it is terrible.

I step forward and I try the handle. The guard, his face completely blank as if his master is not blubbering only yards away, steps to one side. The handle turns but the door does not yield. He has locked himself in. He wants to be alone in the churning ocean of his grief. I don't know what I should do and, judging by the blank face of the yeoman of the guard, he does not know either.

I go back to my own room, close the door, and pull the covers over my head, but nothing can muffle the loud wailing. The king screams out his heartbreak all night long, and none of us, not in his rooms or mine, can sleep for his grief.

In the morning I dress in a dark gown and go to chapel. I am going to pray for the soul of Charles Brandon and for wisdom to help my husband, who has broken under this last loss. I take my place on the queen's side and look across to the royal throne. To my surprise Henry is already there, in his usual place, signing papers for business, looking over petitions. Only his strained red-rimmed eyes betray his emotional vigil. Indeed, of the two of us, I show more signs of sleeplessness, with heavy eyes and a pale face. It is as if he burned away all his grief and fear in one night. As we finish the prayers and say "Amen" he beckons to me. I go round to his side with my ladies following and we leave the chapel together, walking across the courtyard towards the main hall, my hand tucked under his arm, as he leans heavily on a yeoman of the guard on his other side.

"I will give him a hero's burial," he says. "And I shall pay for it all."

I cannot hide my surprise at his calmness, but he takes it as delight in his generosity.

"I will," he repeats proudly. "And little Catherine Brandon need not fear for their sons' inheritance. I shall leave them both in her keeping. I will not take them as my wards. They can inherit their father's estate entire. I will even let her manage it till they are men. I will take nothing from them."

He is cheered by his own munificence. "She will be glad," he announces. "She will be thrilled. She can come to me and thank me personally as soon as she returns to court."

"She'll be in mourning," I point out. "She may not want to serve in my rooms anymore. She may not want to come to court. Her loss . . ."

He shakes his head. "Of course she will come," he says certainly. "She would never leave me. She has lived in my keeping since she was a girl."

I say nothing in reply to this. I can hardly tell the king that a widow might prefer to spend the very first days of her widowhood in prayer, rather than entertaining him. Usually, a widow keeps to her house for the first three months, and Catherine will want to be with her fatherless boys. But then I realize: He will not know this. Nobody told him to wait before summoning me on the death of my husband. He would not imagine that anyone might not want to be at court. He has never lived anywhere but court; he has no idea of a private life or tender feelings that are not watched by the world. Within days of the death of my husband, he commanded me to court to play cards with him and flirt with him. Only I can stop him putting this burden on Catherine.

"Perhaps she would rather stay at her home, at Guildford Palace."

"No, she would not."

Nan comes to me one evening, long after dinner, when the court is closed down for the night and I am ready for bed. She nods to my lady-in-waiting, dismissing her from my bedroom, and takes a seat by the fireside.

"I see you have come for a visit," I say dryly, taking the seat opposite her. "D'you want a glass of wine?"

She gets up and pours us both a glass. We pause for a moment to savor the scent and taste of the deep red Portuguese wine and the light clarity of the Venetian glasses. Each glass, each perfectly blown glass, is worth a hundred pounds.

"What would Mother say?" Nan asks with a little smile.

"*Don't take it for granted.*" I can quote her at once. "*Don't let down your guard. Never forget your family.* And, more than anything else: *How is your brother? How is William? Does William have glasses as fine as this? Can't we get some for him?*" We both laugh.

"She always thought that he would be the making of the family," Nan says, sipping her wine. "She didn't disregard us, you know. It's just that she put all her hopes on William. It's natural to look to the son and heir."

"I know. I don't blame her. She didn't know that William's wife would betray him and our name, cost us so much, and then have to be set aside."

"She didn't foresee that," Nan agrees. "Nor this."

"No." I shake my head with a smile. "Who'd have dreamed it?"

"Your rise to greatness." Nan raises her glass in a toast. "But it comes with dangers."

Nobody knows more about the dangers for a queen than Nan. She has served every one. She has given evidence on oath against three. Sometimes she has even told the truth.

"Not for me," I say confidently. "I'm not like the others. I don't have an enemy in the world. I'm famously generous, I've helped anyone who asked me. I have done nothing but good for the royal children. The king loves me, he made me Regent General and an editor for the English liturgy. He puts me at the heart of the court, of everything he cares about: his children, his country, and his church."

"Stephen Gardiner is no friend of yours," she warns. "And neither are any of his affinity. They would throw you down from the throne and out of the royal rooms at the first moment they could."

"They wouldn't. They might disagree with me; but this is a matter of debate, not enmity."

"Kateryn, every queen has enemies. You have to face it."

"The king himself supports the cause of reform!" I exclaim irritably. "He listens to Thomas Cranmer more than to Stephen Gardiner."

"And they blame you for that! They planned for him to have a papist wife and they thought he had married one. They thought you were for the old church; they thought that you shared Latimer's convictions. That's why they welcomed you so warmly. They were never your friends! And now that they think you have turned against them, they won't be your friends any longer."

"Nan, this is madness. They may disagree with me but they wouldn't try to drag me down in the eyes of the king. They won't falsely accuse me of God-knows-what because we don't agree about the serving of the Mass. We differ; but they are not my enemies. Stephen Gardiner is an ordained bishop, called by God, a holy man. He is not going to seek my destruction because I differ from him on a point of theology."

"They went against Anne Boleyn because she was for the cause of reform."

"Wasn't that Cromwell?" I ask stubbornly.

"It doesn't matter which advisor it is, what matters is if the king is listening to him."

"The king loves me," I say finally. "He loves only me. He would not listen to a word against me."

"So you say." Nan puts out her foot and pushes a log farther into the fire. A plume of sparks flies up, she looks awkward.

"What is it?"

"I have to tell you that they're proposing another wife."

I almost laugh. "This is ridiculous. Is this what you came to tell me? It's nothing but gossip."

"No, it isn't. They are proposing another wife more amenable to returning the church to Rome."

"Who?" I scoff.

"Catherine Brandon."

"Now I know that you are mistaken," I say. "She is more of a reformer than I am. She named her dog after Bishop Gardiner. She's openly rude to him."

"They think she will join them if they offer her the throne. And they believe that the king likes her."

I look at my sister. Her face is turned away from me, fixed on the embers of the fire. She fidgets, putting on dry wood.

"Is this what you came in to tell me? Did you come so late tonight to warn me that the king is thinking of another wife? That I must defend myself?"

"Yes," she says, still not meeting my eyes. "I am afraid so, yes."

The fire crackles in the silence. "Catherine would never betray me. You're wrong to say such a thing. She's my friend. We study together, we think alike. It's really vile, Nan, it's black babbling to say such a thing."

"It's the crown of England. Most people would do anything for it."

"The king loves me. He doesn't want another wife."

"All I am saying is that the king is sentimental over her, he's always liked her, and now she is free to marry, and they will be pushing her forward."

"She would never take my place!"

"She would have no choice," Nan says quietly. "Just as you had no choice. And anyway, some people say that he has been her lover for years. They say that Charles and he shared her. Charles never refused the king anything. Perhaps when he got a beauti-ful young wife, young enough to be his daughter, the king had her too."

I get to my feet and go the window. I want to throw open the shutters and let the night air into the room as if the place stinks like the king's bedroom of corruption and disappointment.

"This is the vilest gossip," I say quietly. "I should not have to hear it."

"It is vile. But it is widely repeated. And so you do have to hear it."

"So what now?" I say bitterly. "Nan, do you always have to be so ill tongued? Must you always breathe sorrows in my ear? Are you telling me that he would put me aside for Catherine Bran-don? Shall he have a seventh wife? What about another after her? Yes, he likes her, he likes Mary Howard, he likes Anne Seymour! But he loves me, he favors me above all others, more than any previous wife. And he has married me! That means everything. Can't you see that?"

"I am saying that we have to keep you safe. There must be nothing that anyone can say against you. No hint against your reputation, no suggestion of disagreement between you and the king, nothing that could make him turn against you. Not even for a moment."

"Because it only takes a moment?"

"It only takes a moment for him to sign a warrant," she says. "And then it is all over for all of us."

Catherine Brandon comes back to court as commanded, and she does not wear mourning. She comes first to my rooms and curtseys before me, and before all my ladies I give her my condolences for her loss and welcome her back to my service. She takes her seat among them and looks at the translation that we are working on. We are studying the Gospel of Luke in the Latin and trying to find the purest, clearest words in English to express the beauty of the original. Catherine joins in as if she is here by choice, as if she does not want to be at her own home, with her sons.

At the end of the morning when we put away our books to go out riding I beckon her to come with me as I change into my riding dress.

"I am surprised that you came back to court so soon," I say.

"I was commanded," she says shortly.

"Weren't you secluded, and in mourning?"

"Of course."

I rise from my seat before the silvered looking glass and I take her hands. "Catherine, I have been your friend since I first came to court. If you don't want to be here, if you want to go home, I will do my best for you."

She gives me a little sad smile. "I have to be here," she says. "I have no choice. But I thank Your Majesty for your kindness."

"Do you miss your husband?" I ask curiously.

"Of course," she says. "He was like a father to me."

"I think the king misses him."

"He must do. They were always together. But I don't expect him to show it."

"Why not? Why should the king not show his grief for the loss of his friend?"

She looks at me as if I am asking her a question to which everyone must know the answer. "Because the king cannot bear grief," she says simply. "He cannot tolerate it. It makes him angry. He will never forgive Charles for leaving him. If I want to stay in favor, if I want my sons to have their inheritance, I will have to conceal the fact that Charles has deserted him. I cannot show him my grief as it reminds him of his own."

"But he died!" I say impatiently to the man's widow. "He didn't leave the king on purpose, he just died!"

She gives me a slow sad smile. "I suppose if you are King of England, you think that everyone's life is dedicated to you. And those who die have let you down."

I don't want to hear Nan's bleak warnings, I prefer to see the gloze of Catherine's false smile as the court is at peace among itself with no quarrels or dogfights, and God's goodness to England shines out in the sunshine and the golden leaves of the trees in the meadows that run beside the river. The country is at peace, the news from France is that they plan nothing against us, the battle season is coming to a close and Thomas has survived another year. It is a blissful end of summer. Every day starts bright and every evening ends in a warm glow. The walls of the palace are golden in the sunset reflected in the river. Henry enjoys a return to good health. His servers haul him onto his horse every morning and we hunt every day, easy runs, through the water meadows alongside the river, and it is like being married to a man of my own age when his huge hunter outpaces mine and he goes past, yelling like a boy.

The wound on his leg is bound tight, and he can manage a limping walk without support, needing help only up and down the stairs that lead from the great hall to his rooms, where I visit him every other night.

"We are happy," he tells me, as if it were an official announcement, as I take my seat on the other side of the fireside from his strengthened throne and his new footstool. Surprised by his formality, I giggle.

"When you have been as troubled as I by unhappiness, you too will take note of a good day, a good season," he says. "I swear to you, my sweetheart, that I have never loved a wife more than I love you, and never known contentment as I do now."

So much for your dark warnings, Nan, I think. "Lord husband, I am glad," I say, and I mean it. "If I can please you, then I am the happiest woman in England. But I have heard some rumors."

"Of what?" he demands as his sandy brows twitch together.

"Some say that you might want a new queen," I say, taking the risk of speaking Nan's warning out loud.

He chuckles and waves a dismissive hand. "There will always be rumors," he says. "While men have ambitious daughters, there will always be rumors."

"I am glad they mean nothing."

"Of course they mean nothing," he says. "Nothing but people talking about their betters, and plain women envying your beauty."

"Then I am happy," I tell him.

"And the children are well and thriving," he says, continuing to list his blessings. "And the country is at peace, though all but bankrupt. And for once I have some quiet in my court for my rival bishops have taken the summer off from their wrangling."

"God smiles on the righteous," I say.

"I have seen your translations," he says in the same tone of smug congratulation. "I was pleased, Kate. You have done well to study, anyone can see how I have influenced your learning and your spiritual growth."

I am sick with sudden fear. "My translations?" I repeat.

"Your prayers," he says. "That's right, it is dutiful and pleasing to have a wife who spends her time on prayers."

"Your Majesty has honored me with your attention." I say feebly.

"I glanced at them," he says. "And I asked Cranmer what he thought. And he praised them. For a woman they are scholarly work. He accused me of helping you but I said—No, no, they are all her own. So you should put your name on the cover, Kate. We should credit them to a royal author. What other king in Christendom has a scholarly wife? Francis of France has a queen who is neither wife nor scholar!"

"I would only put my name on the page as a sign of my gratitude to you," I say carefully.

"You do that," he says, comfortably "I am a lucky man. I have only two things that trouble me, and neither of them overmuch." He eases himself back in his chair, and I pass the sweet cakes and wine closer to his hand.

"What are they?"

"Boulogne," he says heavily. "After all our courage in taking it, the council want me to return it to the French. I never will. I sent Henry Howard out there in place of his father just so that he will persuade everyone that we can keep it."

"And does he convince them?"

"Oh, he swears he will never leave it, says he is dishonored by the very suggestion." Henry chuckles. "And his father whispers to me that he is a boy who should come home and live at his father's say-so. I love it when a father and son disagree. It makes my life so much easier if they are dancing to different tunes, but both of them played by me."

I try to smile. "But how do you know which to believe?"

He taps the side of his nose with his hand to indicate his cunning. "I don't know. That's the secret. I listen to one, I listen to the other, I encourage each to think he has my ear. I weigh them as they bicker, and I choose."

"But it puts father against son," I point out. "And sets your chief commander in France against your Privy Council, and makes a deep division in the country."

"All the better, for then they cannot conspire against me. Anyway, I cannot return Boulogne to the French, whatever the Privy Council wants, for Charles of Spain insists that I keep it, insists that we don't make peace with France. I have to play Spain and France like two dogs in a fight as well. I have to match them against each other like a dog master."

"And your other worry?" I ask gently.

"God be praised, it's just a little worry. It's nothing. Just a plague at Portsmouth."

"Plague?

"Ripping through my navy, God help them. Of course they will take it hard. The sailors sleep on the ships or in the worst of lodgings in that poor little town, the captains and the bo'suns little better. They're all crammed on top of one another and the marshes are pestilential. The soldiers in my new castles will die like flies when it goes through them."

"But your admirals must be safe?"

"No, for I insist they stay with the fleet," he says, as if the life of Thomas Seymour is an afterthought. "They have to take their chances."

"Can't they go to their homes while the plague is in Portsmouth?" I suggest. "It must make sense that the captains and commanders are not lost to the plague. You will need them in battle. You must want to keep them safe."

"God will watch over those who serve me," he says comfortably. "God would not raise his hand against me and mine. I am His chosen king, Kateryn. Never forget it."

He sends me away at midnight—he wants to be alone—but instead of going to my bed I go to the beautiful chapel, kneel before the altar, and whisper to myself: "Thomas, Thomas, God bless you, God keep you, my love, my only love. God keep you from the sea, God keep you from the plague, God keep you from sin and sorrow and send you safe home. I don't even pray that you come home to me. I love you so dearly that I would have you safe, anywhere."

The king's leg swells up again and the wound opens up farther. He cannot bear to put weight on it at all and instead has wheels put under his strengthened chair and has himself wheeled around the palace. Unusually, his spirits stay high and he continues to be the dog master, as he boasted to me. He is going to send Stephen Gardiner to meet the emperor at Bruges to negotiate a treaty with the French that will bring an end to war between the three great kings of Europe; but at the same time, and in complete contradiction, he invites delegates from the German Lutheran princes to mediate between England and France for a secret peace to betray the Spanish emperor. At this rate, we will end up with two peace treaties, one brokered by papists and one brokered by Lutherans, and unable to sign either.

"No, this is a great chance for our faith," Catherine Brandon disagrees, as we sit down behind my long table, assemble our pens and papers, and prepare to listen to the sermon of the day. "If the Lutheran lords from Saxony can bring peace to Christendom, then the reformed faith will be seen as the moral leader, as a light to the world. And they will work for the king, as they want him to save them from the emperor. That papist monster is calling for a crusade against them, his own people, for nothing more than their religion—God save and keep them."

"But Bishop Gardiner will beat the Lutheran lords to it," I predict. "He'll bring home a peace with France before they can."

"Not him!" she says disdainfully. "He's a spent force. The king doesn't listen to him anymore. He's sending him on a fool's errand to Bruges. He wants Gardiner out of the way so that he can talk freely to the Germans. He told me so himself."

"Oh, did he?" I say levelly, and Nan, coming in, notes the edge in my voice and glances across at me.

"Don't think that I have said anything to betray us," Catherine says quickly. "I would never reveal what we study and what we read. But I swear that the king knows, and that he sympathizes. He speaks of your learning with such praise, Your Majesty."

"It was the king who gave the English their Bible," I agree. "That's what the Lutherans want."

"And it was Stephen Gardiner who took it away again. And now the king is meeting with Lutherans and Stephen Gardiner is far away. He can stay away from court forever, for all I care. While he is gone, and while the king supports Henry Howard's captaincy of Boulogne against his father the duke, our greatest enemies are ignored and we grow stronger every day."

"Well, God be praised," Nan says. "Just think if this country were to come to a true faith based on the Bible, not a hodgepodge of superstition based on spells and images and chants."

"Indulgences," Catherine says. She almost shudders with disdain. "That's what I hate most. D'you know that the day after my lord died some damned priest came to me and said that for fifty nobles he could guarantee Charles's ascent to heaven and would show me a sign that it was so?"

"What sign?" I ask curiously.

Catherine shrugs: "Who knows? I didn't even ask. I am sure he could have given me anything that I would wish: a bleeding statue saved from some wrecked abbey? A portrait of the Madonna that spurts milk? It is such an insult to suggest that a man's soul should be saved by half a dozen vile old men bawling out a psalm. How can anyone ever have believed it? How can anyone suggest it now that they can read the Bible and know that we get to heaven through faith alone?"

There is a tap on the door, the guards swing it open, and in walks Anne Askew, as trim and as pretty as if she had just come from the seamstress. She steps in, a gleeful little smile on her face, and dips a deep curtsey to me.

"God bless us!" Nan exclaims and, forgetting herself completely, crosses herself as if she were seeing a ghost.

"You're a welcome stranger!" I say. "It's a long time since we saw you! I was glad to know you were safe, that Bishop Bonner had released you, but we heard he sent you home. I didn't think to see you again at court."

"Oh, yes, I was sent home to my husband," she says, quite matter-of-fact. "And I thank Your Majesty for letting it be known that I am under your protection. You saved me from more questioning, and a trial, I know. They did send me home to my husband, I was paroled into his keeping, but I have left him again and here I am."

I smile at the boldness of the young woman. "Mistress Anne, you make it sound easy."

"As easy as sin," she says cheerfully. "But it is not sin, I promise you. My husband knows nothing of me, nor of my faith. I am as strange to him as a deer in the sheep pen. There is no way that we could marry in the sight of God and no way that such vows could be binding. He thinks as I do, though he has not the courage to say it to the bishop. He does not want me in his home, any more than I can tolerate being there. We cannot be yoked together—a deer and a sheep."

Nan gets to her feet, alert as a yeoman of the guard. "But should you be here?" she asks. "You cannot bring heresy to the queen's rooms. You cannot come here if you have been ordered to stay with your husband, whether he is a sheep and you a deer or both of you a pair of fools."

Anne puts out her hand to halt Nan's anxious torrent of words. "I would never bring danger to Her Majesty's door," she says calmly. "I know who I have to thank for my release. I owe you a debt for life," she adds with a little curtsey to me. Then she turns back to Nan. "They were satisfied with my answers. They questioned me over and over but I did not say a word that was not in the Bible and they had no handle to hold me, nor rope to hang me."

Nan hides an involuntary shudder at the mention of the hangman and glances towards me. "Bishop Bonner has no complaint against you?" she repeats incredulously.

Anne lets out a ringing, confident laugh. "That's a man who would always be complaining about something. But there was nothing he could fix on me. The Lord Mayor asked me did I think the Host was holy, and I did not answer, because I know that it is illegal to speak of the bread of the Mass. He asked me if a mouse ate the Host would the mouse be holy? I just said, 'Alack, poor mouse.' That was the best of his questions: trying to trap me with a holy mouse!"

Despite myself I cannot help but laugh, and Catherine Brandon catches my eye and she giggles.

"Anyway, thank God that they released you, and obeyed the queen," Catherine says, recovering. "We are winning the argument, almost everyone is persuaded by the queen's thinking. The king listens to her, and the whole court thinks as we do."

"And the queen has translated a book of prayers that have come out under her own name," Nan says proudly.

Anne turns her brown gaze to me. "Your Majesty, this is to use your education and your position for the good of all true believers, and especially for the good of women. To be a woman and to write! To be a woman and to publish!"

"She is the first," Nan boasts. "The first woman to publish in England, the very first woman to publish in the English language, the first to be named on the title page."

"Hush," I say. "There are many scholars like me, and many better read. There have been women writers before me. But I am blessed with a husband who allows me to study and write, and we are all blessed with a king who allows the prayers of the church to be understood by his people."

"Thank God for him," Anne Askew says fervently. "Do you think he will allow the Bible back into the churches again for everyone to read?"

"I am certain of it," I say. "For since he has commissioned a translation of the Mass, he is bound to want the Bible to be read to the people in English, and the Bible will be restored to the churches once more."

"Amen," Anne Askew says. "And my work will be done. For all I ever do is recite the words of the Bible that I have memorized, and explain what the words mean. Half the gospelers in London are nothing more than speaking Bibles. If the Bible were allowed back into the churches, we would all be at peace. If the people can read it for themselves again, it will be like the feeding of the multitude. It will be a miracle of our age."

WHITEHALL PALACE, LONDON, AUTUMN 1545

KP

We come to Whitehall as the weather turns cold and the frost in the garden makes the yew trees in the *allées* silvery white on the tips of their branches and green and dark in their shades. The bowls of the fountains are skinned with ice, and I order all the furs to be brought from the wardrobe rooms at my house, Baynard's Castle. Once again they drape Kitty Howard's sables around my neck, but this year I find that they are scented with my perfume and the ghost of the girl queen is gone into the cold twilight.

Nicholas de Vent has completed his great portrait of the five of us and it is waiting for its formal unveiling, fixed in its place, just as we specified that it should be, shrouded in a cloth of gold. Nobody has seen it since it left his studio; we are waiting for the king to announce that he wants to see it.

"Will Your Majesty come and unveil the portrait?" Anne Seymour asks me. "His Majesty asked my lord husband to escort you."

"Now?" I ask. I am reading a book, as simple as a child's primer, that explains the mystery of the Mass, the reality of purgatory. It is a book approved by the Privy Council and it is written in exactly their pompous tone of certainty. I close it, and wonder how it is that men, even thoughtful men, can sound as if they never consider anything but always simply know.

"Yes, now," she says. "The painter is here; everyone is gathering."

"Is the king coming?"

"His Majesty is resting," she says. "His leg is bad. He says he will see it later."

I get to my feet. "I'll come," I say. I see Elizabeth's bright face bob up. She is such a vain child, she longs to see what the painter will have made of her. She sat for him in her best gown, in the hope that in the final design she will be placed center stage, close to her father's hand, an acknowledged Tudor princess. Princess Mary and I exchange a wry look over Elizabeth's head. We may not be excited like a girl at the thought of this portrait, but we are both glad to be publicly acclaimed. This picture will hang in Whitehall Palace for years, perhaps for centuries. People will copy it and have the copies in pride of place in their own homes.

It will show the royal children with their father, and me: seated at his side. It will mark my achievement—a great achievement—of bringing the royal children to their father. I may not give him a child as Jane Seymour did, I will not be his wife for twenty-three years like Katherine of Aragon, but I have done something that no wife has managed to do before—I have put the children at the heart of the royal family. The two girls and the precious heir are in the same portrait as their father. It is a picture of a royal family and I am there as their acknowledged mother. I am queen, I am regent, I am their mother, and the portrait will show my children around me, my husband beside me; and those who doubt my influence and think that they can conspire against me can look at this portrait and see the woman at the heart of the royal family.

"We'll come at once," I say.

I am eager to see how I look. After trying many colors I chose to wear my red undergown, with an extravagant overgown of cloth of gold trimmed with ermine. The painter himself selected it from the royal wardrobe. He said that he wanted the colors of the picture to be all red and gold, to show our wealth, to show our unity, to show our grandeur in royal colors. I did not say that red is my favorite, but of course I know that it sets off my white skin and my auburn hair. He asked me to change my headdress, from my favorite French hood, a semicircular frame that I wear set back on my hair, to the more old-fashioned gable type. Nan brought his choice from the royal treasury and set it on my head. "Jane Seymour's," she said briefly. "Gold leaf."

"I would never wear this!" I exclaim, but he pushed it gently back so that my hair showed a little, so that it framed my face.

"It is a privilege to paint a beautiful woman," he said quietly, and he showed me how he wanted me to sit, perched on the edge of a chair, my gold gown a pool around my feet.

Now I smile at Princess Mary. "I am gripped with vanity," I say. "I can't wait to see it."

"Me too," she says. She takes Elizabeth's hand and I lead the way, with Edward Seymour at my side and the women of my chamber following behind. We get to the great hall, and the men of the court, even some of the Privy Council, are already there, curious to see this great picture that has cost so much to commission and taken so long to produce. No one has seen it assembled. We all posed individually, the painter mostly working from earlier portraits of the king, so this will be a surprise for us all. I see Nicholas de Vent, the artist, looking anxious, as well he might.

"Is His Majesty not coming?" he asks as he bows to me.

I am about to say no, when the great doors to the king's presence chamber open and his wheeled chair comes out, with the king half sitting, half lying in it, his great leg sticking out before him, his face red and swollen stiff in a grimace of pain.

The artist gives a little exclamation of surprise. He has not seen the king since we first discussed the portrait and then de Vent copied the king's likeness from the great portraits by Hans Holbein, which the king prefers above any other. I imagine that the painting behind the screens will show a handsome man of about forty years with his wife and young family around him. He will have two well-shaped legs in ivory hose with the usual blue garter tied under the knee to show off the strong calf. He will not be sprawled like a ship wrecked in dry dock, sweating with the effort of raising his enormous head.

I go to him, curtsey, and kiss his hot cheek. "What a pleasure to see Your Majesty," I say. "And you're looking so well."

"I wanted to see what he had made of us," he says shortly. He nods at de Vent. "Unveil it."

It is a huge picture, nearly five feet high and more than ten feet long, and the cover gets caught on the top right-hand corner so we see it revealed inch by inch from the left, while a page runs to fetch a stool so that he can reach to the corner where the gold cloth is snagged, hiding the full picture.

First a beautifully ornate pillar shining with silver and gold engraving, and a ceiling, bright as stained glass, with red and white Tudor roses. Then a doorway. There is a little gasp of surprise, for there is Princess Mary's Fool, walking past the archway in

Whitehall Palace garden as if to say that all life is passing, that it is a court of fools. In the garden behind her, are the carved heraldic beasts on posts, as if to say that all glory is folly. I glance at the king to see if he is surprised to see Jane the Fool in the top corner of his royal portrait, but I observe his slow nod, and I know that he approved this, even the position of the Fool. He will think that he is making some kind of profound statement about fame and the world. Another pair of matching gold pillars frame the figure of a woman in the foreground. It is Princess Mary in her dark red gown with the greeny-brown overgown, cut square at her throat, trimmed with white silk slashings on her sleeves and white lace cuffs at her wrists. She wears a French hood, pushed back from her pale face, and a crucifix at her throat. I look carefully at the portrait and then I turn and give her a warm approving smile. It is fitting. She looks regal and dignified, her two hands clasped before her, her face turned towards the viewer with a small smile. If anyone copies this to show to a suitor, a foreign prince seeking her in marriage, it will be a fair likeness. She looks both queenly and girlish. The painter has captured her dignity and her charm. I see her rising blush and she gives me a little nod. This is a good likeness; we are both pleased.

The cover drops a little and the court gasps to see Prince Edward, square as his father, standing stocky and bold in a bulky jacket and red stockings, a red hat crammed on his little head, his sleeves ridiculously stuffed. A few people applaud. This could be the Holbein portrait of the king cut down to three feet tall. The painted prince leans with a confident elbow on his father's knee, as Edward would never dare to lean in real life, and Henry's hand is on his shoulder, holding him close, as he has never done. The boy is presented to the eye as if Henry had just given birth to him from between his wide-straddled legs: this is his son and heir, the pose insists. This is the boy of the king's own making, in his image, his little red egg.

Behind them both, as a backdrop and extending over their heads, is the cloth of estate showing the royal crest, above that a gold seal like a holy halo that the old idolatrous church painters used to enamel over the heads of painted saints. In the middle of the picture, still half concealed by the drape, which the pages are desperately tugging, is the king himself. The painter has made him the heart of the picture, plumb center in the blazing colors of a golden sun. His huge puffed sleeves, fat as a pair of bolsters, are in cloth of gold, slashed with white silk, the skirts of his short robe are red and gold, his parted sturdy legs are blazing silver in ivory stockings, the strong calves gleaming, the round knees like two little moons. His gown is trimmed with sable, thrown off the huge padded shoulders, his face is big, pale, and unlined, and his codpiece—"My God," I murmur at the very sight of it. The huge ivory codpiece is boldly erect at the very center of his body, at the heart of the picture. Enormous and gleaming palely, among all the red and the gold, it does everything but announce to the viewer: Here is the king's cock. Admire!

I bite the inside of my lips so that I do not allow even the whisper of a giggle to escape me, I don't dare look at Catherine Brandon. The painter must have lost his wits to be so brash; even the king's monstrous vanity cannot think that this is anything but ridiculous. But then the page finally frees the curtain that has concealed the rest of the portrait, the fabric drops to the floor and at last I see my own likeness.

I am seated at the king's left hand, in the gown that the painter and I chose together, the red underskirt and sleeves complementing the red of Prince Edward's robe, my gold bodice and overskirt matching the king's puffy sleeves, and the white ermine lining and sleeves marking my royalty. The English hood that Nicholas de Vent chose from the royal wardrobe is perfectly rendered, the girdle at my waist done in fine detail, my skin as pearly and as pale as the king's magnificent legs. But my face . . .

But my face . . .

My face . . .

There is a murmur of comment in the court like the whisper of wind through the trees of an autumn wood. I hear people remark, "Oh, I didn't expect . . ." and, "But that isn't . . ." and, "Surely that's . . ." and then everyone bites off the end of their sentences as if nobody wants to observe what is painfully, terribly obvious, and grows more and more obvious, as a silence falls, and someone clears their throat, and someone else turns away, and slowly, though they don't want to stare, no one can resist it any longer: and everyone turns to look at me.

They look at me. And I am looking at Her.

It is not my portrait. It is not my face. I sat for it indeed, and I wore these clothes, the clothes from the royal wardrobe, the clothes that signify a Queen of England. The painter put my hands in that position, tilted my face to the light, but it is not my features under her golden hood. The king has commissioned a portrait of his third wife, Edward's mother, and had me sit in for her, like a doll, so that the painter could get the size and the shape of a wife, any wife. But the face is not mine. The painter did not have to try to capture what he called my luminous beauty. Instead he shows the sharp outline of Jane Seymour's hood and beneath it the bovine blankness of Jane Seymour, the dead queen, who sits at the king's left hand, admiring him and her son, from the grave; and I might as well never have been.

I don't know how I stand, how I smile and remark on what a beautiful picture it is, how well Elizabeth looks, on the left of the woman who supplanted her mother, a stepmother whom she cannot even remember: her mother's lady-in-waiting, the woman who danced the day that her mother was beheaded. I laugh at the portrait of Will Somers in the right-hand doorway, his monkey on his shoulder, the Whitehall gardens behind him. I hear my tinkling laugh and the way that people eagerly join with me, as if to obscure my humiliation. Nan comes to one side of me as if she would hold me up, and Catherine Brandon comes to the other, and they admire the picture and make a babble of noise. Anne

Seymour, my lady-in-waiting, stays at a distance and remarks on the beauty of her dearest tragic sister-in-law.

I keep staring at the portrait. I think it is an altarpiece, an icon like those the reformers have rightly thrown out of the old corrupt church. It is like a triptych with three panels: the two princesses on either side, and the Holy Family, the Father and the Son and the transfigured mother, in the central panel. The two Fools are the worldly fools outside, while the inside world of the royal family glows like gold. Jane Seymour, overcoming death, shines like Our Lady.

Elizabeth comes and takes my hand and whispers: "Who is that? Who is it in your place?"

And I say, "Hush, it is Queen Jane, Edward's mother," and at once her clever little face closes up as if I have told her a secret of shameful doings, something foul and wrong. And at once—and this is how I know she has been corrupted beyond saving—she turns a smiling face to her father and tells him what a beautiful portrait he has commissioned.

Princess Mary throws me a brief glance and says nothing, and then the court falls silent as we wait for the king to speak. We wait, and we wait, Nicholas de Vent turning his cap in his hand, sweating with nerves to see what the great patron of art, Holbein's patron, has to say about this production, this painted lie, this masterpiece of self-aggrandizement, this grave robbing.

"I like it," Henry says firmly, and there is a sort of breeze as the court releases its indrawn breath. "Very fair. Very well done." He glances at me and I see he looks just a little embarrassed. "You will be glad to see the children painted all together, and the honor that I have done to Edward's mother."

He looks at the pale painted face of his dead wife. "She might have sat beside me, just like that, had she had been spared," he says. "She might have seen Edward grow to be a man. Who knows? She might have given me more sons."

There is nothing I can say while my husband publicly mourns a previous wife, gazing into her bleached stupid face as if to find some wit now that escaped everyone during her life. I find that my teeth are gritted to hold a fixed smile as if this is not an insult to me, as if I am not publicly denied, as if the king is not telling the world that all of us who came after Jane—Anne of Cleves, Katherine Howard, me—are ghost queens of less substance than her, the dead wife.

Of course, it is Anne Seymour, the dead queen's sister-in-law, who steps forward and addresses the king as a kinswoman and fellow mourner, taking advantage of his tears as she always does: "It is her to the life."

Except she is dead.

"Just as she was," he says.

I doubt that, for she is in my best gold-heeled shoes.

"She must be looking down from heaven and blessing you and her boy," she says.

"She must be," he agrees eagerly.

I note, dryly, that the sainted Jane seems to have skipped purgatory, though there is a preacher imprisoned in the Tower of London right now facing a charge of heresy for suggesting that purgatory does not exist.

"She was cruelly taken from me," he says, his little eyes blinking out easy tears. "And we had been married little more than a year."

He's not quite right. I could tell him exactly. They were married for a year and four months, a shorter marriage even than Kitty Howard, who lasted only a year and six months before he beheaded her; but far longer than his marriage to Anne of Cleves, now so well regarded, who was pushed out inside half a year.

"She loved you so much," Anne Seymour says mournfully. "But thank God that she left such a wonderful son as her living memorial."

The mention of Prince Edward cheers Henry. "She did," he says. "At least I have one son, and he is handsome, isn't he?"

"The very image of his father," Anne smiles. "See how he stands in the portrait. He is the very image of you!"

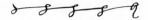

I lead my ladies back to my rooms. I am smiling and they are all smiling. We are all trying to show that we are untroubled, that we have seen nothing that disturbs our position, our sense of entitlement. I am the queen and these are my ladies. Nothing is wrong.

When we get to my rooms, I wait for them to settle to their sewing with a reader opening a book approved by the Bishop of London. Then I say that I have a little flux, something I ate, no doubt. I will go to my room alone. Nan comes with me because hell's own horses would not keep Nan out of my hair right now, and she shuts the door behind us and looks at me.

"Bitch," I say shortly.

"Me?"

"Her."

"Anne Seymour?"

"No, Jane Seymour. The dead one."

This is so unreasonable that not even Nan tries to correct me. "You're upset."

"I am publicly humiliated, I am supplanted before everyone by a ghost. My rival is not some pretty girl like Catherine Brandon or Mary Howard but a cadaver who was not even very lively when she breathed. And yet now she is the wife that he will not forget."

"She is dead, poor lady. She cannot irritate him now. He can think of her at her best."

"Her death is her best! She was never as charming as she is now!"

Nan makes a little gesture with her hand, as if to say stop. "She did the best that she could, and my God, Kat, you would not be so hard on her if you had seen her die in such a fever, crying out for God and for her husband. She may have been a ninny; but she died a woman in lonely terror."

"What is that to me, who will now have to walk past her image every time I go to dinner? Who is not allowed to wear her pearls? But who has to raise her son? Bed her husband?"

"You are angry," Nan says.

"Indeed," I spit. "I see that your studies have not been wasted on you. I am angry. Excellent. Now what?"

"You're going to have to get over it," she says, as steady as our mother used to be when I raged against some nursery injustice. "Because you're going to have to go to dinner with your head up, smiling, showing everyone that you are happy with the portrait, and happy with your marriage, and happy with your stepchildren and their three dead mothers, and happy with the king."

"Why do I have to do this?" I pant. "Why do I have to pretend that I am not publicly insulted?"

Nan's face is very pale and her voice is flat. "Because if you see a dead wife as your rival, you will be a dead wife," she predicts. "People are already saying that he will remarry. People are already saying that he does not like your religion, that you are too much for reform. You have to face them down. You have to please him. You have to walk in to dinner tonight like a woman whose position cannot be questioned."

"Who questions me?" I yell at her. "Who dares to question me?"

"I am afraid that you are widely questioned," she says quietly. "Already, the gossip has started. Almost everyone questions your fitness to be queen."

WHITEHALL PALACE, LONDON, WINTER 1545

KP

In the quiet days before the start of the Christmas feast the king is troubled and openly irritated that neither his traditional advisors nor his new thinkers can get a truce with France. Charles of Spain is now urging that a truce be made so that he is free to turn on his own subjects. He is determined to stamp out the reformers in Flanders and the lands of the Holy Roman Empire. He says that he and Henry must forget their enmity against France to confront a greater danger. They must all three join together to make war against the Lutherans. He says that this must be the new crusade, that they must make war against people who are such sinners they think that the Bible is the best guide to life.

I pray for the safety of the men and women of God in England, in Germany, in every corner of Christendom, who have done nothing wrong but have read the Word of God and study it in their hearts. Then they speak. Why should they not? Why should the scholars of the church and the priests of the church and—yes—the bullies and soldiers of the church be the only ones who can announce the truth as they see it?

Stephen Gardiner, still in Bruges, still desperately trying to gain a peace treaty with France, is passionately for peace with France and Spain, arguing in favor of a bloodstained crusade against Lutherans everywhere, especially in Germany, to start at once.

"God only knows what he is offering, what he is promising on my behalf," Henry grumbles to me as we sit quietly playing cards together one evening.

Around us the court is dancing and flirting, someone is singing, and there is a small group standing around us, watching the play and betting on the outcome. Catherine Brandon is at the king's elbow. He shows her his cards and asks for her advice, and she smiles and swears she will signal to me so that I have the advantage. Most people bet on the king. He does not like to lose. He does not even like someone betting against him. I see a weak card that he plays and I do not trump it. He roars at my mistake and scoops up the trick.

"Shall you summon Bishop Gardiner home?" I ask as calmly as I can. "Do you agree with him that the emperor should make a war against his own people?"

"For certain they go too far in Germany," Henry says. "And these German princes have been no help to me at all. I won't defend them. Why should I? They don't understand the ways of man, why should they grasp the ways of God?"

I glance up and see Edward Seymour, Thomas's brother, watching me. I know that he hopes that I will use my influence to persuade the king that the Lutherans in Germany should be spared, and that the new thinking in England should be allowed. But I walk a very careful course with the king. I have heard Nan's warnings and I am wary of making enemies. I know by now that when the king complains of one side he is often, at the very same time, working against the other. People overestimate my influence when they blame me for reform. I use my influence lightly, and there is a portrait hanging on the wall that denies I even exist.

"Surely it cannot be wrong to think that we should live by the Bible, and that we will go to heaven by faith and the forgiveness of our sins," I remark.

Henry glances up from his hand of cards. "I see you are no better a theologian than you are a card player," he says. His twinkle of a smile takes the sting from his words.

"I don't expect to understand more about religion than you, my lord husband," I say. "And I certainly never expect to beat you at cards."

"And what about my girls?" he asks, turning to Princess Mary, who stands at his elbow, while Elizabeth leans against my chair.

"Cards or scholarship?" Elizabeth asks pertly.

Her father laughs. "Which do you prefer?"

"Scholarship," she says. "Because it is a privilege to be allowed to study, especially with a scholar like the queen; but cards are a pastime for anyone."

"Quite right," he says. "And only the learned and the thoughtful should study and discourse. Holy things should be considered in quiet and holy places, and only by those fit to understand them under the guidance of the church. Cards are for the taproom; the Bible is only for those who can read and understand it."

Princess Mary nods, and he smiles at her. "I take it that you are not one for the wayside sermon, bawled out by any fool perched on a milestone, my Mary?"

She curtseys before she speaks to him. "I think the church must teach the people," she says. "They cannot teach themselves."

"That's what I think," Henry says. "That's just what I think."

The king takes this careless talk at the card table and uses it as the basis for his speech to Parliament. He goes to them on Christmas Eve, as the members are thinking about calling for their horses and going to their homes for the season. He makes a grand entrance, as the nation's father, coming to address his people on the very night before the birth of Christ, like a fat lame herald angel, to tell them how Christ is to be served by them, here on earth. Everyone knows that this is to be a great statement of the king's belief, perhaps the last that he ever makes, and that whether they agree or not, they had better be there. The kingdom knows what I believe—they have read the liturgy that I translated with Thomas Cranmer. They see me as temperate, traditional, but with a focus on personal belief, personal prayer. Some may suspect me of leaning towards reform, but everything I have publicly authored has been approved by the king and cannot be heretical. They have seen Stephen Gardiner's beliefs in the uncompromising *King's Book*, which defines hundreds of true believers as heretics, so they feel the tide is against reform. But always, until now, they have had to guess at the king's beliefs. He has written books and banned them, he has given people the Bible and taken it away again, he has told them that he is the Supreme Head of the church, but never before has he told them what he believes. Never before has the king gone to his Parliament in person, and told them directly what they are to think about God.

Men are moved to tears. The crowds outside, gathered to see the great procession led by the huge king, stand with their heads uncovered as some climb up to peer in through the open windows of Westminster Hall and then shout down what the king, seated like a mountain on his throne under the golden cloth of estate, has pronounced. People are desperate to know if he will be like a German prince and pronounce for reform of the church, or whether he will be like the French king and the Spanish emperor and defend the old ways of the old church and ally with the pope.

"It's bad," Anne Seymour says to me shortly. "We've lost." She is first into my rooms with the news. Her husband, Edward, stood beside the king, his face impassive as the king complained bitterly to his commons that they mangled the Word of God in taverns and took His name in vain. As soon as they got back from Parliament Edward came straight to his wife and muttered his report to her.

"It's very bad for those who think as we do. The king is moving back to the old ways. It will be the Catholic Church as it was, everything is to be restored, and there are some who say that he will join in communion with the Greek Church."

"Greek?" I say blankly. "What has the Greek Church to do with England?

She looks at me as if my husband is as ineffable as God himself. "Anyone but Protestants," she says bitterly. "That's what he means. Anyone but reformers. He told Parliament that he is tired of the constant debate and the questioning of the Bible. He is tired of the gospelers. He is tired of all the thinking and writing and publishing. Of course, he fears that people will question him next. He told them that he had given them the Bible only for men to read to their own families. They are not to discuss it."

"The Bible is only for men?"

She nods. "He says that it is for him to judge between truth and error. They are not to think; they are merely to read aloud to their household and children."

I bow my head under this insult to God-given intelligence.

"But then—just when you think that he is going back to

papistry—he says that he is going to pull down all the chantries, and take their lands."

This makes no sense. "Destroy the chantries and abolish Masses for the dead?"

"He says it is nothing but a hollow superstition. He says that there is no purgatory and so no need for Masses for the dead and so no need for chantries."

"He says that there is no purgatory?"

"He says it has been a way for the old church to make money from the innocent people."

"He's right!"

"But at the same time the service of the Mass is to be unchanged, with all the bobbing and bowing and ducking. And the bread and wine is to be regarded as the true body and blood. And it is heresy to question this."

I look at her with a sort of despair. "What does your husband think that the king actually believes? In his heart?"

She shrugs. "Nobody knows. It is half Lutheranism and half Catholic, it is papist with the king as pope, it is Lutheranism with the king as Luther. It has become a religion quite of his own making. That's why he has to keep explaining it to us. And so heresy, too, is what he says it is. We are all of us—papists and Protestants, Lutherans and gospelers alike—in danger."

"But what does he believe? Anne, we have to know. What does the king believe?"

"All sorts of things, all at once."

The king comes home very tired, and sends for me to visit him in his rooms. They have already put him to bed, and I hesitate on the threshold, wondering if he intended me to come in my nightgown, to bed him.

He beckons me in. "Come in," he says. "Sit with me. I want to tell you all about it before I sleep. You will have heard that they were in awe of me at Westminster? They wept as I told them I was their father and I would have command of them. They said that they had never heard such a speech before."

"How wonderful," I say faintly. "And how good you are to make the effort to go out to them, and on Christmas Eve as well."

He waves a fat hand. "I wanted them to know my mind," he says. "It is important that they are clear. I think for them, I decide for them, they must know what I am thinking. How else are they to find their way through life? How else get to heaven?"

The door behind me opens and the first of the servers comes in with a platter and a spoon and knife. The king is to be served his dinner in bed. One after another the men come in with dish after dish. Henry piles food on his platter as they wrap a great linen napkin under his chin to keep the bedclothes from being spattered with juices from the meats and sauces. I am served in my seat at a table at the foot of the great bed and I eat slowly, so that we may finish our meal together. Henry's plate is constantly replenished and he drinks at least three bottles of wine, the meal takes forever, and when he waves the last dish away he throws himself back against the pillows, exhausted and sweating. I am nauseous just from watching the huge plates of food come and go.

"Should you see the doctor?" I ask him. "Is your fever rising?"

He shakes his head. "Doctor Wendy can attend me later," he says. "Did you know that Doctor Butts is ill?" He gives a wheezy laugh. "What sort of a doctor is that? I sent him a message—what sort of doctor are you, too sick to attend his patient?"

"How amusing. But is he at court? Is he cared for?"

"I think he went home," Henry says indifferently. "He knows better than to bring illness to court. As soon as he had the first symptom he sent me a message to tell me that he would not come near me till he is well again. He begged my pardon for not being able to attend to me. He should be here. I knew I would be overtaxed, going to my people, taking my wisdom to my people, like that. In this cold weather."

I nod to the servers to take everything from the room but to bring the king another bottle of wine and the sweet pastries that he likes to have beside the bed in case he is hungry during the night.

"I was inspiring." He belches with quiet satisfaction. "They listened to me in complete silence. When people talk about preaching, they should have heard me in Westminster this evening! People who call for a new prophet should have heard me speak tonight! I am a father to my people, and a better father than the false priest they call the Holy Father in Rome!"

"Did someone write it down so that others can read it?" I ask.

He nods. His eyes are closing like a sleepy child after a busy day. "I hope so," he says. "I shall see that you get a copy. You will want to study it, I know."

"I will," I say.

"I have pronounced," he says. "That is the end of all argument."

"Yes. Shall I leave you to sleep, husband?"

"Stay," he says. "Stay. I have hardly seen you all day. Did you sit beside old Latimer's bed?"

"Hardly ever," I lie. "He was not a husband to me as you are, my lord."

"I thought not," he says. "You must have had a moment, when he was dying, when you thought you would be free of all husbands. Did you? When you thought you would be a widow, with your own little estate and your own fortune? Perhaps you even picked out a handsome young man?" The little eyes open, twinkle with sly amusement.

It is illegal for a woman to marry the king if she has any hidden love affairs in her past. These are dangerous words for a bedtime story.

"I thought I would be a widow living only for my family, just like your grandmother, Lady Margaret Beaufort," I smile. "But a great destiny called me."

"The greatest destiny a woman can have," he agrees. "But why do you think you have not conceived, Kateryn?"

The question is so unexpected that I give a little start. His eyes are closed; perhaps he does not see it. I think at once, guiltily, of the purse of herbs and Nan's terror that if I do not prevent it, he will give me some monstrous miscarriage. It is not possible that someone in my rooms has told him of the herbs. I am certain that no one would betray me. No one knows but Nan and me. Even the maid who brings the hot water knows nothing more than that she brings a jug of hot water for a morning tisane, now and then.

"I don't know, husband," I say humbly. "Sometimes it takes time, I suppose."

He opens his eyes. Now he is completely wide awake, as if he was never drowsy. "It never took time for me before," he says. "I have three children, as you see, from three different mothers. And there were others, of course. They all conceived at once, within the first months. I am potent, royally potent."

"Indeed." I can feel my anxiety rising. This sounds like a trap, but I cannot see how to avoid it. "I see it."

"So it must be some fault in you," he says pleasantly enough. "What do you think?"

"I don't know," I say. "Lord Latimer was not capable, so I never expected a child from him, and when I married my first husband I was too young, and we were hardly ever together." Pointless to say that you, my third husband, the king, are an old man, sick as a fat dog, rarely potent, probably sterile, and that the wives who you now remember as so readily fertile were the wives of your youth, the first three, and now they are all dead: one was beheaded by you, two died of your neglect. They miscarried time after time, except the third, the one who died in her first childbed.

"Do you think that God does not smile on our marriage? Since he gives you no child, you must think that."

The king's God sent him one dead baby after another in his first marriage until the king realized that God was not smiling. A tiny squirm of protest turns in my mind. It is such blasphemy to call in God when the truth is something that we simply don't understand. I cannot have God in this conversation as a witness against me. God should not bear witness against yet another of Henry's wives. I think God Himself would be unwilling to argue that Kateryn Parr should be put aside. I feel my temper silently rise.

"Who can doubt His blessing?" I assert boldly, gripping my hands on the arms of the chair, nerving myself to go on. "Since you are so well and so strong and so potent, and we have had so many happy months together? Two and a half years of success? Your capture of Boulogne and the defeat of the Scots? Our happiness with your children? Who can doubt that God smiles on you, a king like you? He must smile on your marriage too? A marriage of your own choice when you honored me with your favor. Who can doubt that God smiled on me when you chose me, and when you persuaded me, against my own humility, that I might become your wife? We cannot doubt that God loves you and inspires you. We cannot doubt that you have His favor."

I have saved myself. I see the pleased smile spread across his face as he relaxes into sleep. "You are right," he says. "Of course. And a child born to you must follow. God's blessing is on me. He knows that I have only ever done the right thing."

The doctor, Sir William Butts, does not come back to court as he promised. He died of his fever, far away from the court, and we don't even hear of it until after Christmas. The king says that no one else understands his constitution, no one else can keep him well as Doctor Butts could do. He feels that it was wrong and selfish of the doctor to leave court so abruptly and die in such inconsiderate haste. He takes the drafts that Doctor Wendy prepares for him, he keeps him at his bedside night and day, but he complains that he will never be well now that Doctor Butts is not there to soothe his temper and diminish his fever.

"And we have lost a good friend and an advisor," Anne Seymour remarks to me and to Catherine Brandon. "Doctor

Butts would often ask the king to ignore a piece of gossip against a Lutheran, or to release a preacher. He never declared his own opinions, but he often asked the king to be merciful. He was a good man to have at the king's side."

"Especially when the king was in pain and angry," Catherine agrees. "My husband used to say that Doctor Butts could soothe the king when no one else could do it. And he was a most honest believer in reform." She smooths out her skirt and admires the shine on the satin. "But still we make progress, Anne. The king has asked Thomas Cranmer to make a list of old superstitions in the church that should be banned."

"How do you know? What has he told you?" Anne asks. I hear the hostility in her voice and remember that she is always anxious about someone who might rise in prestige and diminish her, or her husband.

Catherine is trying to manage a difficult relationship with the king: constantly at his side, his favorite flirt, ignored as a councillor but relished as a partner at cards. This is a path that many have trod before her: four ladies-in-waiting have become queen—I am only the most recent. Now Catherine is the most favored lady at court, and Anne Seymour, who never ceases to measure her husband's prestige as the uncle of the prince, is painfully jealous. Surely, the danger is to me, but Anne thinks only of herself.

"He is going to establish two colleges, just as he promised Her Majesty," Catherine says, smiling at me. "One at Oxford and one at Cambridge. This is learned work, just as Her Majesty asked him to do. They will teach the new learning and they will preach in English."

"He's planning to send my husband, Edward, to Boulogne to replace that fool young Henry Howard," Anne says anxiously. "The Howards are in disgrace for Henry's rashness and incompetence—which is all to our good—but with my husband away from court, who is going to keep us Seymours in the king's remembrance? How shall we stay in favor? How can we be influential?"

"Ah, the Seymours," Catherine says sweetly. "The Seymours! The Seymours! Just when we thought we were talking of the friends that we could trust to bring the king and the church closer to God, I find that we are actually talking about the rise of the Seymours, once more. Again."

"We don't need to rise," Anne replies irritably. "We are high in favor. We Seymours are kin to the only Tudor heir, and Prince Edward loves his uncles."

"But it is the queen who is named as regent," Catherine reminds her silkily. "And the king prefers her company, and even mine, to yours. And if Edward is sent to Boulogne, and Thomas is always at sea, who will keep the king in mind of the Seymours indeed? Do you have any friends at all?"

"Peace," I say quietly. But it is not their wrangling that disturbs me. It is that I cannot bear to hear his name. I cannot bear to think that while I am trapped in a court that seems smaller and more confining every day, he is always, always far away.

HAMPTON COURT PALACE, CHRISTMAS 1545

KP

We hold Christmas in the old way, with dancing and music and masquing, and sports and competitions, and huge amounts of food and wine. Every one of the twelve days of the feast the kitchen labors to bring out some new novelty, some great dish; and the king eats and eats as if to satisfy a growing insatiable hunger, as if he had a monstrous worm coiled and fat inside him.

He commands that we invite the former queen Anne of Cleves for Christmas, and she comes to court plumply good-humored, as greedy as the king himself, and as merry and as sweet-tempered as any woman could be who has escaped danger with her life and come out with a royal title, a fortune, and her freedom.

She is wealthy. She comes with a train of horsemen, bringing rich Christmas gifts, carefully chosen to please all of us. She is three years younger than me, fair-haired, dark-eyed, and with a calm untroubled smile. Her rounded prettiness draws admiring glances from people who have forgotten why the king rejected her. She was the Protestant princess and she fell with their leader, Cromwell, when the king turned against reform. She comes to court as if to remind me that there has been a queen before who worshipped in her own language, served God without pope or bishop, took bread and wine not body and blood—and lasted less than six months.

She smiles warmly at me, but she keeps her distance, as if there is no advantage in friendship with a wife. She knows everything there is to know about Tudor queens, and has concluded that there is no point in becoming my friend. They tell me that she was loving with Queen Katherine Howard: she bore no grudge when their roles were reversed, and the lady-in-waiting walked before her queen; but with me she behaves as if it is hardly worth getting to know me. Her cool glance tells me that she doubts I will make three years, perhaps I will not be here next Christmas.

Nan embraces her without hesitation, falling into her arms as if they are two survivors from a secret war that only they remember. Anne hugs her tightly and then holds my sister at arm's length to read her face.

"You are well?" she asks. Her accent is still German, like the cawing of a crow, even after all these years in England.

"I am well," Nan says mistily, as if moved by a kiss from this ghost. "And my sister is Queen of England!"

I can't be the only person to think this rather awkward, given that this rounded, smiling woman was queen one reign before mine, and dismissed from the royal bed and the throne faster than anyone else has ever been. But Anne turns, still holding my sister close, and smiles at me. "God bless Your Majesty," she says sweetly. "And may your reign be long."

Unlike yours, I hope; but I incline my head and smile back at her.

"And is the king in good health?" she asks, knowing that I have to lie, for it is illegal to suggest that he is ill.

"He is in very good health," I say stoutly.

"And inclining to the reform of religion?" she asks hopefully.

Of course, she was raised a Lutheran, though who knows what she believes now? Certainly, she has never written anything of note.

"The king is a great scholar of the Bible," I say, choosing my words carefully.

"We make progress," Nan assures her. "We really do."

That night at dinner I sit on one side of the king, Anne of Cleves on my right hand, honored before the court as the king's sister— as he chooses to call her. I make sure I am smiling as if I am without any care in the world, while beside me I hear him eat, grunt, belch, pant, and eat again. I have become ridiculously sensitive to the noise of him dining; no music can drown it out, no conversation can distract me. I hear the snuffle that he makes when he is tipping a bowl to drink the juices of the meat, the crack of the bones of little birds in his strong jaws, and the loud sucking on sweetmeats and sugar. He makes another noise when he drinks his wine, great gulps and then a sort of pant into the bowl of the wineglass as he catches his breath, as if he is swimming and drinking the lake. I turn my head and speak to Anne of Cleves; I smile down the table at Princess Elizabeth. Catherine Brandon dips her head coquettishly as the king sends down a special dish to her, and Nan glances at me as if to ensure that I have noticed this. I look around the court, at all the people serving themselves onto their heaped plates, snapping their fingers for the servers to bring them more and more wine, and I think: this court has become a monster that is devouring itself, a dragon that eats its own tail for greed.

I am afraid of the cost of keeping this bloated household, the thousands of servants to run after the hundreds of lords, their ladies, their horses, their dogs. It is not that I am cautious—I was raised to run a noble household; I don't like anything mean—but this is extravagance and luxury fueled by the destruction of the churches. Only the wealth of a thousand years of the church could pay for this excess. It is as if the court is a great clockwork toy, with a gear and a great wheel that takes in holy wealth and throws out dross every hour, every minute, just as the king will feast now but will vomit later, or strain in pain on the closestool, clinging to Anthony Denny's extended hand and calling for Doctor Wendy to administer an enema to purge him.

I see that Edward Seymour has an empty place at his side, on his right hand, a seat of honor, and at once I am alert, wondering if he expects Thomas. The noise of the king spooning oyster broth from a golden bowl, and then dipping manchet bread and sucking it, dies away. I cannot even hear the rattle of the golden spoon as he bangs it against the golden dish to prompt the server to give him more. I am watching the door at the end of the hall and, almost as if I have summoned him, as if my desire has created a specter, Thomas, in a dark blue cape, comes quietly into the room, swings the cape from his shoulders and gives it to his page, and comes forward to his brother's table.

He is here. I look away at once. I cannot believe it. He is here.

Edward's warm welcome is unfeigned. He jumps to his feet and hugs Thomas, holding him tightly. The two exchange rapid words, and then hug again. Then Thomas steps away from the Seymour table and approaches the dais where we are sitting. He bows to the king, then to me and to the prince beside his father, and to the princesses, then lastly to Anne of Cleves, whom he escorted to England to be queen. His dark eyes go over us all indifferently, and when the king beckons him forward, he steps up to speak across the high table and stands at a slight angle, so his shoulder is towards me and I see his face only in profile, and he does not look at me.

I remember not to crane my head to listen to their conversation. There are some words about the ships and the winter quarters, and the king tells Thomas to take his seat and dine, and sends a dish of venison stew to the Seymour table at once, and some pastries and a pie and slices of a roast boar. Thomas bows, sits beside his brother, and still does not look towards me. I know this only because when his eyes are on me I feel a heat in my face as if I had a slight fever. I don't even have to see that he is looking at me for this to happen. It is as if my body knows, without my knowing, as if he can touch me without touching.

But tonight I am cool and I look straight ahead as he does, so our gazes go past each other and rest on indifferent objects, at opposite ends of the hall, as if we had never been eyes locked, hands clasped, bodies entwined at all.

After dinner there is masquing in the new way, with the dancers taking partners from the court. I have said that I will not dance and I am glad to stand beside the king, my slim hand on his great shoulder, and avoid the danger of having to go hand-clasped with Thomas. I don't think I could bear to be close to him. I am sure I could not dance. I don't think that I could stand.

The king watches the dancers, applauding one or another. He puts his hand around my waist, while I look fixedly at the windows where a pale winter sun is setting over the trees in the gardens. He slides his hand downwards to pat my buttocks. I make sure that I don't flinch. I don't look at Thomas, I look blindly out of the window, and when the king releases me and I can step aside, I see that Thomas has gone.

KP

At the gift giving for the New Year Princess Elizabeth asks me to accompany her to take her present to the king. Together with Princess Mary we go to his presence chamber, where he is receiving his court and giving and dispensing gifts. He almost always gives a purse of money, and Anthony Denny is at his side, tactfully judging the correct weight of the purse for each smiling recipient. Everyone falls back when the princesses and I enter the room, and I curtsey to Henry but step aside, so that Elizabeth can go forward alone. I look around for Thomas, and see he is standing near to the king, a fat purse in his hand. Carefully, he looks away from me; carefully, I keep my eyes on Elizabeth.

"Your Majesty, my honored father," she says in her clear voice, speaking French. As he smiles at her she changes into Latin. "I have brought your Christmas gift. It is not riches in the eyes of the world but it is a treasure from heaven. It is worthless from the hands of its maker, for that was I, your most humble daughter, who made the translation and the copy for you. But I know that you love the author, and I know that you love the work and that gives me the courage to offer you: this."

From behind her back she brings out her beautifully written translation of my private prayers, translated into Latin, French, and Italian. She goes towards her father, bows very low, and puts it into his hands.

The court bursts into applause and the king beams. "This is a work of great learning and good sense," he says. "Published by my wife and approved by every scholar. And here it is translated by another good scholar into a work of great beauty. I am proud that my wife and my daughter are women of scholarship. Learning is an ornament to a good woman, not a distraction."

"And what do you have for your stepmother?" he asks Elizabeth.

She turns to me and presents my gift. It is another translated book and she has embroidered a cover with the king's name and my own. I exclaim with pleasure and show it to the king. He opens the book and sees the title, written in Elizabeth's meticulous hand. It is an English translation of a book of theology by the reformist thinker Jean Calvin. Only a few years ago this would have been heresy, now it is a New Year's present. It defines precisely how far we have come, what Elizabeth is allowed to read, and that reform is the new religion.

The king smiles at me and says, "You must read this to me and tell me what you think of it, and of my daughter's scholarship."

Archbishop Thomas Cranmer comes to me during the period of quiet study in my rooms and says that he would like to read to us the reforms he is going to suggest to the king, for our thoughts and comments. He glances at Princess Mary, who loves the old ways; but she bends her head, and says that she is sure that the good bishop will suggest only godly reforms, and that, anyway, nothing made by man is perfect. Anne of Cleves looks up with interest. She was raised as a Lutheran, she always hoped to bring sincere religious feeling into England. I have to take care not to look triumphant. This is God's victory: not mine.

There is a small lectern in the corner of my presence chamber where the visiting preachers put their Bibles or their books, and Thomas Cranmer places his sheaf of papers there and looks shyly round at us.

"I feel as if I am about to preach a sermon," he says, smiling.

"We would welcome a sermon," I say. "We have had many godly preachers here, and you, dear archbishop, would be one of the greatest." I take care not to look at Anne of Cleves as I welcome a reformist archbishop to my rooms. If I believed in confession, I would have to admit the sin of pride.

"I thank you," he says. "But today I want to learn from you. I think my task has been to take the church's many additions from the old act of the Mass. The challenge is to cut the words and actions of man and keep the intention of God."

Anne Seymour and Catherine Brandon take up their sewing, but do not make so much as a stitch. I make no pretense of doing anything but listening. I fold my hands in my lap and Princess Elizabeth, sitting beside me, does the same, copying me exactly. Anne of Cleves sits beside her and puts her arm around Elizabeth's narrow shoulders. I have to suppress a little pang of quite unworthy jealousy. Of course, she still thinks of herself as Elizabeth's stepmother. She too cared for the motherless child. So does sin come into the smallest moments of daily life; but really, she was Elizabeth's stepmother for no more than months!

The archbishop reads his list of proposed changes and his explanation. All the ritual of the church, which is nowhere described in the Bible, never required by Jesus, is to go. Curtseying to the cross, kneeling on command, all this must change. Old superstitions, like ringing a peal of bells on All-Hallows Eve to scare away bad spirits and welcome the good saints, is to stop. Statues in churches will be rigorously inspected to see that they have no popish tricks like moving eyes or bleeding wounds. No one is to pray to them as if they might intervene in day-to-day life, and they must remain uncovered during the season of Lent.

"The Bible tells us that Christ fasted in the wilderness," Cranmer says reasonably. "That is all the model that we need to take for Lent."

We agree. Even Princess Mary cannot defend the paganism of binding the statues' eyes, or putting cloths over their heads.

Cranmer takes his changes to the king and then returns to my rooms elated.

"Stephen Gardiner is still in Bruges working on the Spanish treaty, and so the king had no contrary voice urging him to the old ways," he says, delighted. "There was no one there to accuse me of wrong thinking. The Howards didn't like it but the king is tired of them. He listened without argument. He was interested; indeed, he even suggested some more reforms to me himself."

"He did?" Anne of Cleves asks, following the rapid talk.

"Yes, indeed."

"I thought that he might," says Catherine Brandon. "He spoke to me about the danger of setting up a graven image. He thinks the people do not understand that the cross and the statues in church are there to represent God. They are signs, not objects of faith. They are not things to be worshipped for themselves."

Without turning her head so much as an inch, Anne of Cleves slides her eyes towards mine to see if I have observed that Catherine Brandon is in the king's confidence, and that he talks to her about religious reform. Anne of Cleves saw her maid-in-waiting pretty Kitty Howard dancing attendance on the king, absent without permission from the queen's rooms. Now her sidelong glance asks me: Is it the same for you?

I raise my eyebrows slightly. No, it is not the same for me. I have no concerns.

"That's what he said to me!" Archbishop Cranmer says delightedly. "He suggests that there should be no kneeling to the cross, no bowing to the cross on entry to church, and no creeping to the cross from the church door on Good Friday."

"The cross is the symbol for the sacred crucifixion," Princess Mary objects. "It is revered for what it represents. Nobody thinks it is a graven image."

There is a silence. "Actually, the king does," Catherine corrects her.

Instantly, Mary bows her head in obedience to the woman who people think is her father's mistress. "Then I am sure he is right," she says quietly. "Who would know better than the king what his people think? And he has told us all that God has appointed him judge of these matters."

We cannot discuss Thomas Cranmer's reforms without mentioning the Mass, and we cannot discuss the Mass because it is illegal to speak of it. The king has outlawed debate on this most holy event. Only he shall think and speak.

"And yet they can interrogate me," Anne Askew points out after she has delivered her sermon on the miracle of the wine at the wedding in Cana. "I may speak about the wedding wine, and about the wine at the Last Supper, but not the wine that is poured by a priest into a cup in the church in our own days, before our own eyes."

"You really may not," I say quietly. "I understand the point you are making, Mistress Askew, but you may not say it in words."

She bows her head. "I would never speak of things that you wish to keep silent," she says carefully. "I would never bring trouble to your door."

It is like a pledge between one honest woman and another. I smile at her. "I know you would not," I say. "I hope that there is no trouble for you, either."

"And what is your married name?" Anne of Cleves asks abruptly.

Anne Askew's beautiful face lights up with laughter. "His name was Thomas Kyme, Your Majesty," she says. "But I do not have a married name, for we were never married."

"You believe that you can be the one to declare that your marriage is over?" asks the divorced queen who is now named princess, and is to be regarded as the king's sister.

"Nowhere in the Bible does it say that marriage is a sacrament," Anne replies. "It was not God who joined us together. The priest says it was; but this is not true. This is the word of the church, not the Bible. Our wedding, like every wedding, was an act of man, not of God. It was not a holy sacrament. My father forced me into an agreement with Thomas, and when I was old enough and had understanding enough I revoked that agreement. I claim the right to be a free woman, with a soul equal to any man under God."

Anne of Cleves—another woman who was married with no choice, and divorced against her will—gives Anne Askew a little smile.

Thomas Cranmer goes home in triumph to codify the agreed reforms into a new law to put before Parliament; but the king sends a message after to him to tell him to stop his work and do nothing.

"I had to halt Thomas in his tracks the moment that I heard from Stephen Gardiner," he says to me as we watch a game of tennis at the royal court. The conversation is punctuated by the loud thwack of the racquet on the ball and then the delay as the ball rolls down the roof to fall into the court below, and the players run into position to hit it again. I think that the king's religious policy is like this—a great advance in one direction and then an immediate return.

"Gardiner says he is very near to a treaty with the emperor at Bruges, but the emperor insists there are to be no new changes to the Church in England. I don't dance to his piping—don't think that. But it's worth my while to delay reform to please the emperor. I don't want to upset him now. I have to measure what I do, measure like a philosopher, all the time, every little change. The emperor wants a treaty with me so that he is safe to attack the Lutherans in his empire, especially Germany."

"If only—" I begin.

"He'll wipe them out, burn them all as heretics if he can." He smiles. He is always attracted by ruthless means. "He says he will stop at nothing to stamp them out. And where will you get your heretical books from then, my dear?"

I stammer a denial, but the king is not listening to me.

"The emperor needs my help. He wants us to be at peace with France so that he can get on with knocking the Germans into orthodoxy. Of course he doesn't want me stepping any further from the papists as he defends the pope's church."

"But surely, my lord, you would never return England to the power of the pope in Rome," I observe. "You would never fail God in order to please the Spanish emperor? You would not serve the world and risk your honor?"

Henry applauds a shot well played on court. "I shall do as God guides me," he says flatly. "And His ways and my ways are mysterious indeed."

I turn and applaud as he does. "That was hard!" I exclaim. "I never thought he would get it."

"I would have got it easily when I was young," Henry remarks. "I was a champion tennis player. You ask Anne of Cleves. She will remember the sportsman I was!"

I smile past him to where she sits, on his other side, watching the game. I know she is listening; I know that she is thinking what she would have said if she had been in my place. I know that she would speak up for the people of her country who only want to read the Bible in their own language and worship God with simplicity. "Is it the case, Princess Anne?"

"Oh, yes," she says agreeably. "His Majesty was the finest."

"She is a good companion for you." Henry turns to me and speaks in an undertone. "It is pleasant to have a beautiful woman like her at court, isn't it?"

"Why, yes."

"And she is so fond of Elizabeth."

"Yes, she is."

"Everyone tells me I should never have let her go," Henry says with a little self-conscious laugh. "If she had borne me a son, he would be five years old now, think of that!"

I know that my smile has died. I don't know what to think of that, or of this entire conversation. Has Henry forgotten that he never consummated his marriage with the now-desirable Anne of Cleves, telling everyone that she was too fat, and no virgin, and that she smelled so bad that he could not bring himself to do the act?

"Some people say that she had a child by me," Henry whispers. He waves encouragement to the losing player, who bows his thanks.

"They do?"

"Nonsense, of course," he says. "You must pay no attention to what people say. You don't listen to such gossip, do you, Kateryn?"

"No," I reply.

"Because d'you know what they are saying in France?"

I smile, ready to be amused. "What are they saying in France?"

"That you are ill and are going to die. That I shall be a widower and free to marry again."

I force a thin laugh. "How very ridiculous! But you can assure the French ambassador that I am very well indeed."

"I will tell him," Henry smiles. "Imagine them thinking that I would take another wife. Is it not ridiculous?"

"Ridiculous indeed. Ridiculous. What are they thinking? Who is advising them? Where do they get these rumors from?"

"So, no reform," Archbishop Cranmer says to me when I come to church to pray and find him kneeling before the cross. His old face looks tired in the light of the candles from the altar. He had thought and studied and prayed on the reforms that the church needed, and then found that one letter from Bishop Gardiner turned the king around again.

"No reform yet," I correct him. "But who can doubt that God will shine the light of learning on England and its king? I have hope. I have faith, even when progress is so very slow."

"And he listens to you," Thomas says. "He is proud of your scholarship and he takes your advice. If you will keep warning him against the power and corruption of Rome, and advising him to be tolerant of the new thinking, we will go on. I am sure we will go on." He smiles. "He once called me the greatest heretic in Kent," he says. "But still I am his bishop and his spiritual advisor. He will tolerate discussion from those he loves. He is generous to me and to you."

"He is never anything but kind to me," I confirm. "When we first married I feared him, but I have come to trust him. Except for when he is in pain, or when he is angry about something, or when things are going badly, he is always patient and generous."

"We two who are honored with his affection and trust, will work for his good and the good of the kingdom," Thomas Cranmer pledges. "You, with the cause of reform in the court, teaching them the right way with your rooms a beacon of learning, and I will keep the clergy to the Bible. The Word, the Word; there is nothing greater than the Word of God."

"He spoke today of a war on the reformers in Germany," I say. "I am afraid that the emperor is planning a terrible purge of believers, a massacre. But there was no way for me to speak against it."

"There will always be times when he won't listen. Just bide your time and speak when you can."

"He spoke also of rumors that Anne of Cleves had his child, and he said that she was an ornament to our court. He told me that people are saying that I am ill and likely to die."

Thomas Cranmer looks at me as if he fears what I might say next. Gently he rests his hand on my head in a blessing. "As long as you never do anything wrong, then God will protect you, and the king will love you," he says quietly. "But you have to be completely innocent of any sin, my daughter, completely innocent of any imputation of sin. You must always show wifely loyalty and wifely obedience. Always make sure of that."

"I am innocent of sin," I maintain stubbornly. "You don't have to caution me. I am Caesar's wife—no one can say anything against me."

"I am glad of it," replies Thomas Cranmer, who has seen two adulterous queens climb the steps to the scaffold and not defended them. "I am glad of it. I could not bear—"

"But how am I to think? How am I to write? How am I to speak to him of reform without offending him?" I ask bluntly.

"God will guide you," the old churchman says. "You must have courage, you must use your God-given wits and your God-given voice, and you must not let the old papists of the court tame you. You must be free to speak. He will love that in you. Don't waver. You are the God-given leader for reform at court. Take your courage—do your work."

GREENWICH PALACE, SPRING 1546

KP

In February the king's fever returns.

"No one can care for me like William Butts used to do," he says miserably. "I shall die for lack of good doctoring."

He demands that I come to his bedside but he is ashamed of the smell in the room that no oils and herbs can conceal, and he does not like me to see his linen shirt wet in the armpits and stained at the front with constant sweat. But worse than this, he is starting to think that this is not ill health, but old age. He is sinking into a dark fearfulness of death that nothing but the return of his health will lift.

"Doctor Wendy will do his best for you," I say. "He is so faithful and careful. And I pray for you every morning and night."

"And bad news from Boulogne," he remembers miserably. "That young fool Henry Howard is squandering everything I have gained there. He's boastful, Kateryn. He's vain. I have recalled him and I will send out Edward Seymour to take his place. I can trust Edward to keep my castle safe."

"He will keep it safe," I say soothingly. "You need not fear."

"But what if I don't get better?" His eyes, tiny in his puffy face, squint at me as fearfully as a child. "There is Edward, of no age; there is Mary who would turn to Spain in a moment. If I were to die now, this month, the country would be at war again by Easter. I wouldn't trust any one of them not to take arms, and they would say they were fighting for the pope or fighting for the Bible, and all they would do would be to plunge this country into an internal war, and the French would invade."

I sit at his bedside and take his damp hand. "No, no," I say. "For you will get better."

"If I had a second son, I would be at peace," he frets. "If you were carrying a child, at least I would know that there was the chance of another son."

"Not yet," I say carefully. "But I don't doubt that God will be good to us."

He looks dissatisfied. "You will be Regent General," he reminds me. "It will all fall on you. You will have to keep them at peace while Edward grows up."

"I know I can," I say. "For so many of your councillors love you and have promised their duty to your son. There would be no war. There would be a loving care of him. The Seymour brothers would protect him, their nephew. John Dudley would support them. Thomas Cranmer would serve him as he does you. But it will never happen, for you will be well as the weather turns brighter."

"I see you only name reformers?" he demands, his eyes sharp and suspicious. "You are of the reform party, as people say. You are not on my side, you are on theirs."

"No indeed, I acknowledge the good men of all points of view. No one can doubt that Stephen Gardiner loves you and your son. The Howards are true to you and to Prince Edward. We would all protect him and bring him to the throne."

"So you do think I will die!" He crows at having trapped me. "You think you will outlive another old husband and enjoy a widow's estate." His face flushes red as his anger rises. "You sit there, at my sickbed, and imagine the day you will be free of me and free to take some worthless lad as your next husband, the fourth! You, who have wedded and bedded three men, are thinking of the next!"

I hide my shock at his sudden fury and I stay very calm. "My lord husband, I am sure you will recover from this fever, as you have from the injuries of your youth. I was trying to reassure you so that you would not worry on your sickbed. I pray for nothing but your health and I know that it will be restored to you."

He glares at me, as if he would see past my steady gaze and into my heart. I meet his eyes without flinching, for so much that I say is true. I honor him, I love him as a loyal subject and an honorable wife who has promised before God to love him. I never think of his death. It has been a long time since I dreamed of being free. I truly believe that he will recover from this illness and go on and on. This marriage will be my last. I may go to my grave loving Thomas Seymour, but I never think now that we will be together some day. There are no imaginable circumstances in which we could be together. He never looks at me, and I keep my passionate thoughts to myself and see his smile only in rare erotic dreams.

"You cannot doubt my love for you," I whisper.

"You pray for my health," the king says, soothed at the thought of me on my knees.

"I do. Daily."

"And when the preachers come to your room and you read the Bible, do you speak of a wife's obedience to her husband?"

"We do. We all know that a wife worships God in her husband. That is unquestioned."

"And do you doubt purgatory?" he asks.

"I think a good Christian goes to heaven because of the saving grace of Jesus," I say carefully.

"At his death? At the exact hour and minute of his death?"

"I don't know when, exactly."

"So will you pay for Masses for me? Will you establish a chantry for me?"

How to answer this? "Whatever you wish," I promise him. "Whatever Your Majesty would prefer. But I don't expect to see it."

His little mouth trembles. "Death," he repeats. "Thank God I am afraid of nothing. It's just that I cannot imagine the country without me. I cannot imagine a world without me here, without the king that I have become, the husband that I am."

I smile tenderly. "I can't imagine such a thing either."

"And your loss." He gives a little choke. "Yours, especially."

His grief is catching; tears come to my own eyes. I press his hand to my lips. "Not for years yet," I assure him. "If ever. I might die before you."

"You might," he says, cheered at once. "I suppose you might. You might die in childbirth like so many women. Because you are quite old to have a first child, aren't you?"

"I am," I say. "But I pray that God will grant us a child. Perhaps in the summer when you are well again?"

"Well enough to come to your bed and make another Tudor heir?" he asks.

I turn down my eyes and nod modestly.

"You long for me," he says, his mouth moist now and smiling.

"I do," I whisper.

"I should think so!" the king says more cheerfully. "I should think so."

Despite this promise he continues to be feverish and his leg gives him terrible pain for a long dark month. He is no better in spring—which comes slowly to the gardens of Greenwich Palace and makes the trees bud with life and shiver into leaf on the riverside walks, and the birds sing so loudly that they wake me at dawn every morning, which comes earlier and earlier and is warmer every day.

The lenten lilies swell and then flower beside the paths, their bright trumpet blooms like a shout of joy and hope, but the king keeps to his rooms with a table crowded with drafts and tinctures and herbs and jars of leeches, the shutters tightly closed against the dangerous fresh air. Doctor Wendy composes one physic after another, trying to keep the fever down, trying to cleanse out the suppurating wound on Henry's leg, which gapes still wider, like a bloody mouth, as it eats into the flesh towards the bone. Two pages are dismissed, one for fainting at the sight of it, and one for saying in chapel that we should pray for the king as he is being eaten alive. Henry's friends and courtiers gather around him, as if they are all under siege from disease, and each one tries to improve his position with the king in case this is not just another flaring up of fever and pain, but the beginning of a final illness.

It falls to me to dine before the court, to order the entertainments, and to make sure that the royal household runs as smoothly reporting to me as it does when it is reporting to the king. I even confer with the rivals Edward Seymour and Thomas Howard to see that there is nothing troubling, difficult, or dangerous in the Privy Council reports to the king before they take them in to him. When the Spanish envoys visit with a new plan for a treaty against France so that the emperor can move against the Lutherans and Protestants in his land, they call on me in my rooms before they attend the king.

They do this in the morning, in order to avoid the embarrassment of arriving at my rooms when the preachers of reform are there. They would be horrified to bump into Anne Askew: a reformer and an intelligent woman. It is bitter for me to have to smile and greet them, knowing that they are seeking the friendship of England only to be strong enough to hunt down and murder men and women in Germany who believe as we do. But they come and speak of their plans, trusting that I will serve the interests of my country before anything, and I do my duty and greet them with politeness and assure them of our friendship.

It is well known that the afternoon is the time for our sermon and our study. The best preachers in England travel down the river to attend my rooms and speak of the Word of God and how it can be applied in daily life, and how the man-made rituals can be scoured from a clean pure church. In these long weeks of Lent we have some inspiring sermons. Anne Askew comes several times, and Hugh Latimer often. Members of the court come to listen, even one of the Howards, Tom, the old duke's second son, makes his bow and asks if he may sit at the back and listen. I know that his lordship would be appalled to know that his son thinks as I do, but the yeast is spreading through the thick dough of court and the people will rise to holiness. I'm certainly not going to forbid a good young man to come to Jesus, even if he is a Howard.

These are the best theologians that England has, in touch with the reformers in Europe, and as I listen to them and sometimes debate with them, I am inspired to write a new book, one that I don't mention to the king because I know that it will go too far for him. But I am more and more convinced by the rightness of the Lutheran view, and more and more opposed to the superstitious paganism of the old church, and I want to write—I have to write. When I have a thought in my head, when I breathe a prayer in the chapel, I have a great desire to see it set down on a page. I feel as if I can think only when I see the words flowing from the nib of my quill, that my thoughts make sense only when they are black ink on cream paper. I love the sensation of a thought in my head and the vision of the word on the page. I love that God gave the Word to the world, and that I can work in His chosen form.

The king started the reform but now he is old and fearful he has halted. I wish he would go further. The influence of Stephen Gardiner, even at a distance, seems to blight any new thinking. The power of Spain should not dictate the beliefs of English men and women. The king hopes to create his own religion, an idio-syncratic combination of all the views of Christendom, picking the elements that he likes, the rituals that move him, the prayers that strike him. But this cannot be the way to worship God. The king cannot cling to the empty gestures of his childhood for sentiment, he cannot retain the expensive ritual that the old church loves. He has to think, he has to reason, he has to lead the church with wisdom, not with nostalgia for the past and fear of Spain.

I will have to write with care, always aware that my rivals at court will read it and use it against me if they can; but I am driven to tell the truth as I see it. I am going to call this new work *The Lamentation of a Sinner* as an echo of the title of a book by another learned lady, Margaret of Navarre, who wrote *Mirror of the Sinful Soul*. She had the courage to write and publish under her own name, and someday so will I. She was accused of heresy but it did not stop her thinking and writing, and I will not stop either. I will make it clear that the only forgiveness of sins, and the only way to heaven, is through personal faith and a complete commitment to Christ. The lie of purgatory, the nonsense of the chantries, the superstitions of indulgences, pilgrimages, Masses—none of these mean anything to God. They have all been created by man to make money. All that God requires of us was explained by His Son in the precious Gospels. We do not need the long explanations of scholars, we do not need the magic and tricks of the monks. We need the Word. Nothing but the Word.

I am the sinner of the title, though my greatest sin I keep concealed. In my daily life I sin in my constant love for Thomas. His face comes to me when I am dreaming and when I am waking and—worst of all—when I am praying and should have my mind on the cross. The only thing that comforts me for sacrificing him is the knowledge that I have given him up so that I can do God's work. I have given him for my soul, for the souls of all Christians in England that they may pray in a true church. I have surrendered the great love of my life for God, and I will bring reformed religion into England so that my suffering is worthwhile.

I pray for him; I fear he is in constant danger. His ships are commanded to take his brother, Edward, as the new commander, and reinforcements to Boulogne, and I have a long night of vigil when I think that Thomas may attack the French fleet, within the very reach of their shore guns, to clear the seas for his brother's safety. I go down in the morning, white-faced, to see Edward Seymour leave. He is leading his men down to Portsmouth to take ship.

"Godspeed," I say to him miserably. I cannot send him with a message for Thomas. I cannot even name him, not even to his brother. "I shall pray for you and for all in your company," I say. "I wish you very well."

He bows. He turns and kisses his wife, Anne, good-bye and then he mounts his horse, wheels it around, and salutes us all, as if he were a hero in a portrait, and leads his men out, south down the muddy lanes to Portsmouth and over the rough seas, stormy with spring gales, to France.

For several weeks we wait for news from Boulogne. We hear that they have landed safely and are preparing to engage the French forces. We are on the brink of war again with Edward commanding on land and Thomas at sea, but then the king decides that he is not yet ready to fight the French, and orders them all back. He says that John Dudley and Edward Seymour must meet with the French envoys and write a treaty of peace.

I don't think of the small English force trying to defend Boulogne. I don't even think of the fleet on the dark seas with the high spring tides. I just think that my prayers have been answered by a caring God, a God that loves Thomas for his bright courage as I do. God has saved Thomas Seymour because I prayed for him with all my heart, with my sinful, sorry heart, and I go to the chapel and gaze up at the cross and thank God that there will be no war and death has missed Thomas once again.

WHITEHALL PALACE, LONDON, SPRING 1546

KP

I am seated at my table, books all around me, ink drying on the nib of my quill as I try to find the right thing to say, how to express the concept of obedience to God, which is such a central part of the God-given duty of a woman, when Princess Mary comes into the room and curtseys to me. The ladies of my court look up. Each of us has a book or some writing—we could be posing for a drawing of a godly company—but all of us are alerted by Princess Mary's grave face and the way she comes to my table and says quietly: "May I speak with Your Majesty?"

"Of course, Princess Mary," I say formally. "Will you sit?"

She draws up a stool to the table and sits at the head of it so that she can lean towards me and speak very quietly. My sister, Nan, always ready to protect me from trouble, says, "Why don't you read to us, Princess Elizabeth?" and Elizabeth stands at the lectern, puts her book on it, and offers to translate extempore from Latin to English.

I see Mary's doting smile at her clever little sister and then she turns back to me and her face is grave. "Did you know that my father has proposed a match for me?" she asks.

"Not that he was ready to go ahead," I say. "He spoke to me some time ago only of a marriage that might come. Who is it?"

"I thought you might know. I am to marry the heir of the Elector."

"Who?" I ask, completely baffled.

"Otto Henry," she says. "His Majesty my father wants to create an alliance with the German princes against France. I was very surprised but it seems that he has decided to side with the German Lutherans against Spain after all. I would be married to a Lutheran and sent to Neuburg. England will become Lutheran, or wholly reformed, at the very least."

She looks at my aghast expression. "I thought that Your Majesty had such sympathies," she says carefully. "I thought you would be pleased."

"I might be pleased by England becoming fully reformed in religion and by an alliance with the German princes, but I am shocked at the thought of your going to Bavaria. To a country where they might have a religious rebellion, with your father allied to their emperor? What is he thinking? This is to send you into certain danger, to face an invasion from your own Spanish kinsman!"

"And I believe that I would be expected to take up my husband's religion," she says quietly. "There is no intention to protect my faith." She hesitates. "My mother's faith," she adds. "You know that I cannot betray it. I don't know what to do."

This is against tradition as well as respect for the princess and her faith and her church. Wives must raise the children in the faith of their husband, but are always allowed to retain their own faith.

"The king expects you to become a Lutheran?" I ask. "A Protestant?"

Her hand drops into the pocket of her gown where I know she keeps her mother's rosary. I imagine the cool beads and the tenderly carved coral crucifix between her fingers.

"Your Majesty, Lady Mother, did you not know of this?"

"No, my dearest. He spoke of it as one of his plans; no more. I did not know it had gone this far."

"He is going to call it the League Christian," she says. "He will be the head."

"I am so sorry," I whisper.

"You know that they threatened me with death if I did not swear that my father was Supreme Head of the Church," she whispers. "Thomas Howard, the old duke, threatened to smash my head against the wall until it was as soft as a baked apple. They tamed me as surely as they took a whip to me. The pope himself sent me a message to say that I might take the oath and he would forgive me. I failed my mother then, I betrayed her faith. I can't do it again."

Wordlessly, I feel for her hands and hold her tightly.

"Is there anything you can do, Kateryn?" she whispers to me as a friend. "Is there anything you can do?"

"What do you want?"

"Save me."

I am shocked into silence.

"I'll speak to him," I say. "I'll do everything I can. But you know . . ."

She nods, she knows. "I know. But tell him. Speak for me."

That afternoon we have a sermon on the vanity of war, a powerful piece of reasoning from one of the London preachers. He argues that all Christians should live in peace, for whatever their way of worshipping God they are all praying to the one God. Jews also should not be persecuted since their God is our God—though we have a greater insight into Him. He reminds us that Our Savior was born of a Jewish mother. He Himself was born a Jew. Even Muslims, in their benighted darkness, should not be attacked, because they too acknowledge the God of the Bible.

This is so strange and so radical that I check that the doors are locked and the sentries standing out of earshot, keeping all strangers at a distance, before we enter into a discussion. The preacher, Peter Lascombe, defends his thesis and appeals to the brotherhood of man. "And the sisterhood," he says, smiling, though this too is a great claim. I think it must be heretical. He says that, as in Spain in the old days, when the country was ruled by Muslim kings, everyone who believes in God should respect the others' faiths. The enemy should be those who don't believe in God at all and refuse to accept His Word: pagans and fools.

He takes my hand when it is time for him to go and bows over it. I feel between my fingers a little scrap of paper, double-folded. I let him go without a word and tell my ladies that I shall work at my studies for the next hour in silence, and I sit at my table and open my books. Unseen, hidden behind the great folios, I unwrap the note. It is from Anne Askew:

> *I write to tell you that a man came to me saying he was a servant of the Privy Council and asked me when I have preached before you and if you deny the Mass. I will say nothing. I will mention no names, I will never say yours. A.*

I rise from my seat and stand before the small fire that brightens the room as the afternoon grows dark. I hold out my hands as if to warm them and flick the little scrap of paper into the heart of the embers where it flames and curls into ash. I notice how cold I feel and that my hands are shaking.

I don't understand what is happening. On the one hand the king's own daughter Princess Mary is to be betrothed to a Lutheran; on the other hand the forces of popery are gaining power. The Seymours are away from court, Thomas Cranmer keeps to his home, there is no one to speak to the king for the new religion but me. I feel very alone, and I cannot read these contradictory signs. I cannot understand the king.

"Is your hand cramped from writing?" Nan asks me. "One of us could write for you if you would like a clerk, Your Majesty."

"No, no," I say. "I am well, all is well."

Nan is at the head of my ladies as we are about to walk into court. As I enter my presence chamber from my private rooms in a new gown of dark red, she comes to my side as if to straighten the rubies at my neck, and whispers to me.

"Lord Edward Seymour has written to his wife that there is a rumor in Europe that the king is planning to set you aside. Has the king said anything, anything at all to you? Has he even been critical of you?"

"Just the usual," I say quietly. "That he wishes I were with child. Nan—don't you think . . . ?"

"No," she says flatly. "A dead child would be your death warrant. Trust me. Let him long for it, get down on your knees and pray with him if you have to, but don't conceive something that he would take as a sign from the devil."

"But if the child were to be well? Nan, I want a child. I am thirty-three! I want a child of my own."

"How could it be?" she demands flatly. "There's been no healthy child born of a living mother since Princess Elizabeth. And half the court say that she is Mark Smeaton's bastard, from strong young stock. So—no legitimate child since Princess Mary, thirty years ago. He can't get a healthy child on a healthy woman. Last time it killed the mother."

She bends down and straightens the train of my silk gown. "So what shall I do about these rumors?" I ask as she comes up.

"Face them down," she counsels. "Complain about them. And we'll pray to ride them out. There's nothing we can do, anyway."

I nod, my expression grim.

"And even now, even with this gossip spreading we are safe, unless . . ."

"Unless?"

"Unless they come from the king himself," she says unhappily. "If he has said that he is thinking of a new wife, to someone who has repeated it elsewhere . . . if he is the source, then we are lost; but there is still nothing we can do."

I look down the line of my ladies to Anne of Cleves preparing to come in to dinner with her cheerful smile, the former wife he now loves so well that he keeps her at court. She was invited for Christmas and she is still here although it is nearly Easter. Catherine Brandon is behind her, the widow of Henry's dearest friend, the beautiful girl whom he has watched grow into womanhood, perhaps his lover, perhaps his love; and there are the new ones, the pretty ones, the ones young enough to be my daughter, the ones as young as Kitty Howard when he first saw her, young enough to be his grandchild.

"At least Anne of Cleves can go home," I say in sudden irritation.

"I'll see she does," Nan promises.

That afternoon, without warning, Thomas Seymour comes to court to report on the strength of the navy and the gathering danger of the French.

"Come and listen to Tom Seymour." The king beckons me to the table in his presence chamber. He takes my hand and puts it on his, holding my fingers trapped between his, so that I must stand beside him, facing Thomas, as if I am yearning towards the king, my hand resting on my husband's clenched unresponsive fist, listening to Thomas report on ships built and restored, docks dry and wet, outfitters and chandlers and rope merchants and sail lofts. He reports that another effort to raise the *Mary Rose* is being undertaken. She could be raised. She could sail again. Perhaps she might, like our king, defy time itself and go on and on forever, outliving the rest of the fleet, sailing on when all love and loyalty is gone, holding the future hostage, a live fleet yoked forever to her rotting timbers.

"There is an archery tournament in the garden for Your Majesty's amusement," I say. "If you could walk to it?"

"I can walk," he says. "Thomas, you will have seen I have an engine to get me up and downstairs. What d'you think? Should you bring me a crane from your shipyard? Will you fetch me a hoist from Portsmouth?"

Thomas smiles at his king, his eyes warm with sympathy. "If greatness were weighed, Your Majesty, nothing would ever lift you."

Henry cracks a laugh. "You're a pretty fellow!" he exclaims. "Take the queen to the archery butts and tell them I am coming. They can get ready for me. I may take a bow myself and see what I can do."

"Your Majesty must come, and show them how to do it," Thomas recommends, and offers his arm to me and we go towards the door, my hand burning on his sleeve, both of us looking studiously forward, at the guards, at the parting courtiers, at the opening door, never anywhere towards each other.

Behind us come the ladies of my chamber and their husbands, behind them the king's companions wait for him while he is helped up from his chair to his closestool. Someone fetches Doctor Wendy to give the king warm ale and a draft to help with the pain, and guards to help him into his carriage and wheel him out into the garden like a dead boar in a cart.

The double doors to the garden are thrown open by the yeomen of the guard as soon as Thomas and I approach them, and the warm spring air, smelling of the first cut of grass, floods into the palace. We glance at each other—it is impossible not to share our pleasure in the sudden sense of freedom, of release, in joy at the sunshine and the birdsong, and the court dressed in their best and preparing for another nonsensical game in this, the most beautiful palace in England.

I am smiling, simply for the joy of being with him; I could laugh out loud. The sun is warm on my face and the musicians start to play; Thomas Seymour, briefly and unnoticed, touches my hand as it rests on his arm, a swift and invisible caress.

"Kateryn," he says quietly.

I incline my head to left and right as people curtsey to me as we walk by. Thomas is tall, a head taller than me. He moderates his steps to mine but we stride out together, as if we would go all the way to Portsmouth and set sail on his ship. I think that we are so well matched, if we could have been together—what a couple we would have made, what children we would have conceived!

"Thomas," I say quietly.

"Love," he replies.

We need say nothing more. It is like lovemaking, the give and take of few words, the touch of warm skin, even through a thick sleeve, a glance from him to my bright face, my own sense that I am alive now and I have been dead for months. I have been wearing dead women's gowns and I have been dead myself. But now I feel alive again and longing. I feel desire as a sort of trembling wordless need that makes me think: if I could just lie with him once, I would never ask for more. If I could lie beneath him just once and have his long weight bear down on me, his mouth on mine, the scent of him, the sight of the dark hair on the nape of his neck, the smooth bronzed line from his ear to his collar bone . . .

"I have to talk to you," he says. "Will you sit here?"

There is a throne ready for the king when he comes and a chair beside it for me and then lower chairs for the princesses. Elizabeth comes bounding forwards and then smiles and blushes when she sees Thomas. He's not even aware of her as she turns away and strolls back to the archery butts, picks up a bow, and poses: fitting an arrow on the string, and drawing it back. I take my seat and he stands slightly behind the chair, leaning down so that he can whisper in my ear, but we are both facing the green and the competitors testing their strings, and taking aim,

and throwing a few blades of grass in the air to see the wind. We
are completely visible to everyone, we are on show. We are hidden
in plain sight.

"Don't move, and keep your face still," he warns me.

"I am listening."

"I have been offered a wife," he says quietly.

I blink, nothing more. "Who?" I say shortly.

"Mary Howard, the Duke of Norfolk's daughter."

This is a remarkable offer. Mary is the widow of the king's beloved bastard son that he made the Duke of Richmond. If the boy
had not died, he might have been named Prince of Wales and the
king's heir. Edward was not born then, and Henry needed a son;
even a bastard would have done. At Richmond's death the king refused to mention his name and Mary Howard, the little widowed
duchess, went back to live at her father's great castle at Framlingham. When she visits court the king always greets her warmly, she
is pretty enough to attract his heavy gallantry; but I didn't know
that there had been any proposals for her second marriage.

"Why Mary Howard?" I ask incredulously. Someone bows to
me and I smile and nod my head to acknowledge their greeting.
A few archers start to line up for practice shots. Princess Mary
walks towards us.

"So that the Howards and us Seymours should forget our dif-
ferences," he says. "It's not a new proposal. They made it before,
when she was first widowed. So that the Howards can become
kinsmen to Prince Edward. Princess Elizabeth is not royal enough
for them."

"You didn't seek it then?" I can feel a taste in my mouth as
bitter as the morning drink of rue. I realize that this is the flavor
of jealousy.

"I don't seek it now," he points out.

I want to pinch my face as it feels numb. I want to shake my
hands and stamp my feet. I feel as if I am frozen, as still as ice
on my throne, as Princess Mary comes slowly towards me across
the grass.

"Why would you?" I ask.

"It is advantageous," he says. "A set of alliances to link the families. We gain their alliances: they're friends with Gardiner and all who think like him. We would cease the endless struggle over the king. We could agree together how far reform is to go instead of fighting it out step by step. And they'd give me a fortune with her."

I can see it is a good match. She is a daughter of a duke, and sister to Henry Howard, one of the king's young commanders, reckless in Boulogne but still a favorite. If Thomas marries her, she will come to court, she will ask to be one of my ladies. I will have to watch him walk with her, dance with her, whisper to her. She will ask permission to leave my rooms early to go to his bed; she will go away from court to join him at Portsmouth. She will be his wife; I will attend her wedding and hear him swear to love and honor her. She will promise him to be bonny and blithe at bed and board. I think: I will never be able to bear it. I know that I must.

"What does the king say?" I ask the all-important, the only, question.

Thomas shows me his twisted smile. "He says that if Norfolk wants to give his daughter a husband, he might as well choose a man so young and lusty as he will please her at all points."

"Points?"

"That's what he said. Don't torture yourself. It was years ago."

"But the marriage is proposed again now!" I exclaim.

He bows, as if I have made a good remark in an argument that anyone may join. "It is."

"What will you do?" I whisper.

"What d'you wish?" he returns, his eyes on Princess Elizabeth. "I am yours heart and soul."

"Is the king my father coming to watch?" Princess Mary joins us and nods her head to Thomas's bow.

"Yes, he's coming at once," I reply.

As I walk to dinner at the head of my ladies that night I pass Will Somers. He is throwing a ball in the air and catching it in a cup, a foolish little game. We hesitate as we go by.

"Would you like to try?" he asks Princess Elizabeth. "It's harder than it looks."

"It can't be," she says. "I can see, it's nothing but catch."

Will turns and gives her a fresh cup, a new ball. "You try," he says.

She throws the ball high, and confidently she stretches out the cup as it falls. She catches it perfectly and a splash of water from the cup drenches her. "Will Somers!" she shouts, and she runs at him. "I am soaked! I am drowned! You are a wretch and a varlet and a rogue!"

Instead of running, Will drops to his hands and knees and bounds down the gallery, giving tongue as if he were a naughty dog. Elizabeth hurls the cup after him and catches him on his rump. Will howls and leaps up a stair and we all laugh.

"At least you caught him," I say to her. Nan hands me a napkin and I pat Elizabeth's laughing face and the lace at the neck of her gown. "You gave as good as you got."

"He's a wretch," she says. "And I will tip a chamber pot on his head when he next walks beneath my window."

The gentlemen of the court are waiting for us outside the hall. The king, tired by the archery, is dining in his rooms this evening.

"What's this?" Thomas Seymour asks Elizabeth, seeing her damp hair. "Have you gone swimming?"

"Will Somers and his stupid games," she says. "But I flung a cup at him."

"Shall I fight him for your good name?" he smiles down at her. "Shall you have me as your knight errant? Just say the word and I am yours."

I see her color rise. She looks up at him and she is speechless, like a flustered child.

"We will call on you," I say, to spare her.

He bows. "I am dining with the king. I will come to the hall after dinner."

Without any word the ladies align themselves in order of precedence. I go before everyone and behind me comes Princess Mary, and then Elizabeth, then my ladies, in order, Anne Seymour in her place. We walk through the crowded hall and the men stand and salute me and the women curtsey. I go to the dais and my steward helps me into my great chair.

"Tell Thomas Seymour to come to me when he leaves the king's rooms," I say quietly.

The dinner is served far more quickly than when the king is calling for extra portions and sending the dishes all around the room. When everyone has eaten, they clear the tables.

Thomas Seymour comes in through a side door, speaks to one man and then another, and then appears at my side. "Will you dance, Your Majesty?" he asks me.

"No, I shall go to the king shortly," I say. "Was he in good spirits?"

"I thought he was well."

"He is certain to ask me if you are still here, if you are staying for many days?"

"You can tell him that I am leaving for Portsmouth tomorrow."

Nan moves out of earshot and Catherine Brandon and some of the others take their places in a dance.

"What do you think?" Thomas says abruptly. "About my marriage?"

"I have to say this without anyone knowing what I am feeling," I say. "I have to be stony-faced."

"You must," he says. "We have no choice."

"We have no choice in the matter of your marriage either." I turn and smile at him as if I have made an interesting small point of conversation.

He nods courteously and then from the breast of his jacket he draws a little notebook, filled with sketches of rigging and sails. He opens it and shows it to me as if I may want to study it. "You are saying that I have to marry her?"

Blindly, I turn a page. "Yes. What possible excuse could you give for refusing? She is young and beautiful, probably fertile. She is wealthy and she comes from a great family. An alliance with them would be good for your house. Your brother would ask it of you. How can you refuse?"

"I can't," he says. "But what if you were to become free? And I was then married?"

"I would be your mistress," I promise without a moment's hesitation. I keep my face calm as if I am deeply interested in the book he holds out to me. "If I am free and you are married, I will become your sinful adulteress lover. If it costs me my soul, I will do it."

He breathes out. "My God, Kat. I so long for you."

Silently, we turn the pages for a few moments, then he says, "And when I am married and happy and she is with child, and she gives me a son and heir, and her boy takes my name, and I love him and am grateful to her, will you be able to forgive me? Will you be my lover then?"

He does not even hurt me with this picture, the worst that he could draw. I am prepared for it. I close the book and give it back to him. "We're beyond that," I tell him. "We're beyond jealousy and wanting to own each other. It's as if we went down with the *Mary Rose*: we're beyond hating each other or forgiving each other or even hope. All we can do now is try to swim."

"They were trapped," he remarks. "The sailors were trapped by the nets that were stretched over the decks to prevent boarders. They should have dived from the boat as she went down and swum for shore, but they were caught in their own grave and drowned."

I turn my head and blink away the tears. "So are we," I say. "Swim if you can."

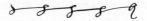

Of course the Howards, always quick to gobble up any advantage, had Mary Howard in their rooms ready for sale, and they visited the king before dinner was even served to ask for his permission for Thomas Seymour and Mary Howard to be married. The king saw them in his privy chamber where he was dining with a few lords and he agreed to the renewed proposal. While I was dining before the court in the great hall, doing my duty as queen, they were agreeing—Seymours and Howards—with the king that the marriage should go ahead. When I told Thomas that we were trapped like his drowning sailors, the king was drinking the health of the young couple.

Anne Seymour brings the gossip to the ladies" rooms. Her husband has told her that the king is pleased that the two great families of England will unite in marriage and content that his daughter-in-law shall remarry.

"Did you know, Your Majesty?" Anne Seymour asks me curiously. "Has His Majesty spoken with you?"

"No," I say. "This is the first I have heard of it."

Anne cannot hide her pleasure that she has this news before me, and I have to allow her the little triumph.

"Just as well," Nan says to me as we go into my bedroom before the nighttime prayers.

"Just as well—what?" I say disagreeably as I sit down before the glass and look at my pale face.

"Just as well to get Mary Howard out of the way. The king has always liked her and they are a family with no feeling but ambition, and no scruples at all."

"She is the widow of the king's dead bastard son," I say with assumed patience. "She is hardly likely to be a temptation to the king."

"She is a beautiful girl and the Howards would propose their own grandmother to him if it suited their purpose," Nan says, paying no attention to my ill humor. "If you had seen them with Anne Boleyn, if you had seen them with all the other Howard beauties—for Kitty Howard was only one of many—you would be glad to see Mary Howard safely settled."

"Oh, I am," I say coldly.

Nan waits as the maid lays my sleeves of gold brocade in the scented chest under the window. "You don't mind for him?" she asks very quietly.

"Not at all," I say clearly. "Not at all."

Thomas leaves court without speaking to me again, and I don't know if he goes directly to Portsmouth or travels to Suffolk to make arrangements for the wedding at Framlingham. I wait for someone to tell me that Thomas Seymour has caught himself an heiress and obliged the cause of reform by making an alliance between the Seymours and the Howards, which will make us all safer at court; to take the Howards from their alliance with Stephen Gardiner is to weaken his power. I wait for Anne Seymour to boast that the match is done and Tom Seymour wedded and bedded. But she says nothing, and I cannot ask. I so dread hearing that he is married that I don't ask.

Catherine Brandon taps on the door to my room when I am changing my gown to go to dinner, and dismisses the maids with a swift wave of her hand. Nan raises her eyebrows to me in the mirror. She is always alert for Catherine to show any sign that she is taking advantage of her growing favor with the king.

"This is important," Catherine says tersely.

"What is it?" I ask.

"Tom Howard, the duke's second son, has been summoned before the Privy Council. They're questioning him. About religion."

I rise up a little from my seat and then I sit down again. "Religion," I say flatly.

"It's a full inquiry," she says. "I was leaving the king's rooms and the door to the Privy Council chamber stood open. I heard them say that Tom was being brought to answer charges, and that Bishop Bonner would report from the Howard lands in Essex and Suffolk. He's been down there gathering evidence against Tom."

"You're sure it is Tom Howard?" I ask, suddenly fearful for the man I love.

"Yes, and they know he has listened to sermons and studied with us. Bishop Bonner has gone through all his books and papers at his home."

"Edmund Bonner Bishop of London?" I name the man who interrogated Anne Askew, a powerful supporter of the old church, hand in glove with Bishop Gardiner, a dangerous man, a vindictive man, a driven man. My influence and power forced him to let Anne Askew go, but there are few who leave the bishop's palace without pleading guilty to whatever crime he names. There are few who leave without bruises.

"Yes, him."

"Did you hear what he had to report?"

"No," she says. She claps her hands together in her frustration. "The king was watching me. I had to walk past the door; I couldn't stop and listen. I only heard what I have told you. That's all I know."

"Someone will know," I say. "Someone will tell us. Get Anne Seymour."

Catherine flits from the room and outside we hear the music of the lute suddenly break off as Anne Seymour puts the instrument aside and comes in, closing the door behind her.

"Has your husband said anything about questioning young Tom Howard?" Nan asks her bluntly.

"Tom Howard?" She shakes her head.

"Well, get to your rooms and find out what the council think they are doing," Nan says furiously. "For Edmund Bonner is looking around Howard lands for heretics and the Privy Council is questioning Tom Howard for heresy, and everyone knows that he has been here listening to the sermons. And many people know that Edmund Bonner released Anne Askew because Her Majesty requested it. How does he now have the courage to question another of our friends? How is he so bold as to go to Howard lands and ask questions about the Howards themselves? Have we lost power without knowing it? Or has Gardiner turned against the Howards? What's happening now?"

Anne looks from my pale face to Nan's furious one. "I'll go and find out," she says. "I'll come back as soon as I know. I may not be able to speak with him till dinner."

"Just go!" Nan spits, and Anne, usually so careful of her own importance, so slow to obey, scurries out of the room.

Nan rounds on me. "Your books," she says. "Your papers, the new book that you're writing."

"What of them?"

"We'll have to pack them up and get them out of the palace."

"Nan, nobody is going to search my rooms for my papers. The king himself gave me these books. I am studying his own writings, his own commentaries. We just completed our work on the liturgy together. This is the king's chosen area of study, not just mine. He is planning an alliance with the Lutheran princes against the Catholic kings. He is leading England away from the Roman Catholic Church towards full reform—"

"The liturgy, yes," she says, interrupting me, forgetting, in the grip of her fear, the respect that she should show. "You're safe working on that, I suppose, as long as you agree completely with him. But what about *Lamentation*? What about that? Would the king think it conformed to *The King's Book*? Is your secret work not heretical against his laws? Gardiner's laws?"

"But the law keeps changing!" I exclaim. "Changing, and changing again!"

"Doesn't matter. It is the law. And your writing is outside it."

I am silent. "Where can I send my papers?" I ask. "Where is safe? Shall I send them to someone in the city? To Thomas Cranmer?"

"To our uncle," she rules. I see that she has already thought of this, that she has been fearful for some time. "He'll keep them safe. He'll hide them and have the courage to deny them. I'll pack up while you're at dinner."

"Not my notes on the sermons! Not the translation of the Gospels! I need them. I am in the middle of—"

"Everything," she says fiercely. "Everything. Every single thing but the King's Bible and the king's own writings."

"You won't come to dinner?"

"I've no appetite," she says. "I won't come."

"You're never going to miss dinner!" I say, trying to be cheerful. "You're always hungry."

"I never ate a single meal in Syon Abbey when I lived there with Kitty Howard under arrest. My belly was stuffed with fear. And I feel like that now."

The king dines in the great hall before his people, sending out the best dishes to his favorites, raising his cup to toast his best friends. The court is crowded, for the members of the Privy Council are all here, having worked up an appetite for their dinner with the questioning of Tom Howard. There are many who would be glad to see the younger son from such a great family take a tumble into the quietness of prison for a while and come out with the Howard pride humbled. Those who have been offended by the persistent rise of his father take a pleasure in humiliating the son. Those of the reformed faith are glad to see a Howard squirm. Those who are traditionalists direct their malice at the ardent young scholar. One swift glance tells me that young Tom is not at dinner: not on the table for the young friends and companions, not at the foot of the Howard table. Where can he be?

His father, the Duke of Norfolk, is completely impassive at the head of his family table, rising to his feet to toast the king when he sends down a massive haunch of beef, bowing respectfully to me. There is no way of knowing what is going through the old man's head. He is a great friend of the old church, devoted to the Mass; but he denied his own beliefs and rode against the Pilgrimage of Grace. Though his heart was with the pilgrims who had enlisted to defend the old church, and fought under the banner of the five wounds of Christ, the duke declared martial law, ignored their royal pardons, and killed them one by one in their little villages. He hanged hundreds of innocent men, perhaps thousands, and refused to allow them to be buried in sanctified ground. Whatever his loyalties, whatever his loves, he cares for nothing as much as keeping his place at the side of the king, second in wealth and honor only to Henry. He is determined that his house shall succeed and become the greatest in England.

I cannot understand why such a man, the head of such a noble house, would sell his own daughter into marriage with the Seymours. Her first marriage was to the king's bastard heir and there is no comparison. As always, Thomas Howard will be thinking one thing and doing another. So what is he thinking when he proposes this match? What will Thomas Seymour have to do when he is the duke's son-in-law?

And how can the duke, knowing that his second son has been questioned by the Privy Council, dine on the king's dishes like a man without fear? How can Thomas Howard frantically thinking where his son might be raise a glass with a steady hand to the king? I cannot make him out. I cannot calculate what long careful game he is playing in this court of old gamblers.

There is to be a masque after dinner with dancers. The king's chair with the footstool is placed on the dais and I stand beside him. Courtiers come and go as the dancers make their grand entrance, and Will Somers skips out of the way as the musicians play and the dancing begins.

Anne Seymour comes quietly to stand behind me, her voice masked by the music. She leans forward to whisper in my ear. "They offered to release Tom Howard without a charge if he would admit that heresy is preached in your rooms. They threatened him with a trial for heresy if he did not assist them. They said that all they need to know from him are the names of those who preach in your rooms and what they say."

It is like falling from a horse: everything suddenly goes very slowly and I can see how this started and how it will end between one beat of the music and another. It is as if the court freezes, the little golden clock in my room freezes, as Anne Seymour tells me that the Privy Council are pursuing me for heresy, hunting me down from word to word. Tom Howard is just bait to lead them to me. He is their first step. I am the goal.

"They asked him to name me?" I glance sideways at my husband, who is smiling at the dancers and clapping in time to the music, quite blind to my descent into terror. "Was the king there? At the Privy Council meeting? Was this in his hearing? Did the king ask them to name me as a heretic himself? Has he told them to find me guilty?"

"No, thank God. Not the king."

"Who then?"

"It was Wriothesley."

"The Lord Chancellor?"

She nods, completely aghast. "The highest law lord in the land has ordered the duke's son to name you as a heretic."

I cancel the preachers who come to my rooms and instead I summon the king's chaplains to give us readings from the Bible. I don't invite them to comment or lead a discussion, and my ladies say nothing, but listen in respectful silence as if none of us is capable of thought. Even when the reading is of great interest to us, something that we would normally study, perhaps even go back to the original Greek to make a new translation, we nod like a convent of orthodox nuns hearing the laws of God and the opinions of man, as if we had no minds of our own.

We go to chapel before dinner and Catherine Brandon, the king's new favorite, walks beside me.

"Your Majesty, I am afraid that I have some bad news," she starts.

"Go on," I say.

"A London bookseller, who has supplied me for years with texts, has been arrested for heresy."

"I am sorry to hear it," I say steadily. "I am very sorry for the trouble for your friend." I make sure that I don't even check in my stride as we go side by side down the gallery to the chapel. I incline my head to a group of bowing courtiers.

"I'm not asking for your protection for him. I am warning you." She has to hurry to keep up with my rapid pace. "This man, a good man, was arrested on the orders of the Privy Council. The arrest was made out specifically to him by name. He is John Bale. He brings in books from Flanders."

I raise my hand. "Better that you tell me nothing," I say.

"He sold us the Testament in French that you have," she says. "And the Tyndale translation of the New Testament. They're banned now."

"I don't have them," I reply. "I have given away all my books, and you had better get rid of yours, Catherine."

She looks as frightened as I feel. "If my husband were alive, then Bishop Stephen Gardiner would never have dared to arrest my bookseller," she says.

"I know," I agree. "The king would never have allowed Charles Brandon to be questioned by such as Wriothesley."

"The king loved my husband," she says. "So I was safe."

I know that we are both wondering if he loves me.

GREENWICH PALACE, SUMMER 1546

KP

The ritual of the court moves on, and I—who once led it boldly—
am trapped inside it, going through my paces like a blinkered
horse, allowed only to run the length of the tilt rail, blinded to the
world outside my narrow, frightened view. We transfer to Greenwich for the pleasure of the gardens in the summer weather, but
the king hardly emerges from his rooms. The roses bloom in the
arbors and he does not smell their scent, heavy on the evening
air. The court flirts and plays and competes in little games and
he does not bellow advice nor award prizes. There is boating and
fishing, riding at the quintain, racing and dancing. I have to appear at every pastime, smile on every winner, and maintain the
normal life of the court, running in its agreed course. But at the
same time I know that people are whispering that the king is ill,
and does not want me at his side. That he is an old man struggling with illness and pain but everyone can see his young wife
watching the tennis, or the archery, or boating on the river.

My physician comes to see me as I am looking at my birds.
Two pairs of canaries have nested and one cage has a row of
adorable chicks, opening their beaks in unison, stretching their
stubby pale wings. "There's nothing wrong with me," I say irritably. "I didn't send for you. I am perfectly well. You will have been

seen coming here, please make sure that you tell everyone that I am perfectly well and that I didn't send for you."

"I know you didn't, Your Majesty," Doctor Robert Huicke says humbly. "It is I who needs to see you. I can see that you are in your full health and beauty."

"What is it?" I ask, closing the cage door and turning from the birds.

"It is my brother," he says.

At once I am alert. Doctor Huicke's brother is a known reformer and scholar. He has attended the sermons at my rooms, has sent me books from London for my studies. "William?"

"He has been arrested. It was an order from the Privy Council naming him, him alone, not the other scholars whom he studies with. None of his circle. Just him."

"I am sorry to hear it."

My blue parrot sidles along his perch as if to listen. I offer him a seed and he takes it in claw and beak, positioning it so that he can crush it and eat the kernel. He drops the husk on the ground and looks at me with his bright intelligent eyes.

"They asked him about your opinions, Your Majesty. They asked him what authors you cite, what books he has seen in your rooms, who else attends the sermons. They searched his rooms for anything written by you. They suspect him of taking your papers to a publisher. I think they may be building a case against you."

I shiver as if I am cold despite the warm summer sunshine. "I am afraid you are right, Doctor."

"Can you speak to the king in favor of my brother, Your Majesty? You know he is no heretic. He has thoughts about religion, but he would never undermine the king's settlement."

"I will speak if I can," I say carefully. "But you see for yourself that I am not influential at the moment. Stephen Gardiner and his friends the Duke of Norfolk, William Paget, and Lord Wriothesley, who were my friends, are working against the new learning, and they are in the ascendancy. This time, while the king is in such pain, it is they who are admitted to his rooms. They are his advisors, not me."

"I will speak to Doctor Wendy," he says. "Sometimes he consults with me about the king's health. He might mention my brother's name to the king and ask him for a pardon, if they charge him."

"Perhaps all these interrogations and inquiries are just to frighten us," I say. "Perhaps the good bishop just wants to warn us all."

The parrot dips up and down as if he is dancing. I recognize that he is hoping for more seeds, and I carefully hand him another. He takes it daintily, turning it round with his black tongue and beak as Doctor Huicke continues quietly: "I wish that were so. You haven't heard about Johanne Bette?"

I shake my head.

"He is one of my congregation, the brother of one of your yeomen. And the Worley brothers, Richard and John, have been taken from your household, too, for questioning. God have mercy on poor Johanne—he has been condemned to death. If this is a warning, it is written in the blackest of ink and addressed to you. It is your men that they are questioning, Your Majesty. It is your man who will have to climb the scaffold."

From the darkened royal rooms comes an announcement: the king is ill again. The fever mounting from his wounded leg burns in his brain and enters every joint of his aching body. Doctor Wendy is in and out of his chambers, trying one remedy after another; the doors are shut to almost everyone else. We hear that they are cupping him, draining the blood from the great bloated body, tapping the wound, grinding gold pieces into it and then washing them out with jugs of lemon juice. The king moans with pain and they station guards to keep people out of the great presence chamber and the gallery beyond, so that no one shall hear him sob in agony. He does not ask for me; he does not even reply to my messages wishing him well, and I don't dare to enter without invitation.

Nan says nothing, but I know that she is remembering when the king locked himself away from Katherine Howard as they went through her little letters and her household accounts looking for a payment or a gift for Thomas Culpepper. Now, as then, the king hides in his rooms, watching, and listening, but never giving himself away.

Some days I wake in the morning certain that today they will come for me, and I will go in my royal barge, my new royal barge, which has given me such foolish pleasure, upriver to the Tower. I will enter through the watergate on the swelling tide, and they will take me, not to the royal rooms, but to the ones that overlook the green, where the prisoners are held. A few days later and I will watch from the barred window as they build a wooden scaffold and know that it is for me. A confessor will come in and tell me that I must prepare myself for death.

On these days I don't know how to get out of bed. Nan and the maids dress me as if I were a cold doll with a set face. I go through the motions of queenship, attending chapel, dining before the court, walking by the river and throwing a ball for little Rig, watching the court at play, but my face is stiff and my eyes are glassy. I think that if the day comes that there is a knock on my door I will shame myself. I will never find the courage to climb the ladder to the scaffold. I will never be able to speak as Anne Boleyn spoke. My legs will fail and they will have to push me up the steps, as they did to Kitty Howard. I will not fight for my life like Margaret Pole. I will not go cheerfully in my best coat like Bishop Fisher. I am as inadequate to this task as I am to my marriage. I will fail at my death as I have failed as queen.

Other days I wake cheerfully, certain that the king is doing what he himself told me is the best way to rule: favor one side and then the other, keep your thoughts a secret from everyone, be the master in the dogfight and let the curs fight it out before you. I assure myself that he is just tormenting me, as he torments everyone. He will get better and send for me, praise my beauty and remind me that I am no scholar, give me diamonds reset from a broken pectoral cross, tell me that I am the sweetest wife a man ever had, and dress me in someone else's gown.

"George Blagge has been arrested," Nan tells me quietly as we walk to chapel one morning. She grips my hand as I stumble. "They came for him last night."

George Blagge is a fat plain adventurer, a favorite of the king because of his round ugly face and his terrible habit of snorting with laughter at a bawdy joke. People compose jokes just to hear Blagge snuffling with laughter, blushing rosy red, and then finally unable to contain his great snorting bellow. The king calls him "his beloved pig," and Will Somers does a fine impression of Blagge hearing a joke that is almost as funny as the real thing. But he will not be doing that trick again.

"What has he done?" I ask.

George Blagge is no fool, for all that he has a laugh like a far-rowing sow. In serious mood he has come to my rooms and listened to the sermons. He says little, and thinks a lot. I cannot believe that he would ever have said anything that might offend the king; to the king he is a playmate, not a philosopher.

"They say he spoke disrespectfully about the Mass, and then he snorted with laughter," Nan whispers.

"Snorted with laughter?" I look blankly at her. "But that's what he does; that amuses the king."

"Now it's disrespect," she says. "And now he's charged with heresy."

"For snorting?"

She nods.

John Dudley Lord Lisle, the rising man and a believer in religious reform, now comes home from France with a peace treaty in his pocket. All the while that Stephen Gardiner was treating with the emperor, aiming for a peace with Spain, selling the reformers to their death in exchange for a renewed loving alliance with the pope, John Dudley was secretly meeting with the French admiral and hammering out an agreement where we keep Boulogne for decades to come and the French pay us a handsome fee. This should be the moment of triumph for John Dudley, for the Seymours, and for all of us who share the reform faith. We have won the race to peace; we have made peace with the French and not with the papist Spanish.

He comes to my rooms to receive my congratulations. The Princess Mary is at my side, putting a brave face on the turn of events that remove England from alliance with her mother's family.

"But, my lord, if we have peace with the French, then I suppose that the king is unlikely to make his new alliance with the German princes and the Elector Palatine?"

The studied blankness of poor Mary's face tells me how anxiously she is awaiting his response.

"Indeed, His Majesty will not need the friendship of the German princes," John Dudley replies. "We have a lasting alliance with France, we need no other."

"Perhaps no betrothal," I whisper to Mary and watch the color flood into her face. I make a little gesture to give her permission to stand aside and she goes to the window bay to compose herself.

As soon as her back is turned, the smile disappears from John Dudley's face. "Your Majesty, what in God's name is happening here?"

"The king is arresting those in favor of reform," I say quietly. "People are disappearing from court, and from the London churches. There's no sense in it. One day someone is at dinner; the next they are gone."

"I hear that Nicholas Shaxton has been summoned to London to answer charges of heresy. I couldn't believe it. He was Bishop of Salisbury! They can't arrest a former bishop."

I didn't know this. He can see the shock in my face. For one of the king's own bishops to be arrested like this is to return to the dark days of the martyred churchmen, and John Fisher walking to the scaffold. The king had sworn he would never allow such cruelty again.

"Bishop Hugh Latimer, who preached before me in the Lent season, has been summoned to explain to the Privy Council what topics he chose," I tell John Dudley.

"The Privy Council are theologians now? They are going to debate with Latimer? I wish them the best with that."

"Stephen Gardiner will certainly debate with him. He is defending the Six Articles," I say. "And that is an easy side to take for there is a new law that nobody may speak against them."

"But the Six Articles are halfway to popery!" he exclaims. "The king himself said—"

"Now, they are the king's express opinion," I interrupt.

"His opinion for now!"

I bow and say nothing.

"Forgive me, forgive me," John Dudley recovers himself. "It's just that I feel as if the Seymours and Cranmer and I are away from court for five minutes and the old churchmen get hold of the king, and when we return we find all the gains we have made and everything we believe are set back. Can't you do anything?"

"I can't even see him," I say. "I can't ask for mercy for the others because I never see him. I am afraid of what they say about me."

He nods. "I'll do what I can," he says. "But perhaps you should limit your studies."

"My books are gone," I say bitterly. "See the empty shelves? My papers, too."

I had hoped he would say that there was no need for me to destroy my library. But he simply asks: "And have you stopped your sermons and talks?"

"We listen only to the king's chaplains, and their sermons are as dull as they can make them."

"What subjects?"

"Wifely obedience," I say dryly, but not even that makes him smile.

Hugh Latimer, ordered to appear as a suspect before the Privy Council where he had once spoken as an authority, admits that he preached a series of sermons before me—undeniable—since half the Privy Council's wives, and some of the Privy Council themselves, attended. He does not agree that he said anything heretical, nor anything tending to reform. He says that he preached on the Word of God, and stayed inside the current teaching of the church. They release him; but the next day they arrest another preacher from my afternoon studies, Doctor Edward Crome, and they accuse him of denying the existence of purgatory.

This, he has to admit. Of course he denies the existence of purgatory. If they asked me, or indeed anyone with any sense, no one could say that there is any evidence for such a place. Heaven, yes—Our Lord speaks of it Himself—hell, yes—He harrows it for sinners. But nowhere does the Bible suggest that there is some ridiculous place where souls must wait and can be bought out of their suffering by a donation to the church or the bawling of Masses in paid chantries. There is simply no reference for this, there is no scholarship to support it. So where has this story come from? The authorship is clear: it is an invention by the church as a way of getting a great income from the suffering of bereaved families, and the fears of dying sinners. The king himself has abolished chantries—how can purgatory exist?

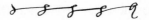

But it is the king who authorizes these arrests, the king who has authorized all of them since the spring herding of scholars and preachers and people related to me. The Privy Council will make inquiries, name names, demand explanations, but the king alone decides who shall be arrested. Either he signs his name, the signature scrawled carelessly, the warrant held on the sheets of his sickbed, or he tells the men he trusts in his chamber, Anthony Denny and John Gates, to use the dry stamp of his signature, and ink it in later. But either way, the warrant is brought to him for his personal express approval. He may be groaning in pain, he may be half asleep, drugged with painkillers and strong wine, but he knows. This is not a plot by papists at his court moving against my beliefs and my friends without the king's knowledge, taking advantage of his sickness and fatigue. It is a plot by the king, himself, against my beliefs and against my friends—perhaps even against me. This is the king setting the dogs to fight, but this time favoring one side against the other, putting a fortune on the outcome. Favoring my enemies against me, putting me, his wife, into the dog pit.

"She's here. Anne Askew is here, right here! Now!" Joan Denny rushes into my rooms and kneels before me, as if her legs cannot hold her up.

"She has come to see me?" I cannot believe that she would take such a risk, knowing that her teachers and mentors are in the Tower. "She cannot come in. Tell her I am sorry but—"

"No! No! Arrested! Summoned to see the Privy Council. They are questioning her now."

"Who told you?"

"My husband. He says he will do what he can for her."

I take a breath. I want to tell her that Anthony Denny must make sure that my name is not mentioned, or at any rate, not repeated to the king. But I am so afraid, and so ashamed of my fear, that I cannot speak. I am so afraid of what Anne might say, what she might tell the Privy Council. What if she says that she preached heresy to us, and that we listened? What if she tells them that I am writing my own book, filled with forbidden knowledge? But I cannot tell Joan, who has listened with me, who studies with me, who prays beside me, that my first thought is to save my own fearful skin. I am afraid and ashamed of my fear.

"God keep her safe," is all I say out loud.

"Amen."

They hold her overnight, somewhere in this great rambling palace. As my maid dresses me for dinner I ask her where Anne Askew might be. She does not know. There are dozens of windowless cellar rooms and attic rooms and treasure rooms that can be locked from the outside. If they don't care for her comfort or safety, they could simply throw her in the guardhouse. I dare not send anyone to look for her. At dinner, Bishop Gardiner intones an interminable grace and I bow my head and listen to him mouthing the Latin words, knowing that half the room cannot understand him; and he does not care because he is completing his ritual, his private ritual, he does not care that they are as children asking for bread and receiving a stone. I have to wait for him to finish his singsong skimble-skamble, raise my head, and nod for the servers to enter. I have to smile and eat and command the room, laugh at Will Somers, send out dishes to William Paget and Thomas Wriothesley as if they are not plotting my downfall, bow to the Duke of Norfolk, who sits at the head of his family table, his face a bland mask of courtier charm, his reformer son still missing. I have to behave as if I have not a single care in all the world, while somewhere in the great palace, my friend Anne eats the cold leavings from the court's dinner, and prays on her knees that God will keep her safe tomorrow.

"They have summoned me to question her." My brother strolls up to my chair while the court is dancing. My ladies, their faces stiff with smiles, form up into sets and go through their steps.

"Will you refuse?"

"How can I? It's a test. I am on trial here too, and if I fail they will move on to you. No, I will question her and hope I can guide her to a plea for forgiveness. I know she won't recant her beliefs; but she might agree that she is ill educated."

"She knows the Bible backwards and forwards," I say. "She knows the New Testament by heart. No one can call her ill educated."

"She can't argue with Stephen Gardiner."

"I think you'll find that she will."

"Then what am I to do?" William exclaims in sudden impatience. At once he throws back his head and laughs, a courtier's laugh, to suggest that he is telling me a funny story. I laugh with him, and I tap his hand, my comical brother.

Will Somers lopes past us with a grimace. "If you are ready to laugh at nothing, you might laugh at me," he says.

I clap my hands. "We were laughing at an old jest, not worth repeating," I say.

"They're the only ones I have."

We wait until he has gone by. "Try to give her a way out, without incriminating yourself," I say. "She is a young woman, full of life. She's not seeking martyrdom. She'll save herself if she can. Just give her a way. And I will try to see the king."

"What is he doing?" my brother whispers. "What does he mean by this? Has he turned against us? Has he turned against you?"

"I don't know," I say. I look at my brother's anxious face and I realize, coldly, that five women have sat here, in this very seat, before me, and not known if the king had turned against them and, if he had, what he was planning to do.

When dinner is over, I send Nan to the king's rooms to ask if I may see him. She comes back surprised: I am to be admitted. She rushes me into my most flattering hood and we pull down the front of my gown, and pat oil of roses into my neck. She and

Catherine attend me as far as the king's bedroom and the guards open the door and I go in alone.

Sir Anthony Denny is there, and Bishop Gardiner. Doctor Wendy is at the back of the room with half a dozen grooms and servers standing around, waiting to move the king from chair to bed, as he wishes, to lift him onto his closestool, or to help him into his wheeled chair so that he can go into his presence chamber and pass like a great statue paraded among his people.

"My lord," I say, curtseying.

He smiles at me and beckons for me to come close. I bend down and kiss him, ignoring the stink. He puts his arm around my waist and squeezes me. "Ah, Kat. Did you and the court enjoy a good dinner?"

"You were very much missed," I say, taking a chair beside him. "I hope you will be well enough to join us soon. It feels like a long time since we had the joy of your presence."

"I am sure of it," he says cheerfully. "This was just the quartain fever that I get from time to time. Doctor Wendy says I throw it off like a boy."

I nod enthusiastically. "Your strength is remarkable."

"Well, the buzzards may hover but there is nothing for them to pick at yet." His gesture indicates Bishop Gardiner as a buzzard and I smile at the bishop's cross face.

"I am more of a lark that goes high to sing your praises," the bishop says with awkward humor.

"A lark, my lord bishop?" I put my head on one side as if to scrutinize his white surplice and black stole. "More like a swallow in your coloring."

"You see Stephen as a swallow?" Henry prompts me, amused.

"He arrives and suddenly it is summer," I say. "He is a harbinger. When the bishop is here, it is high summer for the Privy Council to make an inquiry. Time for all the old churchmen to nest and twitter under the eaves. It is their season."

"Are they not here to stay?"

"The cold winds of truth will blow them away, I think, lord husband."

The king laughs. Stephen Gardiner is quietly furious.

"Would you have him dress any differently?" the king asks me.

I am daring, encouraged by his laughter. I turn my head and whisper in his ear, "Don't you think his lordship would suit the color red?"

Red is the color of a cardinal's robes. If Gardiner could bring the country back to Rome, the pope would give him a cardinal's hat in a moment. Henry laughs aloud. "Kateryn, you have a sharper wit than Will! What d'you say, Stephen? Do you long for a red hat?"

Stephen Gardiner's mouth is pursed. "These are grave matters," he manages to say. "Not fit for a jest. Not fit for ladies. Not fit for wives."

"He's right." The king is suddenly weary. "We must let our good friend defend our church against heresy and mockery, Kat. It is my church, not a subject for debate or humor. These are serious matters, not for foolish mockery. There is nothing more important."

"Of course," I say gently. "Of course, my lord. All I would ask is that the good bishop questions people who speak against your reforms. The reforms themselves should not be questioned. The bishop cannot want us to step backwards, away from your understanding, back to the old days before you were head of the church."

"He won't do that," the king says shortly.

"The chantries—"

"Not now, Kateryn. I am weary."

"Your Majesty must rest," I say quickly, getting up from the chair and kissing his forehead, which is damp with sweat. "Will you sleep now?"

"I will," he says. "You can all go." He retains my cool fingers in his hot grip. "Come back later," he says to me.

I make sure I don't shoot a triumphant glance at Stephen Gardiner. I have won this round, at least.

It is no victory, my whorish triumph. The king is feverish and sleepless, impotent and irritated at his failing. Though I do everything he asks of me, let down my hair, take off my robe, even stand, burning with humiliation, while he passes his hands all over me, nothing can stir him. He sends me away so that he can sleep alone and I sit up all night by the fire in my room and wonder where Anne Askew is in the palace, sleepless as I am sleepless, afraid as I am afraid, and if she even has a bed tonight.

The next round is played out before the Privy Council and I cannot be there. The doors to the Privy Council room are closed and two yeomen of the guard stand before them at attention, their pikes raised.

"She's in there," Catherine Brandon mutters to me in an undertone, as we walk past the wood-paneled door on our way to the garden. "They took her in this morning."

"Alone?"

"She was arrested with her former husband, but she said he was nothing to her and they dismissed him. She's alone."

"They know that she has preached before me?"

"Of course, and they know it was your instruction to Bishop Bonner that she should be freed last time."

"But they don't fear my influence? He did, then."

"It seems your influence has diminished," she says flatly.

"How has my influence diminished?" I demand. "The king still sees me, he still speaks tenderly to me. He commanded me to his bed last night. He promised me gifts. All the signs say that he still loves me."

She nods. "I know he does, but he can do all that and disagree with your faith. Now he agrees with Stephen Gardiner and the

Duke of Norfolk and all of the rest of them, Paget and Bonner, Rich and Wriothesley."

"But all his other lords are for reform," I protest.

"But they're not at court," she counters. "Edward Seymour is either in Scotland or Boulogne. He's such a reliable commander that he is always away. His success is our disadvantage. Thomas Cranmer is studying at his home. You're not admitted when the king is ill, and he has been ill for weeks. Doctor Wendy is not an advocate for reform like Doctor Butts was. To keep something before the king, to maintain his interest in it, you have to be in his company, all the time. My husband, Charles, said he always kept at the king's side because a rival was always ready to take his place. You have to make sure you are beside him, Your Majesty. You have to get into his presence and be there all the time, to put our side of the argument."

"I understand. I try. But how can we defend Anne Askew before the Privy Council?"

She offers me her hand as we go down the stairs to the garden.

"God will defend her," she says. "If they find her guilty, then we will beg the king for a pardon for her. You can take all your ladies in to him, he'll like that, and we can go on our knees. But we can do nothing for her now, as she faces the Privy Council; only God will have her in His keeping there."

The Privy Council sits wrangling with the young woman from Lincolnshire all day, as if she, slightly educated and not yet thirty, should take more than a moment of their time to challenge and discredit. Stephen Gardiner Bishop of Winchester, and Edmund Bonner Bishop of London, argue theology with the young woman who has never been inside a university hall; but they cannot demonstrate her mistake.

"Why would they spend so much time on her?" I demand.

"Why not just order her back to her husband, if they want to silence her?"

I am pacing up and down in my room. I can't sit still to reading or study, but I cannot go and demand that they open those forbidding doors. I cannot leave Anne in there alone with her enemies, my enemies, but equally I cannot rescue her. I dare not go to the king without invitation. I hope to see him before dinner, I hope that he is well enough to come to dinner, and I cannot bear to wait.

There is a noise outside and the guards open the door to my brother and three companions. I whirl round.

"Brother?"

"Your Majesty." He bows. "Sister."

He hesitates, he can't speak. Out of the corner of my eye I see my sister, Nan, rise to her feet, as Catherine stretches out a hand to her. Anne Seymour's eyes widen, her jaw drops, she crosses herself.

The silence seems to stretch for hours. I realize that everyone is looking at me. Slowly I take in my brother's aghast face, the guards beside him. Slowly, I realize that they all think that he has come to arrest me. I can feel my hands tremble and I clasp them together. If Anne has incriminated me, then the Privy Council will have ordered my arrest. It would be like them to send my own brother to take me to the Tower as a way of testing his loyalty, and confirming my fall.

"What do you want, William? You look very strange! Dear brother, what have you come for?"

As if my words have released a mechanism, the clock on my table strikes three with a silvery chime, William steps inside the room and the guards swing the doors closed behind him.

"Has the meeting ended?" My voice is choked.

"Yes," he says shortly.

I see that his face is grave and I put my hand on the back of a chair for support. "You look very serious, William."

"I don't have good news."

"Tell me quickly."

"Anne Askew has been sent to Newgate Prison. They could not persuade her to recant. She will have to stand trial as a heretic."

The room goes silent and everything seems to melt and swirl before my eyes. I grip the chair back to help me stand, and blink furiously. "She would not recant?"

"They sent for Prince Edward's tutor to persuade her. But she quoted them verse after verse from the Bible and proved them wrong."

"Could you not save her?" I burst out. "William, could you say nothing to save her?"

"She confounded me," he says miserably. "She looked me in the face and said that it was a great shame on me that I should advise her, against my own knowledge."

I gasp. "She accused you of thinking as she does? She's going to name the people who believe as she does?"

He shakes his head. "No! No! She was very careful in what she said: meticulous. She named nobody. Not me, not a word against you or your ladies. She accused me of advising her against my own knowledge; but she did not say what my knowledge might be."

I am ashamed of my next question. "Did anyone mention me at all?"

"They put it to her that she preached in your rooms, and she said so do many preachers of many different beliefs. They tried to get her to name her friends in your rooms." Carefully he looks at the floor so no one can say he exchanged a glance with anyone. "She would not. She was stubborn. She would not give any names.

"It was clear, sister, very clear, that the only thing they wanted from her was proof of your meetings, heretical meetings. They would have released her, then and there, if she had named you as a heretic."

"You're saying that it's me they want, not her," I say quietly through stiff lips.

He nods. "It was obvious. Obvious to everyone. She knows."

I am silent for a moment, trying to push down my fear into my churning belly. I try to be brave, as Anne Boleyn was brave. She protested the innocence of her brother, of her friends. "Is there any way we can get her released?" I ask. "Does she have to go to trial? Should I go to the king and tell him that they have wrongly imprisoned her?"

William looks at me as if I have lost my wits. "Kat—he knows already. Don't be stupid. This is not Gardiner running ahead of the king, this is Gardiner doing only what the king wants. The king himself signed the warrant for her arrest, approved her being sent for trial, ordered that she be held at Newgate until she is tried. He will have prepared an instruction for the jury. He will have decided already."

"A jury should be independent!"

"But it is not. He'll tell them what verdict to bring in. But she'll have to stand trial. Her only safety would be to recant at her trial."

"I don't think she'll do that."

"Neither do I."

"What will happen then?"

He just looks at me. We both know what will happen then.

"What will happen to us?" he asks miserably.

To my surprise, the king comes to my rooms with the gentlemen of his household and some of the Privy Council to escort us in to dinner. It has been a long time since the king was well enough to lead me in to dine. They come in noisily, as if celebrating his return to court. He cannot walk, he cannot even stand on his ulcerated leg, but comes in his wheeled chair with his thickly bandaged leg extended before him. He is laughing at this, as if it were a temporary injury from jousting or hunting, and the court takes its cue from him, and laughs too, as if we expect to see him dancing tomorrow or the day after. Catherine Brandon says she will commission a rival chair and there can be a chair joust with the king in the lists, and he swears it must be done and we shall have chair jousting tomorrow. Will Somers dances before him as he is wheeled into the room, pretends to fall and be run over by the inexorable progress of the huge chair and the massive man half reclining inside it.

"Moloch! I have been run over by Moloch!" Will mourns.

"Will, if I had run you over, you wouldn't be here to shout about it," the king warns him. "Keep away from the wheels, Fool."

Will responds with a somersaulting dive that throws him out of the way just in time. My ladies shriek a warning and laugh as if it is extraordinarily funny. We are all on edge, all anxious to keep the king in his sunny mood.

"I swear I will mow you down in my chariot," Henry shouts.

"Can't catch me," Will replies cheekily, and at once Henry bellows at the two pages, sweating behind the handles of the chair, that they must pursue Will around my presence chamber as he dances and leaps, balancing on benches, springing up to the window seat, darting round my ladies, snatching them by the waist and spinning them round so the king charges at them and not him, sending them screaming and giggling out of the way. It is a romp with everyone running in one direction or another and Henry at the center of it all, red-faced, bellowing with laughter, and shouting, "Faster! Faster!" At the end, Will collapses in a heap and snatches up a piece of white embroidery above his head, waving it in a sign of surrender.

"You are Helios," he tells Henry. "And I am just a little cloud."

"You are a great Fool," Henry says affectionately, "and you have disrupted my wife's rooms, frightened her ladies, and caused endless confusion with your folly."

"We are a pair of young fools," Will says, smiling up at his master. "As foolish as we were when we were twenty. But at least Your Majesty is wiser than you were then."

"How so?"

"You are more wise and more kingly. You are more handsome and more brave."

Henry smiles, anticipating the joke. "I am indeed."

"Your Majesty, there is more of you altogether," Will crows. "Much more. The queen has more of a husband than most women."

Henry bellows his deep-throated laugh and loses his breath in coughing. "You are a varlet; go and get your dinner with the hounds in the kitchen."

Will bows gracefully and retires out of the way. As he passes me I catch a quick smile from him, almost as if he was acknowledging to me that he has done his best; all I have to do is to get through dinner. Not for the first time, I wonder how much of a Fool Will Somers can be: a long-term survivor of this knife-edge court.

"Shall we go in to dinner?" the king asks me.

I smile and curtsey, and we proceed, a strange awkward procession, headed by the king in his chair and the panting pages, with me walking beside my husband, my hand on his, resting on the arm of his chair, while he wheezes, sweat pouring from his huge body, staining the armpits of his gold silk jacket and soaking his collar, and I wonder how long this can go on.

"Did you have a sermon this afternoon?" he asks courteously as the server pours water from a golden jug over his hands and another pats his fingers dry with a white linen napkin.

"Yes," I say holding out my hands for fresh scented water. "We had Your Majesty's chaplain talk to us about grace. It was very interesting, very thought-provoking."

"Nothing too wild," the king says with an indulgent smile. "Nothing that would make young Tom Howard argumentative, I hope. He is released from the Tower, but I can't have him upsetting his father again."

I smile as if it means nothing to me but an afternoon's entertainment. "Nothing wild at all, Your Majesty. Just the Word of God and a churchman's understanding of it."

"It's all well and good in your rooms," he says, suddenly irritable. "But they can't go on discussing it in the streets and the
taprooms. It's one thing for scholars to debate, it's quite another
when it's some girl from a farm and some fool of an apprentice
trying to read and wrestle with ideas."

"I quite agree," I say. "That is why Your Majesty was so gracious when you gave them a Bible in English, and they so wish
they could have it back again. Then they can quietly read and
learn. Then they have a chance of understanding. They don't
have to gather to have one recite and another explain."

He turns his big face towards me. His neck is so thick and
his cheeks are so fat that his face is quite square from the white
embroidered collar at the neck of his jacket to the sparse fringe
of his hair at the top of his forehead. It is like being glared at by
a block of stone. "No. You misunderstand me," he says coldly. "I
didn't give them the Bible for that. I don't think that a farm girl
from Lincoln should be reading and learning. I don't think she
should be studying and thinking. I have no desire to advance her
understanding. And I am very sure she should not be preaching."

I swallow a sip of wine. I see that my hand is steady on the
glass. On the other side of the king I notice the small downturned
face of Stephen Gardiner, nibbling at his dinner and straining his
ears to listen.

"You gave the people the Bible," I persist. "Whether you wish
them to keep it in the churches for everyone to read, or whether
you want it to be read only reverently and quietly in the better
sort of houses, must be your decision. It is your gift, you shall
decide where it goes. But there are preachers who have read the
words and learned them and understand them better than some
of the greatest men in the church. And why is that? For they did
not go to college to chop logic, and invent ritual, and pride themselves on their learning; they went to the Bible, to nowhere else
and nothing else. It is beautiful. Your Majesty, the piety of simple
people is beautiful. And their loyalty to you and their love of you
is beautiful as well."

He is a little mollified. "They are loyal? They don't question me along with the teachings of the church?"

"They know their father," I say firmly. "They were brought up in your England, they know that you make the laws that keep them safe, they know that you lead the armies that protect their country, that you plan and direct the ships that keep the seas for them. Of course they love you as their holy father."

He snorts with laughter. "A Holy Father? Like a pope?"

"Like a pope," I say steadily. "The pope is nothing more than the Bishop of Rome. He leads the church in Italy. What are you but the greatest of the churchmen in England? You are the Supreme Head of the Church, are you not? You sit above every other churchman, do you not? You lead the church in England."

Henry turns to Gardiner the bishop. "Her Majesty has a point," he says. "Don't you think?"

Gardiner finds a thin smile. "Your Majesty is blessed in a wife who loves scholarly discussion," he says. "Who would have thought that a woman could reason so? And to a husband, who was such a lion of learning? Surely she has tamed you!"

The king commands that I sit with him after dinner, and I take this as a mark of his favor. Doctor Wendy prepares a sleeping draft for him as the court stands around him, his great bandaged leg sticking out into the concerned circle. Stephen Gardiner and old Thomas Howard stand on one side, and my ladies and I are opposite, as if we would forcibly drag his chair from one side to the other. For a moment I look at the faces around my husband, the set smiles of the courtiers, the self-conscious charm of everyone, and I realize that everyone is anxious as I, everyone is weary as I am. We are all waiting for the king to put an end to this evening, to release us all for the night. In truth, some of us are waiting for a more lasting peace. Some are waiting for him to die.

Whoever wins the battle for the king's wavering attention now will win the next reign. Whoever he favors now will inherit a prime place when Edward comes to the throne. My husband has described these people to me as dogs waiting for his favor, but for the first time I see it for myself, and know that I am one of them. My future depends on his favor just as theirs does, and tonight I cannot be sure that I have it.

"Is the pain very bad?" Doctor Wendy asks him quietly.

"It is unbearable!" the king snaps. "Doctor Butts would never have let it get this bad."

"This should help," Doctor Wendy says humbly, and proffers a glass.

Sulkily, the king takes it and drinks it down. He turns to a page. "Sweetmeats," he says abruptly. The lad dashes to the cupboard and brings out a tray of candied fruits, sugared plums, toffee apples, marchpane, and pastries. The king takes a handful and crushes them against his rotting teeth.

"God knows it was merrier in England before every village had a preacher," Thomas Howard says, continuing one of his slow thoughts.

"But every village had a priest," I counter. "And every priest a tithe, and every church a chantry, and every town a monastery. There was more preaching then than there is now; but it was done in a language that nobody could understand, at a terrible price for the poor."

Thomas Howard, slow of wit and bad-tempered, scowls his disagreement. "I don't see what they need to understand," he says stubbornly. He looks down at the king and sees the great moon face turn one way then the other. "I don't hold with fools and women setting themselves up as learned," the duke says. "Like that stupid girl today."

I dare not speak of Anne by name. But I can defend her beliefs. "Since Our Lord spoke in simple language to simple people, in stories that they could understand, why should we not do so?" I ask. "Why should they not read the stories in the simple words of the Son of God?"

"Because they go on and on!" Thomas Howard suddenly bursts out. "Because it's not as if they read and think in silence! Every time I ride by Saint Paul's cross there are half a dozen of them, cawing away like crows! How many shall we endure? How much noise shall they be allowed to make?"

Laughing, I turn to the king. "Your Majesty does not think like this, I know," I say with more confidence than I feel. "Your Majesty loves scholarship and respectful discussion of the Bible."

But his face is sour. "Sweetmeats," he says again to the page. "You can leave us, ladies. Stephen, you stay by me."

It is a snub, but I am not going to let Stephen Gardiner or that fool Norfolk think I am offended. I rise to my feet and curtsey to the king and kiss him good night on his damp cheek. He does not squeeze my haunches as I bend over him, and I am relieved that all the court does not watch him pet me like his hound. I give a cool nod to the bishop and the duke, who seem to be clinging to their places. "Good night, my lord husband, and God bless you," I say gently. "I shall pray that your pain is eased by the morning."

He grunts a farewell, and I lead my ladies out of the room. Nan glances back as we go and sees that Stephen Gardiner has been given a seat and he is head to head with the king.

"I'd like to know what that false priest is saying," Nan says irritably.

I kneel at the foot of my gorgeously carved wooden bed and I pray for Anne Askew, who will be lying on a stinking pallet of straw at Newgate tonight. I pray for all the other prisoners of faith, those whom I know, since they have been in my rooms talking with me, and those who have been in my service and are now being forced to betray me, and those whom I will never know: in England, in Germany and far, far away.

I know that Anne will endure this for her faith, but I cannot bear to think of her lying in the dark, listening to the rats rustle in the corners and the groans of other prisoners. The punishment for heresy is death by burning. Although I am certain that neither Gardiner nor the king will send a young woman, a young gentle-woman, to such a brutal end, the thought of her facing public trial is enough to make me shudder and bury my face in my hands. All she has said is that the bread of the Mass is bread, the wine of the Mass is wine. Surely they won't keep her in prison for saying no more than everyone knows?

Our Lord said: "This is my body, this is my blood," but he was no trickster like the false priests who dribble red ink from the wounds of statues. He meant: "Think of me when you eat bread, think of me when you drink wine. Consume me in your heart." Thomas Cranmer's liturgy makes this clear, and the king himself supports this reading. We have published this; it can be read in English. Why then should Anne be sleeping tonight in Newgate with a trial before her and the bishop of London demanding that she recant, when she has said no more than the King of England has ruled?

It is late when I finally go to bed and Nan is already asleep on her side. The sheets are cold but I don't send for the maid to warm them. I am ashamed of the luxury of the smooth sheets and the white on white embroidery under my fingertips. I think of Anne on her bed of straw, and Thomas in a cramped bunk at sea, his cabin swaying around him, and I think that I suffer nothing; and yet I am unhappy, like a spoilt child.

I fall asleep almost at once, and almost at once I dream that I am climbing a circular stair in an old castle, not one of our palaces—it is too cold and damp for any of the king's houses. My hand rests on the outer wall and there is icy water beneath the arrow-slit windows. The stair is dark, barred with moonlight, the steps worn and uneven. I can hardly see my way from one window to another. I hear someone whispering from the foot of the stair, his voice echoing up the tower: "Tryphine! Tryphine!" and I give a little gasp of fear for now I know who I am, and what I am going to find.

The stair arrives on a stone landing at the top of the tower facing three small wooden doors. I don't want to open the doors, and I don't want to enter the rooms behind them; but the whisper of my name "Tryphine!" hissing up the stair behind me forces me on. The first door opens with a ring handle that moves under my grip, lifting the latch on the inside of the door. I don't like to think who might hear this, who might be in there, turning their heads, seeing the latch lifting, but I feel the door yield against my hand and I push it open. I can see the little room by the light of the moon coming in through the narrow window. I can see just enough to make out a piece of machinery taking up the whole length of the room.

I think at first that it is some kind of loom for weaving tapestry. It is a long raised bed with two great rollers at either end, and a lever in the middle. Then I step a little closer and I see that a woman is strapped to it, arms above her head, horribly wrenched out of shape, her feet, strapped to the bottom end, turned out as if her legs are broken. Someone has lashed her hands and feet and hauled on the lever so the rollers turn over and the gulf between them widens. This has dragged her arms out of their sockets and her elbows have popped out of joint, her hips and knees and even her anklebones are torn apart. The agony makes a white mask of her face, but even so, I recognize Anne Askew. I stumble back from the torture room and fall against the next door. That room is empty and silent. I draw a breath in momentary relief at being spared any further horror but then I smell smoke. There is smoke coming from the floorboards, and the boards themselves are getting hotter. And now, in the strange life of the dream, I am myself tied, hands behind my back. I am standing, strapped to a stake, and I am lashed with chains so that I cannot move, and my feet are no longer on floorboards but are shifting anxiously on cords of wood. It is getting hotter and hotter and there is smoke in my eyes and mouth, and I am beginning to cough. I gasp and I feel my throat scorched by the hot smoke. Then I see a little flicker of the first flame from the wood under my feet, and I cough again, flinching away from it. "No," I say, but I cannot speak for smoke, and as I breathe in, the heat of the smoke burns my throat and I cough and cough . . .

"Wake!" Nan says. "Wake up! Here." She presses a cup of ale into my hand. "Wake up!"

I cling to the cold cup, my hands covering hers. "Nan! Nan!"

"Hush. You're awake now. You're safe now."

"I dreamed of Anne." I am still choking as if the smoke were still burning my lungs.

"God bless her and keep her," Nan says instantly. "What did you dream?"

Already the horrific clarity of the dream is fading from me. "I thought I saw her . . . I thought I saw the rack . . ."

"There's no rack in Newgate," Nan says, firmly practical. "And she's not a common traitor to be racked. They don't torture women, and she is a gentleman's daughter. Her father served the king, no one can lay a hand on her. You just had a bad dream. It means nothing."

"They wouldn't rack her?" I clear my throat.

"Of course not," Nan says. "Many of them knew her father, and her husband is a wealthy yeoman. They'll hold her for a couple of days, hoping to give her a fright, and then send her home to that poor husband of hers, like they did before."

"She won't stand trial?"

"Of course they'll say that she must face a jury and threaten her with a guilty verdict. But they'll send her home to her husband and tell him to beat her. Nobody is going to torture a lady with a noble father and a wealthy husband. Nobody is going to send a woman as argumentative as that into a public courtroom."

Despite Nan's words I can't sleep, and next morning I have my maids pinch my cheeks and powder me with rouge to try to make me look less haggard. I must not resemble a woman sleepless with fear, and I know that the court is watching. Everyone knows that my woman preacher is in Newgate Prison today; I have to appear completely indifferent. I lead my ladies to chapel and then to breakfast as if we are in good spirits, and the king himself, wheeled in his chariot, meets me at the door to the great hall. There, to my amazement, bounding through the great front doors, is George Blagge, like Lazarus up from the grave, released from prison, fat and cheerful as ever, a man accused of heresy but galloping into the king's presence like a friend returned from an adventure.

Stephen Gardiner has a face like thunder. Behind him Sir Richard Rich scowls as this man, thrown into prison for nothing worse than attending the sermons in my rooms, kneels before the king and looks up to show him a beaming face.

"Pig! My pig!" cries the king, laughing and leaning forward in his chair to pull him to his feet. "Is it you? Are you safe?"

George snorts in his joy, and at once Will Somers triumphantly snorts in reply as if a herd of swine were celebrating George's return. The king roars with laughter; even William Paget hides a smile.

"If Your Majesty had not been so good to his pig, I should have been roasted by now!" George crows.

"Smoked like back bacon!" the king replies. He turns in his chair and narrows his eyes at Stephen Gardiner. "Wherever the hunt for heretics leads you, those that I love are exempt," he says. "There is a line that I expect you to observe, Gardiner. Don't forget who my friends are. No friend of mine could be a heretic. To be loved by me is to be inside the church. I am the head of the church: no one can love me and be outside my church."

Quietly I step forward and rest my hand on my husband's shoulder. Together we look at the bishop who has arrested my friends, my yeoman of the guard, my preachers, my bookseller, and the brother of my doctor. Stephen Gardiner drops his eyes before our gaze.

"I apologize," he says. "I apologize for the error."

I am triumphant at this public humiliation of Stephen Gardiner, and my ladies rejoice with me. George Blagge is welcomed back to court with the king's declaration of his love for him, and the king's declaration of his protection over those who love him. I take it that we are to be reassured by this. The tide that was flowing so strongly in favor of tradition and against reform has gone still, and is now on the turn, as tides ebb and flow, drawn by some invisible power. Perhaps it is the pull of the moon, as the new philosophers suggest. At court, where the tides of power are pulled this way and that by the turn of the expressionless moon face of the king, we know that we reformers are a spring tide once again, flowing strong and high.

"So how can we get Anne Askew released?" I ask Nan and Catherine Brandon. "The king released George Blagge for love of him. Clearly, we are rising high again. How quickly can we set her free?"

"Do you think you are strong enough to act?" Nan queries.

"George's return shows that the king has gone as far as he wants with the old churchmen. Now we return to favor." I am certain. "And anyway, we have to take a risk for Anne. She can't stay in Newgate. It's at the very heart of disease and the plague. We have to get her out of there."

"I can send one of my men to see that she is housed well, and well fed," Catherine says. "We can bribe the guards to let her have some comforts. We can get her into a clean cell and get her books as well as food and warm clothes."

"Do that," I nod. "But how can we get her released?"

"What about our cousin Nicholas Throckmorton? He can go and speak with her," Nan suggests. "He knows the law, and he is a good Christian of the reform faith. He must have listened to her speak in your rooms a dozen times. He should go and see what can be done and we can speak to Joan, Anthony Denny's wife. Anthony is in constant attendance on the king these days—he will know if the Privy Council mean to go ahead against her. It is he who will take the arraignment for her trial into the king for signature, or dry-stamp it himself. He'll take the king's letter to the jury if he means to dictate the verdict. Sir Anthony knows everything, and he will tell Joan what is planned."

"Are you sure he's on our side?" I query. "Are you sure he is faithful to the side of reform?"

Nan makes a little gesture with both hands, like a woman weighing one purse against another. "His heart is with reform, I am sure of it," she says. "But like all of us, he wants to keep the king's favor. He's not going to take a single step that might turn the king against him. Before anything else he is a powerless subject at the court of—"

"A tyrant," Catherine whispers defiantly.

"A king," Nan corrects her.

"But a king who favors us," I remind them.

With a new confidence I go to the king's rooms before dinner and when I find him and his gentlemen talking of religion I give my opinion. I take good care not to be bold or proud of my learning. That's not hard: the more that I learn, the more sure I am that I have very much to learn; but I can at least join in a conversation with those men who have taken up reformation as others take up archery—to please the king and to give themselves something to do.

"So Tom Seymour has no wife," the king remarks in the middle of one of our conversations. "Who'd have thought it?"

It is like a physical blow to hear his name. "Your Majesty?"

"I said, Tom Seymour has no wife," he says, raising his voice as

345

if I am going deaf. "Though I gave my blessing for the marriage and the Howards told me it would go ahead at once."

I cannot think what to say. Behind the king I see the impassive face of Thomas Howard, Duke of Norfolk, father of Mary, who should have been Thomas's bride.

"Was there an obstacle?" I ask quietly as if I am moderately surprised.

"The lady's preference, apparently." The king turns to the duke. "Did she refuse? I'm surprised you allow a daughter such freedoms."

The duke bows, smiling. "I am afraid to say that she is not an admirer of Thomas Seymour," he says. I grit my teeth in irritation at his sneering tone. "I think she is not confident of his beliefs."

This is to imply he is a heretic. "Your Majesty . . ." I start.

The duke dares to speak over me. I break off as I realize that he thinks he can interrupt me—the Queen of England—and that no one has challenged him.

"The Seymours are all famously in favor of reforming the church," Norfolk says, hissing the "s" through his missing front tooth like the snake that he is. "From Lady Anne in the queen's rooms, to his lordship Edward. They're all very intent on their scholarship and their reading. They think they can instruct us all. I'm sure we should be grateful, but my daughter is more traditional. She likes to worship in the church that Your Majesty has established. She seeks no change except as you command." He pauses. His dark eyes flicker downwards as if he might manage to squeeze out a tear in memory of his son-in-law. "And she loved Henry Fitzroy with a true heart—we all did. She cannot bear another man in his place."

The mention of his bastard son trips the king into sentimental memory. "Ah, don't speak of him," he says. "I can't bear to think of my loss. The most beautiful boy!"

"I can't see Thomas Seymour taking our beloved Fitzroy's place," the duke says scathingly. "It would be a mockery."

With mounting rage I hear the old man insult Thomas, and I see that no one says a word to defend him.

"No, he's not the man our boy would have been," the king agrees. "Nobody could be."

Nicholas Throckmorton, my cousin, comes back from Newgate with good news of Anne Askew. She has many supporters in the city of London, and warm clothes, books, and money have been arriving hourly to her little room. She is certain to be released. The importance of her late father and the wealth of her husband count in her favor. She has preached before some of the greatest citizens of London and the city fathers, and she herself has done nothing worse than say what thousands of other people think. There is a general belief that the king has acted only to frighten the more vocal supporters of reform into silence, and that they will all, like Tom Howard, like George Blagge, be quietly released over the next few days.

"Can you talk to the king?" Nicholas asks me. "Ask for a pardon for her?"

"He's in a difficult mood," I confess. "And the churchmen are always with him."

"But he has definitely turned to our side?"

"All his recent decisions are in favor of reform but he is equally irritable with everyone."

"Can you not advise him as you used to do?"

"I will try," I promise. "But the conversation in his rooms is not easy as it used to be. Sometimes when I speak I feel that he is impatient with me, and sometimes he is clearly not listening."

"You have to keep reform in his mind," he says anxiously. "You are the only one at court now. Doctor Butts is dead, God keep him. Edward Seymour is away, Thomas, his brother, at sea, Cranmer at his palace. You are the only one left at court who can remind the king of what he passionately believed only a few months ago. I know he is changeable; but our view is his, and you are the only one who can keep him constant. It is a burden, but you are the only one at court who will defend reform. We are all looking to you."

WHITEHALL PALACE, LONDON, SUMMER 1546

KP

It is midsummer, too hot for being in London. We should be on progress, going down the long green valley of the Thames, staying in the beautiful riverside palaces, or heading to the south coast, perhaps going to Portsmouth, where I might see Thomas. But this year the king does not fear the plague, does not fear the heat in the city. This year he fears that death is stalking him by another route, coming closer and closer like a constant companion.

He is too tired to go far, even in flight from disease. Poor old man, he can no longer ride, he can no longer walk. He is ashamed to be seen by the people who used to line the roadsides and doff their caps and cheer as he went by. He used to be the most handsome prince in Christendom. Now he knows that nobody can look at him without feeling pity for the wreck that he has made of his bloated body, and for the moonlike face.

So, because the king is self-pitying and filled with dread, we all have to stay in the heat of the city, where the narrow streets stink with filth from the central gutters and the pigs and cows nose through the rubbish that is heaped in the streets. I remark that the Lord Mayor should be more active, should get the streets cleaned and fine the offenders; but the king looks at me coldly, and says, "Would you be the Lord Mayor of London as well as queen?"

Everyone is irritable at being detained in town. The courtiers usually go to their homes for the summer months and the northern lords and the western lords are missing their wives and their families and their castles set in the cool green hills of their homelands. The king's bad temper sets the tone for the court: nobody wants to be here, nobody is allowed to leave, everyone is unhappy.

I come across Will Somers as I walk alone in the green *allée* beneath the castle walls. I long, with a wordless ache in my heart, for Thomas; I worry for Anne Askew, still held without trial and without charge; and I wish that the king would listen to me once more as the friend and helpmeet that I swore to be. Will is sprawled, as long-limbed as a fawn, under a spreading oak tree, dappled with shade, in one of the little gardens set between the high hedges, and when he sees me he unwinds his long legs, rises to his feet, bows, and folds himself up again like a jointed puppet.

"How d'you like the heat, Will?" I ask.

"Better than I would like hell," he replies. "Or do you doubt hell along with everything else, Your Majesty?"

I glance around, but there is no one but the two of us in the walled garden. "You want to discuss theology with me?"

"Not I!" he says. "You're too clever for me. And I'm not the only one."

"You're not the only one not to want to discuss theology?"

He nods, lays his finger along his nose and beams at me.

"Who else does not want to talk with me?"

"Your Majesty," he says grandly. "I am just a Fool. So I don't discuss the king's church with him. But if I were a wise man (and I wake every day to thank the Lord that I am not) I would be dead by now. For if I had been a wise man with serious opinions, I would have succumbed to the temptation to discuss these grave matters. Grave because that is where they lead."

"His Majesty has always enjoyed scholarly talk," I say repressively.

"Not anymore," Will says. "In my opinion. Which is to say a Fool's opinion and so not worth having."

As I open my mouth to argue, Will very slowly and carefully goes into a handstand so that he is balancing on his hands and his feet walk languidly up the trunk of the tree. "See what a Fool I am," he remarks, head down.

"I think you are wiser than you appear, Will," I remark. "But there are good people whose safety depends on me speaking for them. I have promised to keep the king in one mind."

"It is easier to stand on your head than keep the king to one mind," Will observes, straight as a yeoman, but upside down. "If I were you, Majesty, I would stand on your head beside me."

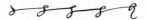

The summer continues hot. We sit beside wide-open windows every afternoon, listening to one of my maids reading the Bible, with the drapes at the windows soaked in cold water, trying to cool down the rooms. In the afternoon, I go to my privy chamber where the shutters are closed against the glare and pray that the king's health mends, and that he releases us from the wearying tedium of hot weather in the fetid city, so that we can go on progress. I long like a swallow to go south, to the sea, to the ocean winds that smell of salt, to Thomas.

Then, one afternoon, as we sit on benches beside the river, trying to get some air, I see the Seymour barge come down the river and tie up at the pier. At once I fix an expression of idle boredom on my face. "Oh, is that the Seymour barge? And who is in it? Is that Thomas Seymour?" I ask.

Elizabeth's head bobs up at once and she jumps to her feet, shading her eyes from the glare from the river. "It is!" she squeaks. "It's Sir Thomas! And Edward Seymour with him."

"My husband?" Anne Seymour asks. "That's unexpected. Your Majesty, may I go and greet him?"

"We'll all go," I say, and we get to our feet and leave our books and our sewing and walk towards the pier where the two Seymour men bow and kiss my hands and then Edward greets his wife.

I hardly see him. I can hardly say the polite words of greeting.

Thomas takes my hand and brushes it with his lips. He straightens up and bows to the other ladies. He offers me his arm. I hear him say something about our sitting out by the river and that surely there are pestilential airs. I hear him say something about the court going on progress. I cannot hear for the thudding in my ears.

"Are you here for long?" I ask.

He leans towards me to reply, his voice low. If I were to lean towards him as he is leaning towards me, we would be close enough to kiss. I wonder if he is thinking that too; then I know that he is thinking that too. "I am here only for one night."

I can't even hear him say the word *night* without thinking of lovemaking. "Oh."

"I wanted to report on the coastal defenses with Edward at my side. We are outnumbered at court. We cannot get a fair hearing. The Howards and their friends dominate everything."

"I heard that you are not to marry Mary Howard."

He slides me a quick smile. "Probably just as well."

"I would have said nothing. She would have been welcome as one of my ladies."

"I know. I trust you completely. But there was something about the whole business . . ." He breaks off.

"Walk slowly," I say passionately. Already, we are approaching the first gateway into the palace and at any moment someone will come and take him away from me. "For God's sake, let us have a moment . . ."

"The Howards insisted that she came to court," he says. "They made me promise I would put her in your rooms. I couldn't think why they would want that, unless to have her spy on you. I doubted their honesty, and she would hardly speak to me. She was furious about something. Clearly, she was coerced. She was very angry."

"So you're still a free man," I say longingly.

Gently he presses my hand that rests on his arm. "I will have to marry," he warns me. "We need an alliance at court. We are losing our influence with the king, we need a greater presence here. I need a wife who will speak for me to him."

"I can't speak for you but I would—"

"No. Never. I never want you to say one word for me. But I need a wife here who can take care of my interests."

I feel as sick as if I have indeed inhaled pestilential airs from the river. "You are still going to marry?"

"I have to."

I nod. Of course, he has to. "Have you chosen a bride?"

"Only if you give your permission."

"I would be very wrong to refuse it. I know that you need a wife; I understand about court. I'll come to your wedding and smile."

"This is not my desire," he stipulates.

"Nor mine, but I'll dance at your wedding feast."

We are nearly at the doorway. The guards salute and open the doors. He will have to go to the king's rooms and I will not see him until dinner. And then at dinner I will not be able to look at him. And then in a month, within weeks, he will be married.

"Who is your choice? Tell me quickly."

"Princess Elizabeth."

I whirl around and look at my stepdaughter, where she follows us at the head of my ladies, as if I am seeing her for the first time, not as a child but as a young woman. She is twelve years old, old enough to be betrothed. In a few years she will be old enough to marry. In one quick glance I imagine her as Thomas Seymour's bride, on her wedding day, as his young wife, as mother to his children. I imagine how she will take to lovemaking and how she will flaunt her happiness. "Elizabeth!"

"Hush," he says. "The king would have to agree, but if he does, then I become his son-in-law. It's a brilliant match for us."

It is. With painful clarity I can see the logic of it for the Seymours. It is a brilliant match for them, and Princess Elizabeth, when she is told of it, will pretend to obedience but will be delighted. She has a childish adoration for Thomas, for his dark good looks and his air of adventure, now she will think herself in love with him and she will talk about him and coo over him and give herself airs and I will lose my love for her in jealousy.

"You don't like it," he observes.

I shake my head, swallowing down bile. "I can't like it, but I don't speak against it. I see that you must, Thomas. It would be a great advancement for you. It would secure the Seymours their place with the royal family."

"I shan't do it if you say no."

Again I shake my head. We go through the doorway into the shade of the entrance hall. The Seymour servants come to greet their masters. They bow and we turn towards the king's presence chamber. It is not possible to speak, and everyone is looking at Thomas and commenting on the admiral's return to court.

"I am yours," Thomas says in a passionate undertone. "Forever. You know that."

I release his hand and he bows and steps back.

"Very well," I say. I know that he has to make his way. I know that Elizabeth is a great match for him. I know that she will adore him and he will be kind to her. "Very well."

Thomas leaves the next morning before chapel and I don't see him again.

"Are you ill?" Nan asks me. "You look . . ."

"Look what?"

She scrutinizes my pale face. "Queechy," she says, using a childhood word with a little smile.

"I'm unhappy," I reply in a moment of honesty. I won't say more but I feel a little eased just by speaking one word of truth. I miss Thomas as a physical pain. I don't know how I am going to bear his marriage to someone else. The thought of him with Elizabeth makes my stomach churn as if I am poisoned with jealousy.

Nan does not even ask me why I am unhappy. I am not the first royal wife she has seen blanched by the strain of being queen.

I am invited to the king's rooms most evenings before dinner to listen to debates. Often I say what I think, and always I remind the king that the cause of reform is his cause, a process that he started in his wisdom, that his people revere him for bringing reform to England. But I can tell from the frosty silence that greets my words that the king is far from agreeing with me. He is planning something; but he does not discuss it with me. I know nothing until the first week of July, when the Privy Council announce a law that makes it a criminal offense to own a Bible in English translated either by William Tyndale or by Miles Coverdale.

This is madness. There is no understanding it. Miles Coverdale translated and improved the Tyndale Bible under the instruction of the king and it was published as the Great Bible, the king's Bible, his gift to believers. This is the Bible that the king gave to his people only seven years ago. Everyone who can afford one has a copy. It would have been disloyal not to have a family copy. Every parish church was given one and ordered to display it. It is the best version in English; every bookcase in England has it. Now, overnight, ownership is a crime. It is a reversal so great that everything is turned around, and upside down. I think of Will Somers standing on his head as I hurry back to my private rooms and find Nan wrapping my precious, beautifully bound, and illustrated volumes in rough cloth and cording up a trunk.

"We can't just throw them out!"

"They have to be sent away."

"Where are you going to send them?" I ask.

"To Kendal," she says, naming our family home. "As far away as possible."

"It's barely standing!"

"Then they won't look there."

"You've got my copy?"

"And your notes, and Catherine Brandon's copy, and Anne Seymour's and Joan Denny's and Lady Dudley's. This new law has caught us all out without warning. The king has made us all criminals overnight."

"But why?" I demand. I am near to crying with anger. "Why make his own Bible illegal? The king's Bible! How can it be illegal to own a Bible? God gave the Word to his people, how can the king take it back?"

"Exactly," she says. "You think. Why would the king make a criminal of his wife?"

I take her hands, pulling her away from tying the knots on the trunk, and I kneel beside her. "Nan, you have been at court all your life; I am a Parr of Kendal raised in Lincoln. I'm a straightforward northern woman. Don't speak in riddles to me."

"That's no riddle," she says with bitter humor. "Your husband has passed a law which makes you a criminal fit for burning. Why would he do that?"

I am slow to say it. "He wants to get rid of me?"

She is silent.

"Are you saying that this new law is directed against me, since they cannot catch me with anything else? Are you suggesting that they have outlawed the Bible just to make me and my ladies into criminals? So that they can come against us and charge us with heresy? Because this is ridiculous."

I cannot read the expression on her face—she does not look like herself—and then I realize that she is afraid. Her mouth is working as if she cannot speak, her forehead is damp with sweat. "He's coming for you" is all she says. "This is how he always does it. He's coming for you, Kat, and I don't know how to save you. I'm packing Bibles and I'm burning papers, but they know you have been reading and writing, and they are changing the law ahead of me. I can't make sure you obey the law because they are changing it faster than we can obey. I don't know how to save you. I swore to you that you would outlive him, and now his health is failing, but he is coming for you just like . . ."

I release her hands and sit back on my heels.

"Just like what?"

"Just like he came for the other two."

She knots the cords around the box and goes to the door and shouts for her manservant, a man who has been with us all our lives. She gestures to the boxes and commands him to take them at once, show them to no one, and ride for home, for Kendal in Westmorland. As I watch him lift the first box, I realize I am longing to go with him into those wild hills.

"They'll pick him up at Islington village if they want to," I say, as the man shoulders the trunk and goes. "He won't get more than a day's ride out of the city."

"I know that," she says flatly. "But I don't know what else to do."

I look at my sister, who has served six of Henry's queens and buried four. "You really think he is doing this to entrap me? That he has completely turned against me?"

She doesn't answer. She turns the same closed face to me that I imagine she showed to little Kitty Howard when she cried that she had done nothing wrong; to Anne Boleyn when she swore that she could talk her way out of danger. "I don't know. God help us all, Kateryn, because I don't know."

HAMPTON COURT PALACE, SUMMER 1546

KP

The king gets worse and it makes him miserable. He agrees that the court shall move to Hampton Court, away from the unbearable heat of the city and the danger of illness, but he does not come out to the garden, or to boat on the river, or even to Mass in the beautiful palace chapel. They tell me that he wants to rest quietly in his rooms, to talk with his advisors. He will not come for dinner, he does not want to visit me in my rooms, I need not come to his. He has shut himself away, excluding me just as he excluded Kitty Howard, when they assured her that he was ill; but in fact he was locked inside his rooms, here, in this very palace, at Hampton Court, brooding on her failings, on the trial he would rig and the execution that he would order.

But, just like Anne Boleyn, who attended jousts and dinners and May Day celebrations while knowing that something was wrong, I have to appear before the court. I cannot withdraw like him. I am in my aviary rooms, feeding my birds, watching their thoughtless chatter and their little busyness as they tidy their feathers, when my clerk, William Harper, taps on the door.

"You can come in," I say. "Come in and shut the door. I have two of them flying free and I don't want them to get out."

He ducks as a canary swoops over his head and comes to my outstretched hand.

"What is it, William?" I ask absently, breaking off seed cake and giving it to the pretty little bird. "Speak up. I have to leave this little beauty and go and dress for dinner."

He glances towards Nan and Anne Seymour, who are sitting in the window seat, side by side, both of them unmoved by my lovely little birds. "May I speak to you alone?"

"What for?" Nan says flatly. "Her Majesty has to go to dinner. You can tell me what it is."

He shakes his head; he looks imploringly at me.

"Oh, go on, and pick out my jewels and a hood," I say impatiently. "I'll come in a moment."

My clerk and I wait for the door to close behind them, and I turn to him. He is a thoughtful man, monastery trained and with a great love for the old ways. He must have regarded half of the books in my closet with pious horror; he has no admiration for the new learning. I employ him because he is a great scholar, he can translate beautifully, and he has a fine hand in writing. When

I want to send out a letter in Latin, he can translate and transcribe in one draft with a beautiful flowing copperplate script. He has never disagreed with anything the preachers have said in my rooms, but I have once or twice seen him bend his head and whisper a silent prayer, like a shocked monk in a worldly school.

"There! No one to hear but me and the birds, and they say nothing—except the parrot, who is a terrible blasphemer, but only in Spanish. What is it, William?"

"I have to warn you, Your Majesty," he says gravely. "I fear that your enemies are speaking against you."

"I know that," I say shortly. "Thank you for your concern, William, but this, I know already."

"Bishop Gardiner's man came to me and asked me to search your closet for papers," he says in a whispered rush. "He said I would be rewarded if I would secretly copy anything and bring it to him. Your Majesty, I think he is assembling a case against you."

The little bird tickles my palm as it shifts its feet and pecks at the crumbs. I did not expect this warning from William. I did not think that they would dare to go this far. I see my shocked expression is mirrored in his troubled face.

"Are you sure it was the bishop's man?"

"Yes. He told me it was to take to the bishop. I could not be mistaken."

I turn away from him and go to the window, the yellow-winged canary clinging to my outstretched finger. It is a beautiful summer day, the sun just dipping below the high red-brick chimneys, the swifts and swallows swirling around. If Bishop Gardiner is prepared to take such a risk in approaching one of my servants to steal my papers, then he must be very confident that he can make a case against me to the king. He must be very sure that a complaint from me to the king will not bring down a storm on his head. He must be certain that he will find something to prove my guilt. Or, even worse, perhaps he has already made a case against me and this is the last stage of a secret inquiry, finding the paperwork to back up the lies.

"It was to take to the bishop? You are sure of that? Not to the king?"

His face is pale with fear. "That he didn't tell me, Your Majesty. But he was bold as brass: that I was to go through all your papers and bring him whatever I could find. He said to copy down the titles of books also, and to search for a New Testament. He said that he knew you had several."

"There's nothing here," I say shortly.

"I know. I know that you have sent everything away, your beautiful library and all your papers. I told him there was nothing, but he said to look anyway. He knew that you had a library for your studies. He said that they guessed you wouldn't have been able to part with your books and that they would be hidden in your rooms somewhere."

"You have been very fair and honorable to tell me this," I say. "I shall see that you are rewarded, William."

He bows his head. "I don't seek any reward."

"Will you go back to this man and say that you have looked and that I have nothing?"

"I will."

I put out my hand to him, and as he bows and kisses it I see that my fingers are trembling and the little bird on my other hand is shaking as he clings to my thumb. "You don't even think as I do, William. You are kind to protect me when we don't even agree."

"We may not agree, Your Majesty, but I think you should be free to think and write and study," he says. "Even though you are a woman. Even if you listen to a woman preacher."

"God bless you, William, in whatever language He chooses, whether through a priest or through your own good heart."

He bows. "And the woman preacher . . ." he says very quietly.

I turn in the doorway. "Mistress Askew?"

"They have moved her from Newgate."

The relief is tremendous. I cry out. "Oh! God be praised! She is released?"

"No. No, God help her. They have taken her to the Tower."

There is a moment of blank silence as he sees that I understand what he is saying. They have not released her into the custody of her husband; they have not bound her over to keep the peace. Instead, they have moved her from the prison where they keep the common criminals, to the prison where they keep those accused of treason and heresy, near to Tower Hill where they hang the guilty, not far from Smithfield meat market where they burn the heretics.

I turn to the window behind me, and I unlatch it and swing it open.

"Your Majesty?" William gestures to the open cages, to the parrot on his perch. "Your Majesty? Take care . . ."

I hold the little canary up to the open window so that he can see the blue sky. "They can go, William. They can all go. Indeed, they had better go. I don't know how long I will be here to care for them."

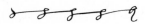

I am dressed in complete silence, my ladies handing me my things without a word, in well-practiced choreography. I don't know how to reach Anne Askew behind the thick stone walls of the Tower. It is the prison for enemies who will not be freed for years, for the gravest traitors, for evil people who have to be held without any chance of escape. For a prisoner, to enter through the watergate, concealed from the City and from all the people who might rise up to defend him, is to set sail on the River Lethe—towards oblivion.

At the heart of my fear for Anne is that I don't know why they would move her from Newgate to the Tower. She has been arraigned for heresy, she has been questioned by the Privy Council, why do they not leave her at Newgate until they send her for trial, or grant her pardon and send her home? Why would they move her to the Tower? What is the point of it? And who has ordered it?

Nan comes forward and curtseys as Catherine stands behind

me and fastens my necklace. The priceless sapphires are heavy and cold on my neck. They make me shiver.

"What is it, Nan?"

"It's Bette," she says, naming one of my younger maids-in-waiting.

"What about her?" I ask shortly.

"Her mother has written to me and asked for her to be sent home," she says. "I have taken the liberty of saying that she can go."

"Is she ill?" I ask.

Nan shakes her head with a pursed mouth, as if she would say more but she is angry.

"So what's the matter with her?"

There is an embarrassed silence.

"Her father is a tenant of Bishop Gardiner," Catherine Brandon remarks.

I take a moment to understand her. "You think the bishop has advised Bette's parents to remove her from my keeping?"

Nan nods. Catherine curtseys and leaves the room to wait for me outside.

"He'd never admit to it," Nan says. "So there's no point in challenging him.'

"But why would Bette leave me? Even if he advised it?"

"I've seen it before," Nan says. "When Kitty Howard was charged. The younger maids, those who didn't have to stay to give evidence, all found excuses to go home. The court shrank like linen on a washday. Same as when the king turned against Queen Anne. All the Boleyns disappeared overnight."

"I'm not like Kitty Howard!" I exclaim in a rush of sudden temper. "I am the sixth wife, the sixth disregarded wife, not the fifth guilty wife. All I have done is to study and listen to preachers. She was an adulteress, or perhaps a bigamist, and a whore! Any mother would take her daughter away from service to a young woman like that! Any mother would fear the morals in a court like that! But everyone says that my court is the most virtuous of any in Christendom! Why would anyone take their daughter away from me?"

"Kitty's maids left in the days before she was arrested," Nan says levelly, not responding to my anger. "Not because she was light, but because she was doomed. Nobody wants to be in the court of a falling queen."

"A falling queen?" I repeat. I hear the words: it sounds like a comet, like something in the night sky. "A falling queen."

"William told me that you opened the window and let your birds fly away," she remarks.

"Yes."

"I'll go and close it again, and call them back if I can. There's no point in showing that we are afraid."

"I'm not afraid!" I lie.

"You should be."

As I lead my ladies in to dinner I look around as if I fear that the court too will be slipping away. But I cannot see any absences. Everyone is there, in their accustomed places. Those who believe in reform do not feel they are newly endangered, it is only those of my household, those who are close to me. Everyone bows respectfully and deeply as I go by. It seems as if nothing is changed from every other night. The king's place is laid, the cloth of state hangs over his great reinforced chair, the servers bow as they come into the room and present the finest dishes to his empty throne as ritual demands. He will dine in his own rooms with his new circle of favorites: Bishop Stephen Gardiner, the Lord Chancellor Thomas Wriothesley, Sir Richard Rich, Sir Anthony Denny, William Paget. When dinner is over, I may leave the great hall to sit with the king in his rooms, but until then there must be someone at the head table. The court needs a monarch, the princesses need a parent to dine with them.

My gaze goes across the room and I note that the Seymour

household has an empty place laid at the head of the table. I glance at Anne. "Is Edward coming home?" I ask.

"I wish to God he was here," she says bluntly. "But I don't expect him. He doesn't dare leave Boulogne: the place would fall in a moment." She follows my gaze. "That place will be for Thomas."

"Oh?"

"He has come to see the king. They can't raise the *Mary Rose*. They're trying some new way, pumping her out as she lies on the ocean bed."

"Really?"

Thomas comes into the great hall, bows to the empty throne and then bows to me and to the princesses. He winks at Elizabeth and takes his place at the head of the Seymour table. I send out dishes to him, to the Duke of Norfolk, and to Lord Lisle, without favoritism. Without looking directly towards Thomas, I can see that he is tanned like a peasant, the skin at his temples lined from smiling into the sun. He looks well. He has a new jacket in velvet—deep red, my favorite colour. Dozens of dishes come from the kitchen, the trumpeters announce each fresh course with a scream of sound. I take a small portion from everything that is presented to me, and I wonder what the time is now, and if he will come to me after dinner.

It takes forever for the feast to be over, and then the court rises from the tables and the men stroll about and talk to one another, and approach the ladies. Some people settle to cards or games, the musicians play, and a few people start to dance. There is no formal entertainment this evening, and I step down from the dais to make my way slowly towards the king's rooms, pausing to talk to people as I go.

Thomas appears at my side and bows. "Good evening, Your Majesty."

"Good evening, Sir Thomas. Your sister-in-law tells me that you have spoken with the king about the *Mary Rose*."

He nods. "I had to tell His Majesty that we made an attempt to raise her but that she was stuck fast on the seabed. We're going to try again with more ships and more ropes. I will send swimmers down to try to make her watertight belowdecks and pump her out. I think it can be done."

"I hope so. It was a terrible loss."

"Are you going to see the king?" he asks, his voice very low.

"I go every evening."

"He seems very displeased."

"I know."

"I told him that since my marriage to Mary Howard is not to go ahead, I am still looking for a wife."

Carefully, I don't look up at him. He extends his arm. I rest my fingers on it. I sense but I do not grip the strength of his forearm. I walk beside him, our paces matching. If I stepped a little closer, my cheek would touch his shoulder. I don't step any closer.

"Did you say that you hope for Princess Elizabeth?"

"I did not. He was not in the mood for conversation."

I nod.

"You know, there was something in Mary Howard's refusal that I still don't understand," he says quietly. "The Norfolks all agreed, Henry Howard the oldest son, and the old duke himself. It was Lady Mary herself who refused."

"I can't imagine her father allowing a daughter to have her own way."

"No," he says. "That's true. She would have had to fight like a wild cat to oppose her father and her brother, acting together. She would have had to defy them openly. It makes no sense. I know that she doesn't dislike me, and it was a good match. There must have been something about the terms of the marriage that were completely unacceptable to her."

"How unacceptable?"

"Unbearable. Unimaginable. Anathema."

"But what could such a thing be? She could know nothing against you?"

His wicked smile gleams. "Nothing of that gravity, Your Majesty."

"And yet you are sure it was her refusal? Her determined refusal?"

"I hoped you might know."

I shake my head. "I am surrounded by mysteries and worries," I say to him. "The preachers who spoke in my rooms are arrested, the books that the king gave me to read are banned, it is even illegal to own the king's Bible, and my friend Anne Askew has been moved from Newgate Prison to the Tower. My ladies are slipping away from my rooms." I smile. "This afternoon I let my birds go."

He glances around the room and smiles at an acquaintance as if he is merry. "This is very bad."

"I know it."

"Can't you speak to the king? A word from him would restore you."

"I'll talk to him this evening if he is in a good mood."

"Your only safety is in his love for you. He *does* still love you?"

I make the tiniest gesture, of denial. "Thomas, I don't know that he has ever loved anyone. I don't know that he can."

Thomas and I cross the king's presence room filled with petitioners, lawyers, doctors and hangers-on watching our footsteps, estimating our confidence at every stride. He pauses at the door of the king's privy chamber.

"I can't bear to leave you here," he says unhappily.

Hundreds of people watch us as I give him a cool smile. I extend my hand to him.

He bows, touching my fingers with his warm lips. "You are a brilliant woman," he says quietly. "You have read and thought more than most of the men in there. You are a loving woman and you believe in God and speak to Him far more intensely and sincerely than they ever will. You can surely explain yourself to the king. You are the most beautiful woman at court, by far the most desirable. You can rekindle his love for you."

He bows formally, and I turn and go into the king's rooms.

They are in the middle of a discussion about chantries and monasteries. To my speechless amazement, I realize that they are agreeing how many religious houses—closed at such cost and with such heartbreak—might be reopened and restored. Bishop Gardiner believes we need monasteries and convents in every town to keep the country peaceful and the people supplied with religious solace and comforts. The corrupt marketplaces that traded in fear and superstition, which the king rightly closed, are now to reopen, as if there had never been a reformation in England. And they are to return to the business of selling lies at a profit. As I come in, Stephen Gardiner is suggesting the restoration of some shrines and some pilgrim routes. Slyly, he suggests that they might pay their fees directly to the crown, not to the church—as if that makes them holy. He says that it is possible to do God's work at a profit. I sit quietly beside Henry, fold my hands in my lap, and listen to this wicked man suggest the restoration of superstition and paganism to the country in order that poor people might be robbed by the rich.

But I make sure that I say nothing. Only when the conversation turns to Cranmer's liturgy do I speak to defend the reform version. Thomas Cranmer was commissioned by the king to translate the Latin into English. The king himself worked on it, and I sat at his side and read and reread the English version, compared it to the old Latin original, checked it for copying errors when it came back from the printers, wrote my own translations. In a low voice I suggest that Cranmer's work is adequate and should be used in every church in the land; but then I get stirred and argue that it is more than adequate, it is beautiful, it is even holy. The king smiles and nods as if he agrees with me, and I am emboldened. I say that people should be free to speak directly to God in church, their contact with God should not be mediated through a priest, should not be undertaken in a language that they cannot understand. As the king is father to his people, so God is father to him. The line between king and people is just like the communion between people and God; it should be clear and open and direct. How else shall there be an honorable king? How else shall there be a loving God?

I know in my heart that this is true; I know that the king believes it too. He has gone so far to drive popery and paganism out of this country, to bring his people to true understanding. I forget to sweeten every sentence with praise of him as I speak earnestly and passionately, and then I realize that his face has grown dark with ill temper and Stephen Gardiner is looking down, hiding a smile, not meeting my bright eyes. I have spoken too passionately, too cleverly. Nobody likes a clever, passionate woman.

I try to retreat. "Perhaps you are tired. I will say good night."

"I am tired," he agrees. "I am tired, and I am old, and it is a fine thing in my old days that I should be taught by my wife."

I curtsey very low, leaning forward so that he can see down the top of my gown. I feel his eyes on my breasts and I say: "I could never teach you, Your Majesty. You are so much wiser than I."

"All of this I have heard before," he says irritably. "I have had wives before, who thought they knew better than me."

I flush. "I am sure not one ever loved you as much as I do," I whisper, and I bend and kiss his cheek.

I hesitate at the smell of him: the stink of his rotting leg, like decaying meat, the sweet sickly smell of old sweat on old skin, the bad breath from his mouth, his constipated flatulence. I hold my breath and I lay my cool cheek against his hot damp face. "God bless Your Majesty, my lord husband," I say gently. "And give you good night."

"Good night, Kateryn Parr," he says, biting off his words.

"Don't you think it odd that every one of your predecessors called herself by her name: Queen Katherine or Queen Anne or—God bless her—Queen Jane? But you call yourself Kateryn Parr. You sign yourself Kateryn the Queen KP. P for Parr."

I am so surprised at this ridiculous challenge that I reply before I can think. "I am myself!" I say. "I am Kateryn Parr. I am my father's daughter, educated by my mother. What else should I call myself but by my name?"

He looks across at Stephen Gardiner—who uses his name and his title without question—and they nod at each other as if I have revealed something that they long suspected.

"What can be wrong with this?" I demand.

He does not even answer me, he waves me away.

When I wake in the morning the privy chamber outside my bedroom is oddly quiet. Usually there is the low reassuring buzz of my ladies arriving for the day and then the tap on the door by the maid-in-waiting for that day bringing in the hot water. As I get up and wash my face and hands in a golden bowl of warm water, the ladies bring my gowns drawn from the queen's wardrobe for me to choose what I will wear, and the sleeves and the bodice and the hood and the jewels. They will offer something to eat; but I will not taste anything or drink until we have been to Mass, for I am uncertain, as everyone is now uncertain, as to whether we are to fast before Mass or not. It may be well known as a meaningless ritual, or Gardiner may have restored it to the court as a holy tradition. I am not sure. It is a sign of how ridiculous the times have become that I—a queen in my own rooms—do not know if I may eat a bread roll or not. It is ludicrous.

Ludicrous, and yet this morning I cannot hear the noise of the baker's boy bringing bread from the kitchen. It is so eerily quiet outside my private chamber that I don't wait for the arrival of my maids-in-waiting; I get up, pull my robe over my nakedness, and open the door to look out. There are half a dozen women outside, three of them holding gowns from the royal wardrobe. They are oddly silent, and when I open my door and stand wordlessly, looking at them, they don't exclaim good morning and smile. They drop into silent curtseys and when they rise up they keep their eyes on the floor. They will not look at me.

"What's the matter?" I demand. I scan the half dozen of them, and then I ask, more impatiently, "Where is Nan? Where is my sister?"

Nobody answers, but Anne Seymour steps reluctantly forward. "Please allow me to speak with you alone, Your Majesty," she says.

"What is it?" I say, stepping back into my bedroom and beckoning her in. "What's the matter?"

She closes the door behind her. In the silence I can hear the ticking of my new clock.

"Where is Nan?"

"I have some bad news."

"Is it Anne Askew?"

At once I think that they are going to execute her. That they have done the thing that we were sure they would not do. That they have taken her to trial, and rushed through a guilty verdict, and they are going to burn her. "Tell me it's not Anne? Has Nan gone to the Tower to pray with her?"

Anne shakes her head. "No, it's your ladies," she says quietly. "It's your own sister. In the night, after you had left the king, the Privy Council sat in judgment, and they have arrested your sister Nan Herbert; your kinswoman Lady Elizabeth Tyrwhit; and your cousin Lady Maud Lane."

I cannot even hear her. "What did you say? Who is arrested?"

"The ladies-in-waiting who are your kinswomen. Your sister and your cousins."

"For what?" I ask stupidly. "On what charge?"

"They have not been charged yet. They were questioned all through the night; they are still being interrogated now. And the yeomen of the guard have entered their rooms, their private family rooms that they share with their husbands, and into their chambers here, in your quarters, and taken their papers away: all their boxes, all their books."

"They are looking at papers?"

"They are looking for papers and books," Anne confirms. "It is an inquiry about heresy."

"The Privy Council is accusing my ladies, my cousins, my own sister, Nan, of heresy?"

Anne nods, her face impassive.

There is a long silence. I feel my knees are weak beneath me and I sink down to a stool by the grate where a little fire flickers.

"What can I do?"

She is as frightened as I am. "Your Majesty, I don't know. All your papers are gone from your rooms?" She glances at the desk where I used to write notes with such pleasure, where I used to study with such excitement.

"All gone. Yours?"

"Edward took them to Wulf Hall when he left for France. He warned me—but I did not think it would be this bad. He never thought it would get this bad. If he were here . . . I have written to him to come home. I have told him that Bishop Gardiner is dominating the Privy Council and that nobody is safe. I have told him that I fear for you, that I fear for myself.'

"Nobody is safe," I repeat.

"Your Majesty, if they can arrest your own sister, then they can arrest any one of us."

I suddenly rouse myself, my temper flares. 'The bishop dares to advise the Privy Council to arrest my sister, Nan? My chief lady-in-waiting? Sir William Herbert's wife? Get my gown. I shall dress and see the king."

She puts out a hand to detain me. "Your Majesty . . . think . . . It's not the bishop who has done this alone. It is the king. He must have signed the warrant for your sister's arrest. This must all be with his knowledge. It may even be at his request."

I lead my ladies to chapel. We put a brave face on it but two maids-in-waiting are missing and three ladies are absent and the court knows, like a pack of anxious hounds, that something is wrong.

Devoutly, we bow our heads to pray. Fervently we take the bread. Quietly we whisper: "Amen! Amen!" as if to declare there is not a thought in our silly heads as to what this really is: wafer or meat, bread or God. We finger our rosaries; I am wearing a crucifix at my neck. Princess Mary kneels beside me but her gown does not touch the hem of mine. Princess Elizabeth kneels on the other side and her cold hand creeps into my shaking grasp. She does not know what is happening, but she knows that something is very badly wrong.

After chapel we take our breakfast in the great hall, and the court is subdued, men talking quietly among themselves and everyone glancing towards me to see how I am taking the absence of my sister, of my two other missing ladies. I smile as if I am completely untroubled. I bow my head for the grace as the king's chaplain reads it in Latin. I eat a little meat, bread, I sip ale; I mime appetite, as if I am not sick with fear. I smile at my ladies and I glance at the Seymour table. I long to see Thomas as if he were a ship with reefed sails waiting at a quayside, ready to sail away to safety. I long to see him as if the sight of him would make me safe. But he is not here, I don't expect him, and I can't send for him.

I turn to Catherine Brandon, the most senior of my ladies at breakfast. "Your Grace, would you inquire if His Majesty the king is well enough to see me this morning?"

She rises from the table without a word. We all watch her walk down the length of the great hall, everyone praying that she will return with an invitation to visit the king's rooms and that we will find ourselves suddenly high in his volatile favor. But she is not gone long.

"His Majesty is in pain with the injury from his leg." She speaks calmly but her face is white. "His doctor is with him, he is resting. He says that he will send for you later and that he wishes you a very good day."

Everyone hears it. It is like a blast from the horns of the hunt. It is open season on heretics at court and everyone knows that the greatest prey, the one who carries the greatest bounty on her head, is me.

I smile. "Then we'll go to my rooms for an hour or two and ride out later." I turn to my master of horse. "We'll all ride," I say.

He bows and gives me his hand as I step down from the dais and walk through the silently bowing court. I smile and nod from left to right. Nobody shall say that I looked afraid.

When we get to my rooms, Nan, Maud Lane, and Elizabeth Tyrwhit are there, waiting for us to come back from breakfast. Nan is seated in her favorite spot in the window seat, her hands folded in her lap, the picture of womanly patience. Something about her powerful rigidity warns me that she has not returned to safety. I walk into the room and I stop myself running to her. I don't fling myself into her arms. I stand in the center of the room and I say very clearly, so that everyone can hear me, and everyone who is appointed to report to the spies of the Privy Council can make their statement: "Lady Herbert, my sister, I am glad to see you are returned to us. I was surprised and concerned to hear that you were explaining yourself to the Privy Council. I will have no heresy and no disloyalty in my rooms."

"None at all," Nan says without a quaver in her voice, without the flicker of an expression on her blank face. "There is no heresy here and there never has been. The councillors questioned myself and two of your ladies and were satisfied that nothing had been said or written by us, either in your presence or in your absence, that could ever be construed as heresy."

I hesitate. I can't think what more can be said for the listening court. "Have they cleared your names and discharged you?"

"Yes," she says, and the other two nod. "Completely."

"Very well," I say. "I will change my gown and we will go out riding. You can help me."

We go into my room together, Catherine Brandon comes in too, and the moment that the door is shut behind us we clutch each other.

"Nan! Nan!"

She holds me with a fierce strength, as if we were little girls in Kendal once more and she had to keep me from jumping out of a tree in the orchard. "Oh, Kat! Oh, Kat!"

"What did they ask you? Did they keep you awake all night?"

"Hush," she says. "Hush."

I find I am choking with frightened sobs and I put my hand to my throat and pull back from her grasp. "I am all right," I say. "I won't cry. I won't go out there with red eyes. I don't want anyone to see . . ."

"You're all right," she confirms. Gently she takes a handkerchief from her sleeve and touches my wet eyes and then dabs at her own. "Nobody must think that you're distressed."

"What did they say to you?"

"They've been questioning Anne Askew," she says bluntly. "They have tortured her."

I am so appalled I cannot speak. "Tortured her? The daughter of a gentleman of the realm? Nan, they can't have done so!"

"They've lost their minds. They were authorized by the king to question her. He told them that they could take her out of Newgate Prison and frighten her into confession, but they took her to the Tower and they put her on the rack."

The terrible pictures of my dream come back to me. The woman with the feet turned outwards, with a hollow where her shoulders should be. "Don't say it."

"I'm afraid it's true. I think they must have shown her the rack and then her courage enraged them and they couldn't resist it. When she wouldn't say anything, they went on and on; they couldn't stop themselves. The constable of the Tower was so appalled that he left them to it and reported it to the king. He said that they had thrown off their jackets in the torture room and racked her themselves. They pushed aside the hangman to do it. One at her head, one at her feet, they turned the wheels. They didn't want the hangman to do it, it wasn't enough for them to watch, they wanted to hurt her. When the king heard that from the constable, he commanded that they stop."

"He has pardoned her? He had her released?"

"Not him," she says bitterly. "He only said that they might not rack her. But, Kat, by the time the constable had got back to the Tower, they had been working on her all night. They carried on while the constable rode to see the king. They did not stop till he came back and told them."

I am silent. "Hours?"

"It must have been hours. She'll never walk again. All the bones in her feet and hands will be broken, her shoulders, her knees her hips will be dislocated. They will have broken her spine or pulled it apart."

Again I see the image from my dream of the woman with her wrists pulled from her arms, her arms detached at the elbow, the strange hollow where her shoulders should have been, her strange poise trying to hold her dislocated neck. I can hardly speak.

"But they have released her now?"

"No. They pulled her off the rack and dropped her on the floor."

"She's still there? In the Tower? With her arms and legs torn from their sockets?"

Nan nods, looking blankly at me.

"Who was it?" I spit. "Name them."

"I don't know for sure. Richard Rich was one. And Wriothesley."

"The Lord Chancellor of England racked a lady, in the Tower? With his own hands?"

At my appalled face she only nods.

"Has he gone mad? Have they all run mad?"

"I think they must be."

"No woman has ever been racked! No gentlewoman!"

"They were determined to know."

"About her faith?"

"No, she speaks of that quite willingly. They had everything they needed about her beliefs. Enough to find her guilty ten times over God forgive them, God help us, they wanted to know about you. They racked her to make her name you."

We are both silent and, though I am ashamed, I have to ask my next question. "Do you know what she said? Did she name us as heretics? Did she name me? Did she speak of my books? She must have done. Nobody could stand that. She must have done."

Nan's smile contrasts with her red eyes. It is the old smile of gritty courage that all women show who have gone through hard nights and come out without betrayal. "No. She can't have done. For see? They released us. We were there when the constable came from London and said what they were doing. They took him in to the king, but the door between the council chamber and the privy chamber was open a crack and we could hear His Majesty bellow at them. Then they came out and questioned us some more. They must have hoped that she would betray us or we would betray her—that at least one of us would name you. But she stayed silent, and we said nothing and then they released us. They have dismembered her, God be with her. They have torn her apart like a boned chicken, but she has not said your name."

I give one sob, like a cough, and then I am quiet. "We have to send her a doctor," I say. "And food and drink and some comfort. We have to get her released."

"We can't," Nan says with a long shuddering sigh. "I thought of this. But she has gone through all this to deny her sisterhood with us. We can't incriminate ourselves. We have to leave her alone."

"She will be in agony!"

"Let it be worthwhile."

"For God's sake, Nan! Is the Privy Council going to release her?"

"I don't know. I think—"

There is a gentle tap on the bedroom door. Catherine Brandon exclaims in irritation and opens it a crack. We hear her say, "Yes, what is it?" and then reluctantly hold it wider. "It's Doctor Wendy," she says. "He insists."

The plump form of the doctor appears in the doorway. "What now?" I demand. "Is the king ill?"

He waits till Catherine closes the door, then he bows over my hand. "I have to speak to you in confidence," he says.

"Doctor Wendy, this is not the time. I am distressed—"

"It's urgent."

I nod to Catherine and Nan to step back to the doorway. "You can speak."

He draws a paper from the inside of his jacket. "There is worse than you know," he says. "Worse than these ladies know. The king told me himself, just now. I am so sorry. So sorry to have to tell you. He has issued a warrant for your arrest. This is a copy."

Now that it has happened, now that the worse thing possible has happened, I do not scream and cry. I am completely still. "The king has ordered my arrest?"

"I regret to say so," he says formally.

I hold out my hand and he gives me the paper. We move slowly, as if we are in a dream. I think of Anne Askew, stretched on the rack. I think of Anne Boleyn taking off her pearl necklace for the French swordsman. I think of Kitty Howard asking them to bring the block to her room so that she could practice laying her head down. I think that I too will have to find the courage to die with dignity. I don't know that I am going to be able to do it. I think I am too passionate for life, I think I am too young, I think I want too much to live. I think I want Thomas Seymour. I want a life with him. I want tomorrow.

Blindly, I unfold the paper. I can see Henry's scrawled signature as I have seen it a dozen times. Without doubt it is my husband's hand. Above it in a clerk's script is the warrant for my arrest. It is so. It is here. It is here at last. My own husband has ordered my arrest on a charge of heresy. My own husband has signed it.

The enormity of this almost overcomes me. He does not want to send me back to widowed obscurity—though he could do that, he has the power to do that. Or he could exile me from court and I could do nothing but obey. He could treat me as he did Anne of Cleves and order me to live elsewhere and I would have to go. He could do that, he is head of the church, he can rule which marriages are valid and which should be dissolved. He did that to Katherine of Aragon though she was a princess of Spain and the pope himself said it could not be done; but Henry did it.

But he does not want me out of his sight or out of his palaces; he does not want me to hand back the jewels and return the gowns of the other queens; he does not want me to leave his children and be forgotten by them. It is not enough for me to surrender the regency and lose my power. That is not enough for him. He wants me dead. The only reason to charge me with a crime that carries a sentence of death is to kill me. Henry, who has executed two wives and waited for news of the deaths of two others, now wants me dead like them.

I can't understand it, I can't think why. I can't see why he should not send me into exile if he has come to hate me, after loving me so much. But it is not so. He wants me dead.

I turn to Nan, standing white-faced with Catherine at the door. "See this," I say wonderingly. "Nan, see what he has done now. See what he wants to do to me." I hand it to her.

Silently she reads it; she tries to speak, but her mouth opens and closes and she says nothing. Catherine takes it out of her powerless hands and reads it in silence, and then raises her eyes and looks at me.

"This is Gardiner's work," Catherine says after a long while.

Doctor Wendy nods. "He named you as a treasonous heretic," he says. "He said you were a serpent in the king's bosom."

"It's not enough that I am Eve, the mother of all sin; now I have to be the serpent as well?" I demand fiercely.

Doctor Wendy nods.

"He has no evidence!" I say.

"They don't need evidence." Doctor Wendy states the obvious. "Bishop Gardiner says that the religion you speak for denies lords, denies kings, says that all men are equal. Your faith is the same as sedition, he says."

"I have done nothing to deserve death," I say. I can hear my voice shake and I press my lips together.

"Neither did any of the others," says Catherine.

"The bishop said that anyone who spoke as you do, with justice, by law, would deserve death. Those were his very words."

"When are they coming?" Nan interrupts.

"Coming?" I don't understand her.

"To arrest her?" she asks the doctor. "What's the plan? When are they coming? And where will they take her?"

Practical as always, she goes to the cupboard and takes out my purse, and looks for a box to pack my things. Her hands are shaking so much that she cannot turn the key in the lock. I put both hands on her shoulders, as if to stop Nan preparing for my arrest will prevent the yeomen coming for me.

"The Lord Chancellor is ordered to come for her. He'll take her to the Tower. I don't know when. I don't know when she'll be tried."

At the words *the Tower* I find that my knees give way beneath me, and Nan guides me into a chair. I bend over till my head stops swimming and Catherine gives me a glass of small ale. It tastes old and stale. I think of Thomas Wriothesley spending all night racking Anne Askew in the Tower, and then coming to my rooms to take me there.

"I have to go," Catherine says shortly. "I have two fatherless boys. I have to leave you."

"Don't go!"

"I have to," she says.

Silently, Nan tips her head towards the door to tell her to leave.

Catherine curtseys very low. "God bless you," she says. "God keep you. Good-bye."

The door closes behind her and I realize that she has said farewell to a dying woman.

"How did you come by this?" Nan asks Doctor Wendy.

"I was there when they were deciding, making his sleeping draft in the back of the room, and then when I dressed his leg, the king himself told me that it was no life for a man in his old age to be lectured by a young wife."

I raise my head. "He said that?"

He nods.

"Nothing more than that? He has nothing more against me than that?"

"Nothing more. What more could he have? And then I found the warrant dropped on the floor in the corridor between his bedroom and his privy chamber. Just on the floor by the door. As soon as I saw it I brought it to you."

"You found the warrant?" Nan asks suspiciously.

"I did . . ." His voice trails off. "Ah, I suppose someone must have left it for me to find."

"Nobody drops a warrant for the arrest of a queen by accident," Nan says. "Someone wanted us to know." She strides across the room, thinking furiously. "You had better go to the king," she advises me. "Go to Henry now, and go down on your knees, creep along the floor like a penitent, beg pardon for your mistakes. Ask his forgiveness for speaking out."

"It won't work," Doctor Wendy disagrees. "He has ordered his doors locked. He won't see her."

"It's her only chance. If she can get in to see him and be humble . . . more humble than any woman in the world has ever been. Kat, you'll have to crawl. You'll have to put your hands beneath his boot."

"I'll crawl," I swear.

"He has said he will not receive her," the doctor says awkwardly. "The guards are ordered not to let her in."

"He shut himself away from Kitty Howard," Nan remembers. "And Queen Anne."

They are silent. I look from one to the other and I cannot think what to do. I can only think that the yeomen are coming and that they will take me to the Tower and Anne Askew and I will be prisoners in the same cold keep. I may walk to the window in the night and hear her crying in pain. We may wait in adjoining cells for the sentence of death. I may hear them carry her out to be burned. She will hear them building my scaffold on the green.

"What if he could be persuaded to come to you?" Doctor Wendy suddenly suggests. "If he thought you were ill?"

Nan gasps. "If you were to tell him that she had fallen into terrible grief, that she might die of her grief—if you were to tell him that she is asking for him, all but on her deathbed . . ."

"Like Jane in childbirth," I say.

"Like Queen Katherine, when her last words were that she wanted to see him," Nan prompts.

"A helpless woman in despair, near to death for grief . . ."

"He might," the doctor agrees.

"Can you do it?" I ask him intently. "Can you convince him that I am desperate to see him, and that my heart is broken?"

"And that he would look wonderful if he came, merciful."

"I'll try," he promises me. "I'll try now."

I remember Thomas telling me never to cry in front of the king because he likes women's tears. "Tell him I am beside myself with grief," I say. "Tell him I cannot stop crying."

"Hurry," Nan says. "When is Wriothesley coming to arrest her?"

"I don't know."

"Go now then."

He goes to the door and I get to my feet and put a hand on his arm. "Don't endanger yourself," I say, though I long to order him to do anything, say anything that will save me. "Don't put yourself in danger. Don't say that you warned me."

"I will say that I heard you were sick with grief," he says. He looks at my strained face and my stunned eyes. "I will tell him he has broken your heart."

He bows and goes out of my bedchamber into my privy rooms, where already the ladies of the court are silently gathering, and wondering if they will be called to give evidence against another of Henry's queens in another death trial.

"Hair down," Nan says briskly. She leaves a maid to unplait my hair and brush it over my shoulders and she opens the door to order another to fetch my best silk night robe with the black slashed sleeves.

She comes back into the room as two maids arrive and straighten the sheets on the bed, and heap up the pillows. "Perfume," she says shortly, and they get a jar of oil of roses and a feather to flick the scent all over the sheets.

Nan turns back to me. "Rouge on your lips," she says. "Just a little. Belladonna in your eyes."

"I have some," one of the ladies says. She sends her own maid flying to her rooms as my maid comes in with my nightgown.

I take off my ordinary gown and put on the silk one. It is cold against my naked skin. Nan ties the black ribbons at the throat and all the way down, but she leaves the top one loose, so there is a glimpse of my pale skin against the dark silk, and he will be able to see the round shape of my breasts. She smooths my hair over my shoulders and the auburn ringlets glint against the darkness of the gown. She closes the shutters just a little so the room is shadowy and intimate.

"Princess Elizabeth is to sit outside in the privy chamber reading the king's writings," she throws over her shoulder, and someone runs to invite the princess to her place.

"We'll leave you alone," she says quietly to me. "I'll be here when he comes in and then I'll go out. I'll try and take his pages out with me. You know what you have to do?"

I nod. I am cold inside the silk nightgown and I am afraid that I will have goose bumps and shiver.

"Start in the bed," Nan advises. "I doubt you can stand, anyway."

She helps me into the great bed. The scent of roses is almost overwhelming. She pulls the gown down to my feet and parts it at the front, so that the king will be able to see my slender ankles, the enticing curve of my calf.

"Don't be too tempting," she says. "It has to be all his own idea."

I lean back against the pillows, and she pulls a lock of hair over my shoulder to fall against the whiteness of my skin.

"This is disgusting," I remark. "I am a scholar, and a queen. I am not a whore."

She nods, as matter-of-fact as a swineherd bringing the sow to the boar. "Yes."

We can hear the rumble of the king's chair across the wooden floor of the presence chamber, and then the doors open to my privy chamber. We hear the ladies rise to greet him and his embarrassed "good morning" to them all and his greeting to Princess Elizabeth, who knows well enough to keep her head down and look devout.

The guards open my bedroom door to him and the king is wheeled in, his bandaged leg sticking stiffly out before him. A waft of stinking flesh breezes in with him.

I flutter a little, as if I am trying to rise but I fall back, too weak and overcome at the sight of him. I turn a tearstained face to him as Nan gets hold of the pages and draws them backwards through the doors then nods to the guard to close the doors on the two of us. In a moment the king finds himself alone with me.

"The doctor said you were very ill?" he asks sulkily.

"They should not have troubled you . . ." My voice dies away into a little sob. "I am so honored that you should come . . ."

"Of course I would come to see my wife," the king says, cheered at the thought of his own uxoriousness, his eyes on my legs.

"You're so good to me," I whisper. "That's why I was so . . ."

"So what, Kate? What's the matter?"

I stammer. I genuinely can't think of what to say most likely to stimulate his pity. I plunge in: "If I displease you, I want to die," I say.

The sudden flush in his face is like the expression he has in sexual pleasure. By luck I have stumbled upon the one thing that delights him above all other, and I did not know it till now. I have fallen, in my desperation, on the very heart of his desire for a woman.

"Die, Kate? Don't talk about dying. You needn't talk about dying. You are young and healthy." His gaze lingers on my arched instep, my ankle, the smooth curve of my leg. "Now, why would a pretty young woman like you talk about dying?"

Because you are Bluebeard, the Bluebeard of my nightmares, I want to say. You are Barbe-Bleu, and your wife, Tryphine, opened the locked doors of your castle and found dead wives laid out in their beds. Because I know you now for a wife killer, I know you are merciless. Because your fat glory in yourself is so great that you cannot imagine anyone thinking for themselves, or being themselves, or caring for anything but you. You are the sole sun in your own heavens. You are a natural enemy of anyone who is not you, not your very self. You are a murderer in your soul, and all you want of a wife is her submission to you or submission to the death you prescribe for her. There is no choice of anything else. You will be master, complete master. You can hardly bear anyone to be other than you. Your men friends have to be your mimics, the only survivor at your court is your Fool, who declares himself witless. You cannot bear anything that is not in your image. You are a natural killer of wives.

"If you don't love me, I want to die," I say, my voice a trembling thread of sound. "There is nothing left for me. If you don't love me, there is nothing left for me but the grave."

He is aroused. He shifts his huge bulk around in the creaking chair so that he can see me. I writhe a little in my grief and my robe parts. I push back the mass of my tumbled hair and the robe slips from my shoulder; but apparently I don't notice that he can see my white skin, the curve of my breast, in my panting distress.

"My wife," he says. "My beloved wife."

"Say that I am your beloved," I insist. "I will die if I am not your beloved."

"You are," he says, his voice congested. "You are."

He cannot get out of his chair to reach me. I scramble over to the edge of the bed, where his chair is jammed, and he stretches his arms out to me. I go towards him, expecting him to embrace me, to wrap his arms around me, but instead he grasps me like a clumsy boy, his hands fumble at the ties of my gown, tear one ribbon, and then I feel his fat hands grasp my cold breasts, as if he were a market trader weighing apples. He does not want to embrace me, he wants to handle me. Awkwardly, I kneel before him as he grasps at me, kneading me, as if he would milk me like a cow. He smiles.

"You may come to my room tonight," he says thickly. "I forgive you."

I lead my ladies in and out of dinner in near silence. Even the most junior, even the most ill informed, knows that something terrible happened and that I took to my bed in a state of collapse and the king himself deigned to visit me. Whether this indicates that all is well or whether disaster has fallen upon us, nobody knows for sure. Not even me.

I leave them in my rooms, whispering and spreading gossip, and I change out of my gown and into my embroidered silk night robe to go to the king's rooms with only my sister Nan and my cousin Maud Lane in attendance.

We walk through the great presence chamber, through the privy chamber, and then to the inner room. His bedroom is beyond. The king is with his friends, but neither Lord Wriothesley nor Bishop Gardiner is there. Will Somers sits before the king's footstool in an odd position, like a dog sitting on its haunches, in complete silence. When he sees me, he stretches out his hands on the floor and lowers himself down, like a dog at rest. His head on his paws is almost under the footrest that supports the king's bad leg. Down there, the stench must be unbearable. I look at Will, all but prone on the floor, and he turns his head and raises his eyebrows to look up, unsmiling at me.

"You're lying very low, Will," I remark.

"I am," he says. "I think it best."

His gaze turns towards the king and I see that Henry, seated above him, is glaring at us both. His gentlemen are seated on either side and Anthony Denny stands up to give me a chair at the fireside so that they can all see the candlelight shining on my face. Obviously, I have to make a public apology. Nan and Maud sink silently onto a bench at the wall as if they are kneeling.

"We were discussing the reform of the church," Henry says suddenly. "And whether the women gospelers who speak so loudly at Saint Paul's cross are making sermons as holy as the clerks who have spent years at the universities."

I shake my head. "I wouldn't know. I have never heard them."

"Never, Kate?" he asks. "Has none of them come to your rooms to sermonize and sing for you?"

I shake my head. "Perhaps one or two came to preach. I don't remember."

"But what do you think of the things they say?"

"Oh, my lord, how could I judge? I would have to ask you for guidance."

"You don't judge for yourself?"

"Ah, my lord husband, how can I judge when I have nothing but the simple education of a lady and the mind of a weak woman? Men are in the shape and likeness of God. I am only a woman, so much inferior in all respects. I consult you in everything, who are my only anchor, Supreme Head and governor next unto God."

"Not so, by Saint Mary, you have become a doctor, Kate, to instruct us," he says irritably. "You dispute with me!"

"No, no," I say hastily. "I wanted only to distract you from your pain. I spoke only ever to divert you. I think it is very unseemly, I think it is preposterous, for a woman to take the office of teacher to he who must be her lord and husband."

Anthony Denny nods judiciously: this is true. Will raises himself slowly on his forepaws as if to confirm that he too has seen this. The king is ready to be placated. He looks around to see that everyone is attending.

"Is it so, sweetheart?" he demands.

"Oh, yes, yes," I say.

"And you had no worse end?"

"Never."

"Then come and kiss me, Kate, for we are perfect friends as ever before."

I step towards him and he drags me onto his good leg so I am practically sitting in his lap and he nuzzles my neck. My smile never wavers, as Will bounds to his feet.

"You can all leave us," Henry says quietly, and his lords bow and take their leave as the pages come in to prepare the room for the night. The candles are new in the candlesticks, spaced around his bedroom so they show a soft and flickering light, the fire is banked up for the night, there is a pleasing smell of cinnamon and ginger.

Nan comes close as if to tidy my hair. "Do what you have to," she remarks. "I'll wait." She curtseys, and leaves me.

Behind me the pages have prepared the king's bed with the usual ritual of plunging a sword into the mattress and rolling on it to detect any hidden murderer, sliding a warming pan over the fresh sheets, and then finally positioning themselves either side of the king to heave him in. They leave a tray of pastries within his reach and a decanter of wine for me to pour.

I straighten my beautifully embroidered night robe of dark silk, and take a seat at the fireside until he invites me to approach his enormous bed. I think, nervously, that it is like my wedding night when I was so dreading his touch. Now I have become accustomed, he can do nothing that would shock me. I will have to accept his damp caresses; I know I will have to kiss him and not flinch from his fetid saliva. I think that he is in too much pain from his leg and too drugged to expect me to mount him so I will have to do nothing worse than smile and seem ardent. I can do that. I can do that for my own safety and for the safety of all who depend on this tyrant for their freedom. I can rack my pride. I can dislocate my shame.

"So we are friends," he says, putting his head on one side to admire my dark blue silk robe and the glimmer of white linen beneath it. "But I think you have been a naughty girl. I think that you have been reading books that were banned and listening to sermons that were not allowed."

Being addressed as a child for my work as a scholar—this too I can endure. I bow my head. "I am sorry if I have done anything wrong."

"Do you know what I do with naughty girls?" he asks, roguishly.

I can feel my thoughts whirling. I have never heard him speak like this before, diminishing me, and being a fool himself. But I must not challenge him. "I don't think I have been naughty, my lord."

"Very naughty indeed! And do you know what I do to naughty girls?" he asks again.

I shake my head. I think he has slipped into his dotage. I have to endure this too.

He beckons me to the side of the bed. "Come a little closer."

I rise from my chair and go to the bed. I move gracefully, like a woman. I take the few steps with my head held high, like the queen that I am. I think, surely he cannot maintain this game that I am a child for scolding, but then it seems that he can. He takes my hand and pulls me a little closer to the bed. "I think that you have read books that Stephen Gardiner would say are heretical, you bad child."

I open my eyes wide as if to assure him of my innocence. "I would never go against Your Majesty's wishes. Stephen Gardiner has never accused me, and he has no evidence."

"Oh, he has accused you," he says, chuckling as if this is funny. "Be sure of that! And he accused your friends, and the girl preacher, and indeed he had all the evidence that he needed to prove to me—or even to a jury, a jury, Kate!—that you are, alas, a very naughty little girl."

I try to smile. "But I have explained . . ."

I see the gleam of his irritation. "Never mind all that. I say you are a naughty girl and I think you have to be punished."

At once I think of the Tower and the scaffold that they can build on the green. I think of my ladies and the preachers who have spoken before me. I think of Anne, waiting in the Tower for release from her agony. "Punished?"

He reaches across his huge barrel of a body and extends his left hand to me. I take it and he tugs me roughly, as if he would pull me across the bed.

I yield. "Your Majesty?"

"Kneel on the bed," he says. "This is your punishment." He sees my aghast face and he laughs so much that he coughs, and tears come into his piggy little eyes. "Oh! Were you thinking that I would behead you? Oh Lord! Oh Lord! What fools women are! But kneel to me."

I gather the skirts of my gown in my free hand and kneel up on the bed beside him. He lets go of my hand now I am positioned where he wants me, kneeling beside him, the stench from his wounded leg wafting up into my face. I put my hands together as if to swear fealty.

"No, not that," he says impatiently. "I don't want you to beg for pardon. Go on your hands and knees. Like a dog."

I shoot one disbelieving look into his face and I see that he is flushed and intent. He means it. As I hesitate I see his eyes harden. "I've told you once," he says quietly. "There are guards outside and my barge will take you to the Tower tonight if I say just one word."

"I know . . ." I say quickly. "It's just that I don't know what you want me to do, my lord husband. I would do anything for you, you know that. I have promised to love . . ."

"I've told you what to do," he points out, reasonably enough. "Go on your hands and knees like a dog."

My face is burning with the heat of my shame. I go on my hands and knees on the bed and I drop my head down so that I don't have to see the bright triumph in his face.

"Lift your gown."

This is too much. "I can't," I say; but he is smiling.

"Up over your buttocks," he says. "Lift your gown right up, your linen too, so your arse is as bare as a Smithfield whore."

"Your Majesty . . ."

He raises his right hand as if to warn me to be completely silent. I look back at him, I wonder if I dare to defy him.

"My barge . . ." he whispers. "It is waiting for you."

Slowly, I pull my gown up to my waist, the silk cool in my fingers. It folds around my waist, leaving me naked from the waist down, on my hands and knees on the king's bed.

He fumbles in the bedclothes and for a horrible moment I think that he is fondling himself, aroused by my nakedness, and that there will be worse for me to do. But he brings out a whip, a short horse's whip, and shows it to me, bringing it to my burning face.

"D'you see?" he asks quietly. "It is no thicker than my little finger. The laws of the land, my laws, say that a husband may beat his wife if the stick is no thicker than his finger. D'you see that this is a thin little whip that I may legally use on you? Are we agreed?"

"Your Majesty would not—"

"It is the law, Kateryn. Like the law of heresy, like the law of treason. Do you understand that I am the lawgiver and the law enforcer and that nothing happens in England without my will?"

My legs and buttocks are cold. I bend my head to the stinking covers of the bed. "I understand," I say, though I can hardly speak.

He brings the whip closer, then thrusts it in my face. "Look!" he says.

I raise my head and look at it.

"Kiss it," he says.

I can't stop myself from flinching. "What?"

"Kiss the rod. As a sign that you accept your punishment. Like a good child. Kiss the rod."

I look at him blankly for a moment as if I wonder if I can disobey him. He returns my gaze, completely calm. Only his scarlet color and his rapid breathing reveal that he is aroused. He holds the whip a little closer to my lips. "Go on," he says.

I purse my lips. He puts the leather plaited thong to my mouth. I kiss it. He puts the thicker leather stem to my face. I kiss it. He puts his clenched hand holding the handle before my mouth, and I kiss his fat fingers too. Then without changing his expression he raises the whip behind me, and brings it down hard on my buttocks.

I cry out and flinch away, but he has tight hold of my upper arm and he strikes me again. Three times I hear the whistle and then feel the blow as it comes down and the pain is quite terrible. There are burning tears in my eyes as he brings the whip to my face again and whispers: "Kiss it, Kateryn, and say that you have learned wifely obedience."

There is blood in my mouth from where I have bitten my lip. It tastes like poison. I can feel the hot tears pouring down my cheeks and I cannot choke down a little sob. He waggles the stick in front of me and I kiss it, as he orders. "Say it," he reminds me.

"I have learned wifely obedience," I repeat.

"Say thank you, my lord husband."

"Thank you, my lord husband."

He is quiet. I take a choking breath. I can feel my chest heave with my sobs. I assume my punishment is finished and I pull down my gown. My buttocks are stinging raw and I am afraid they are bleeding, and my white linen shift will be stained.

"One other thing," he says silkily, still holding me on my hands and knees. I wait.

He pushes back the covers of his bed and I see, like a monstrous erection, he is wearing the ivory silk codpiece from the portrait strapped on his fat naked belly. It is a grotesque sight, huge on his rotting belly, pointing upwards out of the sheets, embroidered with silver thread and stitched with pearls.

"Kiss this too," he says.

My will is broken indeed. I rub the tears from my eyes with the back of my hand and I feel the snot from my nose spread over my face. This, too, I will do for my own safety.

He puts his hand on it and he caresses it as if it can give him pleasure. He giggles. "You have to," he says simply.

I nod. I know that I have to. I put my head down and I put my lips against the encrusted tip. With a single cruel gesture he takes a handful of my hair and thumps the back of my head, so my face is smacked by it and it bangs against my teeth and the pearls scrape my lips. I don't pull back from the pain. I hold my face still as he works it in a parody of abuse against my mouth over and over again till my mouth is bruised by the jewels and the embroidery and my lips are bleeding.

He is exhausted, his face flushed and sweating. The ivory codpiece is smeared with my blood as if he had deflowered a virgin with it. He drops back on his pillows and sighs as if he is deeply satisfied. "You can go."

It is very late when I come out of the king's bedroom and close the door quietly behind me. I walk stiffly across the privy chamber and into the presence chamber where his pages are waiting.

"Go in," I say to them my hand hiding my bruised mouth. "He wants a drink and some food."

Nan and Maud Lane stand up from their seats at the fireside. The double doors between the privy chamber and the bedroom muffled my cry; but Nan can tell at once that there is something wrong.

"What's he done to you?" she asks, scanning my white face, taking in the bruising, the smear of blood at my mouth.

"It's all right," I say.

We walk to the queen's side of the palace in silence, I know that my gait is awkward, I can feel my linen gown sticking to the weals from the whip. I go through the private galleries and into my bedroom. Maud curtseys and closes the bedroom door. Nan unlaces my gown. "Don't call anyone," I say. "I'll sleep in my linen, I'll wash tomorrow."

"The stink of his wound is on your linen," Nan warns me.

"It's all over me," I say tightly. "But I have to sleep. I can't bear . . ."

She shucks off her own gown, and gets into the bed. For once in my life I go to bed without kneeling at the bedside to pray. I have no words tonight, I feel far from God. I slide between the cool sheets. Nan blows out the candle with a quick puff and the darkness forms around us from the shadows in the room and then I can just see the outline of the wooden shutters limned with the dawn light. We lie in sleepless silence for a long time. My little silver clock chimes four. Then she speaks: "Did he hurt you?"

"Yes," I say.

"On purpose?"

"Yes."

"But you are forgiven?"

"He wanted to break my spirit and I think he has done so. Don't ask me more, Nan."

We sleep fitfully, I have no dreams of the dark castle and the woman with the wrenched limbs, or the dead wives behind the bolted doors. One of the worst things that can happen to a proud woman has happened to me, I need not fear my dreams anymore. When the maids come in the morning with the ewer of hot water they find me throwing off my soiled linen and ordering the bath.

I want to get the smell of his suppurating leg out of my skin, out of my hair. I want to get a fetid taste out of my mouth. I feel as if I am soiled, I feel as if I am foul and I can never be washed clean. I know that I am broken.

Shaming me has cheered the king back to health. Suddenly he is well enough to dine with the court, and this afternoon he is wheeled into the garden with me at his side. Nan, Lady Tyrwhit, and little Lady Jane Grey walk with me, the rest of my ladies stroll behind us, and the king holds my hand as I walk beside the chair. There is a spreading beech tree in the center of the king's privy garden, and he stops the chair in the shade and someone fetches a stool for me to sit beside him. Gingerly I lower myself to the seat. He smiles as he sees I cannot sit without pain.

"You are amused, my lord husband?"

"Now we're going to see a play."

"A play? Here?"

"Indeed yes. And when it is over you can tell me the title."

"Are you speaking in riddles, my lord?" I ask. I can feel my fear rising.

The little iron gate to the privy garden creaks slightly, opens wide, and guards come running in, a huge number of them, crowding into the small garden. There are at least forty of them in the bright livery of the king's yeomen of the guard. I rise to my feet. For a moment I think that there is a mutiny against the king and he is in danger. I look round for the pages who wheeled him here, for the gentlemen of the court. Nobody is within calling distance. I stand before him; I will have to shield him from whatever comes. I will have to save him if I can.

"Wait," he cautions me. "Remember, it is a play."

These are not traitors. They are followed by Lord Wriothesley with a rolled letter in his hand. His dark face is alight with triumph. He comes towards me smiling and he unfurls the letter, showing me the seal, the royal seal. It is a warrant for my arrest. "Queen Kateryn, known as Parr, you are under arrest for treasonous heresy," he says. "Here is the warrant. You must come with me to the Tower."

I have no breath. I throw one anguished look at my husband. He is beaming. I think this is the greatest joke, the greatest masque, that he has ever performed. He has broken my spirit and now he will break my neck and I cannot complain, I cannot protest my innocence. I cannot even beg him for a pardon because I cannot breathe.

Even my sight is dim, though I see Nan running towards us across the grass, her face screwed up in fear. Behind her little Jane Grey hesitates, steps forward, shrinks back, as Lord Wriothesley brandishes his warrant and says again: "You must come with me to the Tower, Your Majesty. No delay, please." His face is bright. "Please don't make me order them to take you by force."

He turns to the king and he kneels to him. "I have come. I will do as you commanded," Wriothesley says, his voice oozing contentment. He rises up again, and he is about to nod to the guards to surround me.

"Fool!" Henry bellows at him, full-voiced. "Fool! Knave! Arrant knave! Beast! Fool!"

Wriothesley falls back before the king's red-faced sudden rage. "What?"

"How dare you?" Henry demands. "How dare you come into my own garden and insult the queen? My beloved wife! Are you mad?"

Wriothesley opens and closes his mouth like one of the fat fish in the carp ponds.

"How dare you come in here and distress my wife?"

"The warrant? Your Majesty! Your royal warrant?"

"How dare you show her such a thing? A woman sworn to my interests who has no mind but my mind, who has no thought but mine, whose body is at my command, whose immortal soul is in my keeping? My wife? My beloved wife?"

"But you said that she should be—"

"Are you saying that I would order the arrest of my own wife?"

"No!" Wriothesley says hastily. "No, of course not, Your Majesty, no."

"Get out of my sight," Henry shouts at him as if he is driven to madness by such disloyalty. "I can't bear you! I never want to see you again."

"But, Your Majesty?"

"Go!"

Wriothesley bows to the ground and stumbles backwards through the garden gate. The guards fumble their exit and rush after him, pushing their way out of the sunlit garden, desperate to get away from the furious king. Henry waits till they are all gone and the gate has clanged shut, the guard standing outside it with his back to us. Only when it is all still and quiet again does the king turn to me.

He is laughing so much that he cannot speak. For a moment I fear that he is having a fit. The tears squeeze out of his puckered eyelids and run down his sweating cheeks. He is dangerously flushed, and as he holds his shaking belly he chokes for air. Long minutes pass as he hoarsely cackles before he can steady himself. He opens his little eyes and wipes his wet cheeks.

"Lord," he says. "Lord."

He sees me standing before him, still frozen with shock, and my ladies blank-faced, waiting.

"What's the title of the play, Kate?" he pants, still laughing.

I shake my head.

"You who are so clever? So widely read? What is the title of my play?"

"Your Majesty, I cannot guess."

"*The Taming of the Queen!*" he shouts. "*The Taming of the Queen.*"

I hold my slight smile. I look at his sweating scarlet face and I let the sound of his renewed laughter break over me like the hoarse cawing of the ravens at the Tower.

"I am the dog master," he says, abruptly abandoning his joke. "I watch you all. I set you all at each other's throats. Poor curs. Poor little bitch."

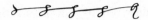

The king sits in the garden till the shadows lengthen along the smooth green grass and the birds start to sing in the tops of the trees. The swallows weave along the curves of the river, swirling above their own silvery reflections and dipping into the water to drink. The courtiers come in from playing games and they walk languidly, like happy children with flushed faces. Princess Elizabeth smiles up at me and I see a scatter of freckles over her nose like dust on marble, and I think I must remind her maid to make sure that she wears a sun bonnet whenever she goes out.

"It's been a beautiful day," the king says contentedly. "God Himself knows what a wonderful country this is."

"We are blessed," I agree quietly, and he smiles as if the credit for the summer and for the weather and for the sun sinking over the glassy river is somehow all due to him.

"I shall come to dinner," he says, "and after dinner you may come to my room and you must talk to me about your thoughts, Kate. I like to hear what you have been reading and what you think."

He laughs as he sees me suddenly go pale. "Ah, Kate. You need fear nothing. I have taught you everything you need to know, have I not? It is my translations that you read? You are my dear wife, are you not? And we are friends?"

"Of course, of course," I say. I bow as if I am delighted at the invitation.

"And you may ask anything of me. Any little gift, any little favor. Anything you like, sweetheart."

I hesitate, wondering if I dare speak of the broken woman in the Tower, Anne Askew, waiting to hear if she is to live or to die. He has said I can ask anything of him, he has just said I am to fear nothing. "Your Majesty, there is one small thing," I start. "A little thing to you, I am sure. But it would be the greatest wish of my heart."

He raises his hand to stop me. "My dear, we have learned today, have we not, that there are no things, not even the smallest things, that come between a husband and wife like us? The greatest wish of your heart could only be the greatest wish of mine. We have nothing to discuss. You need never ask anything of me. We are as one."

"It is my friend . . ."

"You have no better friend than me."

I understand him. "We are as one," I repeat dully.

"Holy unity," he says.

I bow my head.

"And loving silence."

"She's dead," Nan tells me brutally, as they are brushing my hair before dinner. The movement of the heavy brush through my thick hair, the occasional painful pull, seems to be part of her news. I don't put up my hand to stop Susan, the maid, from grooming me as if I were a mare going to the stallion. My head rocks to one side and then the other with the harsh pulling motion. I see my face in the mirror, my white skin, my hurt eyes, my bruised mouth. My head going one way and then another like a nodding doll.

"Who is dead?" But I know.

"Anne Askew. I just had word from London. Catherine Brandon is at her London house. She sent me a note. They killed her this morning."

I choke. "God forgive them. God forgive me. God send her soul to heaven."

"Amen."

I gesture that Susan is to go away, but Nan says: "You have to have your hair brushed and your hood pinned. You have to go to dinner. Whatever has happened."

"How can I?" I ask simply.

"Because she died never mentioning your name. She took the rack for you and death for you, so that you could go to dinner and, when your chance comes again, you can defend the reform of the church. She knew you must be free to speak to the king even if all the rest of us are killed. Even if you lose us all, one by one. If you are the last one left, you must save reform in England. Or she will have died for nothing."

I see Susan's aghast face in the mirror behind my own.

"It's all right," I say to her. "You need not bear witness."

"But *you* must," Nan says to me. "Anne died without admitting that she knew any one of us, so that we would be free to go on thinking, talking, and writing. So that you would carry the torch."

"She suffered." It's not a question. She was in the torture room of the Tower, alone with three men. No woman has ever been there before.

"God bless her. They broke her body so badly that she could not walk to the stake. John Lascelles, Nicholas Belenian, and John Adams were burned at the same time, but the men walked to their pyres. She was the only one tortured. The guards had to carry her tied to a chair. They said her feet were turned in as if she was wearing them backwards, and her shoulders and her elbows were all pulled out. Her spine was disjointed, her neck was pulled from her shoulders."

I dip my head and I put my hands over my eyes. "God keep her."

"Amen," Nan says. "A king's messenger came to offer her pardon as they tied the chair to the stake."

"Oh, Nan! Could she have recanted?"

"All they wanted was your name. They would have taken her down if she had said your name."

"Oh, God forgive me."

"She listened to the priest preaching the sermon before they brought the torches to set the fire, and she said 'Amen' only when she agreed with him."

"Nan, I should have done more!"

"You couldn't have done more. Truly, there was nothing more that any of us could do. If she had wanted to escape death, she could have told them what they wanted to hear. They were clear enough with her what it should be."

"Just my name?"

"All this has been done only so they could name you as a heretic to the king and kill you."

"They burned her?" It must be a terrible death, tied to a stake with the faggots heaped around your feet, the smell of the smoke as the flames take hold, the sight of family and praying friends dimming as the smoke rises and then the terrible crackle as your hair catches and then your skirt smolders, and then the pain—I break off to rub my eyes—I cannot imagine the pain as a gown catches fire, as sleeves take the flames to the arms, to the shoulders, to her delicate white neck.

"Catherine Brandon sent her a purse of gunpowder and she wore it in her gown. When the flames grew hot it blew off her head. She didn't have to suffer long."

"That was all we could do for her? That was the best that we could do?"

"Yes."

"But she had to let them strap her broken arms and legs to the chair, she had to wear a gunpowder purse around her twisted neck?"

"Yes. I don't mean to say that she didn't suffer. Just that she did not . . . cook."

At Nan's simple words I choke on vomit. I put my head on the table among the silver hairbrush and the silver comb and I heave, spilling bile on the table, over the silver brushes and glass bottles.

I get up and turn from the table. Wordlessly, Susan clears up, brings me a cloth to wipe my face, small ale for me to rinse and spit. Two maids scurry in behind her and wipe my vomit from the floor. Then I sit again before my looking glass and see the whey face of the woman that Anne Askew died to save.

Nan waits for me to catch my breath.

"I am telling you now, because the king will know that it has been done according to his orders. When he comes to your rooms this evening, he will know that the greatest woman in England has been burned today, and they are sweeping up her ashes from the cobbles of Smithfield as we walk in to dinner."

I raise my head. "This is unbearable."

"Unbearable," she agrees.

Catherine Brandon returns to court so pale that nobody doubts her story that she was sick. She comes to my room. "She didn't mention your name," she said. "Not when they gave her a chance to get off the fire. Not even then. Nicholas Throckmorton attended and she met his eye and she smiled at him and nodded as if to say that we had nothing to fear."

"She smiled?"

"She said 'Amen' to the prayers and smiled. He said the crowd was horrified at her death. There were no cheers, just a long low groan. He said that this will be the last woman preacher burned in England. The people won't stand for it."

We are waiting in my presence chamber and half the court is here already. The king is wheeled in beaming. We all curtsey, and I take my place beside the chair. He extends his hand, and I take it. The grip is so warm and wet that for a moment I imagine that he has blood on his hands, but then I see it is a flicker of red light from the stained-glass windows.

"All well?" he asks brightly, though he must know that I have learned of Anne's death.

"All well," I say quietly, and we go in to dinner.

HAMPTON COURT PALACE, SUMMER 1546

KP

The fine weather continues and the king himself is as sunny as the mornings. He declares that he is well again, much better, he has never been better, he feels like a young man. I watch him and I think that he will live forever. He returns to the full life of the court and takes every meal seated on his great throne, calling for one dish after another as the kitchen wrestles with cartloads of ingredients that arrive rumbling down the lanes to the huge arched kitchen doors, and sends out one heaped dish after another. The king is in his former place, at the center of the court, the great cog that turns everything, and the machine that is the court becomes once more a huge clockwork engine that takes in food and grinds out amusement.

He even rises from his chair to take slow steps in the garden or in to dinner. The pages walk beside him—he has a heavy hand on each of their shoulders—but he declares that he can walk almost unaided and will do so again. He swears that he will ride, and when I and my ladies dance before him, or when the masquers come in and choose their partners, he says that perhaps next week he will be up and jigging.

He bellows for diversion, and the choristers and the musicians and the players go into a frenzy of creation so that the king can see a new piece or hear a new song every night. He roars with laughter at the slightest joke. Will Somers was never in his life so popular, and takes up magnificently incompetent juggling. At every meal he has rolls of manchet bread spinning around his head and flying out of control around the hall so the dogs leap up and snatch them from the air before Will can catch them, and then he complains that no one understands his artistry, and chases the dogs and goes under the table with them and there is a noisy joyful riot as people place bets on dogs or Will. The king gambles, losing a small fortune with his courtiers, who are wise enough to return it to him in the next game. The king has a lust for life, a joy in life, which people say they have not seen for years. They say it is to my credit that I have made him young and happy again. They ask how I have pleased him.

One evening at dinner I see a stranger, dressed as grandly as a hidalgo of Spain, make his bow to the king and take his place at the table for noblemen.

"Who's that?" I ask Catherine Brandon as she stands behind my chair.

She leans forward so that she can speak quietly in my ear. "That, Your Majesty, is Guron Bertano. Apparently, he is an emissary from the pope."

I nearly shriek. "From the pope?"

She nods, her lips folded together.

"The pope has sent a diplomat, here? To our court? After all that has gone before?"

"Yes," she says shortly.

"This is impossible," I say hastily. The king has been excommunicated for years. He called the pope the antichrist. How can it be that he is now entertaining his messenger?

"Apparently the pope is going to receive the English Church back into communion with Rome. They just have to agree to the details."

"We become Roman Catholic again?" I mutter incredulously. "After all the suffering? Despite all the advances that we have made, despite the sacrifices?"

"Are you not hungry, my love?" Henry booms from my left side.

I turn quickly and smile. "Oh, yes," I say.

"The venison is very fine." He nods to the server. "Give the queen more venison."

I pause while the dark meat is served to my golden plate, the thick dark gravy poured.

"The flesh of the doe is always sweeter than that of the buck," Henry winks at me.

"I am glad to see you are in such good spirits, my lord husband."

"I am at play," Henry says. His gaze follows mine to where the emissary of the pope sits quietly at the table, eating with relish. "And I alone understand the game."

"You are to be congratulated," Edward Seymour says to me thinly as my court of ladies is walking beside the river before the day gets too hot. His lordship is home from Boulogne, relieved of command at last, and taking up his influence at the Privy Council once again. Lord Wriothesley has not recovered from his scolding in the king's garden, Stephen Gardiner has been very quiet, the papal messenger has gone home with only the vaguest of promises, and we all hope that the forces of reform are quietly taking the upper hand once more. I should be glad.

"I am?"

"You have managed something that no previous wife has done."

I glance around but Edward Seymour is not likely to be indiscreet, and nobody is listening. "I have?"

"You displeased the king and then you won his forgiveness. You are a clever woman, Your Majesty. Your experience is unique."

I bow my head. I cannot speak of it. I am shamed, I am unspeakably shamed. And Anne Askew is dead.

"You manage him," he says. "You are a formidable diplomat."

I can feel myself flush at the memory. I do not need Edward to remind me of that night. I will never forget it. I feel as if I will never raise my head up from what I did. I cannot bear that Edward should even speculate about what I did to get the king to tear up the warrant for my arrest. "His Majesty is merciful," I say quietly.

"More than that," Edward says. "He is changing his mind. There are to be no more burnings for heresy. The mood of the country has turned against it, and the king has turned with them. He says that Anne Askew should have been pardoned, and that Anne Askew will be the last. This is your influence, Your Majesty, and everyone who wants to see the church reformed will be grateful to you. There are many who thank God for you. There are many who know that you are a scholar, a theologian, and a leader."

"It's too late for some," I say quietly.

"Yes, but others are still in prison," he says. "You could ask for their release."

"He does not seek my advice," I remind him.

"A woman like you can put a thought into her husband's head and congratulate him for thinking it," Edward says, smiling broadly. "You know how it is done. You are the only woman ever to manage it."

I think that I started my reign as a scholar and learned how to study, and now I have become a whore and have learned whore's tricks.

"It is not ignoble to humble yourself for a cause like this," Edward says as if he knows what I am thinking. "The papists are in retreat, the king has turned against them. You could get good men released and the king to change the law to free people to pray as they wish. You have to work with your charm and your beauty—with the skills of Eve and the spirit of Our Lady. This is what it is to be a woman of power."

"That's odd, for I feel powerless," I say.

"You must use what you have," he says, the advice of a good man to a whore for time immemorial. "You must use what you are allowed."

I take great care not to say one word that sounds like a challenge to the king. I ask him to explain his thinking on the significance of purgatory, and I am interested when he tells me that there is no evidence for such a state in the Bible and that the theory of purgatory was created by the church solely to finance chantries and Masses. I listen with the air of an eager disciple as he propounds things that I have thought ever since I began my studies. Now he is glancing into books that I have read and hidden for my own safety, and he tells me the things that strike him as if they are a great novelty and I should learn them from him. Little Lady Jane Grey knows these opinions, Princess Elizabeth has read them; I taught them both myself. But now I sit beside the king and exclaim when he describes the blindingly obvious, I admire his discovery of the widely known, and I remark on his perception.

"I shall release the men held on charges of heresy," he says to me. "A man should not be imprisoned for his conscience, not if he is questioning reverently and thoughtfully."

Silently, I nod as if I am overwhelmed by the king's vision.

"You will be glad to know that a preacher like Hugh Latimer can be free to speak again?" Henry prompts me. "He used to preach in your rooms, didn't he? You can have your afternoon sermons again."

I speak with meticulous care. "I should be glad to know that innocent men are free. Your Majesty is merciful, and a careful judge of what is right."

"Will you have your afternoon sermons again?"

I don't know what he wants to hear, and I am determined to say only what he wants to hear. "If it is your wish. I like to listen to the preachers so that I may understand Your Majesty's thoughts.

It helps me to follow your intricate thinking if I study the fathers of the church."

"D'you know what Jane Seymour's motto was?" he suddenly demands.

I flush. "Yes, Your Majesty."

"What was it?"

"I believe it was *Bound to Obey and Serve*."

He bellows suddenly: a roar of shocking laughter, opening his mouth wide, showing his yellow teeth and his furred tongue. "Say it again! You say it!"

"*Bound to Obey and Serve*."

He laughs but there is no humor in his voice at all. I make sure that I am smiling, as if I am willing to be amused but too slow to understand the joke, as if I, as a dull woman, can have no sense of humor, but I am happy to admire his wit.

The admiral of France, Claude d'Annebault, who negotiated the peace with Edward Seymour, comes to Hampton Court for a great reception. The royal children, especially Prince Edward, are to welcome him. The king says that he is tired and asks me to watch that Edward does all that he should, and maintains the dignity of the Tudor throne. Edward is only eight, and torn between excitement and apprehension at the part he has to play. He comes to my rooms before the Frenchman arrives and asks me what exactly is to happen and what exactly he is to do. He is so precise, so anxious to be accurate, like a little astronomer, that I call my master of horse and my principal steward and we draw out, on a great sheet of paper, a plan of the gardens. Then, with his old tin soldiers from the nursery, we represent the arrival of the French delegation, and use little dolls to represent us, going out to meet them.

There are to be two hundred French gentlemen and the whole of the Privy Council and the court will come to meet them. We will house them in tents of cloth of gold in the gardens and we will build temporary banqueting houses for the feasts. We draw this little village on our plan, and we take another piece of paper and list the ten days and every reception, hunt, masque, sport, and feast.

Princess Elizabeth is there too, and Lady Jane, and we laugh and call for bonnets and headgear and soon we are play-acting the arrival of the French. Edward plays himself but all the rest of us are Frenchmen and courtiers in great hats, sweeping exaggerated bows and making long speeches until we fail the masque with our laughter and have to be ourselves again.

"But it will be like this?" Edward asks earnestly. "And I will stand just here?" He points at the platform that we have marked on the plan.

"Why worry?" Elizabeth demands of him. "You're the prince and our Lady Mother is regent—whatever the two of you choose to do must be how it is to be done. You're Prince of Wales, you cannot do anything wrong."

Edward gives me his sweetest smile. "I shall follow you, Lady Mother."

"You are the prince," I say. "And Elizabeth is correct. Whatever you do is the right thing."

The visit goes off just as we planned it. Prince Edward rides out with an escort of gentlemen and yeomen of the guard, all dressed in cloth of gold. He looks very small with the great yeomen towering over him, but he handles his little horse well and he greets the visitors with dignity in perfect French. I am so proud of his scholarship that I hug him on his return and dance him around my private chamber.

I report on his good behavior to the king, and Henry says that he will meet the admiral himself, and take him to Mass in the chapel royal.

"You have served me and my family well today," Henry says

to me when I go to his room in the evening to tell him of the visit and the ceremonies, of how well Prince Edward acted as host in his father's absence, of how proud we must be of Jane Seymour's boy. "You have been as a mother to him," the king says. "Far more than his own mother, who never even knew him."

I notice that tonight he speaks of her death as a dereliction of her duty. "You have been as a regent to the country today. I am grateful to you."

"I have done nothing more than I should," I coo.

"I am glad that you are pictured with him in the family portrait," he says. "It is right that you are honored as his stepmother."

I hesitate. Clearly, he has forgotten that it is Jane Seymour, the dead wife, who is in the portrait. I sat for it, but I did not get my face in the frame. There is no portrait of me together with the little boy whom I love.

He continues, regardless. "You have been an honor to your country and to your beliefs," he says. "You have quite persuaded me over these last few months of the rightness of your place at the head of the country and of your convictions."

I glance around the room. There is no one here to disagree. The usual courtiers are in earshot but now they are almost all friendly to me or to the cause of reform. Stephen Gardiner is absent. There was some argument over a small estate of land and the king took sudden offense. Gardiner will have to wheedle his way back into favor, but in the meantime, it is a pleasure to be without him. Wriothesley has not been at the king's side since the day in the garden when he came to arrest me.

"I am always guided by Your Majesty," I say.

"And I think you are right about the Mass," he says casually. "Or do you call it the Communion?"

I smile, pretending confidence while I feel the ground shuddering and weakening beneath me. "I call it whatever Your Majesty thinks best," I say. "It is your church, it is your liturgy. You know better than I, better than anyone, how it should be understood."

"Let's call it the Communion then, the Communion for all

the people of the church," he says, suddenly expansive. "Let us say that it is not literally the body and blood of Our Lord—for how are the common people to understand such a thing? They will think we mean some magic or some trickery. To those of us who think deeply, who meditate on these things, we who understand the power of language, it may be the body and the blood as well as bread and wine; but to the ordinary people we can say to them that it is a form of words. *Likewise also when they had supped he took the cup saying: This cup is the new testament in my blood which shall for you be shed.* It is clear that He gave them bread, He blessed bread, He gave them wine and told them it was a testament. We, who understand so much more than the village dullards, should not muddle them and confuse them."

I dare not look up in case this is a trap set for me, but I feel myself tremble with the strength of my feeling. If the king is coming to this realization, if the king is coming to this clarity, then Anne did not die in vain and I did not throw down my scholarship and take a beating like a slave in vain, for God has brought the king enlightenment through her ashes and my shame.

"Is Your Majesty saying that we should understand that the words are symbolic?"

"Isn't it what you think?"

I will not be tempted into declaring my opinion. "Your Majesty, you will find me a very stupid woman, but I hardly know what to think. I was brought up to believe one thing, and then taught to consider another. Now, as a married woman, I have to know what my husband believes for he is there to guide me."

He smiles. This is exactly right; this is what he wants to hear. This is what a tamed wife parrots to her husband. "Kate, I will tell you—I think we need to create a sincere religion in which the communion is the center of the liturgy but its power is symbolic," he pronounces. The rounded phrase and the sonorous delivery tells me that he has prepared this. He may even have written it down and learned it by heart. Someone may even have coached him—Anthony Denny? Thomas Cranmer?

"Thank you," I say sweetly. "Thank you for guiding me."

"And I am going to suggest to the French ambassador that we work together, France and England, to drive out the superstition and heresy of the old church and create a new church, in France and in England, based on the Bible, based on the new learning, and that we spread it throughout all our lands, and then throughout the world."

This is incredible. "You will?"

"Kate, I want a learned, thoughtful people walking in the ways of God, not a pack of fearful fools plagued by witches and priests. All of Europe but the papal states are persuaded that this is the way to understand God. I want to be part of this. I want to advise them, I want England to lead them. And if the day ever comes, I want to leave you as a regent and my son as a king to reign over people who say prayers that they understand and take part in a Mass—in a Communion that makes sense to them, as Our Lord described—not some kind of mumpsimus-sumpsimus invented in Rome."

"I think it too, I think it too!" I can no longer contain my enthusiasm.

He smiles at me. "We'll bring the new learning, the new religion into England," he says. "You will see this, even if I do not."

WINDSOR CASTLE, AUTUMN 1546

KP

We go on progress after the French visit and the king is even able to hunt. He cannot walk, but his indomitable spirit drives him on and they lift him into the saddle, and once astride he can ride to hounds. At each of our beautiful palaces on the river they build a hide for him, equipped with bows and arrows, and drive the game towards him. Dozens of deer and many stags go down before the royal box, with arrows in their eyes and their faces ripped open. It is more intensely cruel than when we are in the open field. The king takes careful aim with the beautiful beast herded towards him, the animal goes down with a barb in its face and a hound tearing at its hindquarters. Henry is not troubled by the cold savagery of killing a trapped animal. He watches the huntsman cut the throat of a struggling beast with complete calm. Indeed, I almost think that the suffering pleases him. He watches the little black hooves kicking until they are still and then he gives a short laugh.

He is watching the death throes of some poor doe when he suddenly remarks, "What do you think of Thomas Seymour as a match for Princess Elizabeth? I know the Seymours would like it."

I flinch, but he is not looking at me but at the glaze that is coming over the sloe-black eye of the wounded deer.

"Whatever you think best," I say. "Of course, she is still young. She could be betrothed and stay with me until she is sixteen."

"Do you think he would make her a good husband? He's a handsome devil, isn't he? Does she like him? Would he get a boy on her, d'you think? Is she eager for him?"

I hold my scented leather glove to my lips to hide the tremble that I can feel. "I can't say. She's very young still. She likes him well enough, as she should, as her half brother's uncle. I think that he would make her a good husband. His courage cannot be questioned. What do you think, Your Majesty?"

"He's handsome, isn't he? As randy as a dog? He's a terrible man for the ladies."

"No more than many others," I say. I have to take care. I cannot think what I should say to keep myself safe and promote Thomas's hopes.

"D'you like him?"

"I hardly know him," I say. "I know his brother far better, because his wife is in my rooms. When I speak with Sir Thomas, he is always interesting, and he has served you most loyally, hasn't he?"

"He has," the king concedes.

"He has been a great help in the safety of England, the fleet and the ports?"

"Yes; but to give him a daughter would be an exceptional reward. And it would make the Seymours greater still."

"But an English marriage would keep her in England," I say. "And that would be a comfort to us both."

He looks as if he is considering it, as if the thought of keeping her at home moves him. "I know Elizabeth," he says. "She would have him if I let her. She is a slut, just like her mother."

Although our stay at Windsor is in fine weather, suddenly, for no apparent reason, the king withdraws from court. I do not think he is ill, but he takes to his rooms with a small circle of gentlemen and will see no one. The court, accustomed to sunny days of informal sports and pastimes, continues without him as if they hardly care that the lynchpin and the source of all power and wealth is absent. They have become accustomed to his going and then his reappearing. They do not see this as a sign of decline; they think he will come and go forever. But the men who advise him, the men who are watchful of him every day, and hopeful for the future, gather closely around him, almost as if they dare not trust him with each other, dare not trust him alone.

From behind the closed doors the word seeps out, the men in his rooms tell their wives who attend me: he is ill again, and this time he seems deeply tired by the pain of the old wound and the fever. He sleeps for much of the day, waking up to order enormous meals but having no appetite when the servers bring the heaped platters to his bedside.

The old court—the papists like Thomas Howard, Paget and Wriothesley—are slowly, irresistibly excluded. It is the reformers who are in the ascendant now. Sir Thomas Heneage is dismissed from his intimate post of groom of the stool after years of faithful service, without warning and with no reason given. We are quietly triumphant, for the new groom is to be Joan's husband, Sir Anthony Denny, and he joins Nan's husband, Sir William Herbert, to stand beside the king when he labors on his closestool and blows out constipated wind.

With my ladies' husbands in key positions in the king's chamber, with Anne Seymour's husband, Edward, more and more the principal advisor, my rooms and the king's rooms are all but united: husbands serve the king, wives serve me, all of us of one mind. The king's favorites are almost all reformers, and most of my ladies are for the new learning. When the court talks of religion there is a united enthusiasm for change. So there are almost no contradictory voices as the king's quarrel with Gardiner, over some lands, turns dramatically sour. The king flares up into a sudden fury and without another word, Gardiner—once so favored—is not admitted into the inner circle.

No one speaks up for him. His old allies, Bishop Bonner, Thomas Wriothesley, and Richard Rich, are rapidly changing sides and seeking new friends. Of course they follow the royal favor before their loyalty to him. Thomas Wriothesley is Edward Seymour's newest recruit, while Bonner, the persecuting bishop of London, keeps to his diocese and does not dare to come to court. Even the new Spanish ambassador is no friend of Gardiner—he can see that the papist cause is in decline. Richard Rich, with his eye on a new patron, follows John Dudley like a puppy. Only Thomas Howard will still speak to the isolated bishop, but Howard is out of favor himself, his son blamed for the troubles among the English army at Boulogne, and Mary Howard disgraced by her outrageous snub to the Seymours.

Stephen Gardiner's fall is as rapid as a sinner going down to hell. Within a day he is banned from the private royal rooms, forced to stand with the common petitioners in the presence chamber, then, the day after, the guards at the main door are told to exclude him and he can only ride into the yard but not stable his horse. The pitiful thing is that he does not go. He thinks that he will be returned to power if he can just get into Henry's presence. He thinks an explanation or an apology will save him. He looks back on years of service and loyalty and thinks that the king will not turn against such an old friend. He has forgotten that once the king locks someone out, that person is lost, sometimes arrested, often killed. He failed to observe that the only person ever to recover from the king's hatred is me. He does not know what I had to do. He does not know the price I paid. Nobody will ever know. I don't acknowledge it to myself.

Gardiner does all he can. He offers to return the disputed lands, and he dawdles around the stable gates, trying to look as if he is just arriving or just leaving, still the welcome visitor that he was before. He sends in apologies by anyone who will take a message for him. He gets hold of everyone who walks through and tells them there has been a mistake, that he is the king's greatest friend and loyal servant, that nothing has changed, and will they speak of him to the king?

Of course they will not. Nobody wants Gardiner back at the king's side, pouring suspicion into his ear, prompting him to see heresy and treason and to see it everywhere. There is no household that he did not spy on; there are few people who did not feel his bright suspicious eyes on them. There is no sermon that he did not inspect for heresy, no courtier that he did not threaten. Now he has lost the king's favour, nobody has to fear him. And nobody is going to take the risk of mentioning his name to the king, who says that this former beloved advisor is nothing but a troublemaker and he will not hear a word about him.

The frightened old man sees disaster ahead of him. He remembers Wolsey, dropped dead on the York road, returning to London for a trial where they would have beheaded him. He remembers Cromwell, stripped of his badge of office, hacked to death on the scaffold, condemned by the laws that he invented. He remembers John Fisher going to the scaffold in his best coat, certain of heaven, Thomas More trapped by Richard Rich, he remembers the queens—four of them—and how he advised against them as they fell from favor, and he dragged them down.

He gets hold of his former friend and ally Lord Wriothesley and begs him to speak—just once, one word only—to the king, but Wriothesley melts through the bishop's fingers as if he were oily blood from a false miracle statue. One moment he is there, and then he is gone. Wriothesley is not going to risk his uncertain place at court for loyalty to a friend. The king frightened Wriothesley when he shouted at him in the garden, Wriothesley has turned his coat and is working with the Seymour affinity.

In desperation Gardiner begs my ladies to speak to me, as if I would have any reason to return my declared enemy to power; as if he did not promise the king he had evidence of capital treason against me. In the end Stephen Gardiner understands that he has lost his friends, his influence, and his place, and goes quietly to his own palace, to burn compromising papers and plot his return.

The reformists at court celebrate a victory over the dangerous man, but I have no doubt that he will come back. I know that, just as the papists dragged me down and broke my spirit, we are now triumphing against them and they are lying sleepless and fearful at nights; but the king will bait one pack of dogs against another over and over, and we will have to fight it out without principle, without shame, again and again.

WHITEHALL PALACE, LONDON, WINTER 1546

KP

The king's health worsens as the season turns, and Doctor Wendy says that he has uncontrollable fevers that cannot be cooled. While he sweats and rages in his delirium, the heat rises from his overburdened heart to his brain and may prove too much for him. The doctor suggests a course of baths and the court moves to Whitehall so that the king can be dipped in hot water and swaddled like a baby in scented drying sheets to draw the poisons from him. This seems to help and he recovers a little; but then he says that he wants to go to Oatlands.

Edward Seymour comes to my rooms to consult with me. "He's hardly well enough to travel," he says. "I thought the court would stay here for Christmas."

"Doctor Wendy says that he should not be crossed."

"Nobody wants to cross him," Edward rejoins. "God knows that. But he cannot risk his health going by barge on the winter river to Oatlands."

"I know. But I can't tell him that."

"He listens to you," he reminds me. "He trusts you with everything, his thoughts, his son, his country."

"He listens to his grooms of the chamber as much as he does to me," I say stubbornly. "Ask Anthony Denny or William Herbert to speak to him. I will agree with them if he asks me. But I can't advise him against his wishes." I think of the whip that he keeps in a cupboard somewhere in his bedroom. I think of the ivory codpiece stained with blood from the broken skin of my lips. "I do what he commands," I say shortly.

Edward looks at me with a thoughtful expression. "In the future," he says carefully, "in the future, you may have to make decisions for his son, and for his country. You may be the one who commands."

It is illegal to speak of the death of the king. It is treason even to suggest that his health is failing. I shake my head in silence.

OATLANDS PALACE, SURREY, WINTER 1546

KP

With Gardiner absent there is only one group of men surviving at court that still favors the old church, but it is a great family that has survived many changes. Nothing can destroy the How-ards. They will parlay their daughters and throw their own heirs overboard rather than let their house sink. The Howards, Dukes of Norfolk, have kept their place next to the throne even when the kings have changed, even when two girls of their house have risen to the throne and walked to the scaffold. Thomas Howard is not easily dislodged.

But one evening his son and heir goes missing. Henry Howard, recalled from the command of Boulogne because of his terrible arrogance and risk taking, does not appear at his father's table at dinner, and his servants have not seen him; none of his friends know where he can be.

This is a wild young man, a fool who boasted that he could hold Boulogne forever, who has displeased the king with his rowdy grandeur more than once, but always played his way back into favor. He was the best friend of Henry Fitzroy, the king's bastard son, and has always before been able to draw on that brotherly tragic love to win royal forgiveness.

Although everyone is quick to say that it is no surprise that the duke's heir is missing from his father's table, that the Howards are always storming off, everyone knows the young man would not disappear into the stews of London without his retinue and friends. Henry Howard is far too pleased with himself to go anywhere without a full entourage to admire him: somebody must know where he is.

One man knows: Lord Thomas Wriothesley. Slowly, it emerges that his men were seen bundling the young earl into a boat on the river late at night. Apparently there were a dozen of them in the Wriothesley livery and they had the young man between them, carrying him as he struggled and cursed them, and then they slung him in the bottom of the barge and sat on him. The boat went swiftly downstream into the darkness, and then it seemed to simply disappear. It was not an arrest, there was no warrant, and they did not arrive at the Tower. If it was a kidnap, then Wriothesley has somehow found the mad courage to attack a son of the House of Norfolk, and to do it in the precincts of a royal palace. Nobody knows how he could do this, on what authority, nor on what quiet stretch of the dark river the barge with its honored cargo can be moored, nor where the heir of the Howards is tonight.

It is inconceivable that Wriothesley could wage a private vendetta against the young man. Wriothesley and the Howards were conspiring against me only a few weeks ago, and Wriothesley was ready to take me in the royal barge down the river where he has now disappeared with the young Howard heir. So perhaps he was authorized by the king to take the young man. But nobody can think what Henry Howard can have done to invite such an attack, and Wriothesley is absent, and his servants are saying nothing.

His father swears that Henry is innocent of anything. It is his brother, Tom, who was accused of reading heretical books and attending the sermons in my rooms, and besides, that is now allowed. Henry Howard, the older boy, is mostly interested in his own self-importance and his own pleasures. He is too busy with sport and jousting, poetry and whoring to seriously reflect. He will never have engaged in difficult study. Nobody can imagine him as a heretic, people begin to think that Wriothesley has over-reached himself.

Norfolk, after a few days' silence, thinks he is strong enough to challenge the Lord Chancellor. He demands to know where his son is kept, what are the charges, and that he be released at once. He shouts at the Privy Council meeting, he says he must see the king. He even demands an audience with me. Everyone at court understands that nobody, not even the Lord Chancellor, can trouble a Howard without questions being asked. Norfolk rages in the meeting, cursing Wriothesley to his face, and the councillors watch these two powers, the old aristocrat and the new administrator, collide.

As if in a terrible silent reply, without a public command from the king, and without warning, the yeomen of the guard march Henry Howard through the streets of London from Lord Wriothesley's London house to the Tower on foot, like a common criminal. The great gates open as if they are expecting him, the constable of the Tower orders him to be taken to a cell. The doors close on him.

At the Privy Council meeting the duke is foaming at the mouth. Still there is no word of accusation, no charge against his son. This is the work of his enemies, he swears to them; this is an attack by craven men, men of no family or position, men like Wriothesley, who have wriggled their way up into power by a show of learning and cleverness with the law, while old aristocrats, noblemen like the duke himself and his son, the flower of chivalry, are embarrassed by these new councillors.

They don't even hear him out. They don't even answer his bellowed demands. The yeomen of the guard march into the Privy Council chamber and strip the sash of the Order of the Garter from his shoulders. They take his staff of office and break it before him as if he were a dead man and they were going to throw the pieces on top of the coffin as it rests in the grave, while Norfolk swears at them for fools, and reminds them of his nearly fifty years of service for the Tudors—hard service and dirty work that no one else would do. They manhandle him from the room as he bellows his superiority, his innocence, his threats. Everyone can hear the scrape of his boots on the floor and the yell of his protest, all the way down the long gallery.

The door to the king's privy chamber is open a crack; nobody knows if the king has heard. Nobody knows if this is by royal command or if Wriothesley is staging a coup against his rivals. So nobody knows what to do.

Now, two Howards—the Duke of Norfolk and his heir, the earl—are held in the Tower without charge, without accusation, without reason given. The unthinkable has happened to them: the Howards, father and son, who have brought so many innocent people to the scaffold, who have sat high on their horses and watched innocent men hang, are imprisoned themselves.

The news of the fall of their rivals brings Thomas Seymour back to court in a hurry to consult with his brother, and Anne Seymour hovers in the doorway of the Seymour rooms to listen and then reports back to me.

"Apparently the Howard house Kenninghall was searched from top to bottom on the very day that the duke was arrested. They went in at the very moment that he was taken to the Tower. My husband's clerk says that the charge is to be treason."

Joan Denny, whose husband, Sir Anthony, is in the king's confidence, agrees. "The Duke of Norfolk's mistress has signed a paper saying that the duke said that His Majesty was very sick." She lowers her voice. "She will say on oath that he said that the king couldn't last long."

There is a shocked silence: not that the duke should say what everyone knows, but that his mistress should betray him to the Lord Chancellor's men.

Anne nods, avid at this disaster falling on her rivals. "They were planning to alter the royal will, seize the prince, and take the throne."

I look at her incredulously. "No, that's impossible. Take the throne? The Norfolks are creatures of the throne. They have spent their lives jumping like fleas in any direction that any king might take. They never hesitate to obey him, whatever he asks. Their own daughters . . ." I break off but we all know that Mary Boleyn, her sister, Anne, her cousin Madge Shelton, their cousin Katherine Howard, were all Howard girls paraded before the king by their family and given to him as wives or whores.

Anne Seymour bristles at the mention of the Howard young women. Her own lamented sister-in-law Jane Seymour took a swift and dishonorable path from lady-in-waiting to queen. "Well, at least Mary Howard refused."

"Refused what?"

"To be dishonored. With her own father-in-law!"

I don't follow her. "Anne, be clear with me. Who wanted Mary Howard dishonored? And what do you mean by her father-in-law? You don't mean the king?"

She draws closer to me, her face bright with scandalized excitement. "You know that they proposed to marry Mary Howard to my brother-in-law, our Thomas?"

"Yes," I say steadily. "Everyone knows that the king gave his assent."

"But they had no intention of an honorable match. Never! They were planning to marry him and cuckold him. What d'you think of that?"

The thought of someone planning unhappiness for Thomas is like a physical blow. I know what shame is. I would never want Thomas to feel it. "I don't think much of it at all. But what did they mean to do?"

"They were going to marry him, and make him ask you if she could be one of your ladies-in-waiting. He was to bring her to court. And what do you think she was to do then?"

Slowly, a plot is unfolding. I think: How vile these people are, these sneakbills. "I would have granted her a place with me, of course. A Howard girl, a Seymour wife could not have been refused." And, I think, I would have done anything to bring Thomas to court so that I could see him. Even if it meant spending every day with his wife. Even that. They would have drawn me in to hurt him. They would have used me to hurt him.

"They were planning to put Mary Howard in the king's path." She draws back and looks at me. "They planned that she should supplant you."

"How would she supplant me?" I ask coldly.

"She was to flirt with the king, to lead him on, to seduce him. She was to lie with him or do whatever he can still do. She was to be his *maîtresse en titre*, as grand as a French mistress, a whore above all others. They said they could secure that, for certain. You would be all but cast aside and she would be preferred. You would go and live somewhere else, she would rule the court. But they said that if she was clever, there would be more for her than that, something better than that."

"What could be better than that?" I ask, as if I don't know.

"They said that if she were clever and desirable and spoke to him sweetly and did as they taught her, that he would get rid of you and marry her. And then she would guide him back to the old religion and her court would be a center of theology. Like yours, but better, they said: they meant papist. And that when he died she would be stepmother to Prince Edward, and the Duke of Norfolk would be lord protector and rule the kingdom until the prince came of age, and then rule him by force of habit. She would bring the king back to the Church of Rome, he would restore the church and the monasteries in England, and she would be dowager queen over a papist kingdom."

Anne breaks off, her face bright, looking at me with a mixture of horror and scandalized delight.

"But the king is her father-in-law," I object quietly. "She was married to his son. How could they think she might marry him?"

"They wouldn't care about that!" Anne exclaims. "Don't you think that the pope would give them a dispensation? If the bride was bringing England back to Rome? They're devils, they care for nothing but stealing the king back to their side."

"Indeed, I think they must be," I say quietly. "If this is true.

And did they think what would happen to me when pretty Mary Howard was in the king's bed?"

She shrugs. Her gesture says: What d'you think happens to unwanted queens in this England? "I suppose they thought that you might accept a divorce, or they might charge you with heresy and treason."

"I would die?" I ask. Even now, even after being queen for nearly three and a half years, walking through danger for all that time, I find it impossible to realize that anyone who knows me, who sees me at dinner every day, who has kissed my hand and promised loyalty, could coolly plot my death, and conspire to have me killed.

"It was Norfolk who named you as a disciple of Anne Askew," she says. "That was to call you a heretic, that's an offense that carries the penalty of death. It was he who worked with Gardiner to turn the king against you, calling you a serpent. This is not a man who sticks at trifles."

"Trifles?"

"The death of a woman is a trifle to a man like the duke. You know it was he who passed the death sentence on both his nieces? He plotted that they be queen and when it went wrong, he sent them to the scaffold to save himself."

Women's lives do not matter to anyone at this court. Before every queen stands her pretty successor, behind her a ghost.

"So what is happening now?"

"The king is taking advice from us Seymours," she says, unable to hide her rising pride. "Thomas and Edward are with the king now. I expect they will tell me what is happening when they come here before dinner, and then I will be able to tell you."

"I am sure the king will tell me himself," I say, to remind her that I am Queen of England and the king's wife, newly restored to favor. Otherwise she will think of me as the Howards do, as the court does: a temporary occupant of the throne of queen, a woman who might be divorced or killed on a whim.

I dress with meticulous care, sending my gown back once and changing my sleeves. I think I will wear purple and then I see that though it is the color of emperors it drains the flush from my cheeks and tonight I want to look young and lovely. So I wear my favorite red with a golden underskirt and red sleeves with gold slashes. I pull the neck of the gown down, so that my creamy skin is defined by the square cut and my auburn hair flames against the scarlet of the hood. I wear rubies in my ears and gold chains at my waist and looped around my wrists. I paint my lips with rouge and I rouge my cheeks.

"You look beautiful," Nan says, a little surprised at the trouble I have taken.

"I'm showing the Howard household that there is a queen already in place," I say staunchly, and Nan laughs.

"I think we had a lucky escape," she says. "Thank God that they could not agree and Thomas Seymour never brought Mary Howard to court."

"Yes," I say, disregarding the fact that he was ready to marry her. "He saved us."

"It leaves him a bachelor, though," Nan points out. "No man will marry Mary with her father and brother in the Tower, and she giving evidence against them to save her own skin. Thomas Seymour rises up day after day. His family is the leading house in the kingdom and the king loves him. He could choose almost anyone."

I nod. Of course he will marry Elizabeth if the king gives permission. Then he will be married to the third heir to the Tudor throne. Then I can dance at his wedding. Then I will have to think of him as my son-in-law.

"Who knows?" I say lightly. I nod to my ladies to open the doors and we walk from my bedroom into my privy chamber, and into my presence room, and there he is. He turns as he hears the doors open and I realize he has been waiting for me; and there he is.

When I see him a strange thing happens. It is as if I can see no one else. I don't even hear the usual noise of the room. It is almost like a dream, like a slip in time, as if all my clocks freeze and everyone has gone and there is nothing but him and me. He turns and sees me, and I am blind to everything but his dark eyes, and his smile, and his gaze upon me as if he too can see no one else, and I think—ah, thank God, he loves me as I love him, for there could be no smile so warm, so directed, except from a man who loves the woman walking towards him, glowing, her hand outstretched.

"Good evening, Sir Thomas," I say.

He takes my hand, he bows over it, he kisses my fingers. I feel the light touch of his mustache and the warmth of his breath on my hand and the slightest squeeze on my fingers as if to say "Beloved . . ." and then he straightens up and lets me go.

"Your Majesty," he says. "I am so happy to see you looking so well."

As he says the ordinary words his dark gaze is searching my face and I know that he will know that I have put on my best gown and reddened my lips. He sees the shadows under my eyes; he will know that I am grieving for Anne Askew. And he will also know, as a lover always knows, that something very grievous, very bad has happened to me.

He offers me his arm and we walk together, through bowing courtiers, to the window where he gestures with one hand as if to indicate the setting sun and the rise of one penetrating bright star on the horizon.

"Are you hurt?" he asks simply. "Are you ill?"

"I can't tell you here and now," I say honestly. "But I am not hurt or ill."

"The king?"

"Yes."

"What did he do?" His face darkens.

I pinch the inside of his sleeve, the inner part of his elbow. "Not here. Not now," I remind him. I smile up at him. "Is that the pole star? Is that the one that you steer by?"

"Are you in danger now?" he demands.

"Not now," I say.

"Edward says that you were within a hairbreadth of arrest."

I tip my head back and laugh. "Oh, yes! I saw the warrant."

His gaze is admiring. "You talked yourself to safety?"

I think of my stretching my lips to the bloodstained riding whip. I think of the ivory satin codpiece thrust into my mouth, banging against my teeth. "No. It was worse than that."

He makes a little exclamation. "God—"

"Hush!" I say rapidly. "We're not safe. Everyone is watching. What's going to happen to the Howards?"

"Whatever he wants." He takes two impatient steps on the spot, as if he would fling himself out of the room but remembers that there is nowhere that he can go. "Whatever he wants, of course. I expect he will kill them. They were planning treason, without a doubt."

"God help them," I say, though they would have sent me to the scaffold. "God help them."

The double doors are flung open and the king's enormously bandaged foot comes in first, his great chair and his beaming smile next.

"God help us all," Thomas says, and steps back like the courtier he is, so that my husband can be wheeled towards his possession, his chattel, his smiling wife.

Father and son, Thomas Howard and his son Henry, wait in the Tower to hear what charges they will face. No one visits them, no one speaks up for them. Suddenly this old man and his heir, who ruled all of Norfolk, and owned most of the South of England, who rode at the head of thousands of men, who lived their lives like fat spiders in a network of friendships, kinship and obligations, know no one. They are completely friendless and without allies. The evidence of treason against Henry Howard is overwhelming. He was fool enough to boast that he had a great claim to the throne. His own sister Mary Howard, still smarting from his command that she must whore herself out to the king, accuses him. She swears on oath that he ordered her to marry Thomas Seymour to get to court, and to become the king's mistress. She told him that she would rather cut her throat than be so dishonored. Now she is cutting his.

Even his father's mistress, the notorious Bess Holland, gives evidence against him. The young man, well hated by those who should love and protect him, is incriminated daily by his friends and lovers, and finally by his own coat of arms, which Thomas Wriothesley, son of a herald, grandson of a herald, declares has been fraudulently based on the arms of Hereward the Wake—a leader of England five hundred years ago.

"Isn't this rather ridiculous?" I ask the king, as we sit beside the fire in his room after dinner. "Surely Hereward the Wake had no coat of arms to leave to the Howards, even if they are descended from him, which nobody can prove. Does this matter at all?"

Around us the court murmurs and plays cards. I can hear the rattle of dice. Soon the king will assemble his cronies, and my ladies and I will withdraw.

Henry's face is mean, his eyes squinting. "It matters," he says shortly. "It matters to me."

"But for him to claim descent from Hereward the Wake . . . this is like a fairy story."

"It's a very dangerous story," he says. "No one has royal descent in this country but me." He pauses. He will be thinking of the former royal family, the Plantagenets. One by one he has sent them to their deaths for nothing worse than their fathers' name. "There is only one family that can trace themselves back to Arthur of England, and that is ours. Any challenge is going to be met with extreme punishment."

"But why?" I ask, as gently as I can. "If it is an old shield that he has shown many times before. If it is the silly pride of a young man. If the college of heralds saw it years ago, and you have not objected before?"

He raises one fat finger and instantly I am silent. "Do you remember what the dog master does?" he asks me quietly.

I nod.

"Tell me."

"He sets one dog against another."

"He does. And when any single dog becomes big and strong, what does he do with it?

He snaps his fingers when I don't answer.

"He lets the others pull it down," I say, unwillingly.

"Of course."

I am silent for a moment. "It means that you will never have great men about you," I remark. "No thoughtful advisors, no one that you can respect. No one can stay with you and grow great in your service. No one can be rewarded for loyalty. You can have no tried and tested friends."

"That's true," he agrees with me. "Because I don't want anyone like that. I've had men like that before, when I was a young man, friends whom I loved and men who were brilliant thinkers, who could solve a problem the moment they heard it. If you had seen Thomas Wolsey in his prime! If you had known Thomas More! Thomas Cromwell would work all night, every night—nothing ever stopped him. He never failed at anything he set his hand to. I could set him a problem at dinner and he would bring me a warrant of arrest at chapel before breakfast."

He breaks off, his little eyes under the pink swollen eyelids look towards the door as if his friend Thomas More might come in at any moment, his thoughtful face warm with laughter, his cap under his arm, his love for the king and for his family the greatest influence in his life, but nothing in the world greater than his love of God.

"I want Nobody now," the king says coldly. "Because Nobody

gives nothing away, Nobody loves no one. The world is filled with people seeking only their own ambitions and working for their own causes. Even Thomas More—" He breaks off with a little self-pitying sob. 'He chose loyalty to the church over his love for me. He chose his faith over life itself. You see? No one is ever faithful till death. If anyone tells you anything different, they are playing you for a fool. I will never be a fool again. I know that every smiling friend is an enemy, every advisor is pursuing his own interest. Everyone wants my place, everyone wants my fortune, everyone wants my inheritance."

I can't argue against this intense bitterness. "But you love your children," I say quietly.

He looks across at Princess Mary, who is quietly talking to Sir Anthony Denny in a corner. He looks for Princess Elizabeth and sees her peeping upwards into the smiling face of Thomas Seymour.

"Not particularly," he says, and his voice is like cold glass. "Who loved me as a child? No one."

The young man Henry Howard, dearest friend of Henry's dead illegitimate son, sends an imploring letter to the king from his prison in the Tower, reminding him that he and Henry Fitzroy were like brothers, that they spent every day together, that they rode and swam and played and wrote poetry together, that they were all in all to each other. They swore loyalty to one another and he would never, ever conspire against his best friend's father, who had been a father to him.

Henry tosses the letter to me. "But I have read his interrogation," he says. "I have sifted the evidence against him. I have looked at his heraldry and I have heard what he said about me."

If I let him recite his wrongs, he will get angrier and angrier. He will raise his finger and point it at me, he will speak to me as if I am the guilty young man. He draws an intense pleasure in enacting his rage. He prompts himself like an actor to play the part for the thrill that it gives him. He likes to feel his heart race with bad temper; he likes a fight, even if it is in an empty room with a white-faced woman trying to calm him.

"But you are not taken in by all this," I say, trying to appeal to Henry's scholarly, critical mind before he unleashes his temper. "You are sifting the evidence, studying it. You are not believing everything that they tell you?"

"It is you that should be afraid of what they tell me!" he says in sudden irritation. "For if this treasonous dog that you speak for so sweetly had got his way, it would have been you in the Tower, not him; and his sister would have your place. He is your enemy, Kateryn, far more than he is mine. He plotted to inherit my power but he would have killed you."

"If he is your enemy, then he is mine," I whisper. "Of course, Your Majesty."

"He would have had you dead on some trumped-up charge of heresy or treason," the king goes on, ignoring the fact that it would have been his signature on the warrant. "And he would have put his sister in your place. We would have had another Howard queen. I would have had another of their whores thrust into my bed! What do you think of that? How can you bear to think of that?"

I shake my head. Of course there is nothing I can say. Who would have signed the warrant? Who would have sent me to my death? Who would have married the Howard girl?

"You would be dead," Henry says. "And then at my death the Howards would have commanded my son . . ." He takes a little breath. "Jane's son," he says mistily. "In the grip of the Howard family."

"But, my lord husband . . ."

"That was the prize. That's the prize for them all. That's what they all want, however they gurn and gloze. They all want command of the regency on my death and control of the new king.

That is what I have to defend Edward against. That is what you will defend him against."

"Of course, husband, you know—"

"Poor Henry Howard," he says. His voice quavers and the easy tears come quickly. "You know I loved that boy as if he were my own? I remember him as such a beautiful boy playing with Fitzroy. They were like brothers."

"Can't he be pardoned?" I ask quietly. "He writes very sorrowfully, I cannot believe that he does not regret . . ."

He nods his head. 'I will consider it,' he says grandly. "If I can pardon him, I will. I will be just. But I will be merciful too. I loved him; and my boy, my beloved Henry Fitzroy, loved him. If I can forgive Howard for the sake of his playmate, then I will."

The court is to divide. The king is going to Whitehall to oversee the deaths of the Howards, father and son, and the complete destruction of their treasonous house, and the princesses and I are to go to Greenwich. The Seymours, Thomas and his brother Edward, will stay with the king, help him untangle the plot and name the guilty men. Under the king's bright suspicious gaze the interrogations of servants, tenants, and enemies are read and re-read, and then, I am certain, rewritten. All the vindictive spite that was directed at the reformers, my ladies and me, is now turned, like the mouth of a cannon, towards the Howards, and the great guns are ready to roar. The king's sentiment, his mercy, his sense of justice, are put aside in an orgy of false evidence. The king wants to kill someone and the court wants to help him.

The Seymours are in the ascendancy, their religion is the king's new preference, their family is kin to the royal line, their military skills are the saving of the nation and their companionship is all the king wants. All other rival houses are down in the dust.

The court comes to the outer steps of the palace for the lords to say good-bye to their ladies, and for those who are courting to exchange a look, a word, the touch of a hand. The gentlemen of the court come to say their farewells to me, and then finally, Thomas Seymour makes his way towards me. We stand close together, my hand on my horse's neck, the groom holding him steady.

"At least you're safe," he says in my ear. "Another year gone by, and you're still safe."

"Are you going to marry Elizabeth?" I ask him urgently.

"He's not spoken. Has he said anything to you?"

"He asked me what I thought of it. I said what I could."

He makes a little grimace, then he puts the groom aside with one gesture and he cups his hands to take my boot. Just the clasp of his warm hand on my foot reminds me how much I want him. "Ah God, Thomas."

He throws me upwards and I swing my leg over the saddle and my maid comes forward and adjusts my skirts. We are silent while she does her work and then I am looking down on his dark curly head as he strokes my horse's neck but he cannot put his hand on me. Not even on the toe of my boot.

"Will you spend Christmas with the king?"

He shakes his head. "He wants me to look at Dover Castle."

"When will I see you again?" I can hear the desolation in my voice.

He shakes his head, he doesn't know. "At least you're safe," he says, as if that is all that matters. "Another year, who knows what will happen?"

I can't bring myself to imagine that anything good will happen. "Merry Christmas, Thomas," I say quietly. "God bless you."

He looks up, squinting a little against the brightness of the sky. This is the man I love and he cannot come closer. He steps back and puts his hand to my horse's head, gently strokes his nose, fingers his mouth, his sensitive snuffing nostrils. "Go safely" he tells him. "You're carrying a queen." He lowers his voice. "And my only love."

GREENWICH PALACE, WINTER 1546

KP

I think of Queen Katherine, who celebrated Christmas at Greenwich over a divided court while the king was in London courting Anne Boleyn, ordered to behave as if nothing was wrong. This time it is not lovemaking that keeps the king in the city but killing. They tell me that the court at Whitehall is closed to everyone but the Privy Council, and that the king and his advisors are going over and over the evidence that has been gathered against the Howards, father and son.

They tell me that the king has become devoted to scholarship. He studies Henry Howard's careless letters as if they were a text, annotating every guilty admission, questioning every word of innocence. The king has become thorough, pedantic. Spite gives him energy and he follows the interrogations as if he is determined that the young man, the beautiful foolish young man, shall die because of his own light words, spoken without thought.

One night in early January, Henry Howard climbs out of the window of his prison cell, trying to escape the king's mercy. They seize him just as he is about to slide down the chute for wastewater and fall into the icy river. This is typical Henry Howard: daring as a boy. The act should remind everyone that he is an impulsive young man, a bit of a fool, but a brave reckless innocent;

but instead of laughing at him and releasing him, they send for irons and keep him in shackles.

Worse, far worse, is his father's confession. In a desperate gamble to save his wrinkled old skin the old duke writes to the Privy Council that he is guilty of everything that they have put to him. He confesses to bearing arms that were his by right and have been used by the House of Howard for generations. Ludicrously, he confesses to sending secret messages to the pope. He swears that he has done everything they allege, he says anything as long as he can be spared. He pleads guilty as no one has ever been guilty before and offers all his fortune and his lands as payment for his guilt if they will leave him with his life.

As if his son is nothing but an object for barter, he throws Henry Howard into the bargain along with honor and name and wealth. He casts off his son and heir to hell, he all but sends his own hurdle to drag the young man to the scaffold. He says on oath that his son and heir, the twenty-nine-year-old Henry, is a traitor to the king and to his name and to his house. The old duke sends his boy to death as the agreed price of his own freedom. His accusation is the death sentence for his son, and that night the king signs the warrant to send Henry Howard to trial. The king says that it is all the fault of Thomas Howard, and no one can complain of him.

We all know what the outcome of the trial must be. His own father has confessed for him and named him as guilty; surely Henry Howard can say nothing in his own defense?

But he has much to say. He stands in the dock and defends himself. He argues all day until they call for candles in the evening, and the handsome young earl shines in their golden light before the jury of his neighbors and friends. Perhaps, even then, they might have refused to convict him, he was so persuasive and funny and insistent. But William Paget came from the court with a secret message from the king, went into the jury room as they considered their verdict, and when they came out, they said that they had all agreed without one dissenting voice. For who was going to argue? They said "guilty."

In the middle of the cold bright month of January a messenger comes from the Privy Council to inform me that Henry Howard has been beheaded on Tower Hill. His father remains in prison awaiting his own sentence. We hear the news in silence. The king's determination that there should be no more burnings of reformers does not extend mercy to other suspects. Nobody thinks that Henry Howard was more than a foolish braggart, a poet who was too prodigal with his words; but he died for that.

Princess Elizabeth comes to me and puts a cold hand in mine. "I hear terrible things of my Cousin Howard," she says, her dark eyes questioning me. "He was planning to overthrow you, and put another woman in your place. They tell me that he was going to put his sister on the throne."

"It was wrong of him to hope for that," I reply. "Your father and I were married in the sight of God. It would be wrong for anyone to drive us apart."

She hesitates—she has heard enough about her own mother to know that Anne Boleyn did exactly this to Henry's first queen, and her kinsmen were planning to do it again to his sixth. "Do you think it was right that he should die?" she asks me.

Not even for Elizabeth, with Jane Grey standing so solemn and silent, listening behind her, am I going to risk expressing an opinion that is different from the king's. I have kissed the rod. I have lost my voice. I am an obedient wife.

"Whatever your father the king thinks best is the right thing to do," I say.

She looks at me, this bright, thoughtful girl. "If you are a wife, can you not think for yourself?"

"You can think for yourself," I say carefully. "But you need not speak. If you are wise, you will agree with your husband. Your husband has power over you. You have to find ways to think your own thoughts and live your own life without always telling of it."

"Then I had better not marry," she says without a glimmer of a smile. "If to be a wife is to give up your own opinion, I had better never marry."

I pat her cheek and I try to laugh at this thirteen-year-old girl forswearing matrimony. "Perhaps you are right in this world," I say. "But this world is changing. Perhaps by the time you are old enough to marry the world will hear a woman's voice. Perhaps she will not have to swear to obey in her wedding vows. Perhaps one day a woman will be allowed to both love and think."

HAMPTON COURT PALACE, WINTER 1547

KP

The messenger comes by barge, swiftly down the river in the midnight darkness, rowed as fast as the oarsmen can go against the in-running tide, from Whitehall. It's a cold wet journey and the guards take his dripping cape at the entrance of my presence chamber and throw open the doors. One of my ladies, wakened by the hammering on the door of the privy chamber, comes running in to me to say there is an urgent message from the Privy Council at Whitehall and will I receive it?

I am afraid at once, as everyone in this court has learned to fear the uninvited knock on the door. At once I wonder who is in danger, at once I wonder if they have come for me. I throw on my thickest winter robe and go out, my bare feet in my gold-heeled shoes, to my privy chamber, where one of the Seymour men is waiting, shifting from one damp footprint to another, dripping rain on the floor. Nan comes after me and my ladies-in-waiting open their chamber doors and peer out, white-faced in the torch-light. Someone crosses herself; I see Nan grit her teeth, fearing bad news.

The messenger kneels to me and pulls off his hat. "Your Majesty," he says. Something in the appalled shock of his face, in the way he takes a breath as if to make a well-rehearsed speech, the lateness of the hour, the darkness of the night, warns me what he is going to say. I look over his shoulder to see if the yeomen of the guard have come in numbers to arrest me. I wonder if the royal barge is bobbing at the pier showing no lights. I look for the courage inside myself to face this moment. Perhaps now, tonight, they have finally come for me.

He gets to his feet. "Your Majesty, I regret to tell you, His Majesty the king is dead."

So, I am free, I am free and I am alive. When I embarked on this marriage nearly four years ago I did not think that this day would come when I would be free and a widow again. When I saw the warrant for my arrest in the hand of the king's doctor I did not think that I would survive a week. But I have survived. I have out-lived the king who abandoned two wives, left one to die in child-birth, and murdered two others. By betraying my love, my faith, and my friend, I have survived. By surrendering my will and my pride and my scholarship, I have survived. I feel like someone in a town terribly besieged for years, coming out of my house and looking wonderingly around at the breached walls and the broken gate, at the destruction in the marketplace and the torn-down church and yet being alive and safe, though others have died and the danger has passed over me. I have saved myself but I have seen the destruction of everything that I loved.

I sit in the window of my bedroom and wait for the dawn to come. Behind me the fire glows in the grate but I don't allow them to come in and stir it up, bring hot water, or dress me for the day. I am going to watch out the rest of the night and think of them in Whitehall, like the dogs that he said they were, tearing the kingdom apart so that one pack gets one favor and one gets another. They have a will, or at any rate they have something that they are going to declare is the king's will, or at the least they are cobbling together something that they can take as his will, and it honors those who were first at the corpse, as if it is the result of a running race, not the testament of a dying man.

Prince Edward is his heir, of course, but in this will I am not named as regent. There is to be a Privy Council that will guide Prince Edward until he is eighteen years old. Edward Seymour has been too quick for me, too quick for us all. He has named himself as Great Chamberlain of England and will guide the Privy Council with fifteen others. Stephen Gardiner is not among them, but neither am I.

Thomas, late to the division of the spoils, will have to wrest from his brother whatever he can. He will have to hurry. The court is like a pack of hounds, tearing a fallen stag to gory pieces. There are more than eighty outstanding claims that the courtiers swear were promised them, besides the division of the king's estates. He leaves a good dowry to both his daughters, he leaves a fortune to me. But he excludes me from the Privy Council to govern Edward; his last act is to silence me.

Though he was my husband he is to be buried beside Jane Seymour in Saint George's Chapel at Windsor, and he leaves a fortune for people to sing Masses for him and he establishes a chantry chapel with two priests to save him from the purgatory that he did not believe in. When they tell me this, I have to grip the wooden arm of my chair to prevent myself from laughing out loud.

They tell me that he made his confession. He sent for Thomas Cranmer right at the end, and the archbishop gave him extreme unction, so he died a faithful son of the Catholic church. Apparently he told Cranmer that he had little to confess, for everything that he had done had been for the best. I smile as I think of him dying, without fear of the darkness, secure as ever in his own good opinion, dabbled with holy oil. But what was the purpose of his life if not to save his country from these rituals and superstitions? What, at the end, was he thinking?

I have lost my husband and I have survived my jailer. I will mourn a man who loved me, in his way, and celebrate my escape from a man who would have killed me. When I undertook this marriage, against my will, I knew that it would end only in death: his or mine. There were times when I thought that he would have me killed, that I would never be able to survive him. There were times when I thought that his passion to be the one to say the last word would persuade him to silence me forever. But I have survived his abuse, and I have survived his threats. This marriage cost me my happiness, my love, and my pride. The worst price was betraying Anne and letting her go to her death. But this, too, I shall endure; this, too, I shall forgive.

I will publish my translations of the New Testament. I will finish my book of new writing on my faith. I will write my own opionions, without fear, under my own name. Never again will I publish without my name on the frontispiece. I will not send it out into the world without acknowledgment. I will stand up and speak in my own voice and no man will ever silence me again.

I will raise my stepchildren in the reformed faith, and I will pray to God in English. I will see Thomas Seymour walk across the room and kiss my hand without being fearful that someone notices the gladness in my face and the desire in his eyes. I will kiss his smiling mouth, I will lie in his bed. I will live like a passionate intelligent woman and I will bring my passion and my intelligence to everything that I do.

I believe that to be a free woman is to be both passionate and intelligent; and I am a free woman at last.

AUTHOR'S NOTE

PG

It is extraordinary to me that Kateryn the Quene KP (as she signed herself) is not better known. As the last of Henry's queens she survived a wife killer who saw four of her five predecessors into the grave, which must make her one of the most tenacious survivor wives in history. She faced and defeated a series of plots from supporters of the papist side of the English Church who were determined to restore their faith to England, she raised the king's two younger children in the Protestant faith that would be the core of their own reigns, and yet she befriended the king's papist oldest daughter, Lady Mary, and supported her return to royal status. She served the country as regent—the most important person in England—and kept the peace in the absence of the king.

In many ways one can see her similarities to the other wives: she was made regent like the Spanish royal, Katherine of Aragon, she was English born and bred like Katherine Howard, an educated and highly intelligent reformer in religion like Anne Boleyn, and—as a northerner—an outsider like Anne of Cleves. She raised Jane Seymour's son and loved her brother; perhaps if Jane had lived, she would have been Jane's sister-in-law.

But the most interesting thing about her was her scholarship. We don't know the extent of her education when she first came to Henry's court as the young widow of the northern Lord Latimer. It is likely that she had studied Latin and French with her brother's tutor but probably her lessons finished when he left home. So when she came to a court which was alive with debate about the Bible: English or Latin, about the Mass: bread or flesh, about the church: reformist or papist, she set about educating herself.

Her studies in Latin are demonstrated in the letters that she exchanged with her stepson, the little Prince of Wales. Her studies in theology underpin her publications. She was the first woman to publish original work under her own name in English—an extraordinary act, a breakthrough act. Earlier women writers had written in Middle English—more like Chaucer than the recognizable language of Shakespeare that Parr used. A very few published anonymously, mostly they made translations of men's texts. No woman before Kateryn Parr had dared to write original material in English for publication and put her own name on the title page, as Parr did with her book of translated prayers and psalms. Her last work was not only translation, she wrote original material for *The Lamentation of a Sinner*.

Every one of her three books has survived and can be read in a new edition edited by Janel Mueller, listed in the following bibliography. We can even see original copies at Sudeley Castle in Gloucestershire. Down the centuries, remarkably, a woman of the 1500s still speaks to us.

Of course every historian must wish that Parr had chosen to write a chronicle of her times rather than prayers—think what that would have told us about the last days of the Henrician court! But for Parr as for other spiritual women, it may be that her relationship with God was more important to her than her life in this world.

That day-to-day life was filled with incident, danger, and adventure. We don't know, even now, how close she was to the martyr Anne Askew. It looks as if Anne died to keep their connection secret. We know that Anne preached before the queen, and that they may have met when they were girls in Lincolnshire. We know that the queen used her influence to get Anne freed from her first arrest but could not liberate her a second time. We know that Nicholas Throckmorton from the queen's rooms attended the burning and that someone paid for a purse of gunpowder so that Anne's sufferings could be cut short. It looks very much as if the torture of Anne Askew was done to force her to name the queen as a coreligionist, a heretic, and a traitor, to expose her to arrest and death.

The plot against the queen, her quick-witted response, and her humiliation before the court is from the near-contemporary account of Foxe's *Book of Martyrs*, and some of the dialogue is drawn from that account. But the private humiliation that I describe is fiction—we are rarely told what went on behind the closed bedroom doors of the past. I wanted to write a scene in which the legally permitted beating of a wife, and the symbolism of Henry's codpiece, came together to show how men dominate women with their legal powers, with their violence, with their sexuality, and with the myth of their power, then—and now.

We also don't know how intimate Kateryn was with Thomas Seymour while she was queen. Certainly they look as if they were promised to each other—they were writing love letters and making assignations to spend the night together only weeks after the death of the king, and they were married, despite their initial decision to wait, within four months of Henry's death. It may be that their marriage was loving and happy. It is well known that Princess Elizabeth left her stepmother's house after sexualized play with her new stepfather, Thomas Seymour. There were spiteful quarrels with his family about the dowager queen's dower and the royal jewels; Thomas was a jealous and possessive husband. Kateryn and Thomas were to be married for less than a year and a half before she died in childbirth. There were reports of her reproaching him for not loving her, but he was at her deathbed and he seems to have been stunned by her loss, giving up their house and leaving their child to be cared for in the household of Edward Seymour and his wife.

Writing a fictional version of a medieval woman's life has been, as it always is, strangely moving and relevant to my own times. Although she lived so long ago, when I think of the fear she faced and the courage she must have drawn on, I cannot help but admire her. Her careful, mostly self-taught scholarship must resonate with any woman who has tried to enter the exclusive circles of male power: industry, politics, churches, learning. Anyone who loves words will admire Kateryn Parr, thinking of her poring over manuscripts in Latin and Greek, trying to find the perfect English word for translation, and anyone who likes women must warm to her: in love with one man and forced to marry another, a tyrant, but—hurrah—surviving him.

This novel, about a scholarly woman, is dedicated to two great scholars who taught me: Maurice Hutt at the University of Sussex and Geoffrey Carnall at the University of Edinburgh. To me, they exemplify those many teachers throughout the centuries who have knowledge and the grace to share it, who occupy the bastions of male learning and open the gates.

No words can express my gratitude to them—which they would immediately remark is both a cliché and a paradox. Heavens! I miss them both so much.

BIBLIOGRAPHY

Here is a list of the most helpful books and journals I consulted for this fiction. With special thanks for Susan James for her biography and Janel Mueller for her scholarly edition of Kateryn's writing.

Alexander, Michael Van Cleave. *The First of the Tudors: A Study of Henry VII and His Reign*. London: Croom Helm, 1981.

Bacon, Francis. *The History of the Reign of King Henry VII and Selected Works*. Edited by Brian Vickers. Cambridge: Cambridge University Press, 1998.

Baldwin, David. *Henry VIII's Last Love: The Extraordinary Life of Katherine Willoughby, Lady-in-Waiting to the Tudors*. Stroud, Gloucestershire: Amberley, 2015.

Beilin, Elaine V., ed. *The Examinations of Anne Askew*. New York: Oxford University Press, 1996.

Bernard, G. W., ed. *The Tudor Nobility*. Manchester: Manchester University Press, 1992.

Besant, Sir Walter. *London in the Time of the Tudors*. London: Adam & Charles Black, 1904.

Betteridge, Thomas, and Suzannah Lipscomb, eds. *Henry VIII and the Court: Art, Politics and Performance*. Farnham, Surrey: Ashgate, 2013.

Bindoff, S. T., ed. *The History of Parliament: The House of Commons, 1509–1558*. London: Secker & Warburg for the History of Parliament Trust, 1982.

Childs, David. *Tudor Sea Power: The Foundation of Greatness.* Barnsley, Yorkshire: Seaforth Publishing, 2009.

Childs, Jessie. *Henry VIII's Last Victim: The Life and Times of Henry Howard, Earl of Surrey.* London: Jonathan Cape, 2006.

Chrimes, S. B. *Henry VII.* London: Eyre Methuen, 1972.

Cunningham, Sean. *Henry VII.* London: Routledge, 2007.

Denny, Joanna. *Katherine Howard: A Tudor Conspiracy.* London: Portrait, 2005.

Doner, Margaret. *Lies and Lust in the Tudor Court: The Fifth Wife of Henry VIII.* Lincoln, NE, iUniverse, 2004.

Duggan, Anne J., ed. *Queens and Queenship in Medieval Europe: Proceedings of a Conference Held at King's College, London, April 1995.* Woodbridge, Suffolk: Boydell Press, 1997.

Elton, G. R. *England Under the Tudors.* London: Methuen, 1955.

Fellows, Nicholas. *Disorder and Rebellion in Tudor England.* London: Hodder & Stoughton, 2001.

Fletcher, Anthony, and Diarmaid MacCulloch. *Tudor Rebellions.* 5th ed. Harlow: Pearson Longman, 2008.

Gairdner, James. "Anne Askew." In *The Dictionary of National Biography.* Vol II, edited by Leslie Stephen, 190–92. London, 1885; http://www.lu minarium.org/encyclopedia/askew.htm.

Guy, John. *Tudor England.* Oxford: Oxford University Press, 1988.

Hare, Robert D. *Without Conscience: The Disturbing World of the Psychopath.* New York: Pocket Books, 1993.

Hay, Denys. *Europe in the Fourteenth and Fifteenth Centuries.* 4th ed. New York: Longman, 1989.

Howard, Maurice. *The Tudor Image.* London: Tate Publishing, 1995.

Hutchinson, Robert. *House of Treason: The Rise and Fall of a Tudor Dynasty.* London: Weidenfeld & Nicolson, 2009.

———. *The Last Days of Henry VIII: Conspiracies, Treason and Heresy at the Court of the Dying Tyrant.* London: Weidenfeld & Nicolson, 2005.

———. *Young Henry: The Rise of Henry VIII.* London: Weidenfeld & Nicolson, 2011.

Innes, Arthur D. *England Under The Tudors*. London: Methuen, 1905.

Jackman, S. W. *Deviating Voices: Women and Orthodox Religious Tradition*. Cambridge: Lutterworth Press, 2003.

James, Susan E. *Kateryn Parr: The Making of a Queen*. Farnham, Surrey: Ashgate, 1999.

Jones, Philippa. *The Other Tudors: Henry VIII's Mistresses and Bastards*. London: New Holland, 2009.

Kesselring, K. J. *Mercy and Authority in the Tudor State*. Cambridge: Cambridge University Press, 2003.

Kramer, Kyra Cornelius. *Blood Will Tell: A Medical Explanation of the Tyranny of Henry VIII*. Bloomington, IN: Ash Wood Press, 2012.

Laynesmith, J. L. *The Last Medieval Queens: English Queenship 1445–1503*. Oxford: Oxford University Press, 2004.

Lewis, Katherine J., Noël James Menuge, and Kim M. Phillips, eds. *Young Medieval Women*. Stroud, Gloucestershire: Sutton Publishing, 1999.

Licence, Amy. *In Bed with the Tudors: The Sex Lives of a Dynasty from Elizabeth of York to Elizabeth I*. Stroud, Gloucestershire: Amberley, 2012.

Lipscomb, Suzannah. *1536: The Year That Changed Henry VIII*. Oxford: Lion, 2009.

Loades, David. *Henry VIII: Court, Church and Conflict*. Richmond, Surrey: The National Archives, 2007.

Locke, Amy Audrey. *The Seymour Family*. 1911. Reprint, Michigan: University of Michigan Library, 2007.

Mackay, Lauren. *Inside the Tudor Court: Henry VIII and His Six Wives Through the Writings of the Spanish Ambassador, Eustace Chapuys*. Stroud, Gloucestershire: Amberley, 2014.

Maclean, John. *The Life of Sir Thomas Seymour, Knight; Baron Seymour of Sudeley, Lord High Admiral of England and Master of the Ordnance*. London: John Camden Hotten, 1869.

Manning, Anne. *The Lincolnshire Tragedy: Passages in the Life of the Faire Gospeller, Mistress Anne Askew* (novel). 1866. Reprint, Charleston, SC: Nabu Press, 2012.

Martienssen, Anthony. *Queen Katherine Parr*. London: Secker & Warburg, 1973.

Meloy, J. Reid, ed. *The Mark of Cain: Psychoanalytic Insight and the Psychopath.* 2001. Reprint, New York: Routledge, 2014.

Mortimer, Ian. *The Time Traveller's Guide to Medieval England.* London: Vintage, 2009.

Mueller, Janel, ed. *Katherine Parr: Complete Works & Correspondence.* Chicago: University of Chicago Press, 2011.

Mühlbach, Luise. *Henry VIII and His Court: An Historical Novel.* Translated by H. N. Pierce. New York, 1867.

Newcombe, D. G. *Henry VIII and the English Reformation.* London: Routledge, 1995.

Norton, Elizabeth. *Catherine Parr.* Stroud, Gloucestershire: Amberley, 2011.

Perry, Maria. *Sisters to the King: The Tumultuous Lives of Henry VIII's Sisters—Margaret of Scotland and Mary of France.* London: André Deutsch, 1998.

Plowden, Alison. *House of Tudor.* London: Weidenfeld & Nicolson, 1976.

Porter, Linda. *Katherine the Queen: The Remarkable Life of Katherine Parr, the Last Wife of Henry VIII.* New York: St. Martin's Press, 2010.

Read, Conyers. *The Tudors: Personalities & Practical Politics in 16th Century England.* Oxford: Oxford University Press, 1936.

Ridley, Jasper. *The Tudor Age.* London: Constable, 1988.

Rubin, Miri. *The Hollow Crown: A History of Britain in the Late Middle Ages.* London: Allen Lane, 2005.

Scarisbrick, J. J. *Henry VIII.* London: Eyre & Spottiswoode, 1968.

Searle, Mark, and Kenneth W. Stevenson. *Documents of the Marriage Liturgy.* Collegeville, MN: Liturgical Press, 1992.

Shagan, Ethan H. *Popular Politics and the English Reformation.* Cambridge: Cambridge University Press, 2003.

Sharpe, Kevin. *Selling the Tudor Monarchy: Authority and Image in Sixteenth-Century England.* London: Yale University Press, 2009.

Skidmore, Chris. *Edward VI: The Lost King of England.* London: Weidenfeld & Nicolson, 2007.

Smith, Lacey Baldwin. *Treason in Tudor England: Politics and Paranoia.* London: Jonathan Cape, 1986.

Somerset, Anne. *Elizabeth I.* New York: St. Martin's Press, 1992.

Starkey, David. *Henry: Virtuous Prince.* London: Harper Press, 2008.

————. *Six Wives: The Queens of Henry VIII*. London: Chatto & Windus, 2003.

Thomas, Paul. *Authority and Disorder in Tudor Times, 1485–1603*. Cambridge: Cambridge University Press, 1999.

Udall, Nicholas. *Ralph Roister Doister.* 1566. Reprint, Gloucester: Dodo Press, 2007.

Vergil, Polydore. *Three Books of Polydore Vergil's English History: Comprising the Reigns of Henry VI, Edward IV and Richard III*. Edited by Henry Ellis. London, 1844.

Warnicke, Retha M. *The Marrying of Anne of Cleves: Royal Protocol in Early Modern England*. Cambridge: Cambridge University Press, 2000.

Watt, Diane. "Askew, Anne (c. 1521–1546)." In *Oxford Dictionary of National Biography*. Edited by H. C. G. Matthew and Brian Harrison. Oxford: Oxford University Press, 2004; http://www.oxforddnb.com/view /article/798.

————. *Secretaries of God: Women Prophets in Late Medieval and Early Modern England*. Woodbridge: D. S. Brewer, 1997.

Weatherford, John W. *Crime and Punishment in the England of Shakespeare and Milton*. Jefferson, NC: McFarland, 2001.

Weir, Alison, *Children of England: The Heirs of King Henry VIII*. London: Jonathan Cape, 1996.

————. *Henry VIII: King and Court*. London: Jonathan Cape, 2001.

————. *The Six Wives of Henry VIII*. London: Bodley Head, 1991.

Whitelock, Anna. *Mary Tudor: England's First Queen*. London: Bloomsbury, 2009.

Williams, Neville. *The Life and Times of Henry VII*. London: Weidenfeld & Nicolson, 1973.

Wilson, Derek. *In the Lion's Court: Power, Ambition and Sudden Death in the Reign of Henry VIII*. London: Hutchinson, 2001.

Withrow, Brandon G. *Katherine Parr: A Guided Tour of the Life and Thought of a Reformation Queen*. Phillipsburg, NJ: P & R Publishing, 2009.

JOURNALS

Cazelles, Brigitte, and Brett Wells. "Arthur as Barbe-Bleue: The Martyrdom of Saint Tryphine (Breton Mystery)." *Yale French Studies* 95, Rereading Allegory: Essays in Memory of Daniel Poirion (1999): 134–51.

BIBLIOGRAPHY

Dewhurst, John. "The Alleged Miscarriages of Catherine of Aragon and Anne Boleyn." *Medical History* 28, no. 1 (1984): 49–56.

Hiscock, Andrew. " 'A supernal liuely fayth': Katherine Parr and the authoring of devotion," *Women's Writing* 9, no. 2 (2002): 177–98.

Hoffman, C. Fenno, Jr. "Catherine Parr as a Woman of Letters." *Huntington Library Quarterly* 23, no. 4 (1960): 349–67.

Riddle, John M., and J. Worth Estes. "Oral Contraceptives in Ancient and Medieval Times." *American Scientist* 80, no. 3 (1992): 226–33.

Weinstein, Minna F. "Queen's Power: The Case of Katherine Parr." *History Today* 26, no. 12 (1976): 788.

Whitley, Catrina Banks, and Kyra Kramer. "A New Explanation for the Reproductive Woes and Midlife Decline of Henry VIII." *Historical Journal* 53, no. 4 (2010): 827–48.

OTHER

Davids, R. L., and A. D. K. Hawkyard. "Sir Thomas Seymour II (by 1509–49), of Bromham, Wilts., Seymour Place, London and Sudeley Castle, Glos.," The History of Parliament: British Political, Social & Local History, http://www.historyofparliamentonline.org/volume/1509-1558/member/seymour-sir-thomas-ii-1509-49.

Hamilton, Dakota L. "The Household of Queen Katherine Parr." Unpublished doctoral dissertation, Somerville College, University of Oxford, 1992; http://humboldt-dspace.calstate.edu/bitstream/handle/2148/863/hamilton_thesis_complete.pdf?sequence=1.

Letters and Papers, Henry VIII. British History Online, http://www.british-history.ac.uk/search/series/letters-papers-hen8.

Continue for a sneak peek
at Philippa Gregory's next novel

Three Sisters, Three Queens

coming in August 2016 from Touchstone.

I am to wear white and green, as a Tudor princess. Really, I think of myself as the one and only Tudor princess, for my sister Mary is too young to do more than be brought in by her nurse at supper time, and be taken out again. I make sure Mary's nursemaids are quite clear that she is to come and be shown to our new sister-in-law, and then go. There is no profit in letting her sit up at the table, or gorge on crystallized plums. Rich things make her sick and if she gets tired she will bawl. She is only five years old, far too young for state occasions. Unlike me; I am all but twelve. I have to play my part in the wedding and it would not be complete without me. My lady grandmother, the king's mother, said so herself.

Then she said something that I couldn't quite hear, but I know it is that the Scots lords will be watching me to see if I look strong and grown-up enough to be married at once. I am sure I am. Everyone says that I am a bonny girl, stocky as a Welsh pony, healthy as a milkmaid, fair, like my brother Harry, with big blue eyes.

"You'll be next," my lady grandmother says to me with a smile. "They say that one wedding begets another."

"I won't have to travel as far as Princess Katherine," I say. "I'll come home on visits."

"You will," my lady grandmother promises, which makes it a certainty. "You are marrying our neighbor, and you will make him our good friend and ally."

Princess Katherine had to come all the way from Spain, miles and miles away. Since we are quarreling with France, she had to come by sea, and there were terrible storms and she was nearly wrecked. When I go to Scotland to marry the king, it will be a great procession from Westminster to Edinburgh, nearly four hundred miles. I shan't go by sea, I won't arrive sick and sopping wet, and I will come and go from my new home to London whenever I like. But she will never see her home again. They say she was crying when she first met my brother—I think that is ridiculous. And babyish as Mary.

"Shall I dance at the wedding?" I ask.

"You and Harry shall dance together," my lady grandmother rules. "After the Spanish princess and her ladies have shown us a Spanish dance. You can show her what an English princess can do." She smiles slyly. "We shall see who is best."

"Me," I pray. Out loud I say, "A basse dance?" It is a slow, grand, grown-up dance which I do very well, actually more walking than dancing.

"A galliard," she says.

I don't argue; nobody argues with my lady grandmother. She decides what happens in every royal household, in every palace and castle; my lady mother, the queen, just agrees.

"We'll have to rehearse," I say. I can make Harry practice by promising him that everyone will be watching us. He loves to be the center of attention and he is always winning races and competing at archery and doing tricks on his pony. He is as tall as me, though he is only ten years old, so we will look well together if he doesn't play the fool. I want to show the Spanish princess that I am just as good as the daughter of Castile and Aragon. My mother and father are a Plantagenet and a Tudor. Those are grand enough names for anyone. She needn't think that we are grateful for her coming. In particular, I for one don't want another princess at court.

It is my lady mother who insists that Katherine visit us at Baynard's Castle before the wedding, and she comes from the Bishop of London's palace accompanied by her own court, who have come all the way from Spain with her—at our expense, as my father remarks. They enter through the double doors like an invading army, their clothes, their speech, their headdresses completely unlike ours, and at the center of it all, beautifully gowned, is the girl that they call the "infanta." This is ridiculous, as she is fifteen and a princess and I think that they are calling her "baby." I look across at Harry to see if he will giggle if I make a face and say "ba-aby," which is how we tease Mary; but he is not looking at me. He is looking at her with the blank goggle-eyed expression that he gets when he sees a new horse, or a piece of Italian armor, or something that he has set his heart on. I see that expression and I realize that he is pretending to fall in love with her, like a knight with a damsel in a story. Harry loves stories and ballads about impossible ladies in towers, or tied to rocks, or lost in woods, and somehow Katherine impressed him when he met her before her entry to London. Perhaps it was her ornate veiled litter, perhaps it was her learning, for she speaks three languages. I feel so irritated, I wish he was close enough for me to pinch him. This is exactly why no one younger than me should play a part in royal occasions.

She's not especially beautiful. She is three years older than me but I am taller than her. She has light brown hair with a copper tinge to it, only a little darker than mine, which is, of course, annoying; for who wants to match? But I can hardly see it, for she wears a high headpiece and a thick concealing veil. She has blue eyes like mine too, but very fair eyebrows and lashes; obviously, she's not allowed to color them in like I do. She has very pale creamy skin that I suppose is admirable. She is tiny: tiny waist pinched in by tight lacing so she can hardly breathe, tiny feet with the most ridiculous shoes I have ever seen, gold-embroidered toes and gold laces. I don't think that my lady grandmother would let me wear gold laces. It would be vanity and worldly show. I am sure that the Spanish are very worldly. I am sure that she is.

I make certain that I don't show my thoughts as I examine her.

I think she is lucky to come here, lucky to be chosen by my father to marry Arthur, lucky to have a sister-in-law like me, a mother-in-law like my mother and—more than anything else—a grand-mother-in-law like Lady Margaret Beaufort, who will make very sure that Katherine does not exceed the place to which she has been appointed by God.

She curtseys and kisses my lady mother and, after her, my lady grandmother. This is how it should be; but she will soon learn that she had better please my lady grandmother if she wants good service in any of our palaces. Then my lady mother nods to me and I step forward and Katherine and I curtsey together at the same time, to exactly the same depth, and she steps forward and we kiss on one cheek and then the other. Her cheeks are warm; I see that she is blushing, her eyes filling with tears as if she is miss-ing her real sisters. I show her my stern look, just like my father when someone is asking him for money. I am not going to fall in love with her for her blue eyes and pretty ways. She need not imagine she is going to come into our English court and make us look dull and ignorant and plain.

She is not at all abashed by the absence of my smile; she looks right back at me with a quizzical smile, as if she, born and raised in a competitive court with three sisters, understands rivalry. Worse, she looks at me as if she finds my stern look to be not at all chilling, perhaps even a little ridiculous. That is when I know that this is not a young woman like my ladies-in-waiting who have to be pleasant to me whatever I do, or like Mary who has to do whatever I say. This young woman is an equal. I say in French: "You are welcome to England," and she replies in English: "I am pleased to greet my sister."

My lady mother lays herself out to be kind to this, her first daughter-in-law. They talk together in Latin and I cannot follow what they are saying so I sit beside my mother and look at Kath-erine's shoes with the gold laces. My mother calls for music and Harry and I start a round, an English country song. We are very tuneful and the court takes up the chorus and it goes round and round until people start to giggle and lose their place. But Katherine does not laugh; she looks as if she is never silly and merry like Harry and me. She is overly formal of course, being Spanish. But I note how she sits—very still, and with her hands folded in her lap as if she were sitting for a portrait—and I think: actually, that looks rather good, queenly. I think I will learn to sit like that.

My sister Mary is brought in to make her curtsey, and Katherine makes herself ridiculous by going down on her knees so their faces are level and she can hear her childish whisper. Of course Mary cannot understand a word of either Latin or Spanish, but she puts her arms around Katherine's neck and kisses her and calls her "thithter."

"I am your sister," I say, giving her little hand a firm tug. "This lady is your sister-in-law. Can you say sister-in-law?"

Of course, she can't. But she lisps something, and everyone laughs again and says how charming, and I say, "Lady Mother, shouldn't Mary go to bed?" And everyone realizes how late it is and we all go out with bobbing torches to see Katherine leave, as if she were a queen crowned and not merely the youngest daughter of the King and Queen of Spain, and very lucky to marry into our family: the Tudors.

She kisses everyone good night and when it is my turn, she puts her warm cheek to mine and she says: "Good night, Sister." Once again I have such a strong sense of her presence. This is a real princess, as naturally royal as my mother; this is the girl who will be Queen of England. I like her and dislike her, all together, all at once.

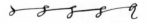

"I hope you will be kind to Katherine," my mother says to me as we come out of her private chapel after Prime, the next morning.

"Not if she thinks she's going to come here and lord it over all of us," I say briskly. "Not if she thinks she is going to act as if she is doing us a favor. Did you see her shoelaces?"

My mother laughs with genuine amusement. "No, Margaret. I did not see her shoelaces, nor did I ask you for your opinion of her. I told you of my hope: that you will be kind to her."

"Of course," I say, looking down at my missal with the jeweled cover. "I hope that I am gracious to everyone."

"She is far from her home and she is accustomed to a big family," my mother says. "She will certainly need you to be a sister to her and you might enjoy the company of an older girl. I had lots of sisters at home when I was growing up. It was fun to have a big family, and when I got older, I found that I valued them, more than I ever thought that I would. When you get older, you know that your women friends are your truest friends, your sisters are the keepers of your memories and hopes for the future."

"She and Arthur will stay here?" I ask. "They will live with us?"

My mother gives a little sigh and puts her hand on my shoulder. "Your father thinks they should go to Arthur's principality," she says. "But I wish they could stay."

"What does my lady grandmother think?"

My mother gives a little shrug. That means it has been decided. "She says the Prince of Wales must live in Wales."

"You'll still have me at home." I put my hand over hers to keep her beside me. "I'll still be here."

"That's the most important thing," she says reassuringly.

THE
TAMING
OF THE
QUEEN

FOR DISCUSSION

1. Discuss the novel's title in relation to Kateryn. Several at the Tudor court feel that she is in need of taming, including her husband. Why do they feel this way? Do you think they are right?

2. When Kateryn becomes queen, she must choose a motto. What is the significance of the queen's mottoes? Do you agree with Kateryn that her motto, "To be Useful in All that I Do," is "'not very inspiring'"? Why or why not? Do the mottoes of Henry's previous queens give you any insight into their personalities and reigns? If so, how?

3. Of her relationship with Henry, Kateryn tells Thomas Cranmer, "'When we first married I feared him, but I have come to trust him.'" Do you think that Kateryn should trust Henry? Why or why not? How does their relationship evolve? Do you think that Kateryn is a good wife? Why or why not?

4. Kateryn thinks, "Sometimes I shock my sophisticated London-bred sister with my ignorance. I am a country lady—worse even than that—a lady from the North of England, far from all the gossip." Compare and contrast Kateryn and Nan. Do you agree that Nan is more sophisticated? Why or why not? How has life at court affected Nan? How does she use her experiences to help Kateryn navigate her new role as queen?

5. Henry tells Kateryn, "'It is not enough to be a queen, you have to look like one.'" What does he mean? Kateryn and her ladies-in-waiting choose her clothing with a great deal of care. Discuss Kateryn's outfits, giving examples of how they help her accomplish her goals. Why are appearances so important in the Tudor court?

6. Edward Seymour praises Kateryn for being able to manage Henry, calling her "'a formidable diplomat.'" How is Kateryn able to cope with Henry's volatile temperament? What compromises, if any, is she forced to make? Is Kateryn a successful diplomat outside her marriage? Give examples.

7. Henry says, "This is the way to rule a kingdom, Kateryn. . . . First you appoint one man, then you appoint another, his rival. You give one a task—you praise him to the skies, then you give an opposite task, a complete contradiction, to his greatest enemy.'" Why does Henry think this is an effective method of governing? What problems, if any, does this create?

8. Kateryn has great respect for Anne Askew, thinking her a woman who "has not been cut down to fit her circumstances." How does meeting Anne affect Kateryn? Do you agree with Kateryn that Anne deserves admiration? If so, why? How are Anne's views revolutionary—and even heretical—in Tudor England?

9. Although Will Somers says he is "'just a fool,'" Kateryn believes him to be wiser than he appears. Do you agree? How has he managed to be "a long-term survivor of this knife-edge court"? What role does the Fool play?

10. Discuss the Nicholas de Vent portrait that Henry commissions. How does each member of the royal family react when

they first see it? Do their reactions give you any insight into their personalities? Explain your answer. Why does the portrait upset Kateryn?

11. Nan tells Kateryn, "'Sometimes, at court, a woman has to do anything to survive. Anything.'" Do you agree? Does Kateryn make any desperate choices in order to survive? Did you find any of the choices that others (for example, the Howards) made particularly shocking? Which ones and why?

12. Anne Askew complains that "'the law does not recognize a woman except when she is alone in the world.'" Discuss the place of women in the Tudor court. When Lady Elizabeth observes Kateryn as Regent of England, she tells her, "'I didn't know that a woman could rule.'" Why is this so surprising to Elizabeth? In what ways is Kateryn's reign instructive to Elizabeth?

13. Henry tells Kateryn that he "'guard[s Edward] as my only treasure.'" Describe Henry's relationship with his three children. Why do you think these relationships are so complicated? How is Kateryn able to help Henry appreciate his children? Do you think she is a good stepmother to them?

14. When Thomas Seymour tells Kateryn that her only chance of safety is "'in [Henry's] love for you,'" she replies that she does not know whether "'he has ever loved anyone. I don't know that he can.'" Do you think that Henry is capable of love? Why or why not?

A CONVERSATION
WITH PHILIPPA GREGORY

Lady Mary tells Kateryn "'If you are a reader, you are already halfway to being a writer.'" Do you agree? How did you decide to become a writer? Is your career the result of your love of reading?

I became a writer rather by default—I was hoping to get a post teaching history in a university when the cuts in university funding meant there were no openings. While I was applying, and waiting, I started my first novel, *Wideacre*, and found that I loved writing. It was a huge success and I have been a full-time professional writer ever since. My love of writing comes directly from my joy in reading. I don't think you can write unless you have read widely and deeply.

As a bestselling novelist, do you have any advice for aspiring writers? Is there anything you wish you had been told at the start of your writing career?

I wish someone had told me that it would get easier—you learn your craft as you write and you solve all sorts of technical difficulties as you go along. It becomes more and more enjoyable too, and it's really important to go with your heart—a novel comes because of a sort of inspiration and you should follow it, however surprising and unlikely. It's a gift, not a conscript.

Booklist has praised your writing, saying, "Nobody does dynastic history like Gregory." Can you tell us how you research your novels? In the course of researching Kateryn Parr, did you learn anything surprising that you incorporated into *The Taming of the Queen*? If so, can you tell us about it?

I read extensively, everything that is newly published and all the older histories, many of them now forgotten and ignored. Then I bring to the story what I have learned from other research—how to locate the women when they are not mentioned in the histories, how to reconstruct their lives from a few clues, what some of the clues mean—the clothes they draw from the wardrobe, their place at court. Kateryn Parr's scholarship was a real surprise to me. I knew that she published, but I had no idea how significant her scholarly work was, nor that she was such a pioneer in women's writing. I have tried to make that clear in *The Taming of the Queen*. Her study of theology and her commitment to religious reform is not especially interesting to the modern reader, but it is a key part of her character that I felt I must show.

You've written extensively about Henry VIII's wives. What first interested you in Kateryn Parr? Was writing about her different from writing about any of Henry's other wives? In what ways?

As one of the wives she's well known and well recorded, unlike one of the mistresses, which makes it easier to re-create her days. But she was involved in meetings with the Lutheran and antipapist preachers, and in plots with others of the court to draw the king towards reform, so a lot of her work was secret and hidden. Foxe's *Book of Martyrs* tells us a lot about this part of her work but he is, of course, very much on the side of reform, so he is biased. I suspect that she was in love with Thomas Seymour when she married the king, but her feelings about him (or about being married to such a physically repellent older man) are completely secret and still unknown.

Kateryn Parr is known as the first English queen to publish under her own name. As an author yourself, did you feel any kinship with her?

I had to restrain myself from assumptions of kinship! She was a far greater scholar than I, a linguist and a woman of deep and regular religious practice. I understand, I think, her love of words and I describe that drawing on my own experience, and I know, as she did, the joy of publishing something that starts its life as a wordless idea in your mind, and then becomes pages and goes out to other people to put ideas in their heads. This is thrilling work that we both have done. But Kateryn Parr was an independently thinking woman when it was dangerous to be a woman like that, publishing anonymously at first, studying in secret. She is a real heroine, while I have all the privileges of the Western women of the twenty-first century—there's no comparison.

Kirkus Reviews **lauds your novels, saying, "Gregory manages to keep us in suspense as to what will befall her characters. . . . Under [her] spell, we keep hoping history won't repeat itself." How do you address the challenge that comes with writing a story where the ending is already well known?**

I have experienced this challenge since *The Other Boleyn Girl* and I found, since then, that by writing the book in first person present tense I get an immediacy and a point of view which is that of the character and which obscures the knowledge of what is going to happen. If the reader can come with me into the here and now of the Tudor world, then they will know only the here and now and not the hindsight of history, which sucks drama and jeopardy from the story.

Many of your novels center around the role that "powerless" women have, and *The Taming of the Queen* is no exception. Kateryn and Anne Askew are powerful figures in their own right, although they are discounted by many in the Tudor court. Why is it important for you to explore this theme?

I didn't realize at the start of my career that this would become a theme for me—it's grown out of the research. So many of the women that we think are "powerless"—following the views of the early historians, all of them men, all of them mainly interested in men and male power—were in fact in continual dialogue with power: gaining ground and losing it. In this novel we see Kateryn become Regent of England, the most powerful person in England, and also in danger of losing her life for thinking independently. I think all women in this period (and probably in all periods) make gains in their personal and political lives and lose them, regain power and experience danger. This is the story of women's history—not one of unbroken oppression and passivity, not one of victimhood. I am drawn to write it because I am a radical historian, a woman, and because I believe it to be the truth—or at any rate a more accurate account than the view of women as inactive victims of male power.

Kateryn has been seen as a divisive figure in the Tudor court because of her interest in religious reform. Do you think that she is remembered fairly by historians? Why or why not?

I don't think she's given true credit for her work as a scholar and reformer, because the big move to Protestantism comes with her stepson, Edward; the movement goes the other way with his heir Mary; and then Elizabeth brings in the Protestant settlement and gets the credit for it. Kateryn is not recognized for her revolutionary religious views because there is less interest in religion now. I think she is largely dismissed by historians as the "last" wife of Henry's declining years, and Victorian historians mistook her for his nurse. I would be very pleased if my novels contributed to a revision of all the wives of Henry. Kateryn is one of six very interesting, very diverse women, who were themselves part of a community of women who were constantly making progress and losing ground in their freedom. They were not feminists in the sense that they argued for women's rights; but they were part of a self-aware community of women whose education and religion persuaded them that they were spiritually and intellectually the equal of men. Once a woman is free to speak to God directly, and not soley through a priest (a male, celibate priest), she sees that her soul is equal to that of a man and then—hurrah—the cat is out of the bag.

Several of your bestselling works have been adapted into films and television series. What has the experience of seeing the adaptations been like? While you were writing *The Taming of the Queen*, were there any scenes that you found particularly cinematic? Can you tell us about them?

I never think about filming when I am writing a novel—the task of writing a novel is too absorbing to admit any diversions to other media. It's always a pleasure when someone takes such an interest in the story that I have told that they want to retell it in another form, and it's always a challenge to let it go fully into that other form and be reinterpreted. Some adaptations I like better than others—like most people who are readers more than they are viewers, I tend to like novels best.

What would you like your readers who are interested in the English monarchy to take away from *The Taming of the Queen*?

I should like them to be aware of the wealth of talent and interest that women brought to English life and expressed in the ways that they were allowed. They are our foremothers and our heroines; they show what can be done in an oppressive world and their lives suggest what we might do even in our own, easier circumstances.

Are you working on anything now? Can you tell us about it?

I am working on a new book set in the Tudor period. More than that I can't say, as I don't yet know!

ENHANCE YOUR BOOK CLUB

1. Kateryn dreams that she is Tryphine, "married against my will to a dangerous man." Research the legend of Saint Tryphine as well as the story of Bluebeard and discuss them with your book club. Do you see any parallels between Kateryn's marriage to Henry VIII and Tryphine's story? What are they?

2. Get a sense of Tudor England by researching Hampton Court, the Tower of London, and Snape Castle, where Kateryn lived with her second husband, John Neville Baron Latimer.

3. Philippa Gregory is the author of several bestselling novels, including *The Other Boleyn Girl* and the Cousins' War novels, which are the basis of the critically acclaimed TV miniseries *The White Queen*. Read some of her other works and watch the adaptations, then discuss them with your book club. Which were your favorites and why? What did you think of the adaptations?

4. To learn more about Philippa Gregory, read about her research, and see a Tudor family tree, visit www.philippagregory.com. You can also follow her on Facebook at www.facebook.com/PhilippaGregoryOfficialFanPage or on Twitter @PhilippaGBooks, for regular updates.

ABOUT THE AUTHOR

Philippa Gregory is the author of several bestselling novels, including *The Other Boleyn Girl*, and is a recognized authority on women's history. Her Cousins' War novels are the basis for the critically acclaimed Starz miniseries *The White Queen*. She graduated from the University of Sussex and received a Ph.D. from the University of Edinburgh, where she is a Regent. She holds an honorary degree from Teesside University, and is a fellow of the universities of Sussex and Cardiff. She welcomes visitors to her website, PhilippaGregory.com.

GARDENS
FOR THE GAMBIA

Philippa Gregory visited The Gambia, one of the driest and poorest countries of sub-Saharan Africa, in 1993 and paid for a well to be hand-dug in a village primary school at Sika. Now—more than 200 wells later—she continues to raise money and commission wells in village schools, community gardens, and in The Gambia's only agricultural college. She works with her representative in The Gambia, headmaster Ismaila Sisay, and their charity now funds pottery and batik classes, beekeeping, and adult literacy programs.

GARDENS FOR THE GAMBIA is a registered charity in the UK and the United States and a registered NGO in The Gambia. Every donation, however small, goes to The Gambia without any deductions. If you would like to learn more about the work that Philippa calls "the best thing that I do," visit her website www.PhilippaGregory.com and click on GARDENS FOR THE GAMBIA where you can make a donation and join with Philippa in this project.

"Every well we dig provides drinking water for a school of about 600 children, and waters the gardens where they grow vegetables for the school dinners. I don't know of a more direct way to feed hungry children and teach them to farm for their future."

Philippa Gregory

Don't miss
PHILIPPA GREGORY'S
other Cousins' War novels

Available wherever books are sold
or at SimonandSchuster.com

TOUCHSTONE

Don't miss any of Philippa Gregory's "mesmerizing and historically rich"* TUDOR COURT NOVELS

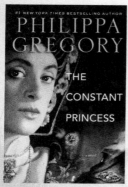

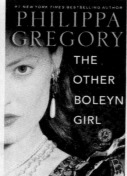

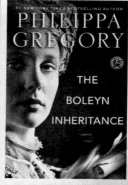

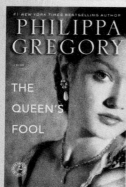

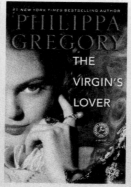

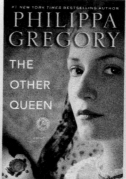

"Sexy...scandalous...smart." —*Redbook*

Available wherever books are sold or at SimonandSchuster.com

TOUCHSTONE

*People

Look for Philippa Gregory's bestselling Wideacre trilogy

Available wherever books are sold or at SimonandSchuster.com

Philippa Gregory

once again brings the past vividly to life...

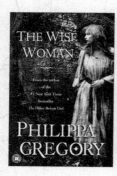

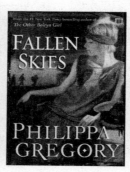

The Tradescant Series

Available wherever books are sold or at SimonandSchuster.com

TOUCHSTONE